Hi there aunty
this is my wacked-up
book about being
a teenager. Hope
you like it; let me
know what you
think!
— Kei

How We'd Look on Film

Kai Gorbahn

iUniverse, Inc.
Bloomington

How We'd Look on Film

Copyright © 2012 by Kai Gorbahn

All rights reserved. No part of this book may be used or reproduced by any means, graphic, electronic, or mechanical, including photocopying, recording, taping or by any information storage retrieval system without the written permission of the publisher except in the case of brief quotations embodied in critical articles and reviews.

This is a work of fiction. All of the characters, names, incidents, organizations, and dialogue in this novel are either the products of the author's imagination or are used fictitiously.

iUniverse books may be ordered through booksellers or by contacting:
iUniverse
1663 Liberty Drive
Bloomington, IN 47403
www.iuniverse.com
1-800-Authors (1-800-288-4677)

Because of the dynamic nature of the Internet, any web addresses or links contained in this book may have changed since publication and may no longer be valid. The views expressed in this work are solely those of the author and do not necessarily reflect the views of the publisher, and the publisher hereby disclaims any responsibility for them.

Any people depicted in stock imagery provided by Thinkstock are models, and such images are being used for illustrative purposes only. Certain stock imagery © Thinkstock.

ISBN: 978-1-4759-0250-1 (sc)
ISBN: 978-1-4759-0251-8 (hc)
ISBN: 978-1-4759-0252-5 (e)

Library of Congress Control Number: 2012905206

Printed in the United States of America

iUniverse rev. date: 4/5/2012

—*For Kirsten Dunst*

On the night you left I came over
And we peeled the freckles from our shoulders
Our brand new coats, so flushed and pink
And I knew your heart I couldn't win
'Cause the season's change was a conduit
And we'd left our love in our summer skin
—Death Cab for Cutie

Part One: Spring

Chapter Zero: Prelude

My future home would look like this, I thought to myself, sitting on the front porch of my childhood friend Brody's house. He lived in a minor-sized mansion on the outskirts of Smithers, our small and sleepy town. One day I'd have a home just like this—for my own. Someplace I could hide away in, somewhere quiet I could relax.

It was an elegant structure, made of stone with a tall slate-roof. Next to it was a barn and shed, even a tree-fort off in the distance. Little animals were all over the place like they'd be in a fairy-tale... like in songs by *Iron and Wine*. Brown squirrels ran up and down branches, hopping from one tree to another, gnawing away at pinecones; and then there was the black-capped chickadees, which dove in and out of the garden, saving it from the insects that would otherwise help themselves to the fresh cabbage and lettuce. My personal favorite were the frogs, that hobbled around the small pond down at the bottom of the meadow. When I was younger I'd catch the frogs every time I came to visit, but now...

Now I just liked to watch them.

There was a bridge by the pond I'd spent entire hours on this last week, looking down on the water at all the tadpoles, frogs and flies. Listening to nothing but the sounds of nature, I'd sit there and think over everything that happened that led me to this point in my life.

✳✳✳

It all begins with Grade 11—back when I knew who I was and how to be happy. Back when things were simple. Sometimes I close my eyes and try to remember how things used to be, but when I think back to those days all I can picture in my head is a girl. Her name: Anna Markus. Thirteen years old and she was the most beautiful thing I'd ever seen. Though we hardly spoke, there was a connection between us that carried me through each day. Whenever I think back to when my life actually made sense, I see her. I close my eyes and suddenly it's like she's right there in front of me, walking towards me in the halls of our old school.

Every morning—as she opened her locker to put away her things—she would look over at me and briefly gaze into my eyes, smiling. And that's how my days used to start off.

With a smile.

Her locker was uncannily next to mine, so everyday I'd see her in the corner of my eye, with us shoulder-to-shoulder, and I'll always remember the looks she gave me in the morning's before school… But that was when she still went to my school, before she moved away and left me here on my own.

Now all that's left is the memory, and that once-happy image of her next to me in the school hallways will always resonate inside me. Two years later I'm seventeen in a world that no longer resembles the one I used to know. Somewhere down the line things have gone wrong. All I see is her. Even though she's gone, she's all that's left of my former self—the one that saw life as something beautiful. My life is now a train-wreck, a disaster, and I'm doing all I can to pick myself back up again.

I was starting fresh.

Today was the day my mom was coming to take me to my new home, to my very own apartment. At any moment now her vehicle would come tumbling up the driveway of the house I'd been staying in. My mom had a big expensive SUV, and when she came to pick me up it would be full of all the things I'd left behind when I moved out two weeks ago.

Chapter One: Scenes and Dreams

Once upon a time I had a close circle of friends. There was me and Eric—best friends—and Cliff and Trent. Together, the four of us were unstoppable. We were like a team, a group of artists on our way to success. In Grade 11 we went downtown each day—usually to Main Street—and filmed outrageous videos of stunts, pranks and jokes. Kind of like *Jackass*, although not nearly as crude.

With dreams of being famous, I'd edit the footage around and upload it on YouTube. Though we never exactly broke through the mainstream, we eventually caused a stir in the town we lived in. The local newspaper even put us on the front page and did a big story on us, interview and everything. Soon enough it seemed as though everyone had seen our videos: all the kids at school, their parents, even our teachers. We were stars. Everyone wanted to know us.

But I guess it's that age-old story about fame—that it never lasts, that people turn on you, that things eventually spin out of control.

The school's hockey players—who began to slowly feel out of the spotlight—started making fun of us by Christmas. They'd call us names in the hallways and post rude comments up on our YouTube page. Suddenly our videos weren't cool anymore. As the months went on we tried to pick it up, tried to be more bad-ass, desperately attempting to gain everyone's respect again. But that, we discovered, did nothing but get ourselves into *real* trouble.

A furniture store went as far as to actually try and press charges, all because we had filmed a prank inside their store and apparently scared off one of their customers. The police were involved and everything. Fortunately we got off with a signed apology and card.

At school we weren't so lucky. One student wanted to be in our videos so badly he came up with an elaborate prank that got himself expelled. He dressed up in black clothes, wearing a mask, and tackled the school's mascot in front of the whole school at a pep rally. Teachers chased him down, took off his mask, and expelled him on the spot. I was suspended—since I'd filmed and initiated it—but that was nothing compared to the guilt I had that our videos had gotten someone kicked out of school, someone who was only expelled because he wanted to be a part of our filming troupe.

The principal of our high school tried to be forgiving. He knew we were nice kids just trying to have some fun. The four of us had all come from good homes. We never drank or smoked or skipped any of our classes. He tried his best to help us, but by the time it was Grade 12 it was a much different story. The school-board told him that if we wanted to stay in high school, our videos would have to be put to a stop.

And so the four of us called it quits, taking our website down and putting away our cameras. That exciting time in our lives was over and done with, and as time would have it, our group gradually drifted apart.

The least concerned over this was definitely Cliff. Throughout all of high school he'd had an abundance of friends, which was unfortunate for me—our senior year—because he was the only friend by then I had left.

Trent was still around, but over the summer—while Eric and I had gotten jobs at 7-eleven—he slid into a different crowd of friends, one that had introduced him to drugs and alcohol. As he edged his way into their group, and as school approached, it was clear to us that Trent was better off sticking with his new circle of friends. I guess it also helped that they were in the same grade he was, because this was our last year and he still had one more to go.

Sometimes we have to go our own separate ways. Even Eric had to do the same and we're as close as friends can be. Nobody can believe it, but Eric and I have only known each other for two years. In the world of high school we started off as enemies: I was the drama-fag; he was the jock. But those lines blurred between us after a bad hockey injury prevented him from being able to play anymore. With no sports, he started hanging with Cliff more often—his long-time friend from elementary school—shocked to find that he was also friends with me. It took time, but as he got to know me he slowly realized how alike we truly were. Through the haze of high school he discovered there was one more person like him. We were almost the exact same. When people saw us together they thought we were twins. In fact, we used to lead people on and tell them we were brothers. We have the same haircuts, the same interests, even the same personalities.

Grade 12 changed everything. Eric couldn't handle school anymore. The fights we got in with the jocks—his former friends—weren't worth it to him. He dropped out of school to get away from it all—and he too, like Anna, had left me all alone. And because he lived out of town, I never got to see him on weekends, either.

The sad thing about Eric and I was that he had already began drifting away from me in the weeks before he decided to permanently leave school. I never took it personally, though, because I knew what was going on in his mind. He thought if he went solo, instead of always being with me, he'd have a better chance at fitting in; without me he might have blended in easier. Maybe people would have stopped talking behind our backs so much, cracking jokes, saying we were gay.

Plus, it never helped that in all of our time throughout high school we had never had girlfriends. There were simply no girls we were interested in.

The only girl that truly intrigued me was Anna, but she was three years younger. It was true that I hoped there was a future between us, but I wasn't worried about it. I believed I had all the time in the world. The last thing I expected was for things to turn out the way they did. The moment she left Smithers, my whole world changed. My senior year was a fraction of the life I used to lead.

✳✳✳

Things all began to change when we got ourselves jobs. When Eric and I first started working at 7-eleven we were looking through a completely new lens, as true observers. It astounded me each shift, how hundreds of people came in like clockwork for a daily pack of cigarettes. I never knew smoking was still such a big deal. Hardly anyone ever smoked in public anymore. Everyone seemed to have been smoking discreetly. I began to wonder what the big deal was. How was smoking worth the ten dollars they spent on it every day?

While walking to work one summer morning, I noticed a guy a few years older than me as he pulled a pack of cigarettes out of his pocket. He was standing on the corner of the street up ahead of me. As he lit a match and drew in the smoke, a thought ran across my mind: *What would it be like to be someone who smoked?*

I used to view my life one way and one way only. It was the life I had been born into: a safe and responsible Mormon lifestyle. My dad was the Bishop of our church, and it was expected of me to follow in his footsteps. That had never bothered me before; but then again, I'd never really thought of it. That morning, before work, the hunger for an alternative suddenly appealed to me. Now that Anna had moved away... *What would make me happy?* I watched him exhale the smoke, and without even the slightest precognition I found myself wishing I was him; or, simply, anyone other than myself.

Then something magical happened: a truck came around the corner and pulled up next to him. After taking one last drag, he tossed the cigarette onto the street, hopped into the vehicle, and drove away, leaving his already-lit cigarette unprotected, at my disposal with no one around. Taking the opportunity at hand, I walked up to it and hurriedly breathed in my first breath of tobacco.

Because I didn't know what I was doing, I of course ended up inhaling far too much, brutally burning the inside of my lungs. But

How We'd Look on Film

that didn't matter; it was exciting! For the first time in a very long time I felt alive.

And that's how it all started.

That summer, while house-sitting for one of my parent's friends, I told Eric that I'd tried a cigarette. Though I expected him to be disgruntled by my actions, it turned out that Eric had had a similar experience. We were on the same page. We always were. A few days before he had gotten one of his older friends to buy him a pack, but so far he'd only smoked one of them.

That night we walked around town, smoking cigarette after cigarette, talking about how great it was that it was now summer, that we had all this money from our new job to blow.

We even went into 7-eleven and I got myself a coffee, which was also against the Mormon religion, the one I used to follow. So what was next? Marijuana.

When I asked Eric if he wanted to smoke weed, he laughed harder than I'd ever heard him laugh before. He couldn't believe what he was hearing; he never saw it coming. It was the one thing he didn't understand—Anna was gone and a part of me had left with her. Nothing mattered the same way it mattered before.

"How are we gonna get weed!?"

"I've no idea," I replied, chuckling. "How does everyone else?"

"People have drug dealers." He smirked and jokingly asked, "Do you know any drug dealers?"

"I'm sure we can find one," I said. "We have the whole night!"

The only place that we could think of was the really sketchy apartment building behind Safeway. Everyone in town knew how dirty that place was. All things considered, it was practically a crack house. When we arrived there, by chance there so happened to be a guy outside his six-foot high porch, minding his own business, having a cigarette. Giving Eric a quick look, I told him, "Here goes nothing," before sprinting across the street and up to him.

"You selling?" I asked the man.

"How much you want?"

My heart was racing like crazy. "I just have twenty dollars," I told him.

"One sec," the dealer said, disappearing inside his apartment. I looked back to Eric and gave him the thumbs up. That's all it took. Getting drugs was *that* easy. *That's the kind of world we live in,* I remember thinking.

Turning back to the dealer's apartment, I heard the screen door open up as he stepped back onto the veranda. He walked up to the ledge and carefully dropped the bag of pot down for me to catch. I put it in my pocket, and as he crawled down on his knees, I handed the twenty dollar bill up to him.

"If this is good, I'll be back," I said, pretending as though I knew what I was talking about. But I had no idea. It was like acting: I was playing the part. As I ran back to Eric with the weed I was practically bouncing up and down with excitement.

On the grounds of my old elementary school, under one of the night lights, we hollowed the tobacco out of one of Eric's cigarettes and sifted weed down the paper tube until it was full again. Once the operation was complete, we lit the thing up and passed it back and forth. Because we never knew how pot worked, we never properly inhaled. We sucked it in like a straw into our mouths and blew out, not even remotely getting high from it. But that didn't matter to us. It wasn't about getting high; it was about experiencing something new.

As fun and exciting as that night was, things came crashing down the next day. After arriving at the place I was house-sitting and surprising us with a visit, my mom immediately recognized that something was up. "What's going on?" she asked.

"What do you mean?" I responded casually, but she could tell I was incredibly nervous. She came through the doorway, looked over, and saw the two empty cups of 7-eleven coffee sitting on the counter. *Two,* not one.

"Are one of those yours?" she asked.

Because I never—*ever*—lied to my parents, I told her the truth. And without even a word more, she stormed out of the house and called my dad over. He arrived moments later. Up until that day I'd never seen him so worked up. And this was only over coffee! While Eric hid in the bedroom he'd slept in that week, my dad lectured me in the living room. He sat me on the couch and towered over me, pacing back and forth, quoting some of the principles of our church. Sitting down, he calmed himself and said, "You get your own job, and now that you're staying somewhere other than home you think you can do whatever you want—is that it?"

"I don't know," I said. *That's all I ever said to my parents.* I never knew how to speak to them so I always kept silent.

"What's next... Smoking? *Marijuana*!?"

He noticed something trigger over my face.

"You've smoked pot," he remarked softly, realizing the cold truth.

I remained silent and so did he. With a sharp exhale he stood up and walked out of the living room. "Dad," I said, standing up, but he'd gone and left already.

After hearing the door slam shut, Eric came strolling down the hallway over to me. "Well this was all a huge mistake," he said, picking up a few things scattered on the floor.

"Come on," I said. "No it wasn't."

"Last night was supposed to be fun," he replied, hanging up a jacket. "Now your parents are going to hate you."

But I didn't care.

No one understood where I was coming from. I was just a kid with nothing going for myself. I never liked my plans for the future. When I turned nineteen I was supposed to go on an excursion with the Mormon church for a whole two years! I didn't want to do that. But everyone thought I did. It was *expected*. I was stuck in a life that had been chosen for me.

My parents blamed the whole thing on depression, which might have been true—maybe I was depressed. But either way, when school started back up they put me in with a psychiatrist, something I was secretly thankful for. After Eric dropped out of school I had no one else to talk to.

✳✳✳

"So now I'm going to ask you a very important question," the psychiatrist asked, after taking me into his office and introducing himself. Pushing his glasses up, he continued, "I don't want you to think about your answer; I want you to say what comes immediately to your mind. Okay?"

I nodded, trying to make myself comfortable in the chair in front of him. His office was cozy and trendy, but very professional.

"If you could have any three wishes granted," he asked, "what would they be?"

I was quiet, thinking of the many possibilities.

"You don't need to think about it," he told me again.

"Money," I began, saying the most obvious thing there was. "To have security," I put straightly.

"And?" he pried, folding his arms.

"To be a famous actor."

"And then what?"

I sighed, knowing the one thing I couldn't allow myself to leave out: "Anna as my wife," I admitted. There was a moment of silence, which left me to think about my last answer more clearly. She'd been gone three months and I was already missing her like crazy.

"Interesting," he said. "Okay. Tell me about Anna."

"She's just some girl I used to know," I murmured dismissively.

"*Used* to know?"

I stopped and thought about what he said, then laughed. "Well I obviously still know who she is—"

"Let me guess," he said, snapping his fingers. "She moved away."

"All the way to Vancouver..."

"Did you two ever have sex?"

Surprised by such an explicit question, I scowled at him.

"I take it from your response that you've never had sex?" he further questioned.

"Anna's only thirteen years old," I told him, then corrected myself, "*fourteen* now."

"But you're interested in sex, right?"

"I suppose, but not really."

"You're almost seventeen," he noted, checking the file on his desk. "Do you think maybe your infatuation with her is because you're afraid of getting older, afraid of the future?"

Everything he said was completely beyond me. "What? No! What are you talking about—"

"Look," he went on, "I'm not a therapist; I'm a psychiatrist. You could tell me everything and it wouldn't make a difference. You're clearly depressed. Just looking at you I can tell you were once a completely different person...

"But Anna has nothing to do with it. Depression is a symptom, a disease," he began to explain. "What bothers depressives has nothing to do with something in particular. If they fulfill something in their lives it just opens up another empty spot. There's always gonna be something wrong; it's just how you look at it. A depressives mind is made to always create problems. Fortunately, modern medicine can change that. Have you done any drugs?" he casually asked. "Do you drink alcohol?"

"I've smoked weed," I told him, "but just once."

"Did it feel good?" he inquired.

After thinking it over, I thought it best to say no, but he laughed and exclaimed, "Sure it felt good! But pot doesn't last, you know. You need something permanent." And that was his segue into telling me how beneficial drugs like Zoloft and Prozac were. But it was Zoloft he put me on, I think. Whatever it was, I quit taking them by the end of my first semester of Grade 12. After dropping out of school, I began my own brand of self-medication.

✳✳✳

I was never meant to work at a gas-station. It's the kind of place that only attracts trouble. Every night the teenage outcasts came rolling in, either stoned or drunk. 7-eleven was like a home for them—a retreat. They were always friendly to me, and so sometimes I gave them extra potato wedges free of charge. By the time I'd left school—now working full-time—they were pretty much the only friends I had. Some nights when I was off work they'd be outside smoking cigarettes or whatever, so instead of heading home right away, I'd hang out with them. Because they all knew me through my job, I blended in easily. It made my days a little more exciting, just to hang out after work.

At first I believed I was above it, that it wasn't about the weed, that all I wanted was the company. But as time went on that was clearly no longer the case: I started buying bags for my own private use, to smoke alone. I'd roll a joint in the 7-eleven bathroom after work, then smoke it in the field near my house. Stepping inside—completely stoned—I'd stumble into my bedroom and mindlessly put on a movie.

That's what I did in the late night hours that my family slept through soundly, in good health. None of them heard the sounds from my TV screen, none of them smelled the smoke. They were the perfect family—and I was the gigantic loser. I just didn't fit in. I lived a separate life from them out of the same house, trying my best to go by unnoticed, with only small appearances here and there. It was really only a matter of time that I left.

By the time it was spring, my parents had simply given up on me. After all the trouble I'd gotten into because of our YouTube videos, it was the last straw that I'd dropped out of school. They never knew how to deal with me anymore, so they guilelessly let me work my full-time job and hide away in my room. I slept through the days and worked late...

I was in need of a change. Though I may have been changing internally, it was my surroundings that needed a full adjustment. I can vividly remember the day my mind went clear, mostly because it was the day the new album by Death Cab for Cutie came out. Narrow Stairs—release date: May 13th, 2008. I'd been waiting months for that CD, literally counting down the days I'd have to wait until I could walk into our local music store and purchase the copy I'd safely pre-ordered. The day it came down to it, Eric was with me, trying his best to carry a conversation as I studied the album artwork and skimmed through its lyrics.

Eric had quit 7-eleven the month before. "Best decision of my life," he told me. "Now I have some time to think, to breathe. I feel free again."

And suddenly it all made sense. Without him even trying to convince me, I'd been convinced. I had three thousand dollars saved up in the bank; there was no point in making any more. I didn't need to work at a job I hated. After working there for almost an entire year, I put in my two-weeks notice the next day.

I thought it might have gotten me on the right track, but my parents were now even more bothered. I'd quit school and now I'd quit working a job. To them I was nothing but a lazy bum.

✳✳✳

"Why are you still in bed?" my mom yelled at me one morning, flicking the lights on in my room. She pestered me again and again: "Church starts in fifteen minutes—you want us to be late? Your dad's already there."

I tried asking her if I could stay home. "Just for today," I tried comprising, but it was pointless. She pulled the blankets off me and told me to get going.

Eventually I did as she said and got out of bed, but when I got out of the shower, I never put on my church clothes; instead—to really rub it in her face—I put on my oldest pair of jeans and a simple, white t-shirt. Though my mom was outside honking the horn with my two brothers and sister waiting—all of them dressed up and ready to go to church—I went upstairs for breakfast anyway.

It must have been strange for her, because for my entire teenage life I'd done everything they'd required. I went to bible study before school, the outings, the picnics; I even helped organize church events. But when my mom came crashing into the house to investigate what was taking so long, none of that mattered anymore. She already knew that I had stopped believing in the religion that meant so much to her and my dad. They were sick of me.

Sick of me and the miserable attitude I had carried day-to-day throughout the past year.

So when she saw me upstairs in my ripped-up jeans, sitting on the counter, calmly having a bowl of yogurt, there was only one scenario left to happen.

"What are you doing?" she asked, stepping into the kitchen.

"I told you—I'm not going to church today."

"Doesn't matter. You *have* to."

"I'm not going," I repeated, shoveling another spoonful of yogurt into my mouth.

"Well then you have to find a new place to live," she told me, and the words cut deep. *You have to find a new place to live.* I already felt unwanted, but to hear it aloud really hurt. Confused by my life with no clue as to what my future would hold, I was in a fragile state and didn't know what to do with myself. I didn't know anything.

"Well then I might as well just move out today!" I yelled unexpectedly, surprising both her and myself. She just stared at me, so I threw my yogurt in the sink, walked downstairs to my room, and did what all teenage boys had done in the movies: I tore down everything that was on my wall and swept everything off my desk. I even threw away my favorite picture of myself. I was about five years old in it, holding a rock, looking on the ground for more. I loved that picture, but I threw it away as soon as I heard the front door slam shut.

✳ ✳ ✳

My plan was originally to hit the road and never look back. A dream I always had was to hitchhike across the country. Stupid—yes, but I thought it glamorous, even heroic. I could take the opportunity and stop by in Vancouver to pay Anna a visit. How impressive would it be—me showing up with nothing but three thousand dollars and a back pack full of clothes? She'd be speechless.

But the money part was a problem, because the day before moving out I'd forgotten my debit card in my bank's ATM machine. I couldn't hit the road just yet. I needed a place to stay until I was able to get my debit card back. The bank was closed on Sundays and it would be closed on Monday as well, due to World Environment Day.

It was unusual how things had turned out. Never in my life had I forgotten my debit card inside an ATM machine, but on that particular weekend I did.

If I hadn't would I have left that morning and begun my trek across Canada? I like to think that I would have. I would have left before anybody could have had the chance to convince me not to. But now all I can do is fantasize about that and what might have happened. That scenario can only exist in my head as a parallel reality. Was it thwarted by blind chance—or was it something bigger? I still question God's presence in my life. There's too many possibilities to be sure of anything. The only thing I was sure of was that my time at home had come to end.

Chapter Two: The Escape

My family went to church for three hours, so by the time they returned I wanted all the stuff in my room gone; but first, I needed to find a place to stay for the next couple of nights. I immediately tried getting a hold of Cliff by calling him on his cell phone, but after receiving no answer I decided to go and see if he was working. I made my way across town to Safeway. When I arrived, the first person I saw was behind the counter of the deli. Her name: Rose Miller.

I'd known her a very long time. Throughout the past few years I'd always had a small crush on her. But that was completely natural: everyone liked her. She had a classical beauty to her appearance, no make-up needed. She was calm and collected, tall and elegant, the kind of girl a guy dreams of introducing to their parents.

Her best friend, Cassidy White, was somewhat the opposite to her. She was the wild one, which motivated Rose to come out of her shell and have fun. In Grade 11 I used to hang out with them all the time. We used to walk up and down Main Street together and hang out in coffee shops. We'd laugh and talk, and they loved watching me film all of the stupid videos I made with Cliff, Eric, and Trent.

Grade 12 was different. Since none of us hung out together, Rose and Cassidy had to rely on their other friends to hang out with, but the only friends they had besides us were potheads.

Here's the twist…

The crowd I used to hang out with after my night shifts at 7-eleven was actually the same crowd that Rose and Cassidy belonged to. The three of us ended up smoking weed together—and we used to be so innocent.

But that was the past—that was Grade 12.

As I talked to Rose that morning in Safeway it was nearing summer break. That meant Grade 12 was over, and that meant things could be different.

"Drayvn Emerald!" she called out, saying my last name as always. She was holding a tray of some food and she had a big smile on her face. "What's wrong?" Her smile withdrew, and she fell serious.

"Well," I began, "my parents just kicked me out."

She furrowed her eyebrows. "When? Just now—like this morning?"

"Just now."

"But what are you going to do?" she asked, taking a few concerned steps towards me. She put down the tray of food and took off her gloves, awaiting an answer from me.

"I'm here looking for Cliff, actually. I'm gonna ask him if it's okay to stay with him for a couple days."

"But, Dray... Then what?"

"I'm gonna go on a bit of a trip, I guess."

More than anything, I wanted her to tell me what to do. I probably would have listened if she told me to march all the way back home, to tell my parents that I was sorry and that I still wanted to live with them. But she didn't know what to say. How could she? She just looked deep into my eyes and gave me an encouraging smile.

"Well, Dray... You call me if you need me, okay? Just call."

I smiled uneasily and gave her my thanks.

"Bye," she said, and that was the last I saw of her before I whipped off to the other end of Safeway, looking for Cliff down each of the aisles. Time was wasting, and I had to keep the conversation short.

"Why aren't you in church?" Cliff asked after greeting me. He was stocking shelves. "Did it end early or something? You're not even in your dress clothes."

"That's what I'm here about, actually."

Cliff laughed. "What, did you get kicked out?"

I paused, and then said, "Yes."

"No way," he muttered, giving me a puzzled look.

Without time for an explanation, I asked, "Do you mind if I stay with you for a couple of days? All I need is a day or two."

"Um, why don't you just go back home?"

"I can't! I've already thrown away half of my stuff. My room's empty."

He scoffed. "Well if you think it's a good idea…"

"It's the only idea I have," I contended. "But right now I've gotta go. When do you get off work?"

"Four."

"I'll just wait at your house with my stuff, okay. *Is* that okay?"

"Of course it's fine by me. My parents won't care, either."

"Alright." I started to walk away, but I stopped myself a moment to turn back to him and add, "Thanks."

✳✳✳

When I got home I packed up everything I needed in three back packs. But even while taking only clothes and toiletries, it was still far too much for me to carry by myself. With church getting out in a half an hour, my parents would be arriving shortly. I never had the time to make two trips. Luckily I also had a foster brother who was my age and he never had to go to church. I creaked open his door and woke him up.

"Andrew… Can you help me carry some of my things? I'm moving out."

He grunted, "Sure," and rolled out of bed. Then he actually realized what I'd just asked him. "Wait, you're moving out?"

"Yes, can you help me?"

He was too tired to think about it. "Okay," he muttered. "Give me a second."

Once he got dressed I explained the situation to him. As he was not much of a talker, he simply took half of my things while I took the other, and together we headed across town to Cliff's house.

Cliff's parents always sort of liked me, so that made talking to them quite easy. I never gave them the full story—I didn't have to; they never asked. All I told them was that I needed a place to stay for a couple of days.

They were thrilled to have me, even giving me a key to the house to keep a hold of. Before I knew it I was settled into the spare room downstairs, unpacking clothes and the rest of my things. When Andrew turned to leave, I asked him not to mention anything to my parents when he got back to the house. He told me that he wouldn't, a promise he clearly hadn't kept.

Moments after he'd gone back home, my mom came knocking on the door. She was in tears and there was no one around but me. Cliff's parents were in the upstairs part of the duplex; I was in the basement.

"Dray, you have to come home," she said as soon as I opened the door.

"It's too late for that, don't you think?"

"What are you gonna do?"

"I don't need to do anything."

"You need a home. You need a job. Need money."

"I don't need that stuff anymore."

"Where will you go? You can't stay here—at Cliff's house forever."

"I won't be. I'm going on a trip across Canada."

Her mouth dropped to almost comic proportions. I would have laughed if she wasn't still in tears. "What do you mean go on a trip across Canada?" She began to shake a little. "You're not nineteen—you can't even get a hotel room. If you wanna go on a trip I can plan a trip for you." She pushed a hand through her hair. "This isn't something a person does," she tried explaining to me, but I knew it better than her.

"I don't have a choice. This is all I can do." I started to get a little mad. "What else am I gonna do?!"

"You can come home?" she suggested.

"You told me to move out."

"You've always known that in our house you have to go to church. You've always known that!"

"Yes and that's why I can't live there."

"Because of church?"

"Because I'm not happy." I was so stern that she began to cry even harder. I hugged her without choice. "Mom, don't cry. This is a good thing. I need to go my own way if I ever have a chance at being happy."

She pulled away from me. "Why can't you be happy at home? In our beautiful home with your loving family. That doesn't make sense to me."

"There's things I've just gotta figure out, I guess. It doesn't make sense to me either! But I'm not happy. I haven't been happy for a long time."

"You would be if you'd see!" she pleaded. "The church is a good thing, not a bad thing."

"To me it's not *anything*," I explained evenly. "It's just a distraction."

"What am I supposed to do, then? While you *go across Canada...*?"

"Don't mock me."

"I don't believe this," she said, wiping away the last of her tears. "Will you just come with me?"

"I've already unpacked," I told her. "I'm not coming home. Not for a very long time."

She scoffed angrily at me and said, "Fine."

✱✱✱

Monday came sooner than I would have liked, the one day I had to kill until the banks opened on Tuesday. I woke up at around ten in the morning, but in the spare room and not the couch I fell asleep in. Did Cliff help me to bed? Was I that tired? He'd already gone to work so I never got the chance to ask, but in the kitchen I could hear someone rummaging around. I decided to get up and say hello, finding Cliff's father grinding coffee beans next to the kitchen sink.

"Sorry," he said, noticing me as I stepped onto the creaky linoleum floor. "Did I wake you?"

"No, no, it's late," I replied. "Time to get up."

"I'm just making some coffee. Would you like some?"

"That'd be great."

"Do you take sugar or crème?"

"Nope. I like it straight up."

"Me too," he said, flicking on the electronic coffee maker.

"My parents, you know, would kill me for this," I said to him, pointing to the coffee machine.

He turned to me, confused. "What do you mean?"

"Nothing. Never mind, it doesn't matter anymore."

"What doesn't matter?"

I paused, realizing the corner I'd put myself into. "Well I moved out now—so now it doesn't matter."

"Moved here?"

"Well, yeah. Just for now, yeah."

"I didn't know that," he softly retorted.

I groaned quietly. "I never really explained myself."

"I thought your family was out of town or something. Something like that!"

"I'm still trying to figure things out," I told him, beginning to feel bad, wishing that I'd told them the full story from the start.

"Tell me—what happened?"

"I felt really trapped, I guess," I tried explaining.

"But that's normal isn't it?"

"I suppose."

"What about yesterday? What was it that happened yesterday?"

"I didn't want to go to church and so my mom told me I had to find a new place to live." I shrugged and added, "Basically *that's* what happened."

"So they kicked you out—because of church?"

"Sort of, yeah."

"Well have you spoke with your parents since? Can't you come up with an arrangement? Like an agreement of something?"

"I've never been too good with talking to my parents. We're kind of like strangers."

"Why?" he asked. Behind him the coffee dispenser made a splurging sound as it emptied the last drops of water through the beans of coffee and into the steaming kettle.

"They don't like me," I said.

"That can't be the truth."

"Maybe not, but that's what it feels like."

Cliff's father turned around and pulled out the kettle, preparing us each a cup. For a moment we drank in silence, both of us lent up against the counter, lost in thought.

"Well I hope things turn out alright for you, Dray. You can stay here as long as you'd like, but you might want to consider talking with your parents. That's important—to be close to your parents, even if you don't return home."

"Thanks. And thank *you* for letting me stay here, by the way. It means a lot. But don't worry, I won't stay here long—"

"No! I'm not worried about that. The only way I'll worry is if you're *without* a place to live. Please, stay here as long as you need."

"Thanks," I told him, and I truly was thankful, but even though I'd found a house I was welcome to stay in, I was still determined to continue on with my plan to hitchhike across Canada—that was until Cliff got off work. He arrived with Eric, who was full of questions. The situation was so messed up—it was a relief for someone to finally react the same way I was feeling inside. I'd been stuck in an unfamiliar home for a full day now, with nothing to do but watch the DVD's Cliff had stored in the cupboards below the television.

It turned out that Eric happened to have his driver's test booked for tomorrow, which if he passed meant he could drive in and out of town from his house by Lake Kathlyn. That kind of freedom would be my freedom, as well. We could finally see each other again and do things together like we used to.

I decided to put my future in the hands of fate: if Eric got his license I would stay at his house; if not, I'd go through with the long and lonely trip to nowhere. Both Eric and Cliff were skeptical as to whether I'd truly leave town, but in the end I never had to.

Eric passed the test and got his license the next day, which made the rest of things seem a whole lot easier. He called me up, full of authority, and told me to get packed, that tonight I was staying at his house.

I got packed as fast as I could, but before I was finished I heard a knock at the front door. I raced to the entrance in excitement, thinking it was Eric. Instead, I found it was my mom. She was holding her car keys up in the air, next to her face. "We're going for a drive."

"I'm kind of in the middle of some things," I told her, annoyed to find her still bossing me around.

"We're going for a drive and you're driving. You have to practice for your driver's test."

"That's in a whole year," I said, and raised my eyebrows at her cold dead stare. After a small pause she lowered her car keys, dropping the whole tough act she was trying so hard to play.

"Please?" she asked. "I want to show you something."

"Fine," I conceded, grievously putting on my shoes. She thanked me as I locked the door.

We walked across the front lawn and got inside her SUV without saying a word to each other. After starting the vehicle up, I asked where we were headed, but she told me just to drive. Complying, I pulled off the side of the road and turned on the radio.

"I thought a lot about what you said yesterday," she spoke, once I'd turned around the corner of the street behind Safeway. "You have no idea what you're doing. Right now, at your age, your brain is still under-developed. You're not able to think things through properly yet."

"What's your point?"

She turned the radio off. "You can't go on a trip across Canada is what I'm saying."

"I'm not."

"You're not?"

"Why should I? I have a home here at Cliff's," I told her, being spiteful, "even a key to the house. Right now I'm staying at Eric's, but I bet even Brody's mom would let me stay with them as well."

"Anywhere but home with your family, huh?"

"A home/family is somewhere you feel like you belong" was close to what I said, but I can't remember the exact words.

"I don't understand why you have all this hate in you," she said, shaking her head at me.

"It's not hate," I told her, keeping my eyes glued to the road. "It's just that... When I look at you and dad—even Cal and Henry—it's as though behind all of your eyes you really just want me to leave. It's this feeling I've always had. With everything and everyone. I've never felt comfortable with myself..." I never intended on getting all *deep* with her, but I couldn't help it.

"You just think that because that's what you want. You dye your hair black and say nothing at the dinner table just because you don't want to be a part of the family. Why do you that?"—I remained quiet—"Dray, you have no idea. Everybody at home is so upset right now because of you. Your little sister cried herself to sleep last night worrying about you! We got home from church and she finds that everything in your room's gone and you never even said goodbye or anything. Nobody knows what to think. Your brother's think you've gone crazy."

At a stop sign, I looked over to her and said, "They've always thought I was crazy."

"You *want* to be crazy," she replied, and it was then that I realized anything I said to her would simply make no difference. She continued on with her lecture, but I quietly ignored the things she was saying as I turned off onto the town's one and only highway. Along each side of the road was the central district of Smithers, and up until that day I'd never looked at it with such melancholy.

Every spot in town was littered with memories.

I hated this place, but I believed in it. I believed things could be good again the way they used to be. And the feelings stirring inside me began to coincide with what came next, because it turned out that my mom had found me an apartment I could move into, and that's where we'd been aimlessly driving to this whole time. She told me to turn off once we reached 7-eleven, to which my mom added that I might want to consider returning back to work there. "You're gonna need a job now," she said. "This apartment's gonna cost you five hundred dollars a month."

"There's no way I'm going back to 7-eleven," I told her.

"It's only a block away…"

"No," I repeated. "There's no way—"

"I get it. You don't have to. But you're gonna need a job."

"I know, I know. Okay, where is this place?" I asked impatiently, eager to see what could possibly end up being my new home.

"This house here," she pointed.

"A house? I thought you said apartment."

"It's a basement suite. The top part's rented out but the basement is available."

"I have to share it?"

"The top and bottom are completely separate. You'll see. Pull over in front of the fence," she told me.

By the time I'd pulled over and walked up the driveway, I'd already fallen in love with the place. It was comparatively nice to the rest of the neighborhood, definitely good enough for me—even if I was used to the luxurious house my parents owned in the suburbs. With all their money they lived in the richest neighborhood there was to offer: tucked away, almost hidden, overlooking the river that circled the outer-length of town. Opposite the river was the mountains; beneath them, at the base, was the railway station. The railway, along with Highway 16, went the long distance it took to go between the two major cities of northern British Columbia.

This here was just the pit stop.

What began as something small, slowly populated its way across the entire valley, making what is now the town of Smithers. The streets by Railway clearly have the oldest of houses, and the further you went from there the more modern things became. My soon-to-be home was in the middle of everything.

"What do you think so far?" my mom asked. "Your Aunt Wendy bought it, and I mentioned you as a tenant. She wasn't sure if it was a good idea or not, but I assured her you would be fine—*that*, and I promised I'd keep an eye out on you."

I ignored her.

My very own place, I thought, dreaming of all the possibilities.

The house was out in the open on a relatively busy street, but the yard to the side of it was secluded by a tall fence, keeping the place somewhat private. The steps down to the basement suite were buried beneath the cement driveway, and I imagined it would look as though no one even lived there. I thought that suited me well.

Once my mom unlocked the door and we'd stepped inside, she began a tour of the rooms. The entrance opened up into the dining room where there was a small table and furnace, some cabinetry and a desk. Easily accessible to the bedroom and living room, the kitchen was in the middle of the suite. Behind it, the bathroom. The suite was small, but big enough for one person.

"This place is perfect for you," my mom said, "because it'll include everything you don't have."

"Everything?"

"All the furniture, the bed, the drawers, dishes and cutlery. Everything in here comes with renting the place out. You wouldn't need to buy anything."

"That's perfect!" I exclaimed, overly-excited in my mom's presence. I'd been trying hard to seem as distant as possible.

"It's available for July, but I might be able to get you in earlier. That is if you do want it."

"I do," I told her.

"Good. If you're not coming home I want you to have an actual place to live in."

I shrugged. "Well I guess this is it then."

When we left the house I was completely lost in thought. Not in the mood to drive, I asked my mom if she would.

"Why don't you?" she asked, but I never answered, so she took the wheel herself and took me back down the highway, back to the temporary life I'd lead until I moved into the basement suite. All I had now was time to kill. Maybe I'd try and find a job.

I was eager to catch up with Eric—to tell him about my new apartment—but when I arrived at Cliff's, I found Brody waiting in the driveway, perched up against the thirty-thousand dollar vehicle his parents bought him. "I told him you were here," my mom said. "He'd been asking about you."

"Well thanks, I guess, " I said, stepping out onto the street. Of course my mom would want me talking with Brody. He was Mormon, just like my parents.

"Wait."

"What?" I turned back to her.

"You're cell," she said, reaching into her purse and pulling out the phone and charger I'd left at home. "Call me sometime. And you should also say something to your brothers and sister so they know you're okay. That too, alright?"

I replied without a word, nodding. Taking the phone from her, I placed it back in my right pocket, where I've always had it up until leaving home. The past couple days had actually felt strange without the weight of it in my jeans. I shrugged one last time before shutting the SUV door, and as she drove off I turned around to Brody, who was looking at me with a strange yet still very familiar expression. I'd known the kid over six years.

"So," he said, "what the hell happened?"

"I don't even know where to begin."

"Tell me," he urged, slouching off his vehicle.

"I got kicked out," I told him. "I'm sure my mom told your mom all about it. Now I'm living here."

"At Cliff's?"

"Tonight I'm staying at Eric's actually."

"Why don't you stay at my house?" he asked, walking towards me.

"Would that be okay?"

"Of course it would. You stay at my house all the time. You have your own room you even decorated. There's still some of your clean clothes in there too."

That was true. Once a month, while his parents were out of town, I stayed at his house to give him some company. He lived a little ways out of town and it scared him to be so far away from everyone. Me: I'd love to be away from everyone and everything.

"How's 7-eleven without me?" I asked, changing the subject.

"Sucks," he replied. "First Eric left—then you. Now it's just me and the new employees, and they only last like two weeks."

"Is Megan still there?"

"Yeah, but she's leaving too."

"Really? That sucks. She was the only nice manager."

He shrugged. "So are you gonna move in with me or what?"

"I'd like to," I told him, "but Eric's expecting me right now. Did you hear he got his license?"

"About time," he said, being the unintentional jerk he sometimes was. Brody got his license the day he turned seventeen, and he always rubbed it in our faces. He also did this for school, proud that he would graduate while Eric and I probably never would.

"Anyway... I gotta get packed," I told him, slinking away.

"I saw your mom hand you your cell phone," he said. "Call me, alright?"

"I will." After thinking about it, I added, "But I want to talk to your mom first and make sure it's alright, though. I don't want to impose."

"It'll be fine! Do you have all your stuff?"

"The important stuff, yeah. The rest is at my parents," I explained, walking towards the front door, "but I guess my mom will drop that off for me when I move into my new apartment."

"What new apartment?"

"The one I'm getting in July," I called from across the lawn, "so I just need to hang out till then."

"What are you talking about?!" he shouted back to me.

"I'll call you!"

✳✳✳

I hurried into Cliff's and finally finished getting ready to head out to Eric's. Almost as soon as I'd finished packing, Eric strolled into the living room I was waiting in with all my things. "You're here," I said, relieved in his presence.

"Is this all you have?" he asked, looking on the floor at the three backpacks.

"It's all I need," I told him as he grabbed two of them off the floor.

"Let's go," he said, so I grabbed the other one and followed him out the door. "Don't make fun of my car," he added once we got outside to where his car was seen parked idly on the side of the street.

"I like it," I said.

"My grandma gave it to me," he replied, defending himself.

"No, I do like it." I *was* being serious. "It's in nice condition."

"Pretty small, though," he asserted, looking it over.

"Oh well. You can only have one passenger right now anyways. You just got your license. This is great!"

"Well, thanks," he said, piling my stuff in the backseat before we got in. As the car started up, country music started playing on the radio. Eric immediately turned it off.

"I was listening to that," I joked.

He laughed and said, "There's no place to put in an iPod so we're stuck with radio."

"Does the cassette player work?" I asked.

"I think so."

"You know you can get a cassette tape that'll plug into the iPod."

"Can you?"

"I'll bet RadioShack will have one."

"Are you sure? I didn't know you could still buy things like that."

"I'm not positive," I told him, "but I'm sure we could find one somewhere."

We took a little spin around town before stopping off at the spot in town where all the major stores were located: Main Street, the busiest place to go in all of Smithers. At RadioShack we found a cassette tape that worked with Eric's car and iPod, which was lucky. Listening to music in his car was the best. After telling him the situation with my basement suite, we went for a drive out to

Telkwa—a small settlement fifteen minutes away from Smithers—listening to the new Cute Is What We Aim For album, which I hadn't heard until Eric put it on. We never talked; we just rolled the windows down and enjoyed the drive, the speakers on full blast—like they'd always end up being—roaring in our ears along with wind that streamed in and blew our hair all around. The song lyrics were fresh and new, inspiring in the way they seemed to read my mind: *if I can keep up with the machine that's in my body, I can do anything, be anything, say anything.*

Even then I knew that drive was only the beginning of all the memories I'd have in that green car, and even now—outside Brody's house—I was correct, even with much more to come in the future. But the day he got his license was the prologue, and the car he could then drive was a portal to the new adventures we'd begin having during the days before school was out.

Up until now.

Summer still on its way.

Chapter Three: Phones and Homes

We played NHL on Eric's PS3 for a couple of hours, but I threw my controller down in defeat when I realized that he hadn't even been trying to beat me. I was so deep into the game but without even trying he won every single time. I thought it was a close game, but it wasn't even close to being that. Disappointingly, I realized if he *had* been trying, the score would have most likely been something outrageous like twenty to nothing—for him, of course. But he liked playing it with me, and so he pretended not being as good as he was. It was kind of him, I supposed, but it did make me feel like an idiot thinking that there was a chance for me to have won...

The last time I'd been in his room was about six months ago, back in winter. It was a two hour walk to his house, but I had nothing better to do. I missed him. After telling him in advance that I was on my way, I made the long trek over. But by the time I arrived, he'd fallen asleep.

I went through the side door, through the dark house, and stepped inside his room—the lights still on—and found him laying sideways on his bed, over the covers. He was curled up with his arms between his knees. Defenseless and vulnerable, it was an image of him I'd never seen before.

I never woke him up. For some reason I liked being there with him as he slept soundly. I grabbed one of his magazines and read while he quietly snored away. It was relaxing, just being inside his room, his house, his life. But I had to get back to Smithers before it was too late; this was when I still had to go to bible-study and school in the morning. After a couple of hours or so, I slipped back out of his room and took the two-hour journey back into town. I would have spent the night, but my parents had a rule that prevented me from ever sleeping somewhere other than home—unless it was Brody's. They didn't want me having any opportunities to go to parties or to meet girls. That way they kept a keen eye on me. But with my parents and I estranged, I would now be spending the night at Eric's for the first time.

Once it got late he went downstairs and pulled a foamy and sleeping bag from out of his garage and put it next to his bed. I was very tired, but the both of us remained awake, talking through the twilight hours, catching up on each others lives. After losing touch with each other for so long we finally began making up for it.

I successfully left out anything to do with what had become an addiction to marijuana. I considered it, but after telling him that I'd tried alcohol a few times and seeing his reaction to just that, I decided to leave the marijuana thing alone. He wouldn't understand. He lived out in the country; I lived in town. Every day I'd have to see a world I no longer belonged in. The people and cars, the friends we used to have—everything constantly reminded me of how distant I was from living a normal life, where I laughed and hung out places, applied for colleges and normal things like that. Eric wouldn't understand. Not yet.

***

The next day we drove back into town for breakfast.

Outside 7-eleven, while drinking coffee in Eric's car, I saw Brody's mom pull in from across the parking lot. With perfect timing to speak with her about my situation, I carefully left my coffee with Eric, rolled out of the car and dashed after her as she entered through the gas-station doors. Inside, she grabbed a newspaper, turned around and saw me. "Look at you," she said.

"What?"

"The Elusive Dray," she titled me. "Here you are."

"What do you mean," I mumbled. Brody's mom had always been a very interesting character. She was always full of unique things to say.

Smiling, she asked what I was up to.

"Oh not much. You?"

"Grabbing a newspaper."

"Which one?"

"The Province."

"I hear that's a good one."

She smiled again. "I hear you need a place to stay."

"I do." I tried my best not to sound awkward. "Not for long, though. I'm getting an apartment in just about a week. It might be a little longer, but I'm hoping for only a week."

"So where are you gonna stay in the mean while?" she pretended to ask, chuckling at me playfully.

"Well"—I nervously laughed—"is it okay if I stay with you?"

She shook her head. "Of course it's okay. You're always welcome to stay at our house."

"Are you sure?" I asked politely.

"When are you coming over?"

I shrugged. "When would be a good time?"

"I'm making pasta tonight at seven, so why don't you come before that so you can join us for supper."

"That would be great! I'll come by around five?"

"Drop be earlier if you want. It doesn't matter to me," she said, leaning over the hundred kinds of gum.

"Thank-you, I will. I just gotta get all my stuff from Eric's."

"That's right! I heard Eric got his license."

"Just his N."

"Don't let him drive with more than one passenger," she warned me. (That was the rule for all new drivers.) "Anyways… I'll see you for dinner tonight." She stepped into line with her gum of choice and newspaper.

"I can't wait," I told her and repeated a thank-you one last time before exiting 7-eleven and dashing back to Eric's car.

"How'd it go?" Eric asked once I'd gotten in.

"She says she wants me to move in today at about six," I told him, putting on my seat belt.

"I guess that works out good until you move into your new place then, huh?"

"Yeah, totally." I thought about it. "Wanna see it? Wanna see the house I'm moving in?"

"The basement suite?"

"It's only like two blocks away from here."

"Okay," he said, switching the car into gear. As we drove out of the parking lot, we both waved goodbye to Brody's mom. She was reading The Province in her vehicle, a car as equally nice as her son's.

In the hours before I was dropped off at Brody's, Eric took me to run some errands. After I showed him where my new home would be, he took me to pick up my debit card from Credit Union. I now finally had access to the three-thousand dollars I had in the bank.

"I'm thinking about getting a job at Wholesale," Eric told me after turning the volume down on his car.

"Why?"

"I haven't had a job in like three months. I'm pretty low on money."

"I've got tons."

"But you should probably get a job, too. Now that you've got your own place you're gonna have to buy groceries and everything."

"It should be fine."

"It'll cost a lot more than you think, I'll bet," he said, pulling into the parking lot beside Gone Hollywood.

"This is where I'd *really* like to work," I muttered.

"Who wouldn't want to work at a video store?" Eric sighed as we got out of his vehicle. "I thought Wholesale would be cool, though, because there's a lot of young people that work there. But not, like, *hundreds*."

"Like Safeway?"

"Exactly."

Smithers had two places to rent videos. Most people went to Movie Gallery, located on the corner of Main Street and Highway 16. It was the cool video store—with the hundreds of copies they offered each new release—but I hated it. I went to Gone Hollywood, the local video store. They had foreign films, anime, television series, and classic films like The Seventh Seal. Cool stuff like that. Slowly, over the past several years, I'd been watching every movie they had. That day with Eric, I rented another huge pile of movies I'd watch throughout the week.

But Eric had been right. I did have to look for a job. I would need one eventually.

After we got my stuff and arrived at Brody's I turned to Eric and told him thanks. "I'll probably see you tomorrow," I said, but I could tell that he was thinking of something. "What is it?" I asked.

"I was thinking, you know, since tomorrow I'm applying for a job at Wholesale... I could take you around town and you could look for a job too."

"Okay."

"Tonight you could print off some resumes or something."

"Okay," I repeated.

"Do you want to?"

I nodded. "Yeah, that's actually a pretty good idea. And that'll give me something to do tonight." I grabbed my stuff out of the back seat.

"I'll call you tomorrow before I come pick you up?" he inquired.

"Sounds like a fun-filled day," I said with a bit of a smirk, then exited his car, which found to be some trouble. With three back packs—two slung around each shoulder, another carried in my arms—I had to balance myself long enough to carefully push the passenger door shut with a foot. Both hands busy, my tight-fit jeans drooped down my legs; in response, I widened my legs, awkwardly making my way to the front door. A voice came from behind me.

"Don't forget to print off some resumes!" Eric reminded me.

After tossing my stuff onto the entrance mat, I turned around to tell him I would, but by that time he'd already rolled his window back up and was pulling out of the driveway. I watched his car tumble away as I tugged my pants back into place.

Brody's mom answered the door. "You're early," she told me, "but you're just in time." Helping with my stuff, she picked up a backpack and led me to their spare room, the same one I'd always stayed in for each and all my monthly visits. She told me I had about five minutes, which gave me a moment to unpack and see what cool things I had left over in the room from my last stay. My guitar, I found, was in the closet, and there was a couple pictures sprinkled on the desk.

Suddenly I remembered something. When I moved out I had thrown away a lot of important things to me. Like that picture I had of me when I was five—that was gone. All I have now are the memories, my clothes, and the acoustic guitar I got for Christmas...

For nostalgia effect, I picked it up and played.

Even after having it for only six months, I had taught myself guitar without a single lesson. I'm sure my parents doubted I would ever actually use it, but they got it for me anyway. They always got me what I wanted. But, for what it's worth, they never took much interest. They never asked me about the songs I wrote or the songs I sang. They didn't even know I was *capable* of writing my own songs. Some nights, even after trying my hardest to play as quiet as possible, my mom would call my cell phone from upstairs and tell me to stop playing. If I had an idea for a song and it was night time, I would have to go out into the forest by my house and play out there. But then again: on those occasions I was usually smoking marijuana, so maybe that was more or less the real reason for always having to leave the comforts of home and embark on such long lonely walks... Kind of like the one I took after dinner at Brody's.

Once it got to be late I said that I had to go out. "Where to?" Brody asked me.

"7-eleven, I guess. I just want to go out."
"I can drive you."
"Thanks, but that's okay."
"Why not?"
"I have a lot to think about," I said.
"Suit yourself—I'm going to bed," he told me, trudging out of the room.

"Goodnight! I'll see you tomorrow!" I called out, desperately trying to act casual, like there was nothing wrong, nothing up my sleeves. The truth of the matter was that Trent was waiting for me in town on the highway. In his pocket: a pipe and some weed.

It was true we never hung out much the past year, but we had reconnected a night not so long ago. Brody and Cliff and I were at 7-eleven getting beef jerky and other supplies for a camping trip when we bumped into him. After telling Trent about the camping trip, we asked if he wanted to come, half-expecting he would refuse our invitation, but it turned out he was ecstatic.

As Brody and Cliff went off into the store to grab all we needed, Trent told me, "I've got a two-six of vodka in my backpack I can bring."

I told him sure—to bring it—even if Brody and Cliff might have been sour about the idea of us drinking. Later, around the fire, I shocked them both by taking a huge swig from out of the bottle Trent had whipped out of his backpack. But they didn't care that much. It was just alcohol, right? Nothing like an illegal, green plant that caused bloodshot eyes and a dazed sense of being.

When they fell asleep in the tent, Trent and I stayed up by the fire, exchanging stories about marijuana: how we got it; who we did it with; funny memories. "We'll have to smoke up some time," he said, and a month later we did.

After dinner at Brody's that night, I texted him and asked if he wanted to smoke up. Next thing I knew I was smoking weed in the trees next to the sign that says *Welcome To Smithers*, telling Trent an incoherent version of how I moved out.

"That's crazy," he said in response. "Now I get"—cough—"why you wanted to smoke a bowl so badly. That's rough."

I shrugged—already high—and lit up another one.

The walk home I called Anna. I know that, but I have no clue as to what we talked about. But that's not what matters to me: it's the fact that although she's in the middle of sleeping, she still picks up her phone and talks to me, that she doesn't ignore my call.

No matter what she's always picked up. And she'll never say goodnight or goodbye, either. She'll talk for as long as I will, never less. For two years of my life, she's been my one and only comfort.

✷✷✷

"Did you even print off any resumes?" Eric asked, after waking me up in the morning. Towering over me, he asked again: "Did you?"

"I was going to," I said, silently remembering what had happened last night, feeling incredibly stupid about it. Was it really necessary for me to have gone out and smoked weed?

"So you never." He sighed and leaned up against the door.

"I thought you said you were gonna call me before coming here," I said. My mouth was dry and my back was sore.

"I *did* call you. You didn't pick *up*."

"What time is it?" I peeked my head out of the covers.

"Almost twelve," he said. "Do you even want to go look for a job?"

"I do. Just give me a minute." I rolled out of bed and put on a pair of jeans.

"I heard Subway's hiring," he suggested.

"Subway?" I asked, my voice peaked with interest. Subway sounded good to me. It was healthy—a real contrast to what I was used to at 7-eleven. They specialized in sandwiches, not cigarettes and junk food. Wouldn't it be a million times better? I thought it would, but Subway ended up being just as awful. I should have known, too, because they hired me without even glancing at my resume. I guess if a place hires you on the spot, that means they're desperate.

The very next day I had my own Subway uniform and hat, and was working a shift from twelve to six. I had to walk into town all by myself, but I didn't mind. It felt good to get up early and make the thirty minute walk to work. Plus, I was trying to keep my mind off marijuana, and having tons to do was helpful. When I got off work I'd head back to Brody's, have dinner, and watch a movie. Eric usually stopped by during the movie, waiting till afterward when the two of us and Brody would go out driving together. Brody would carefully tail behind, chasing after us as we ripped around the countryside. But we wouldn't stay out too late. I tried to go to sleep as early as I could, not wanting to be tired for work the next day.

One night coming home from a nightly venture, Brody's mom was waiting on us in the kitchen. She gave Brody a look and he almost instantly left the room. Something was up. Had she smelled the marijuana on me the night I moved in? I began to feel extremely guilty. They'd let me into their home and I had gone off and done drugs.

"I talked to your mom at church today," she said. "She wants you to call her."

Relieved, I pretended to sound concerned: "Did she? Hmm, okay, thanks." I started to walk off but she stopped me.

"Are you gonna call her?"

"Maybe tomorrow." She gave me a disapproving look, so I tried to defend myself: "It's pretty late, isn't it?"

"She says you've been ignoring her calls all week."

I silently lolled my head to one side and closed my eyes.

"Why don't you want to talk to her?"

I gave up. "You're right—I'll call her."

"Will you really?"

I nodded. "She probably just wants to talk about the new apartment."

"When will you call her?"

"Tomorrow," I decided, thinking it a good day to make the call—it would be my first day-off since I started at Subway.

I was really excited about the day-off too, because work was starting to feel really long and dreary. Three shifts and all I'd done was wash dishes and prepare meat and vegetables in the back. Next week they said they'd start me on the till. But really, was that any better? I guess in the end it's just work. Truthfully, though, I was extremely envious of Eric. He'd finally gotten the job he wanted at Wholesale, and he said it was the best job of his life. I was on my way to visit him, actually, when I made the call to my mom the next day.

"Wow," she said, "you only ignored about fifteen of my calls before calling me back."

"I've been really busy," I said, already annoyed by her—as if I wasn't annoyed enough. It was a busy sunny day and I hated sunny days. It never helped, either, that I had begun to sweat beneath the t-shirt I was wearing that day as I trudged all the way up the hill to town. The cars on the highway were speeding by and the logging trucks roared in my ears loud enough it made it hard to hear what she was saying on the other line. She started saying things like, "You can't even spare a minute talking to me? I'm your mother. You're seventeen."

"I know how old I am," I retorted.

"You're just a kid."

"Mom…"

"Excited about the new home you're living in? Since ours isn't good enough?" She waited for a response, but I gave her none. "Monday you're moving in."

"Today?"

"*Next* Monday," she said.

"That's good. I'll make sure I have that day off work, then."

"I heard you got a job."

"How'd you hear?" I asked, putting a hand over my eyes, giving them a break from the harsh sunlight.

"I know people in this town, Dray," she said. "Word gets around."

"That's right—you know everything," I said, my voice dripping with sarcasm. She paused, then sincerely asked how I was. "I'm fine," I said. "I'll see you next Monday." I pulled the phone away from my ear to end the call.

"Hey!" I heard her say.

I brought the phone back up to my ear. "What?"

"Don't think you can hang up on me like that."

"Like what?"

She paused another time, thinking of something to say. "Why haven't you called your sister?" she angrily investigated.

"I sent an email to Henry," I said. "In it I gave him a message to pass on to Jane."

"That's good enough?"

"For now," I told her. "But I have to go."

"Fine," she said, and hung up.

By the time I reached Eric's work my t-shirt was drenched in sweat. With it, I'd sunk into a terrible mood. Wholesale was not only on the outskirts of Smithers, but on the opposite end of town that I had entered through. Even worse was that I couldn't even find Eric once I got there. I looked up and down all the aisles of the grocery store, but he was nowhere in sight.

I bought a Coke (even that was a drink my parents strongly disapproved of) and sat down in the shade outside the front doors. As I panted and re-gained my strength for the walk back, I watched the loading trucks go in and out of the docking bay. It seemed very busy in the back, but the main store wasn't busy at all. I supposed Wholesale concentrated mostly with deliveries to restaurants and stuff. It sold things in bulk, not like Safeway, the popular grocery store in town.

"Drayvn?" I heard someone say. I looked around and found one of my old stoner-buddies walking towards me from out on the street. I decided not to be annoyed; I'd already been annoyed enough today.

"Hey Ben, what's up," I said plainly, loosening up, finishing my Coke.

"Not bad, not bad, just seeing my mom. Watcha up to?"

"Came here to see my friend, Eric. He just started working here." I tossed the empty pop bottle into the trash can next to the door.

"Cool, cool. I heard this is a cool place to work."

"Yeah?"

"I gotta friend who works here, too—Tyler."

"Hmm, I don't know him." I looked up at Ben, seeing that he'd dozed off. He was scanning the parking lot for some sign of something. "What are you looking for?"

"My mom's supposed to be here," he said. "She's got my money."

"Money?"

"I'll need it if I'm getting drunk tonight."

"It's Monday today, though."

"But it's *summer* time!"

"School's out already?" I asked, shocked to hear that it was. Clearly I'd lost track of time since dropping out of school.

"Today was our last day," he said.

"Why aren't you there?"

He laughed. "Last day of school? Fuck that, I skipped it. Dude I don't give a shit. Hey, what are you doing right now?"

I shrugged. "Chilling out, I guess."

"You should come smoke weed with me and the guys."

"Yeah?"

"Hold on, here comes my mom," he said, walking towards a black van that had pulled into a nearby parking space. As the window of the driver's seat rolled down and and Ben spoke to his mother something turned over in my stomach: *Was I really about to go and smoke weed?*

Apparently I was.

Once Ben returned, forty bucks in hand, we walked across town towards the high school.

"Why are we going to the high school?" I asked by the time we reached Main Street, after he finished a long story about his ventures over the weekend.

"Because," he said, "Lance and Taylor are waiting for us and they've got the weed."

Walking towards us on the sidewalk was a lady holding hands with her young daughter. At the mention of weed, she looked up and glared at us. Ben never noticed, but I did. Ignoring the mother's stare, I pulled out my phone and discovered a text from Anna. '*My plane tickets are booked,*' the text message read, '*I'll be in Smithers in only a couple of weeks.*'

✵✵✵

The next time I looked up from my phone I found myself at the skate park, the place where all smokers and pot-smokers end up at some point each day. By this time I was already high, feeling fine and relaxed in the heat, under the day's bright sun.

I was completely baked.

Sitting next to me was a girl named Kate. My eyes followed her gaze, seeing that she was staring down at the hand I had resting on the bench I was spread out on. Her eyes—I could tell—looked intently at the dirt stuck beneath my fingernails.

"Did you fall down?" she asked. "Your hands are dirty."

"Then I guess I must have."

Sizing me up: "You're really high," she said quietly, barely out of ears-reach from the other people around us.

"I asked you to prom," I responded, caught up in my own world.

She smiled. "I remember."

"Prom is stupid."

"Why'd you ask me to it, then?"

"I don't know," I replied, smiling back at her.

"Dray," Ben said. "Let's go."

"Alright, let's go," I declared, echoing his words.

"By the way, Dray," Kate grabbed my attention as I stood up, "Rose told me about what happened..."

"Nothing happened."

"I hope everything is okay."

"Don't you worry your pretty little head," I said affectionately, and coming from me that was nothing new to her. Under the influence I usually acted like that. After saying goodbye to Kate, I got up off the bench and followed Ben across the surrounding field. He lit a cigar and handed it to me. I took a puff and looked around.

This was where we—the lost teenagers—did our drinking and pot-smoking: the recreational baseball diamonds beside both the skateboard park and children's playground, sometimes even on the slides and merry-go-rounds. For some reason the cops left us alone if we stayed here. Once in a while they'd drive by and flash their lights at us; but still, they always let us be. I guess they thought it better than if we were drinking/smoking up and down Main Street and the rest of town.

***

Later on in the afternoon, as Ben and I were walking down the highway, Eric randomly drove by and pulled up in front of us. "Whose vehicle is that?" Ben asked.

"My friend Eric's," I told him. "He's probably on his way home. I should probably ask him to drive me back home, too."

"Okay," Ben responded sadly. "I guess I'll talk to you later."

As he ran across the highway towards the skate park, I eagerly stepped up to the car. Opening the passenger door, I began to realize how tired and stoned I was. I really did need to go home. Inside, I found Eric toying around with his iPod. I put on my seat belt and waited for him to say something, but he remained quiet. "I came by The Wholesale today," I said, trying to act casual—like I hadn't been smoking up all day. "I couldn't find you anywhere."

"Really?" he questioned disbelievingly, choosing a song.

"Yeah—"

"Who was that you were with?"

"Oh," I said, "that's Ben. Nice guy."

"Ben," he remarked. "How did you meet *him?*" Eric looked over at me, puzzled by such odd behavior.

"He's friends with Rose and Cassidy."

He bit his lip and checked over his shoulder for oncoming cars. Pulling out onto the highway, he said, "I see. So do you want to do anything today?"

"I'd like to, but I think I'm pretty tired. I think I need to take a nap."

He shook his head at me. "You never take naps."

This was true, but at the moment I was feeling more and more tired with every passing second. "I'll text you later," I told him, trying my best not to seem burn out from all the intake of marijuana. "After my nap."

After dropping me off, he speedily drove back down the driveway and out of sight, probably disappointed by my hesitance in wanting to do anything. I felt bad. He must have been excited to get off work and hang out with me. It was my day off, after all. But without any further delay, I headed to my room and passed out, hoping I would wake up soon enough to have dinner with Brody and his mom and follow through with my word in texting Eric like I said I would. But I slept through both things: through dinner and throughout the rest of the evening.

I never woke up until morning, which meant I'd had more than ten hours of sleep.

When I got out of bed and left the room for a glass of water, I stumbled upon Brody's father in the living room. He'd been out of town this last week, and his return, I assumed, must have occurred during my long slumber.

"Good morning," he said, sitting in the lounge chair in front of the television, holding a steaming cup of coffee. Though Brody and his mother were Mormon, he was not—therefore allowed to drink coffee.

"Good morning," I replied back to him.

The TV quietly hummed the day's news while he calmly took a sip of coffee. "I heard you were staying here," he remarked, keeping his eyes on me.

"Not for too long, though. I've gotta place I'll be moving into a few days from now."

"That's quite courageous of you. Moving out, I mean."

"You think?"

"Depends." He leaned back in his chair. "I don't know the full story."

"It's a long one," I told him.

"Always is. But I'll tell you something—"

"Do you—" I stuttered. "Do you mind if I grab a glass of water first?" I pointed towards the kitchen. My mouth was far too dry to continue a conversation.

He waved me off. "Go ahead."

I grabbed a tall glass, filled it full and guzzled the whole thing down. Before returning back to Brody's father, I filled it back up again.

"Thirsty?" he observed.

"Very," I replied. "Sorry, what were you saying?"

"I was about to tell you a story," he began. "I think it has some relevance with you, but I don't know... Like I said, I don't know the full story." He set his cup of coffee down. "But you see, I had a brother, and like you, he left home as well. And it's a good thing to leave. It's good to leave home and begin a new life. It takes courage."

I smiled weakly, and he pressed on:

"But my brother... When he left it was out of anger, not out of something good. He left, and he never looked back. Didn't talk to the family for years. And I think things were never patched up because of it. There's still hate. And what's funny—not funny; what's *sad*, is that I don't even think anyone in my family even remembers what it was that made him leave in the first place. I don't think my brother knows, either. Yet there's still this hate between them."

"Do you remember what the thing was? The thing that made him leave?" I asked.

He smiled. "I do, but that's not the point. The point is that you can't let hate guide you. It has downsides to it. So if there's anything hateful between you and your parents, or maybe even your brothers, I'm telling you to patch it up as fast as you can."

Brody's mother walked in and sat down next to me on the couch. "What are you men talking about?" she asked jovially.

"I'm telling Dray about my brother—how he left home."

"Right," she said, then a look washed over her face. "Dray?"

"Yeah?"

"You smell like smoke," she said.

I froze awkwardly on the spot, but luckily Brody's father spoke before I had a chance to say anything. "That's me," he said. "Went for a smoke just a moment ago."

Pursuing the smell no further—even if unconvinced—she grabbed a National Geographic off the coffee table and began to read. Finishing my glass of water, I stood up and asked if they were hungry for breakfast. "I'll cook," I offered, my way of making up for being such a terrible guest in their home.

Chapter Four: The Now

It turned out there was a party happening the night of my last day-off, which Cliff informed me of when he came over with Eric later on in the evening. Brody and I were playing video games in the basement when they knocked on the door, but his mother answered it for us. "Cliff and Eric are here!" she called down to us. I paused the game, but Brody pleaded me to continue finishing the round.

"Later?" I tried compromising.

"Whatever," he said, tossing aside his controller as Cliff and Eric rushed down the stairs.

"Wow," Cliff exclaimed, "I haven't seen either of you guys in a *long* time."

"Totally," I agreed, getting up off the couch. "What's up?"

"Dude," he ignored me, "what the hell have you been doing?"

"Nothing really," I said. "Working."

"That's right, at Subway. I heard," he told me, taking a few steps into the living room area. "Man, it must *suck* working there."

"It does"—I laughed—"but just a little."

Eric sat down next to Brody and asked what we'd been up to all day.

"We *were* playing Halo," Brody replied, scratching his back.

Cliff spoke: "Julia's having a party tonight. She said to invite you too, Brody."

"I'd rather not," he said, sounding as though Cliff had mentioned the dumbest thing he'd ever heard.

I, myself, was fully interested. "Julia's having a party?"

"You wanna go?" Cliff asked.

"Sure."

"See"—Cliff looked to Eric—"I *told* you he'd wanna go."

A stunned Eric was still not used to the new version I'd made of myself. "I like partying," I said oddly, desperately trying to get it through their heads that the old Dray was gone and that I was a different person now.

"Well hot-diggity!" Cliff exclaimed, using a stupid expression to mask the tension of us going to a party, something we'd never done before. "What about you, Brody? You sure don't want to come and get wasted?"

"Yeah, yeah, yeah..." muttered Brody, giving Cliff the finger. He was obviously pissed off he no longer had a partner to play Halo with.

"Are we going now?" I asked.

"Yeah!" shouted Cliff.

"If it sucks," I said to Brody, "I'll come back, okay?"

"Whatever."

❋❋❋

Before we headed out to the party at Julia's house, Cliff asked to be driven to the liquor store, which confused us because we were still under-aged. Normally, he told us, Cliff's friends got him alcohol, but since none of them were going he was going to have to try and get it himself. I told them that it would be impossible, that they always check ID, but he was insistent.

"I'm going to give it a try, at least," he concluded.

"I really doubt it's going to work," Eric said. "What if they call the cops on you? I'm not even supposed to have two passengers in my car."

"Will you relax?" Cliff said. "Just act casual and nothing bad will happen."

Eric did as he said and turned off into the parking lot of the liquor store, pulling up in the most far-off parking space. "Be right back," Cliff said, getting out of the car and jogging up to the entrance of the liquor store.

"Do you think he'll be able to pull it off?"

"Doubt it."

But our predictions were proved wrong: Cliff *did* pull it off. Somehow he returned to the vehicle with a big bottle of booze in his hands. The person inside apparently never asked for his ID.

And with that turn of events, we thought the night carried a good chance for an amazing time; unfortunately, the party was nothing like what we had expected. The jocks—the ones that hated us—were there, and it was too awkward for us to even bother with.

We headed back home, and being as disappointed as we were, our energy level was way down.

"Is it okay if I go?" Cliff politely asked.

Eric took his eye off the road for a quick look back at Cliff. "What are you gonna be doing?" Eric asked.

"Got stuff," he said.

"Hanging out with Jack and William?" I asked, offended. Jack and William were his other close friends, and they for some reason despised me—even though they'd never even spoken to me before in their entire lives.

"Where do you want me to drop you off?" Eric asked.

"Safeway would be awesome," he replied. "Jack's getting off work soon." After an awkward pause: "Hey Dray?"

"What?" I muttered.

"Can you take care of my Colt 45?" he asked. "Just keep it hidden so I can get it from you for another night."

"Sure," I said, taking it from him and placing it down on the floor, between my feet. After saying goodbye, Cliff ran off and skipped up to the entrance way. As he disappeared inside, my phone vibrated in my pocket with a text message.

"Who's that?" Eric asked as I pulled my phone out.

I checked the text. "Trent wants to do something."

"I haven't seen that guy in forever."

"Want to go pick him up?"

"Sure. Since Cliff apparently would rather hang out with Jack and William than us, even after we had a whole night planned to hang out together."

"I hate those guys."

"They probably wouldn't be so bad if they stopped talking behind our backs."

"No, I *hate* them."

He laughed at me. "So serious!" he exclaimed.

It really was unusual for me to get so worked up, but something about Jack and William really pissed me off. Our crowds were both best friends with Cliff, and yet they'd never made an effort to be friendly towards either me or Eric.

"Let's get Trent," I concluded.

"Text him to wait outside," Eric said, driving out of the Safeway parking lot.

Turning towards the highway, Eric asked, "You know what would be funny? If we just gave away Cliff's alcohol—for ditching us."

"Or drank it!" I added.

He looked over at me and shrugged. "*You* can."

***

"Eric got a car?" Trent shouted in excitement, something that was extremely out of character for him. He was usually quiet and reserved, but right now he was incredibly excited. He knew how long it had been since the three of us had done anything together. Now that we had a car, anything was possible. "We should go on a road trip!" he said, getting into the backseat and taking the spot in the middle.

"Where?" Eric asked.

"I don't know—somewhere."

"How about Houston?" I pondered aloud. It was far away, but not too far. Trent agreed with me, so I turned to Eric and asked, "You want to?"

"I'm down if you guys are." He turned out of the cul-de-sac Trent lived in and sped out of the suburbs, down to Highway 16. "Put on some music!"

"What should I play?" I asked, picking up Eric's iPod.

"Calling All Cars?" Trent suggested.

Both Eric and I enthusiastically agreed. Calling All Cars was the song we used in our very first YouTube video. It was the only one we edited as a group. The rest were done by myself, because they got harder to edit as each video got more and more complex. The final episode, for instance, took me over a dozen hours to complete. But the first one—the one we did together—took just an hour and a half. The four of us crowded around my computer and took turns shouting ideas, cracking jokes, and coming up with possibilities for future videos. But it will always have been Trent's idea to use the song Calling All Cars, and that song will always be our song, the one we will always associate with how much fun we used to have.

And as I tugged the cap off the bottle in my hands, I decided it was as simple as that—the song had given me the motivation. The excitement made me feel like I could do anything.

To make it all even more exciting, Anna had just sent me—in a text—something very romantic, and that made me miss her oh so much. Oh so much as I drank small sips out of the container of beer that neither Eric nor Trent noticed. They were as busy as I was, listening to Calling all Cars and feeling infinite.

'*School's out,*' Anna texted me, '*but it's not summer for me until I see you again.*'

As I drank away, the world around me disappeared. I wandered off into my own personal dreamland. I thought of Anna and I thought about the new life I'd have in my own apartment. Right now was just the waiting period. This summer would be insane. After a year of not seeing Anna, I'd finally have my shot with her.

Reality sank back in when we arrived in Houston. Eric went to gas up, but before he did, I turned over to the both of them and showed them the empty bottle of alcohol. "All gone," I said, and a stupid grin spilled across my face.

"Oh my God you drank the whole thing?"

Eric was freaked out, but Trent laughed it off. "Man, I didn't even know you had any beer," he said in admiration. "You should have let *me* drink some!"

"I'm gonna get some… chicken wings!" I told them, purposefully sounding stupid.

"Hold on—"

"Dray!"

"Don't get out yet!"

Ignoring them both, I got out of the car and wandered over to the trash can. As drunk as I was, I was still able to make out most of their conversation through the door I left open as I disposed of the beer bottle.

"You better take care of him while I gas up."

"He probably isn't *that* drunk," I heard Trent reply.

"He's never drank beer before and he had that whole thing."

"It's a Colt 45, too. Strong beer."

"How strong?"

"The strongest beer there is."

I don't know anything about alcohol. I don't know how much you need to get drunk or anything like that. All I know is that I got really wasted that night in Eric's car. I was putting on an act at first, but by the time I stepped inside the 7-eleven I understood exactly how drunk I'd really gotten myself.

Everyone inside the store seemed unreal—and, more so, *interesting*. I wanted to talk to everybody. "Hey!" I shouted. "What's your name?" And even though they glared silently back at me, it didn't bother me one bit. "I'm Dray," I slurred. "I'm drunk."

"Sorry," Trent would say. "Just ignore him."

At the counter, paying for some chicken wings, I finally got someone to talk to me—the guy working behind the till. "You know, I used to work at 7-eleven!" I excitedly told him.

"Did you?"

"Mhm. In Smithers, though. In the 7-eleven in Smithers."

"How'd you like it?"

"Sucked… *balls!*"

"Dray, shut up—"

"What's your name?" I asked, ignoring Trent once more.

"David."

"Dude—"

"Alright, Dray. Let's *go*."

Trent grabbed our food off the counter and pulled me towards the door. As he ushered me out, I looked around and finally noticed the people who'd been waiting behind me in line. Turning my glance back to the guy working at the till, I saw his attention was still on me. He was laughing in amusement, not even caring that a lot of customers were pissed off that I'd taken up so much of his time.

"Dude, you're awesome!" I shouted across the store, and he laughed even harder. "You're so fucking awesome!"

Violently, Trent threw me out the doors. "You want to get arrested?" he yelled as we strolled onto the pavement of the parking lot.

"Only if you get arrested with me."

"Not tonight."

"Drayvn!" I heard Eric shout, standing by his car, holding his keys. "Get over here!"

"Come on," hushed Trent, beckoning me to follow with his hands full of bags of chicken wings and potato wedges. "Let's eat," he pleaded.

Realizing they were genuinely worried about being caught by the police, I decided to finally listen and run back over to the car. Getting into the passenger seat, Eric said, "Drayvn... I can't believe you. I didn't know you were actually going to drink Cliff's beer."

"I'm *sawry*," I droned, squinting and putting a hand over my face as I lent up against window in the passenger seat.

He laughed, deciding it was funny. "Aren't people supposed to be really honest when they're drunk?" he asked Trent, who laughed too.

"Usually."

"This is gonna be an interesting drive" either Eric or Trent noted. The rest is history. The whole way back to Smithers they asked me questions I answered truthfully, and we all laughed and talked joyfully about past times and what new adventures the summer might hold. When they dropped me off, it was almost twelve o' clock.

"Are you gonna be okay?" they asked. "Don't you have to be at work at eight tomorrow?"

"I'll be fine, you guys," I told them. "Thanks for the awesome time. You guys are the best!"

"Get some sleep," said Trent. "You'll need it."

Brody's driveway was a long enough walk for something to whip through my mind: *I was drunk*. And being drunk was much different than being stoned. Being stoned was whatever you made it. You can disguise the use of drugs easily—all you have to say is that you're tired or stressed. It's easy. But being drunk is different; it's completely obvious. So before I risked the chance of bumping into either Brody or his parents, I immediately ran for the bathroom and turned on the water in the shower. I thought I was in the clear while brushing my teeth, but a knock suddenly came at the door.

"One sec," I said, rinsing my mouth out.

I opened the door as little as I could, but Brody poked his face all the way in. "Don't leave water running," he said.

"I'm just letting the shower warm up."

"You're drunk, aren't you?"

"Just because I went to a party doesn't mean I got drunk," I told him. Even though it was a lie, it was still a valid point.

"I can smell it on you," he said.

"How can you? I just brushed my teeth."

He lit up in anger. "So you *did* drink."

"Wow"—I laughed stupidly—"how did I let *that* slip?"

"You're an idiot."

"I'll agree with you on that."

Not knowing how to respond, Brody closed the door and walked back down the hallway towards his basement. And as I listened to his footsteps trudge down the stairs, I looked at my reflection in the mirror. Everything was wavy. I hardly recognized myself. But then things started getting crazy—the whole bathroom started spinning.

I leaned over the sink, and suddenly found myself puking.

To this day I have to say that puking while drunk has to have been the strangest sensation I'd ever felt. As if the experience of getting drunk wasn't already strange enough! And even though it wasn't exactly my first memory of drinking, it was now my best. Finally my friends were there—my real friends—the way it was meant to be. And even if Brody was pissed off at me, drinking in Eric's car that night will always have been worth it. Even throwing up was worth it. Even the terrible sleep I had that night was worth it.

But so much for work the next day...

When I finally came to, I had only twenty minutes left to get to Subway on time. As fast as I could, I dashed out the door and jogged the whole way there, but by the time I reached Main Street I was still a whole fifteen minutes late. And because I avoided awkward situations, I decided I'd rather not go at all than show up late and hungover. Besides, I still had—and still do have—lots of money left over from working at 7-eleven.

"What are you doing back here?" Brody's mom asked me when I appeared through the side door of their house. "You're out of breath."

The trip back took three times as long because I was exhausted from the lame attempt I made trying to jog my way to work. I shrugged at Brody's mom, looked down and carefully kicked off my shoes.

"What happened?"

"I don't like Subway," I said feebly.

"What happened?" she repeated.

"I don't know."

She looked me up and down. "Is there anything I can do?" she asked.

"I'm sorry," I said. "But don't worry—I'll be out of your hair soon."

"I'm not counting the days down until you leave!"

"My parents probably were."

"Dray..."

"I'm just"—I threw my hands in the air—"*troubled*."

I said the word "troubled" ironically.

Ironic, because I came from a good home with good parents, yet somehow—stuck in my own little world—I was a sappy little cry-baby. "I'm okay," I told her. "I just need to watch a funny movie or something."

"I'm here if you need me," she said, "and that goes for even when you've gone and left for your new apartment. There's a lot of people that care about you."

She saw the disbelieving look I had on my face.

"Believe me," she added.

***

Now that I never had a job to go to, I once again had an abundance of spare time. Lots of time to think, lots of time to wait.

As the days passed by, I watched the rest of the movies I had left over from my last haul of rentals at Gone Hollywood, and when I was through with those I watched what movies I found around the house. My boredom went as far as picking up their copy of Pride and Prejudice and plundering through that.

Eric was working, Brody was mad at me, and I was reading classic literature.

I was hoping to finish it by the time I moved out—still only halfway through—but Monday came sooner than I thought it would. My mom called me in the morning and told me to be ready by noon, which I was.

I was more than ready.

Finally it was time for the next chapter in my life. The past couple weeks had been complete chaos: I lived at both Cliff's and Eric's, then ended up at Brody's; got a job, quit it; drank beer, *puked* beer.

I wish I could have told myself that I was going to smarten up, but I wasn't sure if that was possible. I knew I was still extremely confused about who I was and what I wanted. A pain in my gut told me there was more troubling times ahead.

It was quarter past twelve in the afternoon, which meant my mom was late. I'd already said goodbye to Brody—who was still angry with me—and gave my thanks to his parents. Here I was, waiting uncomfortably on the front porch for my mom to arrive. Each minute made me more and more nervous. I was about to see her for the first time since she showed me the basement suite two weeks ago.

When I heard her vehicle come from beyond the end of the driveway, my heart stopped, but I shrugged it off and readied myself with what little things I had. I picked up my three backpacks and guitar and sauntered towards where she would arrive, watching my mom as her SUV whizzed past the trees and into the clearing in front of me. When she stopped, I walked around the vehicle and opened up the trunk. After throwing my stuff in the back, I climbed up into the passenger seat.

The drive was surprisingly quiet. Though I expected her to have a hundred things to say me, she scarcely said a word. Turning the vehicle around, she exited the driveway and headed down the highway towards town. When she finally did say something, she spoke only of bills and how things would work since I was living without a parent or guardian.

"You're an adult now," she said. "Seventeen, but you're expected to act as an adult."

She also told me about a deposit fee: "It's five hundred dollars, but if you take good care of the apartment you'll get it back when you move out. Then there's rent—it's due at the start of every month. Five hundred and fifty. You'll owe that a week from now, so make sure you have that money ready. You can give it to me in cash or cheque."

So I owed over a grand in bills already. That was more than a third of all the money I had. Maybe quitting Subway wasn't such a good idea, after all... But oh well, I would find a new job soon. Right now I was to enjoy myself. Finally, here I was.

I'm home, I thought to myself as my mom parked out in front of the house, which was now, I guess, *my* house. She was saying something as she turned off the vehicle, but I was in a different world than her.

I was imagining myself ten years down the road, anticipating what life would be like for me then. Whatever happened this summer, in this home, would be a dream, just a shadow of the future. This is where it all starts. This is where it begins. So much was ahead of me. I knew this because when something good is about to happen, I can feel it. And when something bad is about to happen, I can feel that too. I didn't know what was to come, but it was something. For the moment, the only thing I was sure of was that I now had my own apartment. I could do whatever I wanted with it: I could dress the place up whichever way I chose; play music all day; eat dinner in front of the TV. Only seventeen years old, yet I had complete and total freedom.

"Do you need a hand inside with your things?" my mom asked, once we'd finished unloading everything out of the SUV.

"I'll figure it out," I told her, picking up the biggest box there was sitting on my lawn. She nodded and took out a ring of keys from her pocket, preparing to drive off.

"See you in a week, then," she said. "Have the money ready."

I stepped backwards. "Thanks for helping me with my stuff," I said, nodding graciously to the stacks of books and movies she'd boxed up for me.

"No problem."

And then, the two of us went our separate ways. She got into her vehicle and I turned away, towards my new home.

Towards the next chapter in my life.

Part Two: Summer

Chapter One: To Here Know When

In both my bedroom and living room, the windows peek barely above ground level outside the driveway and front yard. Beyond that, on the other side of the street, diagonally across, was a small field that belonged to the town's local college—also the place I told Trent to head to, because he still never knew where I lived. The plan was for me to watch carefully for him, so that when he walked past I could call him over.

Again, I flicked open the blinds and checked to see if he was there, but for the dozenth time I found an empty field, growing darker as the evening went on. While turning off the music I'd put on during the wait, I noticed the clock on the corner of my laptops screen and saw that I'd been waiting a full hour. An hour had passed of nothing but watching and waiting. I could feel myself becoming restless. Even the new music I got today from my brother was failing to interest me.

Because my mom had forgotten a few of my things behind—probably on purpose—I had to make the trip back home to retrieve them. Making use of of the visit, I told Henry to download me some of the new bands I was interested in. Now that I was in my new apartment, I would no longer have the access to internet to get music myself.

While I'd waited for the music to finish downloading, I received a text from Trent. He told me that he got a new pipe, asked if I wanted to 'christen' it with him. I never knew what that was, but he promptly explained to me that when you use a pipe for the first time it gives you the cleanest high. Supposedly, that's the best kind of high. I'm still not sure what he was talking about, but I accepted the invitation. I wanted to show him my new place anyway.

At that thought, I peered outside my window once more. At last, there he was—crouched down on the field, looking around in search of me. Not even bothering to put on my shoes, I dashed out of the car-park and called out his name.

"Nice house," he called back to me, following my voice. "I had a feeling it was this one."

I told him thanks once he'd walked his way over to my front lawn.

"Are you all settled in?" he asked.

"Completely."

"Let me check it out."

Stepping inside, he was taken aback. "You've even got a kitchen table and chairs?" He took a further look around. "Where'd you get all this stuff?"

"Comes with renting the place out," I told him.

"Sweet deal." Taking a walk through the kitchen, and over into the living room, he saw the matching couch and chair, TV, lamps, and coffee tables. "Dude, this is awesome. You've got everything!" Around the corner he stepped into my bedroom. "Pretty big bedroom, too." He looked back at me. "I thought this place was gonna be tiny when I walked in but this is really nice."

"Thanks," I said again.

"Can we smoke in here?"

It was an innocent question, so I laughed it off and said, "Wouldn't be a good idea," though truthfully, I was as eager as him to start blazing. "I don't wanna get kicked out of here, too."

"Getting kicked out once must have been enough," he remarked, sitting down at the kitchen table. After pulling out a bag of weed, he bunched up a piece of marijuana, fitting it perfectly inside his new pipe. "Outside, then?"

"Yeah, let's go." I put on my shoes; Trent did the same and followed me out the door. Outside, in the cement stairwell, we hunched up close together and passed the pipe back and forth as fast as possible, careful not to let any weed go to waste. When it died, Trent turned it over and flicked the ash out.

"Isn't it supposed to be summer," he mused, a slight shiver in his voice. He put the empty pipe in his jacket and warmed his hands up together. "What do you wanna do tonight?"

"I don't know," I grunted, staring off into the night. A couple stars had appeared. "As awesome as my new place is, I'm feeling sick of it already."

"How about we do a few more bowls and go for an epic walk around town?" he suggested. Surprised, I asked him if he really wanted to, but he assured me that he did. Usually, Trent was unmotivated for things like that. He got tired easily, and went home before anyone else did. "Let's do it," he said. "Walking around when you're high is amazing."

✷✷✷

We felt relatively fine as we prepared to head out into the night. Months ago, one toke used to make me feel high; now, after close to a half a dozen, I still felt completely normal. *Almost*, anyway. "Are you high yet?" Trent asked, disappointed, setting the pipe and weed down onto my table.

"Don't do that," I told him, swinging my door open.

"What, you want me to hide it?"

"No," I said. "*Bring* it."

He laughed and did as I said, placing the materials inside the pocket of his jacket.

After locking the door and making our way down my driveway, we watched as a few giggling girls walked past the house, reminding me to ask if Trent knew of anyone out on the town tonight.

"It's a Thursday," he said.

"But it's summer."

"True. I guess some people we know might be hanging out by the skate park. But I don't know for sure. I never walked past it on my way here."

I sighed. "I can't wait till we're nineteen—"

"Then *we* can go to the bar."

"And party with cool, older girls." I pointed down the road to the girls who walked past us a moment ago. They were most likely heading off to the Twin, the most popular bar in town, located across the street from 7-eleven.

"It sucks being under-aged," Trent concluded, and we walked off in the opposite direction of the giggling girls. "Has Eric ever smoked weed?" he randomly pondered.

"He did with me, once."

"He did!?"

"But that was practically a whole year ago."

"What was it like?"

"We didn't know what we were doing."

"Did you get really baked your first time?"

"No," I said simply, remembering how disappointing the experience had been. I thought smoking weed would have changed my life. I thought it would have made me look at the world completely different. All it ended up doing was make my eyes red and give me a sense of dizziness. All it did was wipe away the thoughts that kept me up at night.

"Dude, I'm not high," Trent complained, once we'd made our way down a few blocks. I could tell he was beginning to get tired already.

"Give it a minute," I told him.

"It's been twenty," he said. "We have to do another bowl."

"Alright, another." I looked around us, trying to decide the safest place to pack another bowl. We were in the deadest part of town, by Railway.

He pointed to a plain of grass: "How 'bout there?"

I laughed. "That's someone's back yard, Trent."

"So? Let's do it!"

"What if we get caught?" I asked, though I never really cared. I just wanted to make it seem more dangerous.

"It'll be fine. Come on," he said, stepping off the sidewalk. "Follow me."

After casually passing by, we sneaked into the alleyway and sprinted across the backyard. Cut off from the streets and alleyways, the house had a shed to the side of it, shielded from sight by several tall trees.

"This is perfect," Trent said, and was half-right. No one would see us here from the street. But then again, if the people inside the house took one look out their windows... Well, they'd be staring right at us.

"They're probably sleeping," I said, considering the fact that not a single light was on inside of the house. "We'll have to keep it down, though."

"I'll hurry."

I used my phone as a flashlight, illuminating the Ziploc bag and the pipe as he prepared us yet another bowl of marijuana. I closed up my phone as soon as he was finished.

The lighter clicked on; I looked up at the windows nervously.

"Spooky."

"What is?" Trent asked, blowing smoke out of his lungs.

Paranoia was sneaking over me... "I keep thinking I'll look up and they'll be right there looking at us."

"What are they gonna do?"

"Murder us with an axe?" I joked.

Trent laughed in response, a laugh a little too loud for my liking—given the situation we were in.

"Here." He handed me the pipe. "Take a big one."

Because I was in a rush to get out of the backyard as fast as I could, I took the biggest toke my lungs could manage. Slowly, my body and chest swelled up like a balloon. Trent snickered when he noticed. "Save me some," he said, to which I took the pipe away from my mouth and handed it over to him. Smoke trickled into the air from the funnel; with it, I realized just how much smoke I'd inhaled. And after remembering what Trent had told me earlier today, I understood we had now "christened" this pipe. Maybe that's why we weren't getting high so easily. Maybe clean highs took longer to begin their effect.

When the blood began rushing to my head, I exhaled, but because I breathed out too fast, the smoke was without the space it took to exit my body properly. As a cloud of smoke fumed out in front of my face, some streamed in and out my nose while some remained stuck inside my lungs. I could even feel smoke trapped inside my stomach, meaning I would have to belch it out later.

"*Don't—fucking—cough*," Trent whisper-shouted, but it was too late. I began coughing so hard I couldn't even stop to breathe. Violently, my body shook up and down as I tried clearing the airways down my throat.

"Keep it down!"

A couple dogs barked in the nearby distance.

By the time I composed myself, my coughs were more like muffled hiccups. Between them, I inhaled the fresh summer air. And after wiping away the tears from under my eyes, I told Trent, "That was fucking brutal," but as I spoke those words, we both heard a door swing open in front of us.

We'd been caught.

A man in his thirties came out onto his back porch, looking directly at us.

"Hello!?" was all he could say.

I was too stunned to move, but I managed a whisper: "Trent we should"—I hiccuped—"get out of here?"

But when I looked over, it turned out that Trent was busy—one of his eyes on the man, the other on the pipe he calmly brought to his mouth.

I patronized him: "Seriously!?"

As he inhaled the last of the burning grass, he gave me a condescending look, one that said, "Chill out. Relax."

I supposed, being as high I was, that the man on the porch was beyond my comprehension. Unlike Trent, my initial thought was that he'd hop down and chase after us. But when I looked back, the man did nothing—he just stared at us. Still, I thought it best to get the hell out of there as fast as possible. I was positive that if he got a closer look and saw how unintimidating we truly were, he'd man up and kick our asses. Urging Trent to follow me back into the alleyway, I sporadically tugged on his arm, making him burst into a fit of coughing.

"Oh shit!" I heard Trent say, and as he rubbed a hand through his eyes, I noticed his face was covered in hot ash.

"Are you okay?" I asked.

"Let's just fucking go!" Trent said, coughing and squinting his eyes, trying to find the way out.

"This way," I said with drastic authority, dragging him off the way we came in.

"Hey! Come back here!" the man called timidly after us.

In response, Trent put up his middle finger in the air and said: "Screw you, fucker!"

And while we ran our course back into the alleyway, the man continued shrieking out into the night. We ignored him, laughing and coughing hysterically as we ran the couple blocks it took to get to the isolated railroad tracks. We sat down and caught our breath.

"That guy was hilarious," Trent murmured, sitting down on the rocky terrain.

"I thought he was going to kill us."

"He wasn't gonna do shit."

I laughed. "You see the look on his face?"

"It looked like he was gonna shit his pants!" Trent answered, swaying a hand through his hair. "What the hell?"

"What?"

"I got ash all over my face."

I sat down next to Trent. "You shouldn't have coughed into the pipe."

"That was *your* fault…"

Wiping a hand over his face, he cleared himself of all debris. Done, he went and laid down and looked up at the stars, putting his hands behind his head as a way to keep his hair from the dirty ground. I tried to do the same, but when I looked up into the sky, a major headache occurred.

I closed my eyes instead, letting the headache simmer away.

Years ago I knew all the constellations by heart—their names and where to find them. I used to look up into space often, using a telescope my parents had bought me one Christmas. Before I met Anna, before I had friends, I used to have nothing else to do.

"Look." Trent pointed upwards. "The Big Dipper!"

I dared not even try and locate it. "That all?"

"Hey, I've never found The Big Dipper myself before."

"Amateur."

"What do you see?" he challenged me.

"Right now?" I asked.

He nodded.

"Right now—dude, I'm seeing elephants and whales." We laughed. "Every star looks like it's moving."

✳✳✳

As we did our fifth bowl, I thought it would be the last, but I was made wrong an hour later at the skate park. To my reluctance, we went there to "match bowls" with some of Trent's other friends. Matching bowls, I was told, is when two groups of people—with each their own stash of weed—get together and smoke weed with the same pipe. Though it sounded lame to me, I was in no position to complain. It wasn't my weed; it was Trent's.

After doing two bowls in the dug-outs of the baseball field, my mind was spinning out of control. I couldn't keep up with anything Trent or his friends said to me, so I escaped the mindless chatter and stepped out of the dug-out. Taking in the quiet night air, I checked my phone for the time, but instead found a couple of text messages. They were from Anna.

'Settled in to your apartment, yet?' she asked. *'What are you doing right now?'* read another.

'Reading a book,' I lied.

'Which book?' she immediately texted back.

"Guess what I just realized!" Trent interrupted, stumbling over to me. He put his head on my shoulder and held my neck as a way of balance. "Guess what I just realized," he repeated.

"What?"
"We smoked all the weed I bought today."
"All of it?"
"Forty bucks worth."
"I'm sorry."
"Don't be sorry!" He tripped back a couple of steps. "Tonight's been awesome!"
I halfheartedly agreed.
"I can't believe we smoked a bowl in some fat guys backyard!"
"*Was* he fat—?"
"Hey there!" someone said.
Looking up in the direction the voice had come, we found two girls walking towards us from the playground. They were in tight-loose clothing, not unlike the two girls we saw giggling down the street of my house. The only thing different about them now was the way they walked. Put simply, they were now wasted.
"Hey!" Trent called out to them. "You drunk?"
"Oh ya!"
"Those are the girls," Trent whispered to me. "Those are the girls that were by your house."
"I know," I said, remembering how attractive I had found them to be. "What are you girls up to?" I asked the two of them.
"Saying hello to you," the tall one said, her voice shrill and sloppy.
"Hello," Trent said, overwhelmed. The shorter girl ran up and hugged him, burying her face into his chest. He tried his best not to fall over.
"I'm Amanda," she said.
Suddenly, I then felt the other girl grab a hold of me. She kissed my neck, and as she did I could smell the scent of shampoo permuting from her long dark hair. Sliding her hands down my back, she whispered into my ear, "I'm Tina."
"I'm Drayvn."
"Drayvn?" She looked into my face, trying to recognize me. "I've heard that name before."
"Drayvn Emerald—?"

"You're cute."

I laughed. "Thanks."

"Do you think I'm cute?" she asked, whispering into my ear again.

"Um—"

"Wait, who's this?" the girl named Amanda asked.

"*Drayvn,*" Tina told her.

"I've heard that name somewhere," she replied, but forgot about it and asked, "What are you boys up to?"

"Just hanging out," Trent replied coolly.

"Out here?" She gave us an unimpressed look.

"Where else are we gonna smoke weed?" Trent told her, trying once again to be cool.

"I thought you guys smelt like weed!" Amanda chuckled.

"You *thought* they did?" Tina turned over to us: "You guys smell like you have a pound of bud sitting in your pocket."

"We did," said Trent, "but we smoked it all."

I sighed deeply at Trent's remark, which caught Tina's attention back to me. "Tell me your number, Drayvn," she demanded, playfully basking her dark eyebrows at me.

"Why?" I asked.

"Because I'm going to call you later on tonight."

"Why?"

"Because I like you."

"Why?"

She laughed. "Stop saying *why*! Just give me your number, already."

I smiled, then recited the seven digits while she punched them in on her phone.

"I'll call you in a bit," she affirmed, and the two of them walked back in the direction they came from.

"Who were they?" said someone behind me.

I turned around realized an audience had formed. Trent's friends—guys who'd never had a date with a girl in their life—had gathered together in front of the dug-out to watch both Trent and

I as we had interacted with these gorgeous—and drunk—twenty-something year old girls.

"I don't know who they were," I told them.

"Those girls were fucking hot!" one of them said.

"Did you give that one girl your number?" asked another.

"Yeah."

"They are so drunk—you could totally get laid tonight."

"With both of them!" someone added, and a strange thought occurred:

Now I even had a place to take them to.

When I lived at home with my family, I never would have dreamed of bringing a girl over. My parents religion said that you couldn't even start dating until the age of sixteen. And when I turned sixteen, the only other girls I was interested in were younger than me. No girl my age would be interested in watching a movie and just hanging out… They wanted guys with big trucks, guys to make out with at parties.

I honestly wasn't sure why I was interested in seeing those two girls later on that night. It's not like I wanted anything to happen. I guess it just seemed a whole lot more exciting than hanging out with a bunch of stoners.

***

"I can't believe you gave away my last beer," said one of them. He was pacing around wildly in the dug-out while the rest of us sprawled out stoned on the long bench the baseball players sat on during their games.

"I thought it was *my* beer I gave away," someone—without giving it much care—tried explaining to him.

"Why would you think that," he replied. "You had six beers; I had five."

"Come on," he tried calming him down, "he bought us a pack of smokes."

"With *our* money."

"He still went and got them for us."

"Because you gave him a beer."

"For smokes."

"The ones you smoked."

Pause. "There's some left—do you want one?"

"You know I don't smoke."

"Then what are you complaining about?"

"Because you gave one of my beers away—!"

And just when I thought my boredom had reached its limit, my phone vibrated. "Is that them?" Trent asked.

"I think so," I replied, taking it out of my pocket. It was an incoming call, from a number I couldn't recognize, and it was almost two in the morning—who else could it have been? Trent's eyes widened. He turned to his friends and said, "Guys it's *them*! It's those girls calling!"

They all yelled at me and told me to pick up. "Okay, okay." I calmed them down, then answered, "Hello?"

"Where are you?" Tina asked.

"Um."

The crowd around went quiet, trying to listen in.

"Don't tell me you went home," she sobbed.

"No, I'm by the skate park still."

"You should come to the Twin."

I put the phone away from my ear and told Trent, "They think I'm old enough to go to the bar!" They snickered, disappointed; I brought the phone back to my ear.

"The bar?" I inquired.

"No," she replied. "The motel."

My eyes went as wide as Trent's. "The motel?" my voice cracked, and everybody around went ballistic.

"Shut up, guys!" Trent whisper-shouted at the giggling pack of outcasts.

"Yeah, we got a room," Tina continued. "Just come by—I'll watch for you out the window."

"Are you sure?" I asked.

"Yeah, why?"

"I don't know."

"Will you really come?" she pleaded. "Don't make me wait for you by the window for nothing."

"I'll come," I assured her. "In fact, I'll head there right now."

"Yay!" She gave out a whirly-girlish giggle. "So I'll see you soon, then?"

"Ten minutes," I told her.

When I hung up, Trent's friends piled over me, ruffling my hair and punching my shoulder. I could tell how jealous they were. "You're getting laid tonight," they told me as if it were a fact, not a prediction. But I was certain nothing would happen. If I hadn't smoked nine bowls previous to this, I probably wouldn't have even bothered going to see them at all. But I was high. High and searching for an adventure.

"Are you leaving?" Trent asked.

"I don't have to."

"You should," he said. "I'm going home, anyway." He stood up off the bench. "Come on, I'll walk you to Sev," he offered.

When we got to 7-eleven, Trent bought himself one of their big-bite hot dogs. While stuffing it down his throat, he told me, "Tomorrow you'll have to tell me everything that happens in that motel room. And don't lie!" He finished the hot dog, licked his fingers clean of ketchup, then looked at me confusedly. "Aren't you hungry?" he asked.

"Not really."

"We had like ten bowls tonight—you should be starving. I am. I think I'll get another hot dog, actually."

I laughed. "I better get going, then. Tina's waiting and I really don't want to stand here and watch you demolish another hot dog in less than a minute."

"What?"

I smiled. "Never mind." I turned away and walked off, but as I did, he called out my name. I looked back—still walking away—and inquired. "Yeah?"

"Thanks for the night," he said.

I gave him a scrutinizing look. Trent never gave his thanks to anyone. Something about tonight must have meant a lot to him. *Had we talked about anything personal?* I couldn't remember, so I shrugged it off and made a joke:

"Thanks for all the marijuana!" I shouted, something that clearly bothered him. He looked around, hoping no one heard me. The coast was clear.

"You're gonna get us arrested if you yell that shit out loud!" he warned.

"Coming from the guy who wanted to smoke a bowl in someone's backyard," I retorted.

Trent shook his head angrily at me and then went back inside.

Leaving the parking lot of 7-eleven, the Twin was a block away, and I could already tell in the distance that it had just closed. Drunks stumbled towards me, towards 7-eleven, and I passed by them all as I made my way over to the other side of the building where the motel was.

Just as I thought about going home instead, I heard Tina's voice come from above, calling me by name. On the highest floor of the motel, Tina stepped up to the guard rail and peered down at me.

"What are you waiting for?" she asked. "Come on up!"

"Coming!" I said, and ran up the flight of stairs towards the room they were staying in. By the time I reached her, I was panting pathetically. "I'm stoned," I explained, not wanting her to think I was unfit to simply run up some stairs. She stared blankly at me, so I shrugged and asked, "What's going on in here?" I looked into the motel room, and as I did she ushered me through the door. Amanda, I found, was perched on the bed with a drunk and dazed expression on her face, hardly even recognizing me. I tried saying hello, but all she did was nod her head meekly. The rest of the room looked untouched, so I assumed they'd just arrived from the bar.

I was about to ask why they even got a hotel room in the first place, but that was when I saw, through the open bathroom door, a man preparing drinks by the sink. "Hey bud," the man said, not even bothering to look up at me. "How are you tonight?" he asked.

"I'm good," I told him, extremely confused. *What the hell was going on?* Then it dawned on me... The man was a pimp; these girls were prostitutes!

It was the only logical explanation. They had hooked me here and the man was preparing us drinks before claiming the money. Of course that was it—why else had two twenty-five year old girls been so interested in me?

The man stepped out of the bathroom, two drinks in hand, and looked at me. "You're pretty stoned, man," he said, chuckling, handing over one of the drinks to Amanda.

"Look, I don't know about this—" I started explaining, but was suddenly interrupted.

"Does anyone have any music they can play?" Amanda blurted out.

I shrugged.

"I really feel like dancing!"

I looked over at Tina—who'd put her arm on my shoulder—before turning back to Amanda, who stood up drunkenly and danced her way over to the middle of the room, between both me and the man standing next to the bathroom. Watching her intently, the man casually sipped his drink as she chugged back hers. Once she drank the whole thing down, she lolled her head with a smile and sat her glass down on top of the TV set before stepping up close to the man. She kissed his cheek, ear, and neck. He took another sip of his drink and led her into the bathroom, closing the door behind them.

Relieved, I realized he wasn't a pimp. These girls were *not* hookers. But even that revelation never made the situation any more normal. *What am I even doing here?* I thought to myself, but asked aloud, "Is that her boyfriend?"

Tina laughed harshly. "No," she murmured.

"How do they know each other?"

"They just met."

"At the Twin?"

"Yeah." Tina went and sat down on the bed. In the background, I heard Amanda moaning from in the bathroom. They turned on the fan to filter the noise, but we heard it all. Amanda and that guy—they were having sex.

In the bathroom of a motel with some random guy she met at the Twin.

"Why weren't you at the bar tonight?" Tina asked.

I went quiet.

Her mouth dropped. "You're not old enough, are you?"

"To be honest with you," I said carefully, "no, I'm not."

"Sit down," she told me, padding the mattress she was sitting on. "So then how old are you?" she asked.

I sat down next to her and said, "Seventeen."

"Shitty age."

I agreed with her and looked down at my feet, but the room was too quiet—except for the continuous grunts and moans coming from the bathroom—so I looked up to try and start a conversation. When I looked over I found that she was lost in thought, staring at me with what looked like a grim and blank face—but I knew what it really was; I knew she wanted me. Her eyes fluttered. She moved close to me.

But I hesitated, without even meaning to.

She pulled away. "We don't have to do anything," she said, smiling. "But I warn you, they might be in there for awhile."

"That's okay," I said.

"We can *talk*," she thought to herself, then laughed. I could tell the idea of talking seemed elementary to her.

"Is that okay?"

"Of course."

I felt like I owed her an explanation. "I've never been with a girl before," I explained, trying to be cool about it the same way Trent had tried to be cool.

"Drayvn. I'm not trying to have sex with you."

"No, like really—I've never even kissed a girl."

She was dumbfounded. "You haven't kissed a girl? Why not?"

"The right time just never comes along."

"But you're so good-looking. The girls should be chasing after you." Studying me up and down, she then said, "I would love to be your first kiss. But I don't think you'd *want* me as your first kiss."

"I don't know what I want," I said flirtatiously, thinking dangerously to myself. *Why shouldn't I kiss her?* She was just some random girl. Just some girl I'd never see again. My life was no longer a storybook story—what was I waiting for? Nothing. I had nothing left to hold onto.

Ready to make my first kiss, I scooted closer to her on the bed, so close that our shoulders were touching. Adapting to my movements, she put an arm around me, and because I was tired, I closed my eyes, feeling comfortable for the first time in almost a year. The moans from the bathroom seemed to have died down, and for a moment everything went quiet. I felt her roll a finger along my shoulder, then a hand through my hair. I was so relaxed. A chill crept down down my spine.

I would open my eyes and kiss her, I decided. I'd push her down lightly onto the bed, crawl over her body, look into her eyes and kiss her. I knew exactly what to do, but once again, my plans were thwarted. They always are. This time, someone came knocking on the door. Despondently, I opened my eyes. "Who's that?" I asked, still stoned.

"That's them—the boys that rented out this motel room." Tina jumped up off the bed, raced across the room and swung open the door. "Hey there!"

Four guys in their late twenties entered the room passively. One of them kissed Tina on the cheek.

"Hey Mark," she said gleefully

"And who's this?" he asked, looking up from Tina to me.

"That's Drayvn," Tina told everyone, closing the door as they scattered around the room.

"You wanna drink?" Mark offered, pulling out a large bottle from the inside of his jacket.

"No thanks. But thanks, though."

"You're being polite. I'm pouring you one, anyway." He went over to the desk and unwrapped a set of plastic cups.

"Wait," someone behind me said. "Where'd this kid come from? What's he doing in our motel room?"

"Chill out," said Tina. "Me and Amanda met him on our walk—"

"You two were pretty drunk tonight," noted someone else.

"Whose fault was that?" Tina said, annoyed. "You guys kept buying us drinks."

"How else"—the same voice came behind—"were we going to get you girls to come party with us?" Walking in front of me to the desk, he took a freshly poured drink off the counter and sat down beside me. "How old are you?" he asked.

"Nineteen," I told him casually.

"Hey!" Tina glared at me. "You told me seventeen."

"I did" was all I could think to say. An awkward pause followed.

"He can be whatever age he wants to be," the guy next to me spoke, a surprisingly nice thing for him to say. At first, he'd seemed like a complete douche to me. "I'm Daryl, by the way," he said.

"He's getting *married*," Tina remarked.

Daryl and I shook hands. I asked, "When are you getting married?"

"Three days from now," he replied.

I surveyed the scene around me. "Is this a bachelor's party?"

"Sort of," he told me. "We're from Houston."

Tina grabbed two drinks off the counter: one for herself, the other for me. I took an awkward sip.

"Why'd you come to Smithers for a bachelor's party?" I asked, trying not to grimace as I swallowed down whatever the drink was.

"We heard the Twin was a great place to party."

"Was it?"

"No." He took a drink. "Anyways, the wedding is this Sunday."

"How long have you known each other?"

Confidently: "Eight long years."

"Were you high school sweethearts?" I asked

"Kind of," he explained. "We lost our virginity's to each other, but we've gone out with other people since. Just a year ago we started getting serious and now"—he shrugged—"now we're ready to commit."

His story disappointed me, but I nodded and said, "That's awesome."

After weighing the idea around in his head, he took a drink and assured me it was. Past his head I noticed Tina. Apparently, during my conversation with Daryl, she had fallen onto the bed across from me and was now making out with Mark.

"Are you a virgin?" Daryl asked, yanking my attention away from Tina. "You're still in high school, right?"

"I'm not in high school, actually."

"But he *is* a virgin," said Tina, looking up from Mark, dabbing her wet lips with an open palm. "He told me."

Daryl turned back to me. "That's okay," he said. "Big deal—it doesn't actually matter."

Tina burst out laughing, but continued kissing Mark through her laughter.

"Where's that other girl?" one of the guys asked.

"*Amanda*," I said. "Her name's Amanda."

"Where is she?"

"Bathroom."

Daryl nudged my arm. "Is our friend Paul in there with her?"

"I never caught *his* name."

The guys laughed. Daryl stood up and sauntered over to the door. He looked back at us as he knocked and called out his friend's name. A faint voice came from the other side and said for him to come in. Opening the door, Amanda was revealed alongside the guy I now knew as Paul. She was leaning over the sink, throwing up.

Paul mouthed to us, with a smile, "She's fucked." One of his hands was carelessly holding back her hair.

Quietly looking back on Tina, I discovered she'd chosen to continue making out with the stranger next to her instead of helping her friend out.

I took this all as a cue for me to head home. Burn out, the façade of excitement had vanished away completely. The whole ordeal gave me something to think about, though, as I left the room and headed down the stairs of the motel. *Why did I even go there?* I wondered, walking across the parking lot of the Twin, up the alleyway and onto the street my basement suite was on.

Chapter Two: Good to Sea

The morning's clean light, pouring in through the window above me, nuzzled me back into a state of consciousness. Though I smelt terribly like smoke, I felt totally fine. It was as though last night's grand adventure had never occurred. I wasn't strung-out, tired, or anything like that. In fact, I felt good. I was ready for another night of partying! It was a Friday, after all, which meant a lot more people would be out on the town drinking. I'd probably even see Rose and Cassidy.

Excited for the day—and the night ahead—I threw some eggs on the frying pan and eagerly had myself a quick shower. Once I hopped out, I rushed back to the stove and flipped the eggs over. While they continued to fry, I put on a change of clothes and texted Rose, asking if she had any plans for the night. But as I did, I finally remembered that I'd forgotten to text Anna back last night when she asked me what book it was that I lied to her about reading, something I felt pretty bad about.

But it's not like I could have told her the truth. I was supposed to be her knight in shining armor, not the high-on-drugs boy who hung out in the baseball dug-outs at two in the morning.

'*Sorry for not texting you back. I fell asleep,*' I replied, then added, '*The book's called Thumbsucker, by the way. It's really good.*' It wasn't a complete fabrication. I really have been reading a book called Thumbsucker. When my mom brought me and my things here, I looked through my book collection and found the one book I hadn't read yet. What's strange is that while I'm usually a fast reader, this particular book was taking me forever to get through. I'll read a couple of pages, then doze off thinking about something else. It's an amazing book; I just can't keep my head focused on it. Life's too exciting right now.

Apparently so exciting I'd forgotten all about the eggs I had cooking over the stove.

Luckily—after I pulled them off the burner—they were still in decent shape, still edible, especially after dowsing them in salt and pepper. It was a great breakfast. I enjoyed it, sitting at my kitchen table, contemplating the day ahead. Now all I needed in front of me was a nice, warm, steaming-hot cup of coffee. Maybe today I'd go and buy a coffee-maker to have for when I was at home. But more importantly, I needed to find a job. That was my mission for today.

'I'll be around,' came a text from Rose, along with the winking emoticon she sometimes used. *'Hope to see you out and about."* And as I thought of a reply, I received yet another text, this time from a different girl. *'You must be a heavy sleeper, then,'* said Anna, her words dripping with disbelief. Thinking it over, I realized how unusual it must have been for her that I never said goodnight. The past couple years I'd always given her my complete and full attention. So not knowing what to say—to either of them, actually—I put my my phone down and finished my eggs.

✳✳✳

Trent unexpectedly dropped by a little later on in the afternoon, which was a cool feeling for me. No one had ever showed up like that when I lived at home with my parents. If I ever did let anyone over—and I sometimes did—I had to make sure they never swore around my parents or brought up anything slightly suggestive. But even though I tried so hard to remind them, they'd sometimes go off and say, "Oh my God," or something like that, and then that would get me into trouble and my parents would no longer like my friends. So the whole experience of having somebody over was just embarrassing. I never bothered. But now that I had my own place, if people went knocking on my door all they'd find was me.

Without even a hello, Trent blurted out, "What the hell happened last night?!"

"Who knows," I said with a smile as Trent stepped into my kitchen. "Last night was ridiculous."

"Do you remember smoking a bowl in that guys backyard?" Trent asked, and I could tell from his voice that he couldn't believe the fact of the matter himself. I chuckled. I *hadn't* remembered it, but now that I did, I realized what an amazing time it had been last night. "That's all I can remember," Trent continued as he sat down at my table. "The whole night's a blur for me right now."

"Me too."

As I sat down with him he looked back up at me. "Let's do it again, tonight," he suggested.

I grimaced. "I think Eric will want to hang out tonight. It's a Friday, after all."

"Whatever. If he doesn't want to smoke weed—who cares, right?"

"I guess so."

Trent stood up. "I gotta go to work," he said, pulling out a pipe and lighter out of his jacket. "I thought I'd drop this off so I don't have to get it later." He placed them down on the table in front of me. "We *will* have to get more weed, though. Wanna come by my work?" he asked, getting up and putting on his shoes. "I'm off at five."

"That sounds good."

Once he went out the door, I watched him leave down the street through my window. He worked at Zellers, which I thought might be an alright place for me to work. But the job I really wanted was at Wholesale, with Eric. Two days ago I'd tried getting a job there, but the manager told me all the positions were filled. After that, I thought I'd wait it out and make sure I found a job I actually liked, but with my money running low I was starting to get desperate.

Back in the kitchen, I picked up the pipe on the table—the one responsible for all that happened last night—and inspected it carefully. There was still some weed encrusted on the inside, enough there I believed to take a hit from. Using the lighter Trent left behind, I took in a quick drag. Surprisingly, a large amount of smoke came tumbling through its funnel and down my lungs. Sitting down, I relinquished in a nice head-rush, but it was interrupted by another knock at the door. I got up and checked it out.

As I opened the door, I'd expected Trent, but it was Cliff, I found, instead.

"I thought this was your house," he said.

Without him noticing, I sneakily put the pipe and lighter in my pocket and said, "How'd you know?"

"Eric gave me directions." He stepped in, then flared his nostrils. "What's that smell?"

I tried being as inconspicuous as I could. "I was trying to fix the stove," I said, coughing slightly, not wanting Cliff to know I was *that guy*.

The guy that smokes weed at twelve in the afternoon.

"The burner wasn't working, so it's probably the gas you smell."

He gave me a condescending look, then walked over to the stove and turned it on. "It works fine—are you stupid?"

I threw my hands up and said, "I guess I'm just not used to a stove like that."

"Right, your parents have a fancy one, don't they?"

As he took a look through the rest of my apartment, I still wasn't sure if he knew or not that it was marijuana he could smell, but he dropped it nonetheless. In his hands, I noticed a couple movies. "What movies did you rent?" I asked.

"That's actually why I came by," he said, stepping back over to me. "The new movie by Gus Van Sant came out, and I know he's, like, your favorite director."

"He made a new movie?"

"It looks really good," he said, handing me the cover. "Want to watch it?"

"Wow"—I took it from him—"I haven't even heard of this."

"Me neither. The only reason it caught my eye was because on the cover it said it was the director of Elephant."

"Do we have time to watch it now?"

"Only if you put it in right now," he replied. "I've got work at four."

***

"So was the kid gay or something?"

I laughed, hitting the pause button on my DVD remote, cutting the credits off from strolling up the screen. "What do you mean?" I asked, at first not taking Cliff's statement seriously.

"The kid," Cliff clarified. "Do you think he was gay?"

"I never thought of it. What—did you?"

Cliff leaned forward on his knees, sitting across from me on my large couch. "He *had* to have been gay. He was having sex with a girl and yet the whole time he's having sex he's acting like someone's just died."

"Someone *did* die. Remember?"

"Still," he grunted, "he obviously wasn't into girls from the very start. The movie would have been so much better if that came full circle in the plot—if, for instance, he met some cute skater-boy instead of that dumpy girl at the coffee shop."

This was regular routine for Cliff and I. Throughout the years we've watched thousands of movies and argued endlessly over a number of them. Our interpretations are almost always different.

"Sorry Cliff," I told him, "but I'm still not convinced he was gay."

"Dude," he said, shaking his head at me, "it's a Gus Van Sant movie for crying out loud! Even the high school killers of Columbine were homosexuals according to him."

"They weren't gay, either," I reproached. "They'd just never had the chance to be with girls before."

"Well maybe that's what the director was trying to tell us," Cliff said, now giggling a little as he'd realized his interpretation had gone a bit too far. "Boys who don't get pussy end up turning gay and killing someone."

"Bravo!" I shouted sarcastically. "That *has* to be it..."

"Okay, I'm being stupid, but hear me out... The movie was like a metaphor for being gay, being *Paranoid*—as the title implies—that people *know*..."

"Interesting observation, but I think you're over-analyzing."

"I have to over-analyze these boring art films or I'd just fall asleep."

I gasped, concealing an amused smile. "I liked it!"

"I did, too," Cliff finally admitted. "But I think they could have taken the plot in more interesting directions."

"Fair enough," I said, coming to an agreement with him. "You hungry?" I then asked.

"Little bit."

"You rented the movie; I'll buy us lunch."

✱✱✱

After grabbing a burger at our favorite restaurant—The Aspen—Cliff and I parted ways. While he went to work at Safeway, I continued across the parking lot over to Zellers. "What are you doing here?" Trent asked, surprised to see me walking through the toy aisle he was busy sorting through. "I don't get off for another half-hour."

"I know, but I was thinking of applying here."

His eyes lit up. "Really?"

"I don't know—should I?"

"Totally!" He stood up. "It would be amazing if I got to work with you!"

"Is there someone here I could talk to?"

Trent waved a hand behind him, towards the other end of the aisle, and told me to follow him as he directed us across the store. Making our way through the clothes and furniture, he showed me into an office space where an older man sat crookedly staring up at our arrival. "Who's this?" he asked, referring to me.

"He's looking for a job," Trent answered. "I thought you might want to talk to him."

The eyes of the man sitting in his desk lit up the same way Trent's had moments ago. Hopping out of his chair, he stepped up to me and shook my hand, and as he did, he might as well have told me I was hired from the get-go because he almost instantly gave me the job, anyway. Just like Subway had. It was depressing, because when I was hired at 7-eleven, I was so proud of myself for getting a job. I used to think it took a lot to impress an employer.

"Can you start this Sunday?" he asked, after going through a couple of his usual procedures—asking what hours I preferred and how many I would need to support myself. I'd already explained to him that I lived on my own.

"Sunday would be perfect for me."

He smiled. "I'm guessing you've got some weekend plans?"

"Not sure yet," I said, smirking. He surprisingly seemed like a really cool boss to have.

"Parties to go to?" He stretched back in his seat. "Or throw?"

"Not really." I thought about it, then added, "Maybe."

He laughed. "No sense in having your own apartment and not throwing any parties in it. Have fun, I'll see you on Sunday at four."

✳ ✳ ✳

Patiently standing outside the entrance, I watched and waited for Trent as he finished up the last of his work, but in my waiting, I noticed a different Zellers employee—wearing one of their striking red uniforms—come strolling through the automatic doors. He was my age, maybe a little older, and looked kind of familiar. Though I only assumed we went to high school together, he saw me and seemed to recognize me at once.

"Trent just told me you got a job here. That's awesome." Pulling out a pack of smokes from his pocket, he added, "Trent will be right out," before putting one of the cigarettes in his mouth.

"Wait, so who are you?" I asked, trying to be as friendly as I could.

Through his teeth, he answered, "James," as he lit the cigarette hanging out of his mouth. "You're Dray, right?" He exhaled. "We'll be working together."

"You're friends with Trent?"

"Trent hasn't mentioned me before?" James gave me a puzzled expression. "Me and him have become good friends since he started working here."

"Really?" For me it was strange—Trent wasn't the kind of guy who attracted cool friends.

"You want a cigarette?" he asked.

"Actually," said a voice from behind us, "you should buy us a pack of cigars." I looked over and found Trent stepping towards us. "We'll need some for tonight," he said.

"Sure."

"Would you?" I asked for assurance. It was pretty generous for someone to go out of their way to illegally purchase a pack of smokes for minors.

"Totally," James said, puffing out a large cloud of smoke. "Let's go for a walk and get them."

Just across the street was Petro, the most popular gas station in town besides 7-eleven. Together, the three of us headed across the large and busy parking lot—shared between Zellers and Safeway—to pick up the pack of smokes. The whole way there, Trent and James were arguing amongst themselves on what brand of cigars to buy. I didn't care a whole lot, but when we got there I was the one that had to give James the ten dollars it costed to buy a pack. Trent, it turned out, never had any cash on him. Even though I knew Trent would most-likely smoke most of the cigars, I didn't mind paying. After all, Trent had bought us the forty bucks of weed we wasted away the night before.

"What are you guys up to, tonight?" James asked, returning back to us from inside of Petro. After making sure no one was looking, he handed me a pack of Prime Time Vanillas.

"Just hanging out," Trent said.

"That's cool. You know, I'd totally come hang out with you guys, but tonight I've gotta date with someone."

"With who?" Trent asked.

From the look on James' face, I could tell he was considering not to say, but he discarded the thought and told us anyway. "Carli Tollifson," he said.

"Doesn't she have a boyfriend?" retorted Trent.

"Kind of. I guess." James shrugged sheepishly. "Just don't tell anyone I'm seeing her."

"Fuck, James," Trent exclaimed with a chuckle.

"Fuck you!" he replied playfully. "Like *you* wouldn't."

Uninterested, I interrupted their conversation: "Thanks for getting us the cigars, James."

"No problem," he replied. "Hey, what are you doing *next* weekend? We should hang out, get drunk."

"That would be cool," I replied, nodding. "I've got my own place, too, you know. A basement suite. It's got a backyard and everything."

"Does it have a fire pit and chairs or anything like that?"

"It does, actually."

"Next weekend, then, all right? We'll have a fire. Roast hot dogs or something. Drink some beer."

I looked at Trent and nodded, then turned back to James. "Sounds good," I said, tearing off the plastic sleeve that the pack of cigars were wrapped in.

✳✳✳

James went back to his vehicle and Trent and I walked in the other direction, through the summer heat, across town to my house. "Want to grab a sandwich at Subway?" Trent asked as we crossed the highway and reached Main Street.

"That might not be such a good idea," I told him.

"Why not?"

"I used to kind of work there, actually."

"You did?"

"Believe it or not," I answered.

"And...?"

"And," I began a response, "I kind of walked out on them and didn't show up to one of my shifts."

Trent laughed. "So it would be pretty awkward, then, if you went in there now?"

"If the manager that hired me is inside, yeah."

"Well, I'm really hungry. Can we stop by Sev—or will it be awkward going in there too?" Trent joked. "You also worked there, you know…"

"Yeah, yeah," I chuckled, "that'll be fine."

Instead of Main Street, we continued our walk down the highway towards my house and 7-eleven. On the way, I sent a text to Eric. *'Coming over?'* I asked. By the time we got there, I received a response. As we entered through the doors of 7-eleven, I pulled out my cell and read what Eric had sent me. *'Do you actually want me to?'* was his reply. Looking up from my phone, I thought of what I would send back to him, but was subsequently distracted by a girl at the other end of the store. It was Rose. She was wearing a t-shirt with a Pikachu on it, pouring herself a cherry slurpee. Next to her was Kate, the girl I'd asked to prom, who already had a slurpee in her hands. Casually sipping on it, she bobbed her head up and down to whatever music she had playing through her white iPod headphones. Waiting on Rose, she looked around the store and noticed Trent and I as we sauntered towards them. She pulled out her music and gave us a big, happy, summer smile. When we got closer, I realized that she was just stoned.

"Look," said Kate to Rose, "it's *Dray*."

Rose spun her head around—spilling some of her slurpee on the floor in the process—and said my name, using the same emphasis on it as Kate had.

"Hey girls," I said, happy to see them.

"What are you up to?" Kate asked, moving close to me.

"Trent's hungry and—"

"And we're trying to find some weed," Trent interrupted.

Kate raised her eyebrows. "Yeah?"

"Know where we can get some?" he asked nonchalantly. Unlike me, he thought smoking weed was cool.

"I could hook you guys up," Kate told Trent. "Lance and Taylor are getting some today. If you give us the money, we can get you in on the bag we're getting."

"How much are you planning on buying?" I heard Trent ask, but I drowned out their conversation and leaned over to Rose.

"Cool shirt," I complimented her.

Rose smiled darkly at me. She knew how much I loved Pokémon. In one of our internet videos, Brody and I had sung the whole theme song and even did a dance routine we came up with all by ourselves. It was a spoof/horror film, featuring a haunted house and invisible friends. At the end of the video, I credited Rose as one of the invisible characters, which made her ecstatic to be included, even if it was just her name at the end. Later, she told me it was her favorite video I ever made.

Kate: "If we get you a separate bag it'll cost more."

Trent: "That doesn't matter…"

"So what are you doing tonight?" Rose asked, swaying my attention away from Kate. I knew in the back of her mind it probably bothered her a little that I'd asked her friend to prom and not her. Truthfully, I knew then and now that Kate was going to say no, and that Rose would have said yes, but I didn't really *want* to go to prom. The thought of being rejected sounded a lot better than not going because I simply never fit in.

"Nothing much today," I told her, "but tomorrow I'm thinking of having a party."

"You are?"

"Maybe. I just finished getting settled into my new apartment, so…"

"So it'll be a house-warming party?"

"Is that what they're called?"

Rose nodded with a smile. "By the way, thanks for not texting me back this morning!" She looked a little upset but she continued smiling.

"I am so sorry!" I tried to say, but she told me not to worry about it.

Why do I keep forgetting to text people back? First Anna, then Rose, and I still haven't replied to Eric yet, either.

"Also," Rose said, "Cassidy told me to tell you that she misses you and that she can't wait to hang out with you and see your new place."

"Are you hanging out with her tonight?"

"No, but tomorrow for sure."

"Really?"

"Yeah, so you should really have that party you're thinking of having."

"Hey Rose, we've gotta go." Kate stepped over to where we were having our private conversation. "Trent just gave me forty bucks to get another bag, so we've gotta catch up with Taylor before he goes to get the weed for tonight." She turned over to me. "We'll come by your house later on and drop the bag off there, all right? Trent gave me directions."

"Fine by me," I said, then looked back to Rose. She smiled at me as Kate pulled her away to pay for their slurpee's. Behind me, I heard Trent say, "I'm starving," as the two girls embarked into the hot summer evening. Once they left, I pulled out my phone to finally text Eric back while Trent bought himself a box of chicken wings. *'Of course I want you to come over,'* I began, *'but I should warn you, Kate and Rose are buying Trent a bag of weed.'*

Eric never responded; instead, he surprised us with a visit...

Trent and I were in the backyard about to light up the Prime Time's when Eric's car came bouncing up my uneven driveway, a song loudly playing from inside the vehicle. When he came into view—after he'd parked, got out, and came hastily walking through the car port—I saw that he was in a bad mood, which probably had something to do with me, I thought, since I'd been avoiding him for the past week. Thinking we were inside, Eric headed down the stairwell to my basement suite.

"Eric," called Trent, "we're over here!"

Thump thump thump back up the stairs and Eric's head bobbed back up into vision. He looked up and caught sight of us sprawled out in the green, green grass. I turned over and saw that Trent had put one of the Prime Time's in his mouth, letting it hang there lifelessly.

"Cigarettes?" he noted, looking down on us.

"Cigars," Trent corrected him. "Want one?"

Eric sighed. Instead of walking around the car port fence, he climbed over the tall ledge and sauntered towards us. "Sure," he said, not caring. Trent passed him a silver cigar and lit it once he sat down next to us. Eric and Trent smoked theirs like pros; I coughed trying to get mine started.

"Here," said Trent, taking the lighter from me, "I'll help you light it."

"You haven't smoked in a while, I'm guessing?" Eric assumed, looking up at the bright blue sky.

"Not cigars," Trent answered for me.

Eric dropped his head back down and looked at me awkwardly.

"Cigarettes are easier to smoke," I said.

"Sure," he said blankly, "but what's this I hear about you guys getting a bag of weed from Kate?"

"For later tonight," Trent told him, "if we're in the mood."

"I'm not smoking weed," Eric huffed.

"You don't have to," Trent said.

Eric turned to me. "What about you, Dray?"

"What?"

"Are you going to smoke weed?" he asked.

"I don't know," I told him. "Maybe."

"So that's a yes?"

"Leave him alone," Trent said, coming to my defense. "Don't make it such a big deal."

"Fine." Eric relaxed, took a drag, and asked whether or not I had found a job yet.

"I was hired at Zellers today—happy?"

He stared back at me, and in his stare I momentarily flashed back to Grade 11. I see the boy I used to be, lying down on my bedroom floor, laughing on the phone with Eric. Back then we called each other every night to talk about our day. We'd talk about the girls we liked and the teachers we hated. We told each other every one of our secret thoughts—the quiet things no one ever knows—until it got to be too late and I'd fall asleep on him.

"Whatever," Eric said, tossing away his cigar. In the corner of my eye, I saw it crash into the shed and disperse into several tiny embers. I threw mine next to the remains of his where they hung together in the blades of grass, slowly burning away until there was nothing left but the filters... Behind me, the fence-door creaked open. As it were expected, Kate and Rose came strolling through my backyard.

"Good evening, gentlemen," Kate said, waving a bag of weed above her head as though she were casting a magical spell.

"You're flattening it," said Trent.

"I'm letting oxygen into the buds," she told him, smiling. "It'll burn longer this way."

"That sounds... *untrue*," I said.

"Fuck you both!" Kate giggled. She quit spinning the bag of weed around and chucked it down at Trent. "You got a pipe?" she asked, and sat down next to him.

"Don't you?" he replied.

"Coming right up!" After lifting her bag onto her lap, she delved through it until she came across a bright, blue pipe. "Here you go," she said, handing it over to Trent.

Meanwhile, Rose had sat herself down between Eric and I and was digging through her own bag. She took her phone out, and from the looks of it appeared to be sending a text to someone.

"Hey Rose," Eric was first to say.

Suddenly it registered to her: "I haven't seen you in forever!" Rose touched his shoulder as if to make sure he was really there.

"You haven't?" Eric pretended to ask, though he knew it was true. *Just a year ago we saw Rose every day.*

"I thought you'd moved to Prince George or something," said Rose, the girl who had once been our closest friend.

"Not yet," was his reply.

My phone vibrated and Eric and Rose continued talking. Quietly, I checked my phone's activity, finding which person it had been that Rose had texted while she sat here next to us. She had texted me, the boy sitting beside her, meaning whatever the text message read, it was meant to be read in private, just for me.

'I'm really excited,' she told me.

'For what?' I replied immediately, then looked back up at the crowd around us. Eric was telling Rose the plans he had for the future; Trent and Kate were preparing the pipe; and Rose was

secretively texting me back. By the time she closed up her phone and placed it back in her pocket, my phone vibrated once again. *'That I get to see you more often now that you don't live at home anymore,'* she explained, placing a smiley face at the very end.

"Are you two, like, texting each other?" Kate blurted out, pointing at Rose and I. "As soon as Rose puts her phone away, Dray pulls his out!"

"I thought that's what you guys were doing," Eric murmured.

"Well aren't you guys the detectives," I said slyly.

They laughed, including Eric. Rose turned to me and smiled provocatively. My heart fluttered.

"Pipe's ready," said Trent, raising it up for us to see. We all, but Eric, scooted closer together in the circle and crooned over the pipe.

"Are you having any?" Kate asked Eric, noticing his lack of interest.

"No," he told her.

"Sure?"

Eric never bothered to answer any further.

✳✳✳

Giggling and flirting, Rose and I slowly made our way down Main Street, trailing behind Eric—the leader of the pack—and Trent and Kate, who struggled to keep up with the un-stoned Eric. Someone had music playing—on their phone maybe—and it hummed through the night undetected. Rose closed her eyes and rested her head on my shoulder, the streetlights were blurry, my head felt like a balloon; still, I managed to successfully tune in on the conversation ahead.

"So are you coming tomorrow night?" Kate asked Eric.

"What do you mean?"

"The party," she said.

Nothing registered across Eric's face.

"At Drayvn's house," Kate further explained. "He's having a party."

"No one told me."

She sighed. "You're not much of a partier."

He scoffed. "I am."

"I find that hard to believe—you wouldn't even take a look at the bag of weed we brought over," she said, egging him on.

"That's because I don't approve of it," Eric declared, making sure we all heard.

"What about drinking?" Trent asked.

"I don't have a problem with drinking," he said, a surprise to us all.

"Why not?" Kate asked, stunned.

"Because it's legal."

"Then why don't you drink?" Trent asked.

After briefly thinking it through, he said, "Because I haven't had any opportunities worth drinking."

"What about tomorrow night at Dray's?" Kate suggested.

Eric turned around and looked back at me. "Are you actually having a party tomorrow?" he asked, trying to ignore the fact that Rose—a girl he'd always adored—was cuddled up in my shoulder.

"Think it's a good idea?" I asked innocently.

"Only if you drink with me," he replied.

"How would we get the alcohol?"

"The same way everyone does."

※※※

"I don't know about this," said Cliff—the next day—as he looked out his window from the backseat of Eric's car. The parking lot around us was busy, not ideal for teenagers who were attempting to illegally purchase alcohol.

"Work your magic," I told Cliff.

"Fuck my life," he kidded. "You know the only reason I was lucky last time was because the guy working never even gave a shit."

"He knew you were under-aged?"

"*Everyone* knows we're under-aged. And if someone sees me go in there they're gonna recognize me." He sighed and looked out the window again.

Turning to me for an answer, I gave Eric a look as if to say, *if this is gonna work, Cliff's gonna need some serious motivation.* Surprisingly, Eric found just the words to say: "Cliff," he said, "if you pass on this opportunity, who knows—you might never get to drink with your two good friends, Dray and Eric."

"This is a one-time deal?"

"Maybe."

"Fine, fuck you guys, I'll do it. If I get arrested it's all your guys' fault."

Cliff slammed the door shut on his way out, and Eric and I laughed at him as he disappeared behind the rows of cars leading up to the Twin's liquor store.

"I can't believe you convinced him like that."

"It was easy enough. He's excited—probably even more excited than we are."

"Yeah," I said simply, suddenly realizing that we hadn't even had a moment alone together to really discuss the whole matter of drinking. Last night he left early—probably sick of being around the stoned group of us—and this morning, when he told me all about getting the alcohol, he'd arrived with Cliff.

"Kind of weird," I begun the conversation, "knowing you and I will drink together tonight."

"Happy?"

"I guess that depends on how tonight goes."

He let out a stifled and sombre laugh. "It could be a really fun night," he said. "Then again, it could also turn out really lame."

"Drinking isn't really the kind of thing we do, is it?"

"We used to say we'd *never* drink," he said, more to himself than to me. "But those days might be over."

"You think that?"

"Well you've got your own place now, somewhere safe to drink. We won't have to be like other teenagers: drinking on the streets, going to lame parties." He looked up at me and placed his hands over the steering wheel offhandedly. "Besides, you might like drinking more than smoking weed, and then maybe we can hang out more."

I smiled grimly. "It's not that I like weed," I said defensively, "it's just something to do. But I get what you mean." Eric turned away and tried to spot Cliff in the parking lot. "Tonight'll be fun," I quietly concluded.

Behind us, the door Cliff got out of sprung back open. A few bottles of what I assumed to be alcohol were tossed across the backseat. Cliff followed them through and sat himself down in the middle.

"Holy!" we exclaimed, leaning over into the back and observing the goods Cliff had gotten a hold of. "You did it again."

"What can I say?" Cliff asked rhetorically. "I'm the shit."

✻✻✻

'We're getting so drunk tonight,' I sent to Rose as we exited the liquor store parking lot while Cliff and Eric listed off all of the things we had to do before tonight's party could unravel. First of all, it was decided we'd start drinking early. That way we could ease our way into drunkenness before people started showing up at the house. "Invite everyone," they told me, but I never really had anyone to invite—no one but Rose and Cassidy and their group of friends.

'We're still invited, right?' Rose asked.

'Of course! What time should we expect you over?' I asked, and moments later I received a response. She said they planned on arriving sometime around nine, which was now only a few hours away. Meanwhile, the three of us were at A&W, filling our faces with as much as we could possibly eat. Cliff had told us that the more you eat during the day meant the more you could drink at night. He also said that it was best not to drink water during the day, because then you wouldn't be thirsty for the alcohol. It was interesting for us to hear this, because we didn't know anything about drinking and there was so much to learn. We didn't even know what kind of alcohol it was that Cliff had gotten us. He had to explain it all: the difference between whiskey and vodka; what drinks mixed well together; the cost of alcohol; and all sorts of other cool facts.

"There are certain kinds of tequila," he told us, "that can fuck you up like crazy, but not give you a hangover. But that stuff is rare. Usually when you drink tequila you're hung-over no matter what."

Of course, after he had said this, I couldn't help but ask another series of questions, trying to understand what a hangover was. Weed had never done that to me, and I'd only ever had a few drinks of alcohol before, so the idea of being hung-over actually sounded exciting, which was funny, I knew, because to almost anyone else, it was a normal part of life. But to me—and to Eric—it was much more than that. It was a whole new world we were uncovering.

✳✳✳

Nine o' clock rolled around faster than we expected. We had been waiting on Trent to get off work, but even with him here, we were still reluctant to delve into the drinks we had expertly mixed into each cup in front of us. Eric and Trent had darkened the color of their Dr. Pepper with Fireball whiskey while Cliff and I had brightened our Cream Soda with Smirnoff vodka, a strange and transparent liquid that seemed to slither its way through the cup. Everything was ready; still, none of us were prepared to take a drink. Not even Cliff, who was used to drinking alcohol. "I should have gotten beer," he said.

"Why didn't you?"

"I wanted to get alcohol that we'd all like," he explained, staring blankly at the cup in front of him.

"We might have liked beer," said Eric.

"You wouldn't have," Cliff assured him. "Beer tastes terrible until you're used to the taste."

"I can drink beer," I noted.

"No you can't."

Pause. "Dude, I drank your Colt 45 that one night."

"That's right, you drank the whole thing!" Cliff punched my shoulder playfully.

"I almost forgot about that," Trent said, laughing.

"You were so wasted," Eric reminded me.

"I know," I said, thinking back to how goofy I had acted on our trip to Houston. "That was my first time getting drunk."

"And this'll be your first time drinking with your friends," Eric cheerfully added.

"Let's do it, guys," said Trent. "Let's take a drink together before anyone else gets here."

"Cheers?" I offered, looking around the table at my three best friends. They returned my stare with nervous glances and together we took the next step in our lives, tapping the four of our plastic cups together, a joyful moment before the terrible taste that followed.

"Cliff, this tastes like puke," Eric said, putting his cup back down on the table. "Why would anyone drink this?"

"Because it gets you drunk," Cliff told him.

I drank in silence, not letting the taste bother me.

"And how many cups," Eric further questioned, "do we have to drink until we're drunk?"

"Five, at least."

Eric sighed and took another small sip. "Is it actually worth it?"

Cliff was busy chugging back his drink, so Trent answered for him: "Oh yeah," he said, grinning. "You'll see."

"By the way, Dray," Eric grabbed my attention, "I'm gonna have to stay the night here."

"Why?"

"Obviously he can't drive home if he's drinking," Trent explained, rolling his eyes at me.

"Well, *sorry*"—I made a gesture—"but this is the first time this scenario has ever come up, so… I didn't think of it like that."

"I'll only need to stay here if I get really drunk."

"You will," Cliff assured him, jumping out of his seat. "Let's get some music going in this place. I assume your laptop is in your room?"

"Dray?" someone said.

"What?" I asked, momentarily distracted.

"Where's your laptop?" Cliff asked again.

"Oh!" I shook my head back into the moment. "Yeah, it's in my room." I turned back to Eric and Trent and raised my cup at them once more.

"Cheers," Trent agreed, and the three of us tapped our cups together again. We took another big drink and Cliff walked back into the kitchen carrying my laptop, a long cord trailing on the floor behind him.

"There's a car outside," Cliff said, plugging the cord into a nearby outlet.

"Eric's?" I asked.

"No, dumb-ass," he remarked, placing the laptop down on the kitchen table. "I know what Eric's car looks like."

"Then whose is it?"

"I don't know—that's why I mentioned it."

"Rose?" thought Eric.

"She doesn't have any friends that can drive."

"Go check it out, then."

I put on my shoes and left the basement suite. Behind me, through the door, I heard Cliff put on a Pinback song as I went up the stairwell and looked down the driveway. Sure enough, a car was parked out in front of the house. Walking closer, I discovered an old friend of mine sitting in the passenger seat. It was Jacob Hurwitz. He looked over and saw me, smiled, and got out of the vehicle. Racing over to give me a warm and familiar hug, I saw from over his shoulder another old friend of mine: Nick Foreman, who appeared from the driver's seat, strolling around the car, hands in his pockets.

"Long time, no see, you guys," I said as Jacob took his arms off me.

"You dropped out of school and off the face of the earth."

"Did I?" I wondered.

"You did."

"So what are you doing here?"

"Just driving around, thought we'd stop by," Nick said, sitting down on the front lawn.

"Henry told us where you lived," Jake added.

Henry and Cliff and I knew Jacob because of our school's Drama club. The four of us had been in numerous theater productions together, and because Jacob was as involved with acting as much as we were, we all became friends on a professional level, working our best to put on the best show we could. Through this friendship, I was also acquainted with Nick, who was Jacob's best friend, and not at all interested in school theater, quite similar to Eric.

Not that Eric wasn't interested in acting. He liked the arts, but as a former jock, the school's theater productions just weren't cool to him.

"Drayvn! Have you been drinking?"

"What?"

"I can smell it on your breath." Jacob leaned closer to me and whiffed me up and down. "Vodka?" He pulled away. "That stuff is rank."

"You drink now?" asked Nick.

I laughed. "I'm having a party tonight, actually."

Jacob took a look at the house, then turned back to me. "A real rager," he joked.

"Gotta start somewhere," I said. "Why don't you guys come join?"

"Yeah?"

"Hell yeah," I exclaimed. "We got alcohol—you can have some."

They snickered. "Don't worry. We have our own."

"We always carry some in my trunk," Nick said, wiping grass off the back of his jeans as he walked over to behind his car. The trunk door opened, revealing dozens of bottles, all of different kinds and sizes, wrapped in bags or placed in boxes.

"Holy!" I stared in amazement.

"I hope you're ready to get shit-faced, Dray," Jake said, "because it's happening."

Not sure what he meant, I smiled at the gesture and helped carry in some of their alcohol, showing them the way to my basement suite. "Who's living upstairs?" they asked, carefully taking their time down each step, making sure not to drop any of the precious booze.

"No one yet," I told them.

"So we can be as loud as we want to?"

"I guess we can, yeah," I said, quietly realizing the very thing I'd confirmed. It was true: *we could be as loud as we wanted...*

Consequentially, the party got as crazy as Jake had hoped. For me—and for Eric—the party would have been amazing no matter what the case. Even if no one came and it was just the four of us, the experience would have remained unforgettable. But when Rose and her friends arrived, the party immediately kicked into high gear. Suddenly my basement suite—that had seemed rather large and spacious before—was crammed full of drunk and hyper teenagers, going in and out the door to smoke bowls or cigarettes. In the space of only a half an hour, the place practically exploded. The four single drinks that had been mixed at the kitchen table had multiplied into a dozen, and the rest of all the glasses and cups I owned were scattered around the living room, now empty and forgotten.

A couple beers had fallen sideways on my kitchen counter, dripping the small remnants down the cabinetry below, but I didn't care or clean up the mess; I was happy just to be throwing my very first party. The chaos, instead of a restriction, was more like a freedom. I felt so strangely free—alcohol coursing its way through my body—as each new person came into the house and said hello, complimenting the party I was throwing or the awesome basement suite that now belonged to me. And as soon as I thought no one else was coming, another girl came strolling in through the entrance.

"Cassidy!" I said, shouting her name across the kitchen.

"Drayvn!" she called back, closing the door shut. After taking her shoes off, she charged at me, letting me catch her in my arms. Briefly, I lifted her up into the air and shook her around.

Laughing, she said, "I'm gonna throw up!" so I safely set her back down on the tiled kitchen floor.

"When did you get here!?" I inquired.

"I got here with Rose, Dray—you just never noticed me!"

"I didn't?"

"No, but that's okay."

"No it's not! I'm sorry!" I hugged her again.

"It is and I'll tell you why…" ("Why?" I asked.) "…Because you and Rose are completely in love with each other."

I stared at her for a delayed second, as though I was realizing it for myself. "No we're not," I said, shrugging.

"Yes you are!" With a quick hand, she swayed a couple strands of hair from out of my eyes. "Go for a walk with her," she advised. "Just talk to her."

My long dyed-black hair fell back into sight.

"Sure," I said, "but you're crazy! We're not in love with each other. You know how long we've been friends for…"

"For as long as you and I have." She looked at me like I was missing something, but the moment came and went.

"Dude, you gotta come play this card game," interrupted Eric, who came running over. Cassidy slinked away; Eric grabbed a hold of my shoulders. "It's getting everyone completely wasted," he continued, "including me!"

"That's okay, man, I gotta make sure the rest of the party is doing alright."

"True," he said, looking around at the havoc surrounding us. "This party is awesome, though!"

I laughed, having never seen Eric drunk before. "I know, right!"

"We've been missing out," he decided. "This is so much fun. And dude, Rose is obviously in love with you. She's been at the table with us, playing the card game, but she's not even paying attention."

"Huh?"

"She just keeps looking at you."

"Me?"

"See!" Cassidy shouted at me, walking off to the table.

"Yeah, dude." Eric shook his head. "I keep saying *dude!*" He laughed at himself and ran back over to the table.

Turning around, I saw Trent sitting alone on the couch, nodding off to the song that was play on my laptop. I went over and joined him. "How's it going, Trent?" I said, sitting down.

"Not bad. I think I'm gonna go smoke a bowl, though."
"Yeah?"
"Want to?"
"No, that's okay—I'm pretty drunk already."
"Suit yourself," he said, standing up. "Later."

My eyes followed Trent as he walked off into the kitchen and around the corner to where the entrance was. Looking over at the table, I caught sight of Eric, who was leaning over to Rose, whispering something in her ear. Abruptly, I felt a strange burst of jealously surge through me, but almost as suddenly, he pulled away. Following this, Rose looked down at her feet, thinking hard about something. With a smile, she hopped out of her seat and walked over towards me.

"What did he say?" I asked, once Rose stood close enough to hear through the loudness of the party.

"What?" she said cutely, pretending she had no idea what I was talking about.

"Come on, tell me—what did Eric say?" I asked again, trying my hardest to keep cool.

"He said you looked lonely." Rose sat down next to me. So close that our legs were touching. I looked at her and realized what Cassidy had said maybe wasn't as crazy as I initially thought. Maybe I did like her more than just a friend. Seeing that I was lost in thought—and not about to say anything—she started the conversation: "Have you heard the new Death Cab for Cutie album?" she asked.

"Of course," I said flatly.

She giggled. "What a dumb question. They've only been your favorite band for what, four years?"

"Long time, yeah." I smiled. "Not that long, though."

"You know what's crazy?"

"What?"

"They played a Death Cab for Cutie song on the radio."

My jaw dropped. "What!"

"I knew you'd be pissed to hear that," she said in admiration.

"Death Cab does not belong on the radio."

"Sorry, Dray, but their new album is totally radio-friendly." She laughed at the stunned expression on my face. "We should listen to them right now!"

After thinking for a second, I thought of something witty to say. "They might be radio-friendly now, but that doesn't mean they're party-friendly too," I told her, sneering.

"No," she replied, shaking her head. "Just the two of us should listen to them." Rose dug through her designer bag and pulled out an iPod and white headphones. She stuck an ear-bud in my left ear and put the other in her right, then asked what the song should be.

"Steadier Footing?" I suggested.

"That's way too short," she said, clicking through the different albums.

"Kay, then which?"

"I Will Possess Your Heart."

"That's like ten minutes long!" I informed her, even though I knew she was fully-aware of the matter.

"It's perfect," she said, looking back down at the iPod. After highlighting the song and pressing down on the center button, a single note seared through our ears, getting louder and louder through the constant chatter surrounding us. Together we observed the party, quietly concentrating on the atmospheric whistle as the piano set in, anticipating the infamous bass line that would continue for the next several minutes. It was bliss.

✳✳✳

"Kiss her," came a whisper in my ear. I whisked around—standing at the entrance of my basement suite—and the voice came again, this time in a much more recognizable tone: "You have to," Cassidy—I realized—was urging me, watchfully keeping her eyes on Rose, who was putting her shoes and jacket on behind me. "She told me to tell you."

"Who did?" I pretended to ask.

She nodded her head towards Rose, glaring at me insistently.

"What did she say?" Playing stupid, I threw my hands in the air like I never heard a word she said, but Cassidy called the bluff and ended the conversation. With a slight smile, she turned her back to me and joined the crowd around the table, leaving me breathless, somewhat confused, and extremely nervous. All I planned on was going for a simple walk, but according to Cassidy I was now leaving the house with a girl that supposedly wanted me to kiss her.

"Ready to go?" Rose asked, smiling passionately at me.

Beaming back at her, I was just about to respond, but Cliff came flying over and hopped on top of me, forcing me to carry him even though he was much heavier. "You're spilling your drink on me!" I shouted, embarrassed, not feeling cool at all in Rose's presence.

"Sorry man!" Cliff rolled off my back and tried to rub his drink off the shirt I was wearing. "It'll come off," he said, desperately grinding his fingers on the wet stain above my chest.

"Dude, fuck off."

"You just said the f-word." Rose stared at me disbelievingly. "That's so unlike you."

"I'm sorry," I told her.

"What about me?" Cliff asked, putting on a show.

"Go die?" I suggested.

"Hey Dray," said Jacob, who was sitting at the kitchen table. He put his cards down and stared up at me.

"Jacob," I said, getting more and more impatient. "What's up?"

"Are you and Rose going somewhere to have sex?" he asked, thinking he was saying a joke or something. In any case, everyone considered the remark hilarious. Laughter erupted from the table, making Rose turn a soft shade of red. Condescendingly, I shook my head at them all—noticing that Eric was probably the only one who wasn't laughing—and put on my shoes.

"You know what your problem is?" Cliff asked.

"What, Cliff?" I finished tying my last shoe and stood up straight. "What's my problem?" I asked carelessly.

"You need to drink more."

Ignoring him, I turned back to Rose: "Let's just get out of here," I said, to which she agreed, almost laughing herself through the embarrassment of it all. Together, the two of us raced out the door, not even bothering to take a last look at the party behind us.

※※※

Half an hour later, in the alleyway behind Rose's house, I thought hard about what Cassidy had said to me; still, no matter how I played it through in my mind, the scenario remained absurd. Rose and I had been friends for far too long for anything to happen between us now. Cassidy, I figured, just wanted something exciting to happen tonight, that's all. No big deal. Cassidy had always been like that.

"Dray?" I heard Rose whisper-shout.

"I'm over here," I quietly called back to her. "Marco polo!"

Rose giggled heart-fully, sneaking her way around the shed I was lent up against. "I made it!" she squealed, wrapping her arms around me.

"How much longer are you allowed out tonight?"

"For as long as I want!"

"I thought your mom only let you out until one, though," I said, leading us back towards the street.

"She was in bed sleeping, so I checked in with her and told her I was going to sleep, too."

I looked back at her, stunned. "You lied to her?"

"I snuck out the window," she elaborated.

Below, at our feet, we reached a small pool of water, which was shimmering in the moonlight. "Careful," I told her, pointing to the puddle.

"Thanks," she replied, carefully making her way around as I jumped across.

"I can't believe you lied to your mom!" I exclaimed, thinking it over. She had now gone to extreme lengths to be here with me now. "You're trouble, aren't you?" I flirted.

"Hey now," she said, "at least I don't *swear!*"

Lost in thought, I slowed the pace of my walking and Rose appeared next to me, barely to be seen in the darkness of the alley. "Was that really the first time I've ever sworn in front of you?" I asked.

She brought a finger to her lip, trying to remember. "I'm not sure," she decided. "Hey, what's that?"

"What?"

"Up ahead!"

Dashing off towards the end of the alleyway, she ran out onto the nicely paved street and into the bright-orange hue of the surrounding streetlights. Following her out of the darkness, I saw as she picked up and unraveled a scrunched-up piece of paper.

"Look what I found," she shrieked. "A flier!"

"For what?" I asked, catching up to her.

"I can't read it," she whined. "It's all wet. You have to help!" She handed the tattered leaflet over to me.

"The ink's everywhere," I said, trying to decipher the dribbled out words.

"Can you understand it at all?" she asked, peering over the thing as I held it high in the air.

"It's for a garage sale," I uncovered, laughing in amusement. "That's awesome—I've been trying to check out all the garage sales in town."

"What are you looking for?"

Handing the flier back to Rose, I said, "An old typewriter, maybe."

"Well we should check this garage sale out. Who knows—maybe they'll have just the thing you need."

"We don't know where it is, though."

"Well, looky here..." She pointed to the flier. "We have directions!" After glancing once more at the fuzzy print, she added, "I think."

"You wanna go tomorrow?"

"Tomorrow?" She made a face. "I wanna go right now!"

"It's still open? At this time?"

"Oh yeah, didn't you know? Midnight garage sales are all the rage these days." She giggled softly at her own joke.

"Well what are we waiting for!?" I cried out, taking the flier back from Rose to figure out an address. "Toronto Street—here we come!" Grabbing Rose's hand, I tugged her with me down the street, towards the highway.

"How fast can you run?" she asked, jogging alongside me.

"Faster than you, I'll bet."

"We'll see about that," she retorted, winking kindheartedly at me before we took off, running as fast as we possibly could until we started laughing so hard we had to stop.

✳✳✳

"So you went for a walk," Cliff said, once we returned back to the party. "Don't you know that sobers you up?"

"Dude, believe me—I'm drunk."

"Not drunk enough," he said, pacing backwards to the kitchen table where the party continued to rage. "Take a shot with me. You too, Rose."

"I'm down if Drayvn is," she replied, returning a wave to someone who was calling her name in the living room.

"Let's do it," I said, putting an arm around her as Cliff pushed his way through the crowded table.

"Your hair is so long," said Rose, who was looking me up and down.

"I'm getting it cut," I told her. With a swift tilt of my head, I shook the hair out of my vision.

"How short?"

"Short enough so there's no black dye."

"Cool," she said. "I miss your old hair color."

"I do too."

"By the way," she whispered, "I'm noticing you're not wearing any eye-liner."

"I stopped—"

"Thank God for that," said Cliff, who apparently overheard.

I took my arm off Rose.

"That was just embarrassing," Cliff continued, handing me two light party cups.

"Not like you let yourself be seen with me anyway," I replied, passing one cup over to Rose as I looked down into my own. "How about putting some Coke in these, Cliff?"

"I said *shots*!"

"Shots don't have mix," Rose explained, seeing the confused look on my face.

"Gross."

"You can do it," Rose encouraged.

"But—"

"No *buts!*"

I peered back into the cup and an aroma of a deep cinnamon, coated with the smell of Listerine, floated up my nose, making me gag slightly.

"You don't have to," said Rose, standing tall next to me.

"Oh no," I replied. "I do."

Chapter Three: Couches in Alleys

Laying in bed, I lazily turned over and grabbed my cell phone off the nightstand beside me. Expecting to send off a couple of texts before I had to get up and get ready for my first day at Zellers, I instead—after flipping it open—discovered that the wallpaper I previously had in the background of the main menu had been replaced by a completely new picture: a penis. Someone, at one point during the party last night, had taken a picture of their penis with my phone's camera and set it as the background.

Nauseated, I let out an unimpressed laugh and tossed the thing across my bed. *Now who would have done that?* I thought to myself, ducking beneath the covers. I couldn't believe morning had come—the night seemed to stretch on forever.

The party just kept going.

I skimmed over in my head the details: me and my friends got drunk, we threw a party, and... *Rose and I had begun a romance?* Was that really what had happened? After getting out of bed and staring into the mirror I hung next to the closet, I thought it over, searching my reflection for some sort of answer. My face, looking back at me, held no such thing, but there was something odd about the way I looked this morning. Was I happy...?

Not sure on the matter, I shrugged the idea off my head and wandered into the living room. Whatever it was that happened last night seemed to have done me good. But the house! I'd forgotten all about what a wreck the place had been before going to bed. Last night Eric and I hadn't bothered cleaning at all. When we finally got back from walking around and taking people home, we were too tired to do anything except lay down and chat while he sobered up enough to drive. I told him to stay, but he hadn't had a drink in almost four hours, so after grabbing himself a Coke out of the fridge, he drove his way home at around six in the morning, leaving me to sleep through the early morning hours.

✳✳✳

"Yeah?" Eric said, answering my call.

"Just checking to see you're still alive."

He let out a soft laugh. "I wasn't drunk. If I was, I would've stayed over."

"I know."

"What are you doing?"

"Going to work," I told him. Just now I was making my way across the highway.

"You know," he began, "if you'd like, I could drop by Zellers, grab your key, and clean up the house for you."

"No need to," I said. "I already cleaned it all up."

"Swept and mopped?"

"Yep."

"Wow," he scoffed, "that's impressive."

"I woke up and felt really motivated for some reason."

"Really?" Eric laughed and compared: "I woke up and felt really fucking tired."

I laughed, too. "Maybe I'm tired but don't know it yet. It'll probably hit me halfway through my shift."

"Get yourself an energy drink at Petro or something."

"Good idea."

"Last night was fun," he said.

I smirked happily, looking down at my feet as I trudged down the sidewalk that wrapped around the firehall. "By the way," I said, "know of anybody that used my phone last night?"

"No, why?"

I laughed coldly. "Someone took a picture of their penis with it."

After a brief flutter of silence, an eruption of laughter flew from the other end of the line. "Oh my God, I actually remember that now!"

"Who was it?" I asked hastily.

"It was Trent!" he told me. "I went into your room and walked in on him pulling his pants down."

"Gross..."

"And it was Cliff that took the picture," he added, much to my dismay.

"Cliff?! What the hell!"

"I guess he thought it'd be hilarious to put it as your screensaver or something."

"Yeah," I said sarcastically. *"Hilarious!"*

"It's completely gay," he made clear. "Who the hell would even wanna look at Trent's penis?"

"Cliff, apparently."

Eric laughed some more and said, "We definitely gotta bug him about that next time we see him."

"Agreed."

"Alright, I better let you go. Have fun at work."

✵✵✵

Zellers wasn't as terrible as I thought it would be; but then again, it wasn't at all what I expected. I thought they were going to have me running one of the cash registers, but apparently the store closed just an hour after my shift started, which meant I worked alone in the empty and dimly-lit store with only two other guys. Together we unloaded shipments from the back, checked their invoices, and stocked the shelves with all of the new merchandise.

The coolest part about this was that I never had to wear a uniform. Because we had no customers to deal with, I was free to wear whatever I wanted. But that was only one real perk to it. It may have seemed laid back, but it was still hard work. When we finally had our break, I had already begun to sweat.

"You smoke, Dray?" asked my night-time supervisor, watching me as I chugged back a bottle of water.

"Sometimes," I said, wiping my forehead dry. "But that's not why I'm so unfit. I haven't been to gym class in a long time."

"Me either," he replied, laughing. "But that's not what I meant. If you smoke, now's the time for a smoke-break. We've only got another fifteen minutes and it's back to work."

"Oh," I replied, too tired to be embarrassed. "I would, but I don't have a smoke on me."

"Want one?"

"Sure," I said coolly. "If you don't mind."

He handed me a cigarette and lighter. "Here you go."

"Thanks," I said, smiling in excitement. For some reason I'd actually been craving one for the past few hours.

After tossing my bottle into the recycling container next to the staff-room vending machine, I placed the cig fixedly in my mouth and made my way through the store, all the way to the back-entrance, out to where we took the garbage and cardboard. Once outside, I flipped my long hair back and let the evening's wind cool me down while I lit up and sucked in the cigarette.

'How's work?' I read, checking my phone to find a text from Anna, one she must have sent sometime during the last four hours.

'I feel tough,' I replied, wandering down the grassy hill, towards the empty street that trailed behind Zellers. *'They're making me do some hardcore heavy-lifting.'*

I sat down and relaxed on the warm pavement sidewalk, enjoying my smoke as I waited for a response, watching Highway 16 as cars continually whispered by, the only noise to be heard on a Sunday evening such as this.

'So you'll be big and strong in time to see me next week?' came the next text, making me smile as I took in a nice, long drag.

'Next week?' I began. *'That's plenty of time. I'll be completely ripped by then. If only you were coming sooner…'*

As soon as I had sent the text away, I almost immediately began to feel guilty. What about Rose—had last night truly changed things between us? Was she now counting on me to be her new guy—to be her first boyfriend? Of course I knew that Anna and I were only friends; but on the other hand, that was exactly what I used to think of Rose and I. Was flirting with Anna over a text going against my moral obligations?

A better question: Did I even have morals anymore? And if I did, what were they? After moving out and getting my own place, I seemed to no longer know where I stood with anything anymore. But instead of over-thinking it all, I decided to just watch it with what I said to Anna, even to Rose. I didn't want anyone hating me; I wanted things to work out the way they were meant to.

After crushing my spent cigarette with the heel of my shoe, I stood up and headed off to finish the last of my eight-hour shift.

Right as I went through the doors, I received another text, giving me another thing to look forward to: *'I got another bag of weed if you're interested,'* I was told, here by someone who was definitely not Anna.

✱✱✱

"Wait a second," I said, after work as I paced around Trent, who was lounging about on a large tree-stump by the Walnut Elementary School. "Just wait a second, here!"

"Say what you wanna say already." Trent laughed and closed his eyes. "How are you liking Zellers?" he asked, opening them back up again. "It was your first shift today, right?"

"Hey!" I shouted angrily.

"What?"

"You interrupted me?"

"Sorry," he grunted.

"Now you tell me this for real"—I pointed a finger at him—"and don't lie... Did Eric actually smoke weed with you last night?"

"God's truth."

I stopped my pacing and thought deeply about it for a moment. "I don't believe you," I decided, and began pacing back and forth once again.

"Ask him yourself," said Trent, defeated.

"Maybe I will."

"Man, you're baked," he observed, getting off the tree-stump. "You're starting to wig me out."

"Sorry," I said. "I've got way too much energy."

"Watch a movie," he told me. "Chill out."

I agreed, watching him as he picked up his backpack and threw it over his shoulder. "Are you going home?" I asked.

"It's *only* two in the morning," he said sarcastically.

"True."

"Shitty you have to get off work so late. Why didn't you ask for morning shifts? You could have worked at the same time as me."

"Hopefully they'll switch me sometime soon."

"You should ask them to," he suggested, then turned around and sauntered his way across the soccer field.

"By the way," I called after him, "thanks for the picture."

"What picture?" he called back to me.

Through the tone of his voice, I realized he honestly couldn't remember leaving me the picture. Amused, I decided not to tell him.

✳✳✳

The next day, before my second shift started at Zellers, I finally got a haircut. While dropping off some movies at Gone Hollywood, I went across the street to book an appointment for one, but they had a spot available and there was still enough time for me to have the hair-cut and get to work on time.

"What kind of cut were you thinking?" the hairdresser asked, sitting me down and wrapping me up in the tarp-like cloth.

"I want all the black gone," I told her, staring into the large mirror in front of us.

"That'll be short," she said, swaying her hands through my long and thick hair.

"I'm tired of having black hair."

"You got it. I'll go get the buzzer."

Once she went into the back, I reached in and pulled my phone out of my pocket. Entering camera mode, I snapped a quick photo of myself, then put it as the screensaver (finally replacing the all-too revealing picture that Trent and Cliff had left me.) Ever since I got a cell phone, I'd been taking numerous photos, collecting the very best from all the good times I've ever had. Right now, I have two-years worth of memories on my phone; still, I planned on taking a whole bunch more, preparing for a day down the road where I can make a scrap-book out of them all.

Taking one last look at myself in the mirror and another at the picture I'd taken of the very same thing, I said goodbye to my long and black hair just as the hair-dresser reappeared, plugging the buzzer in and starting it up. Quietly, she then cut it all away, while I sat still, staring into my shifting reflection.

When it was over—and I had paid her a clean twenty-dollar bill—I asked the time, discovering that the hair cut had taken longer than I expected. Running a bit late, I called and asked Eric for a ride, because I knew he was getting off work right about now. Fortunately, I'd called him in time before he left out of town back to his house.

"Holy shit," he exclaimed, moments later as I climbed into his small, green car. "You look so different with short hair."

"I know," I agreed, putting my seat-belt on.

"You know what you look like?"

I looked at him and guessed, "Like I did in Grade 11?"

"Exactly, yeah." Eric put the car back into drive. "It's weird."

"Speaking of things that are weird," I segued the conversation, "I heard you smoked weed on Saturday."

Disgruntled, he asked, "You want a ride to work or not?"

I laughed. "So you really did?"

"Not 'cause I actually wanted to."

"Because you were drunk?"

"No," he explained, "because I wanted to understand why you've become so obsessed with the stuff."

"I'm not obsessed with it. I never had any on Saturday," I told him, not bothering to mention the fact that I smoked up last night.

"Yeah, but only because Rose was there to entertain you."

"What?"

"Doesn't matter." Eric shrugged against the steering wheel, dipping down the intersection past Petro.

"I don't actually care," I said lightly. "Trent told me but I had to ask you before believing him."

"You can never be too careful with what Trent says."

"For sure." I leaned back in my seat. "How's the Wholesale going?" I asked, quickly continuing with the change of subjects.

"It's amazing," he told me, nodding his head. "Every day I keep expecting it to be awful, but I always have a good shift." Taking a sharp corner, Eric whizzed into the parking lot of Zellers. "You should apply there," he added.

"What about the job I have now?"

"Do you like it?"

Pause. "I'm not sure yet," I told him truthfully.

After stopping the car in front of the entrance, he said, "See how it goes, but I'll try and get you a job with me at Wholesale. We can work together like we did at 7-eleven."

"Like the old days…"

"And besides," he continued, "it sucks that you start work when I'm getting off."

"I'm free on weekends," I said, staying positive. "At least I get those off." I got out the door and bent over, ducking my head beneath the frame of the car, looking in on Eric.

"But it's the summer," he complained. "You should have *every* night off in the summer."

"But I think they need me on nights."

"Alright," he said, putting the car into drive. "I guess this weekend we'll have to do something awesome or something."

"For sure," I said, smiling as I then slammed the door shut.

Maybe it was because of mine and Eric's conversation—the knowledge that there was another job out there that might have suited me better—because for some reason, my next shift at Zellers seemed much more tiresome than the day before. The physical exertion that had at first felt refreshing now made me feel restless. All I wanted to do was hang out, do something. I knew I needed a job, but I also knew I still had close to two thousand dollars sitting in my bank account.

"You're still on this pallet?" my co-worker asked, glaring down at all I'd accomplished the last few hours.

"I can't tell the detergent's apart," I told him. "They all look the same."

"Scan them and they'll tell you their official names—you know, the ones that correspond with the prices on the shelf."

"I know," I said gruffly, eying him as he stared condescendingly back at me.

"Then get on it."

I took in what he said and pretended to switch into a quick working pattern, but only long enough so that he'd bugger off. As soon as he did, I tossed the scanner on top of the pallet and wandered down a nearby aisle, hiding in the back to discreetly send a text message to Rose, who I'd been texting regularly—along with Anna—throughout the past couple days.

'I probably won't have another party this weekend,' I responded, *'but we should hang out sometime soon anyway, sober or something.'*

✳✳✳

"You called," said Anna, her voice soft and taint from coming out of sleep, waking up only to answer my call.

"You sound shocked."

"It's been a while…"

"I know," I admitted. "I've been busy, believe me—"

"You used to call me at least a couple of times each week."

"I know," I said, swaying forwards on the swing I was sitting on. Once again, I was stoned on the grounds of Walnut Elementary School at two in the morning. Trent had drifted to sleep, listening to his music on the grass next to the playground, so I thought to call Anna.

"How's Subway?" she asked, yawning briefly.

"Um," I stammered, "I guess I forgot to mention it to you, but I work at Zellers now." She said nothing, so I added an explanation: "I got the job over the weekend."

"I'm behind the times," she reflected sadly. "But that makes sense—I was wondering what kind of heavy-lifting there was to do at Subway."

I laughed. "All I did *there* was wash dishes."

"So you like Zellers better?"

"I guess, but I don't know—it's all work." I fidgeted in the swing I was hanging off of, already not looking forward to work the next day.

"Tell me," she said dreamily, "what's it like living all on your own?"

"It's still sinking in," I contemplated. "I keep expecting my mom to barge through my door and tell me to get up and clean my room."

Anna went quiet, considering something, then spoke: "Have you spoken with your mom lately?" she asked.

"Briefly. She called me just the other day."

"And how was that?"

"She was only… *slightly* obnoxious."

Anna giggled. Her voice cackled into my ear and then she coughed.

"You alright?" I asked.

"I might be sick."

"Then you better get back to sleep," I told her. "Sorry to wake you up so late."

"It's fine," she replied. "I'm just glad you called."

"See you next week?"

After a brief pause, she quietly said, "I can't wait."

Swiftly, I closed my phone shut, and as I did, I realized how excited I truly was to be seeing her again. Before moving out, Anna had been the one and only thing I had to look forward to, but now that there was so much going on at once, I'd forgotten how much her presence in this town meant to me. Smithers wasn't the same without her, and even if I'd busied myself with a basement suite and new life, her return was bigger than any of that.

"Dray!" called Trent, interrupting my thoughts.

I pulled myself off the swing and walked over towards my friend, who was writhing around in the grass, rubbing his eyes with both palms. "What is it?" I asked, helping him up.

"You should walk me home," he mumbled. "I don't feel good."

✳✳✳

A vehicle pulled into my driveway at around twelve in the afternoon the next day, waking me up from a deep and comfortable sleep as it hummed noisily above my window. Once the engine clicked off, it was the sound of footsteps that came next, echoing through the carport while I grimaced at the thought of getting out of bed, hating the arrival of morning which had now become as late as twelve.

Several loud knocks suddenly came crashing over my door. This, I assumed, had to have been Eric, who had an entire lunch hour at his job to go and do whatever he liked.

I ran across the suite, wearing nothing but my underwear, and answered the door to find Eric like I had predicted. Unfortunately for me, he was not alone. Although Jacob and Nick were there, it was the presence of a girl I'd never met that caught me off guard. She was standing a couple steps up, her eyes avoiding me.

"Get some clothes on, Dray!" Nick joked.

"We have virgin eyes here," Jacob added, nodding towards the unknown girl, who laughed noisily.

I looked to Eric, who apologized: "Sorry to show up like this."

"It's fine," I told him. "I'll get some clothes on."

They piled in through the doorway as I raced back to my bedroom and tried finding some clothes to wear. This took longer than usual to accomplish. Because I never had a laundry machine, I was running low on clean clothes.

"This is Alice, by the way," said Jacob, greeting me as I opened my bedroom door. He was sitting down on the couch with Nick and the girl I now knew as Alice.

"How come I've never seen you before?" I asked brightly, trying my best not to sound rude.

"I'm from Houston," she explained. "I just came here to visit Nick and Jake for the day."

"Even though I'm working," said Nick, sounding disappointed.

"Where do you work?" I asked.

"Dude," said Eric, sitting on the chair beside my kitchen, "look at his shirt."

Following his words, I looked over and realized that Nick was wearing the same thing as Eric: a dark blue t-shirt with the words 'Bulkley Valley Wholesale' written in white across the chest.

"You work with Eric?" I asked, dumbfounded.

"Started today," Nick replied.

"And they're still hiring," Eric continued. "That's why we're here. Do you still have a spare resume laying around? We wanna apply you."

"Yeah," I said, "I got a few kicking around."

Back into my room, I quickly pulled out one of the resumes I'd thrown into the orange cabinet that had come with the basement suite. It was a little crumpled up, but it was good enough. Once I returned to the living room, I saw that the four of them had stood up, preparing to leave.

"Me and Nick gotta get back to work," Eric declared, resting his hands toughly over his hips.

"And me and Alice are gonna grab some lunch," added Jacob, "but we gotta party this weekend or the next, alright? The party you threw on Saturday was amazing."

"What party?" asked Alice.

"Dray threw a party here on the weekend," Nick explained, leading the way through the kitchen.

"Here? Really?" Alice looked all over the house and exclaimed, "This would be *such* a cool place to have a party!"

"Next time we'll bring you," flirted Nick.

"I'd love to," she replied, "but then again, that's up to Dray."

"I don't care," I said, smiling as I realized she probably had assumed that I was popular and had a ton of friends.

"If Nick's kind enough to actually give me a ride, I'd love to be here if you do decide to have another party."

"Well"—I shyly put my hands in my pockets—"I'll let Nick and Jake know in advance."

"Yeah!" yelled Jacob. "Don't be a stranger."

They waved goodbye and piled back out the door. Once they left, I checked the time on my cell phone, which was plugged in beside the bedroom closet. In four hours, I once again would have another eight hours of work to attend to.

Chapter Four: After The K.M. Taper

The work-week—as awful as it was—zipped by faster than I expected. Before I knew it, it was the weekend again. My first day off was a simple day of relaxation. I thought about asking Rose to hang out, but decided not to. At this point in time my mind was set more on Anna, and I never wanted to be out on a date with a girl while thinking of someone different. Instead, I chilled out alone in my backyard, barefoot in the grass, smoking the leftover Primetimes that James bought me.

Out of boredom—and to get out of the sun for a moment—I opened up the shed and tip-toed my way through it, finding all sorts of yard tools and supplies. In the corner, I discovered a large pile of uncut firewood, ideal for the fire pit that was in the center of the backyard. With a smoke in my mouth, I dragged some of it out beneath the tree next to the shed and grabbed the ax. On top of a large root, I sturdily prepared a piece of wood to cut as smoke sifted upwards into my eyes.

"Don't cut your toes off," came the familiar voice of Trent.

"You're right," I said, setting the ax back down on the ground. "I should get some shoes on." I took a large drag of the cigarette as Trent came around the carport to where I was, beneath the one and only tree.

"Don't tell me you smoked all the Primetimes," he said, walking over to the picnic table to set his backpack down.

"Two left," I told him. "Want one?"

"Keep them for yourself, actually. You seem to enjoy them more than me."

I went over to the fire pit and slipped my shoes back on, using one of the lawn chairs for balance.

"Did you bring any weed?" I called back to him.

"Yeah, man, but just enough for two more bowls. Then I'm done."

"You're quitting?"

"No," he said, shaking his head as he sat down in the grassy shade. "Then I have to get another bag."

"Gotcha." I walked back over to the shed, to Trent, and grabbed the ax again. "Well shit. Sorry. I've been smoking all your weed." With a clean swing, I sliced the piece of wood straight down the middle, breaking it into two perfect pieces.

"How about..." said Trent, thinking of some sort of settlement. Meanwhile I propped up one of the leftover pieces to cut into kindling. "How about you pay for the booze tomorrow and we're square?"

"Tomorrow?"

A look of concern spread across his face. "You're still down to have James over tomorrow, right?"

"I dunno—are you sure he still wants to?"

"Well, yeah," he said, pulling a bag of weed out of his pocket. "He says he's really excited to party with you and Eric."

Something didn't sound right to me. "You sure?" I asked formidably.

"I'm serious," he assured. "James called me today and asked if you were still down."

"I'm down."

"I knew you would be—that's what I told him."

I laughed. "How about you load up a bowl?"

"Coming right up."

I went into the shed and grabbed some more firewood. Behind me, I heard Trent ask, "Is it alright if I crash here, tonight? I gotta work early in the morning and it's such a long walk from my house."

"Yeah, man, that's fine," I called back to him. "We can watch a movie or something."

***

When I woke up the next morning, Trent was already gone. The house was left quiet. Outside, the sun had reached high enough to sear down into the basement suite, illuminating the carpet in my living room, raising its temperature to such an uncomfortable level it almost hurt to walk over. I closed the blinds and turned on my computer. Breaking the silence, I turned on iTunes and played a song at top volume, then danced my way through the kitchen and flicked on the stove.

Midway through breakfast, Eric called me up and asked what I had planned for the night. I told him that James and a couple of his friends were coming over to party with Trent and I, but he never believed me. "Those guys are pulling Trent's leg," he said. "They wouldn't hang out with us." Normally I would have trusted Eric on such matters—James was older and much more popular than us—but after meeting James a week ago, he seemed to me like an extremely friendly kind of guy, not who I'd expect to lie and say he wanted to party with us while he actually never.

"Even if they don't come," I explained to Eric, "I cut up some firewood yesterday and I'm gonna have a fire. We can all just... hang out, you know, around a fire."

"You and Trent won't be smoking weed, will you?"

"Don't worry," I snickered sheepishly, "he's all out."

"Yeah, yeah," mumbled Eric. "See you tonight, maybe."

Once Eric clicked off, I realized how important today was. As my last day-off, it was the final opportunity to get my laundry done and to go grocery shopping. Surprisingly, I found, living expenses were more than I thought they'd be. Doing two loads of laundry was over ten dollars! And without a car, I had to carry all my heavy clothes in a garbage bag back and forth across the highway. Then there was grocery shopping, which was was even worse—carrying three bags in each hand for ten blocks was death. By the time I got home, I was exhausted. But without a moment to waste, I got down to business and made up dinner. Feeling ambitious, I cooked up some pork and rice, which was more than I'd ever cooked before. I was still adjusting from a life at home, where it was my mom that prepared dinner each and every night. I'd never even done the laundry when I had lived at home, either.

After eating and tidying the suite up, I had nothing left to do, so I went outside and lit the fire.

'Come on over!' I told Eric, via text, *'The fire's lit!'*

'It's… early.'

'Trent will be here soon. He gets off work at five. Why don't you pick him up there at Zellers?'

'I'm thinking of sitting this one out.'

Tired of Eric's pessimistic attitude, I never bothered texting back; instead, I flipped open my pack of Prime Time's. Seeing I only had one cigarillo left, I savored each inhale I made, slouching comfortably back on my favorite of the lawn chairs I owned.

Behind me, I heard two cars interrupt the moment as they pulled into the driveway. I stood up on my tip-toes, peeking over the tall surrounding fence to catch a glimpse of the newly-arrived vehicles. One car I never recognized, but the other, I found, was a bright and silver SUV—my mother's. I spat the Prime Time out of my mouth and walked to the back, entering around the driveway through the carport. My mom, who was now standing outside the SUV, gave me a momentary look before closing the driver door. Further down the driveway, a girl in her late twenties appeared, walking from the car I never recognized. Awkwardly, my mom introduced us: "This is Dray," she said, "my son. He lives downstairs."

"Hi, Dray," the lady said. "I'm Kara."

I was quiet, so my mom spoke: "Kara might be moving in upstairs."

"Cool."

"What are you doing out here?" my mom inquired, taking a few steps forward. She looked in the backyard and observed: "Having a fire?" she asked.

"Yeah," I said, looking into the backyard as well. To my reluctance, I saw that my Prime Time—the one I'd spat out in a sudden rush—had a stream of smoke floating noticeably up into the air. Luckily, my mom never noticed.

The two of them walked onto the footpath that lead to the front entrance as my mom chatted noisily about the house. Hopping over the carport ledge, I quickly took one last drag of the Vanilla Prime Time and tossed it into the fire. Waiting uncomfortably for my mom to leave me in peace, I sat back down and decided to text Eric back.

'Please,' I said, *'just come over.'*

Moments later, I heard the front door swing back open. My mom and my supposed new-neighbor came strolling back into the carport, still stuck in constant conversation. Eventually they said goodbye, someone got in their vehicle, and the car took off. I was hoping this someone had been my mom, not Kara, but of course it wasn't. How could my mother pass up an easy opportunity such as this and not talk to me?

"Drayvn?" came her voice. She crooned over the carport ledge and said, casually, "You're still outside."

"Can't let the fire go out," I told her, spinning the lawn chair around so that I was facing towards her.

"You have a couple friends coming over?" she asked.

"I just like sitting here alone."

I'm not sure if my mom took me seriously or not, but she changed the conversation: "Kara's nice," she told me, as though she thought I was worried or something. "She's moving in with her sister."

"Cool."

"Anyway, I just wanted to catch up with you on rent."

"It's due. I know."

"I'm going to be around here all next week, getting some work done upstairs for your Aunt, so you can come up and give it to me whenever."

"That works out well. I thought I was gonna have to walk all the way to your house and give it to you there."

"You know it's still your house, too."

"I know."

"Have you gotten a job?" she asked, trying to sound cheerful.

"Yeah."

"Where?"

"Zellers."

"Like it?"

"It's not bad."

"Good," she exclaimed, pulling her keys out of her sweater pocket, a sign that she'd given up on trying to have a conversation with me.

※※※

Seeing Trent was a relief. Once my mom left, I sat alone for an entire hour, killing time as I fiddled with my phone. I was texting Anna and Rose, but mostly I was trying to convince Eric to come out. Funny enough, I never even texted Trent to check if he was still gonna show; I just assumed he would.

"You started the fire already?" he said, tossing his large black backpack on a lawn chair before sitting down on another.

"Got bored," I explained truthfully.

"It's only five-thirty. I hope you have enough wood to last the whole night." Trent raised his hands up and felt the heat of the fire bask over them.

"I don't know if we'll have the fire going that long, anyway. Eric says he's not even coming."

"Why not?"

"Not in the mood, I guess. What about James?" I hopefully inquired. "Have you talked to them?"

"Not yet," he said, pulling out his phone. "I'll give James a text now."

After Trent received a couple of texts back from James, I judged from the look on his face that the odds of having a good night were low. "It's just gonna be you and me tonight, isn't it?" I asked.

"And we don't even have any weed."

I punched his shoulder playfully. "We have a fire, though."

"Fuck this." Trent tossed his phone across the fire on top of his backpack.

"You know," I began, now being serious, "I could go and try buying us booze."

"Would you do that?"

"The liquor store's only a block away. I could go to the corner of Sev and ask someone walking by to go in and get it for us. I've got cash."

"Want me to come?" asked Trent, now considering what his place was in all of this.

"Someone's gotta look after the fire," I explained.

"Dude, I don't know anything about fire's," he murmured. "I don't wanna be in charge of the *fire*."

"What, you wanna be responsible for illegally getting booze and then walking here with it?"

Trent laughed. "I'm used to getting illegal things."

✳✳✳

In the corner of my backyard, beside the alleyway, Trent slid back through the tall fence door. "Guess what I got," he said. From out of his backpack, he revealed a package of drinks wrapped in a plastic bag.

"No way!" I hopped out of my seat and ran across the yard to look through the bag. "How'd you do it?" I asked him, but received the answer through the presence of someone else:

"What's up, Dray?"

"You made it," I said, looking up as James pushed the fence shut.

"I have to leave again, though," he said, shrugging, "but I'll be back before the liquor store closes, alright? I just gotta take care of a few things."

"Well thanks for getting us alcohol," I said. "I take it that's how Trent got a hold of this."

He smiled. "Trent said not to get beer, so I got you guys some Fireball and some coolers."

"Coolers?" I asked, confused. "We've had Fireball before, but what's coolers?"

James snickered, but then realized it was a serious question. "Oh," he said, thinking of an answer.

"Coolers," said Trent, "are like pre-mixed drinks already put in bottles."

"I think it's more complex than that," James pondered.

"Whatever," he replied. "It all gets you drunk."

"Damn straight." James looked over at the fire. "I'm psyched to drink here tonight. This'll be great, guys. I'm sick of drinking at the bars."

"Is that what you're doing now?" Trent asked.

"Yeah." He tossed his head back as though he wished he could stay. "I told someone I'd go and have a couple with him."

"Come on," Trent urged.

"Sorry, dude, I keep my promises."

"You promise you'll come back here, then?" I said, finally saying something. "Before the liquor store closes?"

"I promise," he said, giving me a cool and hip fist-bump. "And I'll pick you guys up some more alcohol, too. I expect you guys to be finished with what I've got you by the time I come back."

***

Blasting music with his windows down, Eric fashionably showed up in the driveway without even mentioning beforehand that he'd planned on arriving. When he got out of his vehicle, he found me and Trent laughing and joking around, drinking next to each other by the fire pit.

"You guys are drinking?"

"You're missing the party, man," I said, taking a large swig from one of the cooler's that we'd gotten a hold of.

"What?" Eric sauntered forward, taking his sunglasses off. "Where'd you get the alcohol?"

"James!"

"Thanks for telling me—"

"Come and have a seat," I said. "Have yourself a"—I pointed to my drink—"*Mike's Hard Lemonade.*"

Eric peered over us. "Is that what you've got here?" he asked.

"And Fireball," Trent concluded.

"Really?" Eric took a seat. "Well I hated Fireball, so I think I'll take a Lemonade if that's alright."

"Pussy!" Trent laughed and showed him his bottle of Fireball. "See how much I've drank?"

Eric grabbed the bottle from Trent and observed it. "Why's this bottle so much smaller than the one we had last weekend?"

"The one we had was a 2-6," Trent clarified. "This here"—he took the bottle back—"is called a mickey." As he explained all about the different prices of different sizes, I reached down and pulled out another Mike's Hard Lemonade from the case we had lying down in the grass beside us. After prying off the cap, I turned to Eric and handed the drink over to him. Once Trent saw this, he interrupted his own conversation and drunkenly shouted, "Cheers!" as he hurriedly twisted the cap off his own drink, the half-empty mickey of Fireball.

Eric and I exchanged glances, enjoying Trent's peculiar behavior. "Cheers," we said, tapping our bottles together as Trent chugged back more of his whiskey.

"That's delicious!" Eric shouted, surprised. He smacked his lips around and looked down on the drink in his hands. "This actually tastes… *good.*"

"All alcohol tastes good to me," Trent confessed, making Eric and I burst into laughter, even Trent himself. The idea of us all drinking together came full circle: here we were, this is what we did now.

Once we settled down, the three of us leaned back in our chairs and stared deep into the fire, all of us with drinks in hand. Eric spoke—not for conversation—saying, "Now this is what summer's all about."

***

When James and his two friends showed up, it was almost a surprise to see that they had arrived. Caught up in our own fun, we'd forgotten that James had promised to swing by and join us. Even after only a few drinks each, we were already beginning to feel pretty drunk.

Through the corner of my eye, the guys came strolling into my vision as they picked their way through the awkward and tall fence-door. Being the first one to notice, I hopped out of my chair and rushed over to greet them. Once I was close enough, I saw that the three of them were all carrying bags by their sides. Putting two-and-two together, I realized that they'd come with a large supply of alcohol, which got me super excited—not that I needed anything more to drink; it was just cool to see that they were truly prepared to party with us.

"Finally," Trent blurted out, looking over to us. "We're dying to start drinking some more!"

"You finished the Fireball?" James asked disbelievingly.

"Ages ago."

"More like ten minutes ago," I quietly corrected.

Even in the scarce and fleeting bare sunlight, it was bright enough to look over the two new guys that James had brought with him. They were like opposites: one was tall and buff, wearing a white muscle-shirt; and the other was small and skinny, almost scared-looking. James' look fell in between them as the more moderate type. Together, the three of them made an interesting group of friends—kind of reminding me of our own clique: Eric, the buff one; Trent, the skinny one; and me, the guy in the middle.

"I should introduce you guys," said James. "This is Drayvn. It's his house."

"Really?" said the smaller one of the two. "How old are you?" he asked in an accusing sort of way. I guessed absentmindedly that it was hard for him to believe that someone as young as me had their own house. Instead of being offended, I took his skepticism as a compliment.

"That's Sam," James added. "Dray, you're what—eighteen?"

I shrugged. "Seventeen."

"*Seventeen?*"

"Believe it or not," I said coolly.

"Thanks for having us over," came a gruff voice. It was the guy wearing the muscle-shirt, and even with his intimidating look and deep voice, his speech had an element of friendliness lingering beneath his words. "I'm Ryan," he said. "Where should we put all of the booze?"

"Oh, wherever," I replied, turning back towards the fire to spot a decent location. "You can put it on the picnic table by the shed if you want."

"Sounds good."

"What's up, Eric?" James called out. He grabbed a chair I had lent up against the fence while Ryan and Sam made their way to the picnic table to quickly unload their bags of alcohol.

"You recognize me?" Eric asked.

"Oh, yeah," James said, pulling the chair up between Eric and Trent. "It was a small high school, man. What, you don't remember seeing me at all?"

"I remember seeing you, I guess."

"We never had that many friends in high school," I admitted.

"And they both dropped out," said Trent.

Clarifying, I added, "We've always been out of the loop."

The look on James' face was pure astonishment. "You guys dropped out?" he asked, staring back and forth between Eric and I.

"Who cares?" said the boyishly-sounding Sam, still over beside the picnic table. "High school education is a joke."

"But you need high school for college."

"Um, James," he replied, prying the cork out of a bottle of wine, "GED?"

"Well, sure, but that's high school education. And besides, a GED isn't worth nearly as much credit as far as graduating goes."

"Says who?"

"You know it's not."

"High school's a joke," Sam repeated, sitting down next to James where they continued bickering away. Behind me, Ryan stepped up and handed me two cases of coolers.

"This is for us?" I asked.

"James said you liked coolers."

"We do, but this is a lot here."

"Drink as much as you can," he advised, "and save what you can't for next time."

After giving Ryan a cheerful nod, I turned over to Eric and Trent and asked, "Who wants some more Mike's Hard Lemonade?" As expected, they instantly complied. Handing a cooler to both Eric and Trent, I took one myself and sat down. Ryan did the same, creating a perfect circle around the fire as James and Sam maintained their prolonged conversation on schooling. "So are you guys in college, then?" I asked, subtly interrupting them.

"In Prince George, yeah. We're just back in town for the summer," James told me, then noticed the fresh new cooler in my hand. "I got you guys two packs." He motioned to the other case of Mike's Hard on top of the picnic table. "I hope that's enough."

"Oh, yeah," I said. "That's plenty."

"Rock and roll."

"Are you guys," Sam asked, "like, new to drinking?"

Trent laughed. "Eric and Dray *never* drink."

"Why not?!"

Eric answered first: "Never had the right times to."

"Oh," exclaimed James, "but now that Drayvn has his own place...?"

"Pretty much."

James thought it over and set his beer down in the grass. From out of his pocket he pulled out another small bottle of liquor and asked, "Have you two ever had Root Beer Schnapps before?"

"What's that?"

"Dude," Ryan said to James excitedly. "Give them a swig!"

"What is it?" I asked again.

"It's the easiest kind of hard liquor to drink."

"Oh no." Eric groaned. "Is it like Fireball?"

"No way," James tried to convince him. "This is *way* better."

"I dunno," Eric said, clinging tightly to his bottle of Mike's Hard Lemonade. "I think I'll pass."

"Dray will have some," said Ryan. "Won't you?"

"Can't say no."

"And what about Trent—where'd he go?"

I looked beside me, discovering an empty seat where Trent had sat only moments ago.

"He stood up and left?" Eric pondered conversationally.

"Washroom?" someone figured.

"I dunno."

I got out of my seat and spun around, seeking Trent out in the timid darkness. What was left of the skyline—a shimmering piece of blue hanging above the mountains—twisted above me, through my drunken motions as I curved through the shed and picnic table, making my way towards the basement suite. Just as I was about to enter the carport, I heard voices, which I quickly turned my head towards. On the other side of the fence, I saw Trent. He was being lectured, or pestered—or something—by an older lady. I ran to the fence and peeked my head over-top. "What's going on?" I called out to them. "Trent, what are you doing?"

"Your friend," the lady said, standing in front of the steps of her back porch, "decided to drop by and help himself to some of our firewood."

"Trent?"

"I'm sorry," I heard him grunt. Slowly, he backed up further from the lady I now knew as my neighbor. Even drunk, I realized what a terrible first impression this was for me.

"You might as well take the firewood you came for," she insisted.

"That's kind," I intervened, "but honestly, we have all the firewood we need."

"Well Trent here thinks you need more." She walked up her porch and looked back down at us. "Take some now so you don't have to try stealing some again."

We stared at her, dumbfounded, not sure what to do.

"And please," she added, "walk around and use the fence-door."

Trent apologized again, trying his best to sound as authentic as possible, and picked up a few pieces of firewood that lay disorganized near his feet. Piecing it together, I assumed he'd hopped over the fence and grabbed the wood quickly, only to drop it on his way out, probably in surprise that he'd been caught.

Fully embarrassed, I gave my apologies as well and rushed back to Eric, Ryan, James and Sam. As surprised as they were to hear the sad tale of Trent being a dumb-ass, I was even more surprised to see, when I first walked over, that Eric was chugging back the bottle of Root Beer Schnapps. Tonight, I knew, was about to get crazy, maybe even crazier than last week. At least that's what I was hoping for.

***

"Get-back-here-motherfucker's!" James yelled, hanging off the tall-fence that overlooked the street I lived on. Placing my hands on his bare shoulders, I pleaded him to drop back down in the yard; but Ryan, interested in getting into a fight, drowned me out, leaving me with nothing to do but watch the scene unfold.

"You pussy or something?" Ryan asked the opposition. "Get back here!"

Unfortunately for me, the two drunk guys—standing on the corner of the block with a girl the same age as them—came stumbling back down the street towards us.

"Come on!" I begged, tapping James insistently.

Finally realizing that I was there, he fell down next to me. "It'll be fine," he said, smiling casually. "Don't worry."

Through the cracks in the fence, I watched the group arrive closer and closer, the two guys shaking their heads angrily, hopped up and ready to fight. James crawled back up the fence and hung there with Ryan.

"What the fuck you yelling about?" one of them asked, his voice louder and stronger-sounding than I expected.

I turned back to Eric and Trent and Sam, who were all standing shirtless by the fire, hoping they might have some idea of what to do, but all they had to offer was the same identical look they had plastered across their faces, one of wide-eyed fear and deep, drunken confusion.

"You fucking," James said, "poked your fucking head over the fence and called us gay."

"Yeah," the same guy replied, "I was letting my friends know what a gay-ass party you were all having."

James trembled in anger. "What's gay, huh? What's gay?"

"Well we saw the fire and everything and expected there to be a real party happening—"

"Fuck you," mumbled Ryan.

"You're just a bunch of dudes without shirts on!"

"We work out, douche bag." Ryan quickly loosened up a tight fist and slipped his middle finger up, waving it ferociously in the air at them. "We compare workouts."

"With a bunch of dudes?" added the voice of another guy. "That's not gay at all," he said, his voice dripping with sarcasm.

"Oh what," James said, "and you think you're fucking cool or something? Look at the girl you're with—she's a fucking ugly tramp."

As James's last remark took a moment to sink in, everyone around went completely silent. Mentally, I prepared myself for what I knew would come next. James had gone too far, and now there would be consequences. Once again, I did my best to interfere: "He doesn't mean it!" I lied, waving my hands up and down over the fence. "He doesn't know what he's saying!"

But it was too late.

The two guys started hollering and attacking the fence, trying to take swings at Ryan and James who were shouting back at them.

Then, a spot of luck—the girl spoke up: "*Let's just go!*" she said tiredly. "You're acting like a bunch of little kids."

I breathed a sigh of relief, but there were protests from both sides, refusing to leave things unsettled. The girl unwaveringly continued to lecture us all, and through her words and reasoning, she was eventually able to grab hold of things and drag the two of her friends away from the situation. Happily, I watched as the silhouettes of them dispersing slipped through the cracks in the fence until they'd gone back where they came from. Ryan and James, meanwhile, continued cat-calling them until I angrily told them to shut their mouths.

"What was that about?" Sam inquired.

"Don't worry, they're gone," James answered as we sauntered back into the light of the fire.

"I'm not *worried*," replied Sam.

"Really?" asked Ryan. "Because it looks like you've all shit your pants."

Fully irritated, Eric, Sam and Trent—crowded behind the fire from us—glared heatedly at both Ryan and James.

"Fuck you, Ryan."

"You guys are crazy," added Eric.

"How 'bout we all just chill out?" I demanded, using the most serious tone of voice I knew how to use.

"Sorry," said Ryan, grabbing another beer off the picnic table. "Where the fuck's my shirt?"

James nudged me and quietly asked, "Dray, do you smoke?"

"Sure," I replied.

"Can I talk to you in private? We'll go for a smoke."

I nodded and followed him out the yard. On our way, we picked up our shirts off the picnic table and threw them on as we exited out the carport. Stepping out on the edge of the street, James lit up a cigarette and handed me another. "First of all," he said, "sorry for all that shit back there." Using his right shoulder, he motioned towards the tall fence where the whole ordeal had taken place.

"It's done. I'm over it."

"When we drink like this," he said contemplatively, "we sometimes get real rowdy, you know?"

"I'm pretty wasted, too."

"Yeah, man, that's good. This has been great. That's why I wanted to talk to you—I wanted to say thanks for having us over. It's been a blast."

"I'm glad you came."

"And you know I actually wasn't going to, hey? There's this girl, man. I've been trying to hook up with her forever and I thought tonight I might actually have a chance. But whatever, I'm glad she blew me off. This is where it's at!" He tried punching my shoulder playfully, but his blow ended up leaving a small sting of pain; still, it never bothered me one bit. "Oh shit," he said, realizing something. "I forgot to give you a light!"

"No problem," I said, laughing as I rubbed the sore spot on my shoulder.

After giving me a light, we noticed a pack of giggling girls who came strolling around the corner of my street. They were drunk—or does everyone just seem drunk in my mind when it's me that's drinking? In any case, they stopped mine and James's conversation long enough to admire them as they came walking right in front of us.

"Now would you look at that…" James stomped out his cigarette and gave me a look as though he were expecting me to say something, but I remained quiet, sucking away on the cigarette he'd given me. "You wanna go talk to them or what?" he asked.

"Sure," I said. "I'm down."

"Ladies!" James called out, and they stopped dead in their tracks, staring at us confusedly.

"Who's this?" I heard one of them ask.

As James took off to go and meet them, he waved me to follow. "We got this, alright? Be cool," he whispered. Right smack in the middle of the street, we approached them. "My name's James and this is Dray."

"We don't know you," they accused us.

"I know," James said, taken aback. "That's why I'm telling you our names. We've got a fire and drinks—just wanted to see if you'd wanna come join us."

"That sounds wonderful," one exclaimed sarcastically. I assumed she was the leader of their group.

"Does it?" James asked, not sure what to think.

"Yeah," she replied. "But how about we meet ten years down the road when you two aren't still in middle school?"

The three girls laughed hysterically. I almost laughed with them before I realized I was supposed to be insulted instead. I knew James was. He was shocked, completely dumbfounded as they nudged past us and walked off in the opposite direction.

"You bitches!" James shouted after them. "I'm in college!"

Still standing in the middle of the street, we watched the girls in their high-heels and mini-skirts as they disappeared down the road, turning off into the parking lot of the Twin.

"Fucking bitches," James repeated.

I flicked ash off my cigarette and inhaled one last drag, then tossed it aside.

"They were whores. Obviously."

"Of course," I agreed halfheartedly, looking over at James who continued to stare down the road where the girls had been.

"Fuck it." He turned to me and said, "I'm just pissed that girl blew me off today."

"She was a whore?"

"No, not her." James looked at his feet and I noticed as a faint smile appeared on the corners of his lips. "What about you, man? Who's the hottest girl in your life right now? You got anyone?"

"There's a girl, yeah." *Two*, possibly.

"Still trying to get to her, huh?"

"Basically."

"Well don't give up. It's summer. This is when things happen. But then again, you gotta make sure you make them happen yourself."

"Yeah."

"Know what I'm saying?"

"Maybe," I replied, realizing how late it had gotten all of a sudden. The town was getting more and more quiet, but the nice and comfortable silence was broken by the sound of someone puking. By my side, I turned and found James knelt down, hurling up his supper all over the street.

"You alright?" I asked, softly tapping him on the back.

James stood up and casually said, "We gotta party again sometime." He chuckled and punched me in the same spot he'd punched me before. "And we both need to get laid," he added. "Agreed?"

I laughed and without a word more helped him back into the yard.

Chapter Five: The World At Large

On the top floor of the house there was something going on, something loud and noisy. For a few hours, I never gave it much thought, sleeping through it mostly, but as I came to consciousness I remembered what my mom had mentioned to me on Saturday. I realized that it was probably the new tenants, renovating and getting their furniture moved in, maybe even painting some of the walls. Me: I was in bed, burnt out from smoking weed with Trent, still a little high and dazed, trying to ignore the sound of hammers and the creaking of footsteps back and forth above me. I knew I needed at least a couple more hours of sleep, but a knock at the door gave me no choice but to get up and get on with the day.

"Still sleeping?" Eric questioned, stepping through the doorway. He was wearing his shiny-blue Wholesale uniform, clearly on his lunch break. "You smell like weed," he added

"Do I?"

He nodded.

"Trent dropped by last night," I confessed.

"What about Saturday?" Eric kicked his shoes off and sat down at the kitchen table. "Wasn't that awesome?" he inquired. Between the lines I knew what he was getting at, and he was right: getting drunk was monumentally more exciting than pot. But after so many months of habitually smoking the stuff, it had built itself into my routine. Getting high was nature to me.

"I know, I know," I mumbled tiredly, sitting down with him. "But Trent's always doing it."

"Big deal."

"It's hard to say no," I tried explaining.

Eric ignored me, leaning back in his chair to look out the windows in my living room. "Have you met your new upstairs neighbors yet?" he asked.

"One of them," I remembered.

"How old do you think they are?"

"Twenty-five or something…" For the first time I really thought about it—how awesome it would be to share the same house with some cool and older girls. "You think they'd ever come party with us?" I asked.

"Doubt it." Eric smirked offhandedly, now looking up through the kitchen window as the sun poured down on him. "Anyway"—he looked at me—"the reason I came here was to tell you that I got you an interview at Wholesale."

My jaw dropped in excitement. Eric continued: "They're looking for someone to help me out in the freezers."

"No way!"

"Yep."

"When's the interview?"

"Now. If you wanna have a shower I'll drive you."

"For sure! Totally," I said, getting up and walking towards the bathroom. Before entering, I turned back to Eric and asked, "Do you think I'll get the job?"

"You'll have to do some lying—are you up for that?"

"What kind of lying?"

"Well," he considered, "for starters, don't tell them you already have a job."

"Piece of cake."

I closed the bathroom door shut, then skipped into the shower without even letting it warm up a little.

***

"We need a full-time worker," said the manager of Wholesale, sitting behind his desk. Behind him, in the window, cars whizzed by on the highway below. "That's forty hours a week. Can you commit to that?"

"Of course," I responded confidently. "That's exactly what I'm looking for."

"So you don't have any previous commitments during the week, Monday to Friday?"

"Nope, nothing."

"No other jobs?" he investigated, just as Eric had predicted.

"Nothing," I repeated. Though I felt guilty about lying, I knew it was something I had to do. If there was any chance of me getting this job, I would have to quit Zellers without giving them any notice.

"Great, that's fantastic," he said. "You're exactly what I'm looking for."

"And this is exactly where I want to work. Ever since Eric started here, I've heard nothing but good things."

"Right," he said. "*Eric*. That brings me to another point I wanted to bring up. You and Eric are good friends from what I've put together, and since you'll be working in the same division I hope that won't get in the way of you two getting your work done."

"Oh no," I said, pretending to sound appalled. "We've worked together before. If anything," I coerced, "it helped us be even better workers."

He gave me a big and bright shining smile. "That's what I like hearing."

Warmly, I grinned back at him.

"Come in on Friday," he continued. "I'll get you all set up, and then on Monday you can get started on a regular work schedule."

After giving me a few more details—dates and times—I was set to leave. I got up and shook his hand, thanked him, and stepped outside the office. Down the hall, I headed down the stairs to ground level where all of the cash registers were. After passing a couple of aisles I found Eric waiting for me around the corner beside the staff room.

"How'd it go?" he asked.

"How do you *think* it went?"

His face lit up. "You got the job."

"It was beautiful," I told him. "I was so charismatic in there. Worked my magic and now I've got a full-time position with you."

"*Dray, the actor.*"

"You should have seen it."

"I wish I had. But listen," he said, looking down the nearby aisles, "I gotta get back to work. Are you okay to walk home?"

"Of course. Come by my house when you're off?"

"Don't you work tonight at Zellers?"

"I'm not going," I told him, shaking my head enthusiastically. "Let's go do something fun."

"To celebrate your new job?"

"Fuck yeah!"

Eric covered his mouth, concealing a loud laugh. "You sound so weird when you swear," he told me, which I knew was true. But as unusual it was for me to swear, it was even more unusual to see Eric legitimately burst into laughter like I had just made him. "Don't swear like that around here," he added, still trying not to laugh. "This is your new workplace now."

✳ ✳ ✳

The walk from Wholesale to my apartment was longer than I previously thought out in my mind. By the time I reached the Zellers and Safeway parking lot, I was already bored and tired. Wishing I'd brought my iPod along, I realized that that was what I'd have to do in the future for each and every walk to work in the early mornings. But it wouldn't be so bad, I decided. Some time to listen to music would be a great way to start off the day.

Since it was on my way, I briefly considered doing the right thing by actually going inside Zellers and telling them that something had come up and that I would have to resign, but I knew they'd probably ask me a hundred questions and I was in too good of a mood to be in such an awkward situation. If anything, I'd get Trent to explain it all for me.

Another thought crossed my mind as I continued the walk, an idea so great I couldn't believe I hadn't thought of it before. My whole life I'd always wanted a cat, but my family could never get one because Henry, my brother, happened to be allergic. Now that I had my own place, there was nothing that could stop me! That was, if my landlord allowed it. Luckily, my mom was at the house, helping the new girls move in, available for me to ask permission to bring home a kitten—if I were to find one somewhere. Hesitantly, she called her sister—my aunt; the official landlord—who said it was okay as long as I was careful with litter box and such. My mom, of course, gave me a huge lecture on the responsibilities of having a pet to take care of.

"I know," I told her naively. "*I know.*"

She glared at me, not even remotely amused. "You think things are easier than they are."

I agreed with her. "Because I *make* them easy."

"How?"

"By doing them my own way."

After some noise subsided from inside the U-haul trailer parked outside the house, Kara poked her head out of it and said, "You should listen to your mom, Dray. She knows it all."

"Doesn't know me," I replied, smiling.

"Parents know a lot more about what's going than you'd think. You learn this as you get older." Kara nodded her head, waiting for me to say something back, but I kept quiet and so she went back to moving things around in the trailer. I turned to my mom, who was putting her gardening gloves back on. Behind her, I noticed what work had been done by the front entrance.

"Looks good," I said, nodding towards the fresh mounds of dirt and the plants nestled over top.

"Thanks," she said, now looking it over herself. "Soon flowers will start growing."

"Cool." For conversation, she turned back to me and asked how I was liking the place. Plainly, I told her how nice it was, how well it suited me.

"It'll be just one more thing you'll have to worry about, you know…"

"What will?"

"If you get a cat."

I shrugged. "That's alright. Maybe I need something to worry about."

✳ ✳ ✳

"I wish there was pet store in town," I told Eric, being casual, secretly steering the conversation the way I wanted it to play out—the way I'd planned it as I waited for him to get off work. After speaking briefly about the new job, I segued the conversation from money to the possibility of affording a pet. Being my best friend, he of course already knew how much I'd always wanted a cat.

"Terrace," he pondered, "is basically the closest place around that has a pet store—that, and then there's Prince George…"

"How far is Terrace, you think?"

"Two hour drive, easy."

"Well if you're ever in the mood for a road trip," I threw out, "would you ever take me to Terrace to get a cat?"

In response to my question, Eric thought about it as he paced through the living room. After sitting down on the old and ratty couch, he looked up and asked, "You're set on getting one, aren't you?"

"It'd be great," I said, sitting down opposite of him on the chair I put beside the door to my bedroom. "Having a cat around would keep me company."

After a quick pause, Eric said, "I don't work tomorrow."

"Would you wanna go then?" I eagerly asked, smiling excitedly. "I'll pay for gas and everything."

"No, man."

"No what?"

"Why go tomorrow when we can go tonight?"

"I don't get it—what are you trying to say?"

Eric looked at me as though I was misunderstanding the punch-line of a good joke. "Let's spend the night in Terrace," he told me.

"And come back tomorrow?"

"Want to?"

"Of course I do," I said, thinking it over, "but we'd have to reserve a hotel room and stuff."

"That'll be easy," he told me. "Think about it—we could spend the night there, and in the morning you'd have all day to choose a cat and get whatever else you need."

"A litter box…"

"Little toys."

"Let's do it," I said, sitting up.

"Well hold on," Eric said, waving me to sit back down.

"What?" I asked, doing as he said.

"Because it's my car," he began, "and I'm the one driving—"

"What do you want?" I hastened him.

"I want you to stop smoking weed," he said, and as serious as he was, he still retained the upbeat nature of our conversation. He was the only person I knew that could do that—to speak in two different tones of voice. It was impressive.

"That's the condition?" I asked.

"I think it's fair. You get a cat and I get my best friend back."

"Can you be anymore melodramatic?" I stood up and gathered my keys and wallet.

"It's the deal—take it or leave it."

Answering him, I said, "I'll call my parents to book us a room."

"What about the deal?"

"I'll *think* about it," I told him. "Can we just get going?"

"Well are you sure?" he asked, checking the time on the display screen of his cell phone. "It's only four o' clock—you could still make it to work on time at Zellers, you know…"

"They're gonna be so pissed when I don't show," I exclaimed—the rebel I was; the rebel I'd become.

Grabbing a backpack out of the living room closet, I went into my room and began stuffing it full of clothes. And as I packed up my things, Anna was doing the same from across the province, preparing for her long drive up to Smithers… *'I'll see you in a few days,'* she told me, which put me in an even better mood for the trip ahead. Our first real road trip, and also our first time staying in a hotel without any parents. Now that I'd thought of it, there seemed to be a lot of first-times occurring. Who knew what would come next…?

✳✳✳

"You still think of her, don't you?" Eric asked heedlessly, once our conversation had died away and I was looking out the window, staring at the mountains as they towered over us. I turned to him, not sure how to reply. Sunglasses on, he quickly peered sideways at me and said, "You have a look," and smiled, guiding the car through the curvy Highway 16 roads.

"What kind of look?"

"When you think of her, when you text her… You have this look on your face that just gives it away."

"That gives what away?"

He ignored my question and continued: "You never forgot about her, did you? Not once."

"No," I said, quitting the ploy of acting stupid as I realized there was no point, not with Eric.

"And she's been gone how long? What, a year?"

"Basically."

"She was your girl," he told me dreamily.

"Still is."

"Even though she isn't?"

"Basically," I repeated, half-smiling.

"And Rose?"

"She does what she wants," I mumbled, defining her my own way.

"She's there, but not really there. I know. I always thought she'd have made the most perfect girlfriend." After a brief pause, he asked, "You know what my biggest regret is?"

"What?"

"That I never dated someone in high school."

"Things were complicated back then," I told him, and the flashbacks of Grade 11 came strolling through my mind all over again.

"We always had this idea stuck in our heads of a perfect girl…" Eric shook his head at himself in quiet disgust, obviously thinking back to Grade 11 the same as I was. "I bet if we had just dated someone everything might have been better. If we'd actually gotten to really know a girl, we might have saw them as something perfect."

"Instead of judging them from first impressions?"

Eric shrugged. "I think that's what I mean."

"But we tried dating girls," I defended us, trying to make him feel somewhat better about it. Down the road, I noticed a small town and gas station in the distance.

"Not hard enough," he replied.

I chuckled. "But we *tried*."

"What if you have a shot with Rose?" Eric blurted out wearisomely. "What if *she's* your future wife?"

"I don't get what you're trying to say."

"What if you fuck that up?!"

Quickly, I told him, "If it's meant to be, I won't."

"What if things aren't meant to be the way we used to say they were?" Eric exhaled and cocked his head backwards on the headrest. Registering that we had arrived in the only town there was to get gas on the way to Terrace, Eric changed the subject: "We better fill up here."

I agreed hesitantly, half-wishing we could continue the conversation, even though it wasn't really an enjoyable subject. "And I'm paying for gas."

"We'll split it."

The sun in full blast, close to setting behind the mountains, Eric handed me his second pair of sunglasses to wear once we'd pulled up to the pump. It felt so cool, filling up his car, shades on as vehicles ripped by. I felt strangely like an adult—opposite to how I'd always felt before—living my own life the way I wanted. Everything felt… awesome.

When I walked into the gas station I had a fantasy that Anna would be inside, watching me as I suavely paid for gas and a couple of waters. I wanted her to see how cool I was, how cool I could be. But thinking of Anna also reminded me of what Eric had said about Rose—what he said about having a girlfriend. I wasn't quite sure what to think. And besides, it was a depressing conversation anyway. Walking back to the car, I decided not to bring it up again, and for the rest of the drive we spoke of nothing but the good things. Love and romance—and all that—was still yet to arrive, if at all.

✳ ✳ ✳

The next morning in the hotel room we looked through the phone book to find our way through the city. It was easy finding the hotel—which was directly on the highway—but any further from where we were now was a whole new world, not at all what we were used to from living in our small hometown. In the yellow pages we found two different places to go: a PetCetera and an animal shelter. We both agreed that saving an unwanted animal would be a better way to go than buying one, even if the shelter happened to be another hour off into the middle of nowhere. After calling and getting directions, we checked out of the hotel and continued our adventure down the highways.

Once again, it was a warm sunny day, which made me realize how deep we were into summer, how great it'd be this year. The last all I did was mope around and work at 7-eleven. Now we had a car and an apartment to do whatever we wanted.

"When will she be here?" Eric asked.

"Who?"

"You know who…"

"You-Know-Who?" I joked. "Like… Voldemort?"

"Alright, fuck you."

I laughed an apology. "She's coming in like two days or something."

"Does she plan on actually hanging out with you? Or will she blow you off at every last second?"

"I don't know." I smirked. "We'll have to wait and find out."

Eric had never been a fan of Anna. But, thinking about it, maybe it wasn't Anna that bothered him, but instead the dazed and day-dreaming boy she made me out to be. He had always been more realistic about these kinds of things. He knew better than to get attached.

"You're crazy," he mumbled. "There's so many other girls you could have fallen for."

"It's not like Anna was the *only* one," I defended. "I tried dating *lots* of girls."

"But you couldn't *because* of Anna. You were always stuck on her."

I opened my mouth to speak... yet no words escaped me. Eric was probably right. He usually was.

✸✸✸

The shelter was located in what looked to me like a ghost-town. Lots of pavement and buildings, but no cars or people. When we found the address, I was surprised to see that it was even open. Fortunately for us, it turned out being the most amazing animal shelter that I'd ever been to. There was dozens of dogs, birds, and rabbits available; and for cats it was even more impressive—there was at least a hundred to choose from.

My eye first caught a beautiful and fully-grown female, but when I tried to take her from the kennel, she meowed defensively until I placed her back down. The vet accompanying me—a young attractive woman—explained that the cat had just given birth to two kittens and couldn't stand being apart from them. As tempted as I was to take all three of them, I knew it best to keep looking. Hoping I'd find another cat I liked just as much, I looked into another kennel filled with a much larger amount of kittens. They were scrambling all over the place, hopping on top of each other, trying to jump up at me.

It was as though they were each pleading me to choose them, trying to stand out from the others. But it was the kitten in the back I noticed immediately: a loner, sitting crouched in the corner, its head staring thoughtfully into the distance until I reached down and picked it up.

"Is this a boy or girl?" I asked the vet, who was cleaning up a nearby cage.

"Female," she told me, giving my kitten a quick glance. "What do you think of her?"

She laid limply in my arms, staring up at me with the same relaxed stare she'd held down in the kennel. "I think I'm in love with her."

The vet giggled playfully at me, and stood up to get a better look at the cat I'd chosen. "God she *is* pretty! Look at those eyes."

"Adorable."

"All yours if you want her," she said, and then walked out of the room to give me a quiet moment to think it over.

"You won't believe this," came Eric's voice—unusually expressive—as he stepped into the room. "In the other room over there there's two gay cats having sex. It's messed! They're both males."

"No way," I said, half-amused, still in the moment as I cradled my cat, which Eric caught notice of.

"Did you find a cat you liked?"

"I did," I replied, smiling brightly.

"Know what you'll name her?"

"I think so," I told him. "I'm thinking *Esme*."

He stepped up and looked down on her with me. "She's very calm," he noted. "She'll suit you really well."

I murmured a soft agreement, still focused in on my tiny and fragile kitten. Small enough to fit into the palm of my hand, she was clearly a newborn, possibly only a few weeks old. Of all the places Eric and I could have gone we'd come here—to an animal shelter in the middle of nowhere. Somehow we had found the kitten I always wanted.

"You sure you don't want to get those two gay cats?" Eric asked in a facade of seriousness.

I burst into laughter.

"Come on," he said, chuckling with me, "let's take you and Esme home."

Chapter Six: Never Heart

The white-fluorescent lights in 7-eleven—a huge contrast from the darkness outside—flared painfully into my eyes upon entering through the entrance way. Quickly, I used a hand to block it out, letting my eyes adjust as I tripped around to the candy aisle for a chocolate bar. To read the labels, I dipped down on my knees, but someone interrupted—calling me by name—and so I stood back up. "Who are you?" I inquired, focusing in on a girl a couple of feet shorter than me, a girl I'd never seen before. She dressed and looked my age, but I knew through her eyes that she couldn't be much older than thirteen.

"You don't know me, but I know you," she said, wise in her tone.

"How's that?"

"I watched the videos you put up on Youtube," she explained, enunciating each word as clear as possible. She could obviously tell how stoned I was.

"That was years ago," I told her. "It's been *years* since I've made a video."

"I know." She smirked and continued: "I was in elementary school at the time. Me and my friends loved you."

My confusion finally turned into a sudden sense of cheerfulness. "For real?" I asked. "You really liked them?"

"You were hilarious. The one with the paper airplanes—I think I watched it over a hundred times."

Speechless, I took a look at my surroundings, realizing that I'd forgotten where I even was. The drugs, and the excitement of someone actually having seen the videos that had once meant so much to me, had now put me in a strange state of mind. "You want something?" I asked the young girl, who stared up at me with a puzzled expression.

"What do you mean?"

"Whatever you want; I'll buy it for you."

"Really?"

"I've got three thousand dollars in my bank account," I told her, but then realized that probably wasn't true. At the rate I was going I must have been down to at least half of what I had when I first moved out.

"Three thousand dollars?" she questioned, impressed. "Well aren't you Mr. Money Bags."

"Today's your special day," I said, smiling comically. "Ice-cream, slurpees, chocolate, whatever... My treat!"

The girl giggled, too flattered to say no, and skipped off to grab a few things off the shelves. Me: I went for a bottle of water, feeling the weight of gravity begin to pressurize my sense of being. The fluorescent lighting seemed to get brighter and brighter... After grabbing a Dasani, I snapped the bottle cap off and took a sip right then and there, unable to wait any longer for something to drink. Even after gulping half of it down, my mouth was still unbelievably dry.

"Ready?" I asked the still-nameless girl, who came strolling around the aisle I was in. She had all the treats her arms had the ability to hold. She giggled again, pleased with her haul, and we followed each other up to the till. Unfortunately for me, the employee working just so happened to be a friend of mine. My Mormon friend, Brody. "What's up, man?" I asked him, full-knowing how pissed off he still was after I'd gotten drunk that one night while staying with him.

"Not much. What are *you* doing?"

"I'm buying this girl here some candy!" I pointed to the girl next to me, and saw that she still had everything in her arms. "What are you waiting for?" I asked. "Put 'er up on the counter!"

She laughed some more and did as I said; meanwhile, Brody kept a stern expression as he continually rang her items through. The total came to something ridiculously high, but I didn't care; I whipped out my debit card and handed it over to Brody, who glared at me restlessly.

I was high enough that I gave up trying to disguise it. "Don't tell me, Brody, I know—you're very disappointed in me, right?" I motioned towards my red-glazed eyes and nodded up and down, waiting for a response from him, but he remained quiet and passed me the debit machine. "He thinks I'm a *loser*," I whispered to the girl beside me, just loud enough for Brody to hear as I punched in my pin number. I set the debit machine back down on the counter, expecting anything from him, but all he did was ask if we wanted a bag for all the stuff.

"Yes, please," she replied, gleaming, finding the awkward situation all very amusing.

Brody grabbed a plastic bag and stuffed it full of all the candy, pop, and chips she'd picked out. Handing it to her, he looked to me and calmly asked, "Do you think you're funny or something?"

"I've never told a joke in my life," I told him, quoting Andy Kaufman. "*I don't even know what's funny!*"

"You're just stupid," he said, cutting me off, and then it was me that remained quiet. I never knew whether to feel hurt or angry. My feelings were blurred into one huge bundle of nothing, the way they always were under the circumstances I so often put myself under.

"Drinking? Smoking pot? There used to be so much more to you."

"And there's not anymore?"

"Doesn't look like it."

"Come on," the young girl said, dragging me away from the till. "Let's go."

"See you, Dray," Brody said. "Have a good life."

I turned away from him, smiling defensively. "See you," I murmured. The girl put her hand on my back and lead me out of the store.

"Your friend's an asshole," she told me once we were outside in the cool-night air. I held my head low but she ducked beneath me to catch my attention. "What's his problem?"

"He's been responsible his whole life," I told her, putting it plainly.

"He should be kinder."

"You know," I retorted, muttering, "you're much too mature for your age."

"Thanks," she replied, taking a step away from me, "and thanks for the candy." Decisively, she reached into the 7-eleven bag and pulled out my half-empty bottle of Dasani. "Drink some more water," she said, handing it over to me. "I hope you remember me in the morning."

"I'll try."

I turned around and headed off towards my basement suite, eagerly awaiting a nice and comfortable bed to fall asleep in. Stumbling up and down the street, I regretted ever leaving the house in the first place. My trip to 7-eleven wrecked the night completely. My high was now faint and abstract; thoughts buzzing all over the place, opposite to how I liked them. To keep myself focused and secure, I sent a text to Anna when I'd finally laid under my covers. Her reply took me off guard: *'What's going on with you?'* she asked abruptly. When I asked what she meant, she repeated herself: *'Seriously, Dray... What's going on with you?'*

'Um, nothing.'

'I heard about you... How you're smoking weed every day.' At the mention of weed, my heart stopped. I couldn't believe it had come to this. *'What's this about?'* Anna kept on.

'It's not something I'm proud of,' I tried telling her.

'Of all people... You.'

'Poetic, isn't it?'

'No. It's pathetic,' she said, her words cutting deep, almost as deep as my mom's had when she told me I had to move out three or four weeks ago.

My body froze, my head spun. The only thing I ever counted on was what Anna told me. She was my crutch, and now her words were turned against me. What did I have left? What did I have worth saying back to her? How could I ever fully explain myself? She would never understand. '*Well you don't have to make me feel bad,*' I told her. '*I'm used to this feeling already.*'

'*What feeling?*' she asked.

'*Being a disappointment.*'

'*…But I'll bet you're not used to disappointing me.*'

'*I guess there's a first for everything,*' I told her, thinking it was a smart thing to say, but it most-likely wasn't. She never responded, and twenty minutes I waited. Nothing came.

I had to use all my willpower to put my phone on the floor and force myself to sleep. I dreamed of nothing.

✳✳✳

Morning began with the sound of an electronic coffee-maker/alarm clock, a present from Trent, who'd showed me how to work it the night before. When the alarm is set, the coffee maker will start brewing the coffee-beans moments before the alarm comes on, so in the morning when you go to turn it off, there's a fresh pot of coffee waiting for you.

I hopped out of bed and stormed into the kitchen, absorbed by the scent of coffee as I turned off the alarm. It was the perfect gift for today, which happened to be the morning of my first shift at the Wholesale. With a steaming cup in hand, I leaned against the counter and considered all that had transpired between Anna and I last night. I felt like a piece of shit, but it all seemed to make sense. I had my own place and a job I actually wanted now. I never had time to be getting high and lazy, sleeping throughout each day. Wholesale was five days a week, all early-morning shifts. Smoking weed was past me. It was time to get back on track.

I even had a cat I needed to take care of—even if that cat was still hiding beneath the couch, the spot she'd ran to and remained in over the past couple days. Setting my coffee down, I set out once again to try and coax her back out. On my stomach, I reached out, trying my best not to scare her, but she was too far away. "Come here," I pleaded. "Come here, Esme..."

Her shiny feline eyes stared back at me like I was some sort of monster, someone not to be trusted. But I knew she would understand eventually, that I wasn't all that bad... Once she got to know her surroundings, she'd warm up to me. All it would take was time.

※※※

"Excellent, you're on time. Now that's a good start."

My new boss stood out of his chair and grabbed a small box off his desk-stand. After reaching inside of it, he pulled out a shirt and name-tag. "There you go." He handed them to me. "I almost forgot!" he bellowed, turning back towards the desk-stand. I could tell he was obviously in a hurry to send me off and get on with his day. When he returned, he passed me a box-cutter. "And there's that," he concluded. "Any questions?"

"Sure," I said awkwardly, confused with so many things I didn't even know where to start. "What'll be my... duties?"

"Right, right, of course. You'll be working in the freezers with Eric. Any questions—you ask him."

But it turned out Eric had just as much of a clue of what we were supposed to be doing as me. "There's so many people working here," he told me, once I'd put on my uniform and found him in the staff room, "that you just wander around until someone asks you for help with something."

"But we're supposed to work in the freezer rooms, though, aren't we?"

"Technically"—Eric shrugged—"but no one's ever told me what I'm supposed to actually be doing in there. And it's cold, so..."

"Basically you just mess around and you get a check every week?"

"Best job ever."

"Well now I get why you wanted me working here with you so badly," I said, smirking as I looked around the warehouse. This kind of job would definitely make life easier on me, and since I was about to start making some adjustments, the timing couldn't have been any better.

The rest of the morning went great. We walked around, and like Eric said, eventually one co-worker or another would call us over and ask for help unloading something—that, or carrying a large package somewhere. We were like errand boys for all the adults. Luckily for us, though, there were some teenagers our age as well. Two boys—Brendan and Tyler—were the shelf-stockers, and two girls—Chelsea and Carli—worked as cashiers. And then there was our friend from high school, Nick, who worked in grocery, but he got every Friday off so we wouldn't see him until our shift on Monday.

When lunchtime rolled around, Eric and I bought ourselves a couple of TV dinners and went to the staff room, pleased to find that the whole troupe was in there on their lunch break, as well. I went over to the table while Eric ripped open the packaging off our Hungry-Man frozen suppers.

"You guys hear about the new Batman movie?" asked Tyler, who was looking down on a newspaper between taking large chomps of an apple.

"The Dark Knight," Eric replied, looking up from the microwave as he dialed in a set time.

"Check this shit out." Tyler tossed me the newspaper to read from across the long table.

"What's it say?" Carli asked. I looked down at the paper and scanned over the headline: **The Dark Knight, Breaking New Grounds After Possibly Breaking the Architecture of Chicago.**

"Who cares?" interrupted Brendan. "Batman—isn't that kid stuff?"

"Fuck that," Tyler said. "You never saw the last one?"

"Nope."

"It was awesome! Definitely not for *kids*."

Carli hopped out of her seat and paced around the table towards me. "Do you mind?" she said politely, bending over me to catch a glimpse of the newspaper. Her hair draped over my shoulder as she read aloud: "The Dark Knight, breaking new grounds, after possibly breaking the architecture of Chicago."

"Right, I heard about this," Eric said, sauntering over.

Skimming through the article, Carli quickly continued: "... Director Christoper Nolan has finally succeeded his plan in flipping a real-life semi through the air and onto the pavement of one of Chicago's most famous streets. After a full month of investigation and tests, three engineers concluded that if the stunt was pulled correctly, new developments on the sewer system below would prevent any permanent damage. Warner Brothers estimated the single stunt, which will only last a total of seven seconds of screen time, will have costed the production twenty million dollars, possibly more. But Christopher Nolan and his studio aren't worried. Analysts suggest The Dark Knight will gross over ten billion dollars worldwide, making it the biggest film of the decade. Premiers July 18th 2008."

"Crazy, hey," said Tyler.

"That does sound pretty fucking awesome," Brendan admitted.

"Tyler," said Carli, moving back towards her seat next to him, "we should go together and see it."

"Yeah?"

"If you want," she flirted.

Chelsea turned to me, hidden from Carli and Tyler, and pretended to puke, motioning a finger down her throat. I laughed quietly and she smiled. But then, behind her, a co-worker of ours waltzed exasperatedly into the staff room.

"Carli! Chelsea!" She was one of the older cashiers. "It's busy out there. We need you! When you're on break you gotta keep your eyes out on the floor in case we need your help on till."

The two girls sighed and packed away their almost-finished sandwiches back into their lunch pails. "We'll be right there," Carli told the lady, getting out of her seat.

"Bye guys," said Chelsea.

"See ya," Carli added, resting her hand briefly over Tyler's shoulder.

The two of them piled out the door, following their wanna-be-supervisor back to work. Once they'd left, Brendan leaned over the table towards Tyler and said, "Well Carli obviously wants *your* dick."

Tyler shrugged, then laughed. "Sorry, man."

"I called dibs on her!" Brendan shouted, half-serious but mostly joking.

"You can have her when I'm through with her," Tyler said, making himself laugh so hard he almost fell out of his chair. Normally, this kind of talk wouldn't have interested either me or Eric, but we laughed anyway. These guys had some real character—however crude it made them.

✳✳✳

And after four more hours of walking around and socializing, our time was up. We were off, making today the easiest day of work I'd ever had in my whole life. To top it all off, when Eric and I headed out to his car, I told him how I was now through with smoking weed—for *real* this time. I did feel kind of bad that I never fell through with the promise I made before our road trip together, but I was certain that I could now.

"What made you change your mind?" he asked, revving up the engine of his small and old green car.

I shrugged. "It's not even fun anymore."

"And getting drunk...?"

"*The best.*"

Eric laughed. "Well I'm pretty happy to hear that. I honestly think that stuff was starting to make you forget about things."

"I think that was part of the appeal," I mused.

I then turned away from him, smiled, and looked out the window, watching the Wholesale disappear behind us through the rear-view mirror. Oddly enough, I couldn't wait to get back there for Monday's day of work. *How strange,* I thought, *I'd finally found a job I liked.*

"You hungry?" Eric asked. "I'm buying."

"Sure," I replied. "What are you hungry for?"

"I was thinking sandwiches at Safeway."

I looked forward into the distance at the towering sign above, which read the logos for both Safeway and Zellers, the biggest attraction we had in our small town.

"Sound good?" he asked.

I chuckled and replied, "You're buying; I 'aint complaining!"

Before missing the turn off, Eric quickly zipped the car into the parking lot.

✳✳✳

When I entered through the doors, I immediately peered into the deli, hoping Rose would be the one working. I couldn't believe how long it had been since I'd seen her and was hoping to get a chance to at least say hi. But today looked as though it were her day off. This meant I'd have to a throw a text her way at some point during the evening.

Eric waved his hand in front of my eyes, taking me out of a trance of thought. "You sure you haven't quit smoking weed?" he asked jokingly. "What kind of sandwich do you want?"

"Sorry," I said, and told him, "whatever you're getting..."

Eric stepped up to the sub-station and waited for someone in the deli to come and help while I went for a small stroll, pacing around the bright and noisy store. I stayed nearby, though, just close enough in case Eric had something to ask me—and then...

In the corner of my eye, she appeared.

Anna Markus came through the automatic doors like it was no big deal, like it was a regular occurrence. Like she still lived here or something. And even after she'd skipped off the entrance mat and onto the linoleum floors, she still hadn't noticed me—I, who stood there, frozen to the spot, my vision tunneled in on her as my life flashed back on me. Like a ghost, she took over all surroundings. Voices faded. Everything went quiet. And when she looked into my eyes, there it was again—that face, the one that smiled up at me every morning before school started.

Over the last year she may have changed a bit: she might have grown a couple of inches; her hair may have been colored; the clothes she wore I'd never seen before... But her eyes—they hadn't changed a bit. She was still the thirteen year old girl that lived inside my heart.

I ran to her as fast as I could.

Before she knew it, my arms were wrapped around her, holding her entire body tight up against me. I closed my eyes, taking it all in as she slowly let herself loose, placing her hands down onto my back. One second at a time, her fingers pressed deeper along my spine.

When she pulled away, her eyes looked over my chest, onto the logo above my heart. "Another job already," she noted. "What happened to Zellers?"

"Wholesale hired me?" I told her, realizing what a loser I was. Having three jobs in the span of two weeks came off pretty bad. "Did you just get into town?" I asked, reversing the conversation away from being about me.

"Yeah," she said, looking down at her feet, which was completely out of character for her.

At once, I knew just how upset Anna was. The gravity of the situation finally dawned on me. The choices I'd made over the past year had severed what was left of our connection together. I was no longer her perfect man: the healthy and happy person I'd always been. I was a lie, a fabrication. How could she tell me apart from what was true and real? How was she to ever count on me again? Trapped inside my own world I'd even gone as far as forgetting to text her back, something I never would have done previous to the mess of a life I'd begun living. Now here she was, standing in front of me, looking down at her feet, unable to look back at me.

"It's still me," I told her.

"I know." She looked up from her feet and used all her courage to look me in the eye without looking away, without blinking.

"It's been a weird year," I explained.

"You think *you've* had a weird year..."

"What do you mean?"

Someone behind me called Anna's name, making our awkward moment even more pitiful. Taking a look around me, she waved to someone down one of the aisles, motioning them to give her a quick moment. After switching her focus back to me she said goodbye, and without even a chance to say anything back to her, she nudged past me towards her friends, leaving me to enter reality all over again. Voices and footsteps came echoing throughout out the store like before, attacking me as I tried to think things over.

I remained there until Eric came and led me out of the doors ahead, back to his car. "Want to eat at your house?" he asked. Within that simple question, I noticed a rare spark of kindness ingrained between each word. He must have seen me talking to her, I realized.

✸✸✸

"Don't you see?" said Eric, who was sitting down at my kitchen table with me. "That was her plan all along. It's exactly like before: '*I'm in love with you—oh wait, I'm moving.*' She strings you along, man. All she wants is to be missed."

"That's not such a bad thing."

"What part?" he asked, moving aside our sandwich wrappers.

"Being missed," I murmured, letting my eyes roll up to the ceiling, which had now turned a faint orange through the filter of dawn sinking in through the kitchen windows.

"That's not the main point here..." Eric put his elbows up on the table, looking at me with an intensity he'd almost never shown before. "You think this is all a part of one huge love story, but it's not."

"Then what is it?"

Eric sighed, searching himself for some sort of answer. "I know why you love her," he quietly remarked. "She's poetic and quotes Death Cab lyrics to you—I get it. But she'll never love you."

"She doesn't have to love me. That's not the point."

"Yes it is! There's love out there and you're wasting your time dreaming of someone who lives on the other side of the province."

"It's not a waste of time."

"You said it so yourself," he commented. "You said she turned her back on you today."

"Because I let her down."

"And now she's let *you* down, right? Call up Rose or you'll regret it for the rest of your life."

I laughed out loud and fell back into my chair. "So that's where this was all leading?"

"You know I'm right," he replied, attempting to conceal a tiny smile from formulating at the corner of his lips. "Text her."

Eric had had me convinced.

Rose was not only my friend, but a high-school sweetheart. She'd always been there, through thick and thin—friends with my friends the same way I was friends with hers. We fit. We had each others trust. If anybody was meant to be with anybody it was us, and if she was prepared to go down that road with me, then I surely would, too.

For starters, she was positively thrilled when I did as Eric said by sending a text her way. After asking if she wanted to hang out with me—just the two of us—she replied, '*Of course!*' which put me in a completely new mind-space. Rose made things so much less complicated.

I had to wait through the evening, though, because she was with her friends and didn't want to ditch them so suddenly. '*Wait up for me,*' she told me, and so that's what I did.

"Don't stay up too late," Eric said, walking up the cement stairwell. And after wishing me luck, he got into his car and drove home, leaving me to prepare for my first official night-out with Rose.

I felt so riled up it was insane. Compared to the last year of my life—where I was depressed for every second of it—I was on top of the world. My feelings of isolation had disappeared; I felt connected to things now. There was something that I felt I could offer, something inside me I wanted to share. I wanted to talk to people again and I especially wanted to talk to Rose.

No later than ten o' clock, three flat knocks thrashed on the door—the kind of knock police would use, one full of authority. Could that have been Rose? Opening the door, I found it was, but then realized disappointingly that her timely knock must have been done out of much concentration, trying to conceal the state she was in. Put straightly, she was wasted.

"Are you drunk?" I asked.

She scrunched up her face, embarrassed. "Little bit."

"So that's what you and your friends were up to…"

"Yeah," she hesitantly admitted. With her shoes off, she hopped over and flailed her arms around me, the smell of alcohol ever-looming over her. "You're not mad at me, are you?" she asked.

"No, I'm—"

"Oh my God!" Her eyes lit up, seeing something over my shoulder. She let go of me and darted off into the living room. I looked around and saw that Esme had finally peeked her head out from beneath couch, but when Rose toppled down to pet her, the poor thing shot back down into hiding. "You got a kitten?!" she called out to me, reaching after Esme.

I sighed. "She's kind of afraid of everything."

Rose gave up and sat upright, laying against the couch. I sat closely next to her, as close as we had sat together at my party. She closed her eyes—tired—and smiled. "I've been trying," she said, eyes still closed, "to act as normal as possible…"

"Have you?!"

"Yes!" She giggled. "But I think I may be a little drunker than I'd hoped."

"Really, well—"

"Oh my God!" Her eyes flicked open. "Where's my phone!?"

"In your—?"

"It's not in my pocket," she confirmed, slapping both thighs. "I must have dropped it in the park. We have to go there! If I don't find it I'm gonna be in so much trouble. I already lost my last phone and my mom was so mad." Rose looked at me, pleading for help with a cute and pouting expression.

"Don't worry," I told her. "We'll go and find it. Where were you—"

"What's this?" she interrupted—suddenly not worried anymore—picking my copy of Thumbsucker off the couch. I'd been reading it earlier today.

"Great book," I told her, realizing how hard it was going to be to carry an actual conversation with her. "Reminds me a lot of my life."

"Why?" she asked, smiling. "Do you suck your thumb in secret or something?"

I laughed, and so did she.

But then, abruptly, something whipped through her mind. Her face switched to something sour and cold. Catching on to what was happening, I quickly grabbed something out of the kitchen for her to puke in.

Though this wasn't necessarily the night I'd mapped out in my mind, it didn't bother me all that much. I didn't mind holding her hair back, making sure she was comfortable. It felt like she needed me.

✳✳✳

"I have to pee," she said, running off to the other end of the baseball field. "I'll be right back!" From across the pale horizon—discolored by the shiny fluorescent night light—I watched as her silhouette reached the chain-link fence and hunched low to the ground. I looked away, towards the the sky, and saw Orion stretching above me. After seeing it in a movie as a young teenager, I went and found the stars in real life. Since then, it's remained my favorite constellation. There's so much in it that reminds me of so many things...

Rose and I had come here to find her phone, but that task had turned out impossible. The light shining against the ground created too many shadows in between the blades of grass. To make her feel better, I explained that I'd come and look for it in the morning, at first light. She of course said that I was sweet for offering, but that I never had to. In response, I promised her I would—I'd set my alarm clock for six in the morning and make sure it was found. How cool would it be for me to be the one to find it?

When she returned to me she never said much. All she did was tell me to lay with her on the grass. Doing as she said, she curled up over my chest, gently caressing one of my shoulders. To my dismay, I could feel an erection coming over me—but after carefully slowing my thoughts down, I reminded myself how drunk she was and that I was there to help. I relaxed, keeping my eyes on the ever-shifting constellations above.

A moment later, she began to cry. First came a sniffle, then a couple of tears, and then a whole lot more. The harder she cried, the tighter she held me. She started saying weird things, weird drunk things she probably would never remember—only me, who listened and listened.

Looking up into my eyes, she asked if I wanted to kiss her. I replied by kissing both of her cheeks and then forehead. I wanted so badly to kiss her on the lips, but she was drunk, and I never wanted her to wake up and regret anything.

With a soft palm, I tenderly wiped away what tears hadn't rolled off onto my shirt. She chuckled dreamily, and after she'd buried her face back into my chest, she started saying my name over and over.

"Oh Dray," she'd say. Again and again.

But as time went on, her buzz faded away into a bleak tiredness—she started feeling dizzy. I took her home, holding her up the whole way, making sure she didn't fall...

"I'll look for your phone in the morning," I promised, whispering to her in a hushed voice. We were being careful not to wake her mother, whose room was by the window next to us. "Sleep well."

"Sorry I threw up."

"Don't worry about it, Rose."

She blew me a kiss—standing from the top stair of her porch—and said, "I like it when you say my name."

"*Rose,*" I repeated gingerly.

She giggled, then quickly quieted herself. Smiling at me one last time, she creaked the door open and slipped inside.

Chapter Seven: Nothing Gets Crossed Out

Never in my life had I been up so early. Stepping out onto the street in the earliest of morning light was like stepping onto another planet. The feel of the air, the whisper of the wind, and the sound of birds chirping was unlike anything I'd ever experienced. It was all very different. Nothing huge, but it seemed as though everything had a new and unique quality to it.

I was still in my pajamas when I left the house. Mostly this was because I half-expected myself to fall right back asleep when I returned home, but also because I was eager to start looking for Rose's phone. When I got to the baseball diamonds, I realized sadly how big of a job it was going to be. It was too large an area for me to scrounge over the entire field. I checked the obvious places: both of the dug-outs and all around the playground, but no such luck—it was simply nowhere to be found.

By the time I got back inside my cozy and warm basement suite, I was wide awake. *Time to get on with the day*, I decided, grabbing my phone off the kitchen counter. I had a text, but right as I was about to check it, I became distracted by something in my living room. My kitten was rolled up in a ball, sleeping soundly on top of my couch. She'd come out of hiding!

Careful not to wake her, I slowly settled myself on the couch. My plan was for her to wake up, find me there, and finally realize how harmless I was. After making myself fully comfortable, I finally checked my cell and read the text. Turns out it was more than a text; it was practically an essay, the longest text I'd ever received. At first, I thought it was from Rose, but nope...

It was from Anna.

'Dray, you've no idea how bad I feel about yesterday... I don't know what came over me. Seriously. I haven't been able to sleep all night thinking about it. Thing is, it's just been really tough on me, coming back here, with all the memories I have in this town. I took it out on you. As bad as I feel towards alcohol and drugs, it's harder on me just imagining you not in my life. I'm so sorry. Please forgive me. I need you. I need you now more than ever before in my entire life.'

What a twist.

This had to be the biggest surprise of my life. What Anna was saying had been the last thing I ever expected her to. She was saying everything I ever wanted to hear from her. *'I don't see how this makes any sense,'* I replied, uncaring—not that my real-life response was anything close to being along the lines of uncaring.

Anna always had to be so damn epic.

'You're awake?' came her second text. *'Have you been thinking of me, as well?'*

'I've been up partying,' I lied—just for the hell of it.

But she replied, *'I don't care. I'm not gonna hate you ever again. When Eric told me that you were smoking weed, throwing big parties and running off with other girls, I snapped. But I don't care. Not anymore. The past is the past and I need you.'*

Eric. It was him.

I couldn't believe it. Not once had I given a thought over who had been the one to break the news to her that I was a different boy than the one she'd left behind. Thinking about it now... Obviously it had been Eric! Who else would have cared enough to go to such extreme lengths to wreck my relationship with her? He'd always disapproved of Anna. It was his belief that all she ever did was try and make as many boys fall in love with her as she could—which seemed true enough, but it was my naive belief that I was special that made me forget about that. Her locker was next to mine, she smiled at me every morning—wasn't I special?

Instantly, I realized what to tell her next.

'I loved you differently than any other boy,' I punched in. As I hit send, I shook my head and scoffed at myself, holding back a set of tears from surfacing.

Her response came immediately. *'Then have me.'*

As much as I loved her for saying it, I just couldn't see us together as a possibility anymore. There was too much anger between us. How could I give up on Rose, who had spilled her heart out to me the night before? I was sick of pain; I was sick of hurting—I needed the road to happiness.

In thought, I looked down and saw that my cat was now awake, staring up at me with a disillusioned expression. "Hey Esme," I said in a hushed voice, putting my hand around her collar. As she began to purr, my phone vibrated with another text, also from Anna, who apparently wasn't even going to give me the time to reply to the last. *'That was the first time you ever hugged me, yesterday,'* it read. *'Please don't make it the last.'* And after that, it simply hurt too much to respond. I slid my phone back inside my pocket and tried discarding the thought of her.

I so badly wanted to return to the morning buzz I had, the feelings I'd awoken with. But I remained distracted. Nothing felt right. If only Rose hadn't have been drunk—then I may have felt more sure of what was going on between us.

With a yawn, Esme pounced off the couch and leisurely made her way through the door to by bedroom. I followed her in and saw the message Rose left on my whiteboard. Last night she cutely snapped off the cap from one my markers and said, "Read this in the morning, when you wake up, and text me it so I can remember…"

Doing as she told me, I texted her as promised, repeating the drunk scrawl she'd left behind: *'Good morning, beautiful. It's a beautiful day.'*

Beneath it, she signed her name with a heart. If I never knew any better, I'd say there was a good chance she may have really liked me… But girls were complicated. I could never be too sure.

How We'd Look on Film

∗∗∗

"Tell me everything," Eric said, coming in through my door. He threw his hoody onto one of the chairs of the kitchen table and waited excitedly for me to say something. "Well...?" he implored.

I stood there, arms crossed, staring darkly at him.

"What?"

"What do you want to talk about—my night with Rose, or the conversation I had this morning with Anna?"

Finally, he got where I was getting at.

"You're gonna be pissed off at me for that, aren't you?" he asked.

"No," I told him reluctantly, "I'm gonna cook you dinner to say thanks for making the night with Rose possible."

Eric smiled.

"But I am still pissed off at you," I made clear, pulling a frying pan out of one of my cabinets, "for going behind my back."

Eric's smile withdrew, but he was still pleased with himself. "I know it wasn't the most honest thing for me to do. But I had to! Only Anna could have stopped you from smoking weed."

"What about telling her about the parties I'm throwing or the girls I'm running off with? Thanks dude," I sarcastically exclaimed.

Eric shrugged apologetically—his way of saying sorry. "That might have been over-kill... But it made you go for Rose, right? Two birds, one stone."

I laughed, flicking the stove on. "Such an asshole," I muttered.

"What's for dinner?" he asked, chuckling along with me.

"Pork."

"Pork?"

"It's cheaper than steaks." Grabbing the pork-chops out of the fridge, I showed him the price off the label I'd bought at Safeway.

"Don't you have, like, three grand?" he questioned.

"Believe it or not," I told him, "I've basically used it all up. I think I may be down to a thousand."

Eric shook his head in a sympathetic tone, probably realizing for himself how much money this basement suite had taken out of me.

There was the five-hundred dollar deposit and another five-hundred-fifty for July's rent. Soon I would have to pay for August's.

"At least you'll get a paycheck on Thursday," he told me. "Wholesale pays every week." Suddenly, something caught Eric's eye in the living room. "Esme's come out of hiding?" he asked, shocked.

"Apparently."

"Congratulations! You might have a normal cat, after all."

I smiled, malcontent. At the same time I was looking at him with both affection and hate. The truth of the matter was that I previously had planned on ambushing him with a series of allegations when I opened the door moments ago. I wanted to show him what a big deal it was that he'd interfered with mine and Anna's relationship, but when I saw him at the door, I couldn't help but be happy to see him.

He did care about me, after all, probably more than either Rose or Anna ever would.

✳✳✳

The work-week went as good as I could have hoped for. Since I worked at a grocery store, I was able to find some good deals for my lunches and dinners. When I got off work, I could cook up a nice meal, complete with potatoes and vegetables. I'd began going through the entire series of The OC again, so that's what kept me busy through each evening I spent alone, making up these elaborate dinners. Trent normally would have been coming by, but I told him I wasn't smoking pot any longer and I couldn't be around him if *he* was, which seemed to have steered him off. And then there was Rose, who could only handle seeing me for small amounts of time, still very embarrassed by her behavior on Friday. She asked me to visit her at work a couple of times, but we never really got to hang out in the evenings. She told me I'd probably see her over the weekend.

I still hadn't said anything back to Anna. There was already enough going on. At work we finally found out who our supervisor was, which was kind of a bummer because we then ended up getting a ton of work handed over to us. Turns out he'd been doing all of the work we were supposed to be doing, not realizing that they'd hired Eric and I to help him out. This meant five hours a day—at least—of being trapped inside the four-room freezer, unloading new shipments and putting set amounts out in the displays for customers. We had to wear big winter-suits, gloves and tuques. But it wasn't so bad; we never cared all that much. We still went for ridiculously long breaks, hanging out with our slacker friends, Brandon and Tyler, listening to them bullshit back and forth all day. We made it fun. Sometimes in the freezers—to keep warm—we'd pretend to work out, punching boxes full of frozen-foods, seeing who could do the most damage to the cardboard box.

After work one day, while sifting through my cell phone, I saw Rose's number in my contacts and decided to give her lost phone a call—just out of boredom, just to see what would happen. What harm could it possibly do?

An older man answered, "Hello."

"Hello?" I croaked, speechless.

"Yes, hello. Who is this?"

"Who are *you*?" I said in an awful-sounding, accusing kind of manner.

"I'm trying to get rid of this damn phone I found laying around on the ground. Want to help me out here?"

"Yes!" I suddenly shouted, finally realizing how awesome this was. I was going to be the one to find Rose's phone! "Where are you?" I asked the man, who was beginning to sound very annoyed. "I can come get it!"

"How about I meet you somewhere?"

"7-eleven?" I offered.

"Sounds good," he said gruffly. "See you in fifteen minutes?"

"For sure, I'll see you then."

I hung up, grabbed my wallet and key and sprinted for the door, horrified to find—when I opened it—that my mom was in the process of walking down the cement stairwell. My excitement dropped to zero. "Mom," I whined. "What are you doing here?"

"We need to talk." She strolled down the stairs, onto my entrance mat.

"Rent's not due for another week," I told her. I was hoping that I'd only have to see her one month at a time.

"I'm not here about that. I want to know what's going on with you. I've been hearing things all over town."

"Mom, I'm busy."

She glared at me, exasperated. After inviting herself in she told me to sit down with her. "What is it?" I asked, sitting down. With a groan, I slouched backwards into the chair.

"So you've had three jobs since you moved out... Three!"

I let out a booming laugh. "I think it's kind of impressive. Three employers thought I'd be a benefit to their company. I must be really good at interviews. Clearly I could get a job *anywhere*!"

After a pause, she replied, "You think this is funny?"

"I know how to take care of myself," I said, clapping my hands together as if I were giving myself an applause.

"What about staying up till six in the morning, wandering around town in your pajamas? What's *that* about?"

I laughed again. "Are you spying on me?"

"What were you doing?!"

"I was going for a drug run!" I threw my hands in the air abrasively. "You caught me."

She went quiet, tearing up. "Why do you do this to me?"

"It's not all about you, you know," I told her, but was now beginning to feel bad. She *was* my mom. "You have nothing to worry about," I assured her. "Those jobs I got sucked—the one I have now is really good. They're nice to me and it's a good paying job, okay? I'm doing really good right now. All I had to do was a find a job I actually liked." I leaned over the table and gave her an encouraging smile, but there was something still brewing in that brain of hers...

"Are you smoking pot?" she asked. "And don't lie to me. I know you've smoked pot since you've moved here."

It was time to come clean, and so I told her, very seriously, "Yes. This past month I started smoking weed."

Her mouth dropped in shock.

I continued: "But I've stopped. Now that I have a place to take care of and bills to pay, I've decided to be responsible. I don't do it anymore. You can judge me or hate me for it, but I don't care. I'm living my life the way I want to now."

She exhaled, looking over me, her son, and then over my basement suite. "It's nice and clean in here," she said, pulling keys out of her pocket. "The place looks good.

"Mom..."

"You obviously don't need me," she said.

When she stood up to leave, I went and gave her a hug—even going as far as telling her that I loved her. "I'm sorry I'm so weird," I said, which made her laugh, successfully cheering her up. After walking her to the SUV outside the carport, I continued my journey to return Rose's phone.

✳✳✳

She was obviously happy to have it back, but there was something off-putting about the way Rose responded. It wasn't at all what I expected when I handed it to her from over the counter of the Safeway deli. She uniformly smiled, giving her thanks.

"I never thought I would see this thing again," she said, nodding her head up and down.

Did she acknowledge the fact that I ran across town for the sole purpose of giving it to her—how excited I was that I'd come through with my promise of finding it? Had she realized how big of a thing it was for me to get out of bed at six o' clock on a Saturday morning? Or, a better question, did she even believe that I really went and looked for it that early in the morning? When I told her I had—but that I couldn't find it—she never gave me much of a reaction then, either. It was like she never believed me. She may have had it in her mind I already found her phone long ago and kept it for some reason, only just deciding to give it back to her now.

Maybe she didn't trust me...

✳✳✳

Friday night after dinner I was deep into one my favorite episodes of The OC. It was the one at the carnival, where all sorts of plot-lines were now intersecting.

Seth Cohen, trying to get Summer Roberts to fall for him, is getting advice on how to do this from his good friend, Anna, who secretly happens to be in love with him the whole time. (It's all very cheesy and melodramatic, but I love every second.) Together, Seth and Anna try to make Summer jealous by going to the carnival and pretending to be a couple, only Seth doesn't realize that Anna really does like him, and that she isn't going along with the plan in trying to make Summer jealous anymore, even though they are succeeding in doing that very well.

Meanwhile, Ryan Atwood is trying to win over Marissa Cooper—and that's where it gets really good. As Marissa is about to hop onto the Ferris Wheel with her date, Ryan takes his spot as the ride takes off. Marissa gets upset with him, but Ryan starts pouring his heart out to her, which isn't something he normally does and so she begins to find it charming. Then, the ride stops abruptly, and Ryan starts to freak out, looking down on everything below. Apparently he's afraid of heights. *"Look, maybe you just need something to take your mind off it," Marissa says.* And then just as she goes in to kiss him for their very first kiss...

Someone knocked on my door.

With my remote on the coffee-table I pressed pause right as the music began to swell up. If it was my mom again I was going to be really pissed off. Whoever it was had ruined my favorite part. If it was Eric that wouldn't be so bad because he could quickly come join. He was a fan of The OC, as well.

Surprisingly enough, it was Brody.

"So this is where you live," he said plainly. "Kind of small."

I let him in, unsure of what he had under his sleeves. Did he come here to sniff the place out for marijuana so he could report back to my mom? I thought he hated me—what was he doing here?

"This is kind of cool," he commented, pacing around. After sitting down on the couch, he looked up at the living room windows and asked, "You have a cat?"

Looking over, I noticed that Esme had gotten herself up on the windowsill. She must have pounced from the couch and then from the TV to get there, a huge leap for such a small kitten, which was pretty impressive. "That's my cat, Esme," I told Brody proudly.

We then heard something crackle, and with a closer look we noticed as she gnawed a small, plastic piece off from the venetian blind.

"She's tearing your blinds apart, dude," Brody said, laughing.

"Oh my God!"

"You never noticed?" Brody went over and looked on the carpet by the lamp. "There's huge chucks all over the floor." He stood up to my kitten and tried playing with her, but Esme automatically took tiny swipes back at him.

"I guess I was so into my TV show I didn't even see her up there."

Brody turned back to me. "What show were you watching"

"The OC."

"Hit play," he said, looking at the paused screen-shot on my TV. "I wouldn't mind watching a bit."

After hitting the play button, the show resumed. Ryan: *"Fifty-feet in the air, how am I supposed to keep my mind off—"* And just as Marissa suddenly interrupts with a big and passionate kiss, the Ferris Wheel starts back up again. And as the camera slowly pans out, the cool indie-music gets louder and louder. *Boom!* The credits roll.

Best episode ever.

"What's up in this place?!" someone shouted into my basement suite.

Brody looked over at me. "Who's that?" he whispered.

"I don't know," I replied, getting out of my chair. "Hello?" I inquired, walking through the kitchen. At the entrance I found it was Nick and Jacob. They'd let themselves inside.

"Dray!" Jacob ran over and gave me a hug.

"Your shoes, man," I told him, seeing as they muddied up the dining room floor.

"Sorry, sorry..." After kicking his shoes off, he went around into the living room. "Brody!" he shouted, using the same emphasis as he had with my name. "I thought that was your vehicle outside," I heard him say.

Nick quietly took his shoes off and stepped over to me. "Hey man."

"How's it going?" I asked. Over the past week, Eric and I had became pretty good friends with Nick. He was a surprisingly nice guy. After some brief small-talk, we went and joined Brody and Jacob in the living room.

"Watching The OC?" Jacob asked.

I smirked.

"I would suggest we all watch it," he said, "but Nick and I came here on a mission."

"What kind of mission?"

"We're looking for people to come party at Cameron's house tonight."

"Yeah," Nick added. "My brother's gonna be there and he's booting. If you want any alcohol now's the time to make your order."

"Awesome," I said excitedly. Truthfully I was beginning to feel somewhat restless being cooped up in here over the past week. Attending someone else's party where I wouldn't have to worry about the mess was just what I needed. Cameron's house would be great, too, because he was one of the few other friends I had in high school. I knew him through Cliff, of course. "Hey, will Cliff be there?" I wondered.

"Oh yeah," Nick replied. "He's drinking already!"

"It was his idea to come and get you," added Jacob.

I laughed. "Really? Well let's go, then."

"What about you, Brody?" Jacob went over to him and pulled him up off the couch. "Wanna come party?"

Like hell, I thought. He stopped talking to me for an entire month all because I drank that one single night while staying at his house.

"Okay," he grunted. "Let's go." Brody looked at me and saw the stunned expression I had plastered over my face. "I honestly don't care anymore," he told me, shrugging. "My life has gotten really boring this summer."

✱✱✱

While Nick took Jacob and I to the party, Brody kindly made the drive out of town to pick up Eric, which I'd asked—practically begged—him to do. There was no way I wanted Eric to miss out. If he made it, tonight would be our first official party that we ever attended together—another first. To top it off, Brody would even be there, the last person we would have expected to want and come out. Not to mention, Cliff was partying as well, and we hadn't seen him in weeks.

When we arrived at Cameron's house, Nick's older brother, Roger, was waiting out in the driveway for us. Getting outside the vehicle, Jacob and I both rummaged through out wallets for some cash. We each gave him twenty bucks.

"What do you guys want?" Roger asked.

"Could we—?"

"Nope!" Roger took the money and hopped into the passengers seat of his younger brother's car. *"You get what you get,"* he said comically, swinging the door shut. Through the metal and glass, I heard him shout over to Nick, "Drive!" who responded by hitting the gas hard, doing a burn-out right in front of the house. Leaving tire-marks all over the driveway, it echoed loudly through the neighborhood.

"One of these days," Jacob said, "Nick is gonna lose his license."

"That'll be hilarious," I replied, watching as the car sped down the hill towards Safeway.

"No it won't!" Jacob shook his head at me. "*Then* who's gonna drive me places?"

"You'll have to start walking again, I guess."

Jacob considered it, then said, "Never!"

"*Hey you two*," a voice from behind us said. Jacob and I turned from the street and looked up the front-entrance stairs, discovering Cameron, who stood there, already smashed, holding a large drink in his hands. "Get your asses inside." He took a slurp from his glass and smacked his lips. "Let's take some shots!"

We laughed rowdily and ran up to Cameron.

"Dray," he noted, blinking profusely as he looked over my face. "Holy shit! Long time, no see."

"Yeah man, thanks for having me over—"

"Have a sip," he urged, handing me his glass.

I looked down into it. "Why's it red?"

"It's a Caesar," he explained.

"Have you ever had one?" Jacob asked.

"No, I haven't."

"That drink is *yours*," Cameron said, pointing to it as he stepped backwards into the house, almost tripping through the door. "Enjoy it, man."

And after taking a sip, I delved into the party, pleased to find people that were drunk, fun, and actually friendly. It was a much more mature environment for drinking than I'd ever been in before. The only thing that may have dropped it's maturity level down a small bit was our friend Cliff, who was drunk to such an incredible extent it was ridiculous. I could hardly recognize him as my clever and self-educated movie-buff friend who knew who someone like David Cronenberg was. Normally he could name every Johnny Depp film that existed, in order of year; now I'd be surprised if he even knew the name of whose house it was we were in. The whole time he constantly ran around, unable to sit still, calling girls rude names and making fun of Brody.

Brody never took too much offense. He enjoyed watching Cliff make an ass of himself. After an hour, though, Brody said goodbye to me and Eric and left the party without a beat. I had no clue how he did it. How could he miss out on all of this? How could he miss out on these kinds of experiences? I knew how much better I was than partying and acting dumber than I was, but like Cliff, I didn't care. Making an ass out of myself was better than staying home and doing nothing. Throughout the night, I remained in a very good mood now that I knew Brody was no longer mad at me. We weren't as close as we used to be—true—but he was my oldest friend. We grew up together.

At the end of the night, Eric and I were sitting sprawled out on the big poofy couch in front of the TV in Cameron's basement.

How We'd Look on Film

Everybody had left except for us. We were very tired, but we wanted to be the last one's standing. Cameron was with us, sitting on the couch at the other end of the room, still sipping away on one last beer. "Wanna play some Rock Band?" he asked us.

Eric laughed out loud, paused, and said, "I think it's a little too late for that."

"You got Rock"—hiccup—"Band?" I asked.

"Want to play?"

"Um." I gave it some thought... "Maybe another time," I decided.

"Yeah," Cameron complied, probably already forgetting what we had been referring to. "Another time."

Eric: "We're all pretty messed up, aren't we?"

"I think we might be," Cameron agreed. "You guys like Star Wars?" he randomly asked.

We popped our heads up in unison and explained promptly that we were *huge* Star Wars fans.

"Alright, that's it," Cameron responded, jumping out of his seat. "I'm putting it on." Looking over his movie collection, he asked which one we preferred.

"Return of the Jedi," I demanded, trying not to slur. "My favorite. It's just so awesome. Like when Luke shows up to save Leia and Han Solo—and he's got the green lightsaber... The green lightsaber was the best."

"Return of the Jedi?" Cameron made a face. "I want to kill whose ever idea Ewok's were."

"Why does everyone hate the Ewok's?" I pondered to myself.

A New Hope was Eric's suggestion. "Nothing beats the original," he said. "Obi-Wan Kenobi and all his words of wisdom; Luke learning the force; the Death Star blowing up. By far the best of the series."

"Maybe. But come on, you guys... The Empire Strikes Back!"

"No," I whimpered.

"Come on," Cameron argued. "What about the ending where he finds out Darth Vader's his father?"

"Best scene in movie history," I agreed, "but we won't make it that far."

"Speak for yourself," Eric remarked. "Cameron, let's do it—let's watch the whole thing."

"That's the spirit! You in, Dray?"

"Alright, let's do it."

Right as Cameron was about to flick off the lights, he looked up and saw as someone came trudging down the basement stairs. I looked over and found Roger a couple of stairs up, standing there as he looked over us. His arms were crossed and his hair was disheveled. He looked really, *really*, drunk.

"How was your night, Roger?" Cameron asked.

Casually, he replied, "I just broke up with my girlfriend."

"So not a good night?"

"No, it was pretty fun." Roger fake-grinned, showing his shiny, white teeth. "Good party, Cameron. I'm gonna go sleep on your bed now."

We honestly never knew whether to laugh or to console him as he tripped down those last couple stairs and through the living room. Eric and I exchanged looks and shrugged. Passing by Cameron, he disappeared down the hallway and into a room at the end.

"Is he going to regret breaking up with his girlfriend?" I asked Cameron, who flicked off the lights.

"Definitely," he replied. "That's Roger."

And as we laughed together, the main menu of The Empire Strikes Back popped up on screen. After starting it up, Cameron sat down and the three of us got as comfortable as we possibly could—just in time as the main theme commenced in beautiful surround sound. I thought I'd fall asleep, but the set-up Cameron had kept us so in tune with the movie we forgot all about the time.

✱✱✱

The next day an even bigger adventure unraveled. After spending the whole day sleeping in and recovering, I was revisited by Jacob and Nick. With a knock at the door, I checked out the window. Sure enough, it was them. That golden car of Nick's was parked outside in the driveway next to the red car that belonged to Kara. I thought about not answering the door, but decided I still had Sunday night to relax and try and get a hold of Rose. My hopes were high that I would see her this weekend.

"What are you doing tonight?" Jacob quickly asked the moment I swung open the door.

I exhaled. "You on another mission?"

"Yes," Jacob began, "but a different kind of one..."

Their plan was to break into Chandler Park school. Illegal—yes—but not as bad as it sounded. Chandler was the middle-school we went to for our seventh and eighth grade, but it so happened to close down the year we began at the high school. Now it was nothing but an old and creepy abandoned building. For the past four years it had been collecting dust, being broken into every couple months or so by bored teenagers. I'd heard the stories, but never thought I'd be one of the infiltrators.

I'm not sure how they did it, but somehow they convinced me. It must have been the fact that Eric told them he'd be up for it, too—but only if I came as well. They texted him back and said I was and twenty minutes later he showed up at the basement suite to join us. By the time he arrived, it had finally began to get dark outside; but still, now that we were in summer, dusk came much later, and we had to wait until it was dark enough to be doing the risky, illegal things we had planned. This meant Eric and I were headed for another late night.

At eleven, I got into Eric's car and we followed Jacob and Nick to the other end of town. "Think this is a good idea?" I asked.

Eric glanced sideways at me. "No," he replied, "but it'll be memorable." He parked his car behind Nick's in a nearby suburb, which we knew would look a lot less suspicious than if we parked them out in front of the scene of our crime.

As we walked towards Chandler, my heart was beating so hard it literally hurt my ribcage. I'm pretty sure everyone was feeling as scared as me, but none of us acted like it. We were trying to be as brave as we could. Jogging down the sidewalk, we turned into the alley where the school buses used to come in after school.

Splitting up, we went our own way to try and find the easiest route to get inside. I did the most obvious thing—I checked to see if any of the doors happened to be unlocked, but it evidently wasn't about to be that easy for us.

Eric tried prying off one of the boards they'd used to cover up a broken window, but that was no use; we'd have to break one ourselves. As soon as the thought came to mind, it was apparent that Jacob had already figured that out for himself. He came running over, and with a small grunt he tossed a boulder up into one of the windows, smashing it into a hundred pieces.

After the ear-splitting noise, we all paused—looking at each other—and listened very carefully. I thought we were done for—but no sirens flicked on in the distance, no alarms shot off inside. A helicopter spotlight never came shining down on us, either. Nothing. *Let's get to it then*, was my first reaction.

"Lift me up," I told the team, and together they helped carry me up into the window. With a couple of bruises and scrapes, I crawled through the broken glass and fell down into the dark classroom. After standing up, I experienced the eeriest sensation of my life. This was one of my old classrooms, and here it was now—old, unused, and forgotten. The desks—lit up by the pale moonlight—were covered in cobwebs; the tile-floor was falling apart; and the whole place had a musky smell. It was like a nightmare. Like a scene from a horror movie.

I hurriedly got myself out of the classroom and found my way down the hallways. I couldn't believe how well I could remember where to go. I unlocked the nearest door and called after the group. "Over here," I whisper-shouted. They followed my voice and joined me inside.

"Oh my God," Eric exclaimed, looking down the ghostly hallway. "This is like deja-vu..."

"I know," I whispered aside to him.

"Let's go explore," said Jacob.

"We should stay close, though " Nick added, "so none of us get lost."

Together, we wandered through the school, using our cell phones as flashlights, careful to remain quiet. Just because we were inside didn't mean we couldn't get in trouble anymore. By the time we got to the other end of the school, the four of us had taken our own individual trip down memory lane. Everything about middle-school flooded back to mind.

I almost forgot where the bathroom had been, or which spot in the school I used to eat my lunch. I'd even forgotten where my first locker was. Now, I remembered everything.

In the mirror inside of the mechanics room, I got the four of us to huddle together and take a photo with me. *Never will I forget this*, I thought to myself, snapping the picture with my phone. Afterward, I immediately set it as my wallpaper.

"Should we get going?" Eric suggested, which I was about to agree with but I noticed that something had caught Jacob's eye.

"Check out these computers," he said, stepping away from us.

I looked over onto the ground and saw a bunch of computers, monitors, and keyboards stacked up by the wall. "Those don't even look that old," I noted.

"They still use this place as storage for the high school, you know. It's not *completely* abandoned."

I took another look around and noticed there were a bunch of kitchen appliances on the other side of the room. "Look," I said to Eric, pointing over to the rest of the storage. "I wonder if they have any microwaves."

"Today could be your lucky day."

Rummaging through blenders, bowls, and toasters, I finally came across a microwave, the one thing my basement suite didn't include. "I'm totally taking this," I said, pleased with my find.

"Want some help?" Eric asked.

"Sure."

Eric called after Jacob and Nick from across the large mechanics room, and told them, "We're gonna bring this microwave out to the car. See you two soon?"

They agreed, and Eric and I lifted up the microwave, cantering our way outside the room. We got to the door closest to us—unlocked it, and stepped outside into the back. "Alright, quickly," I ushered.

"What's that?" Eric asked.

"What?" I lifted my sight up and saw as headlights came shining into the back-alley. What was a car doing driving through the old and over-grown back-alley at this time of night? We must have exhausted our sense of danger, because the last thing we expected was there to be a police car doing a patrol of the area.

"Oh fuck," Eric realized as it came darting in front of us.

Not thinking properly, I let loose of the microwave, which fell to the ground and smashed to pieces, making our presence inevitably known to the prowl car, which hit the breaks hard, coming to a full stop.

"Run!"

Eric and I sprinted for the door. Behind us, we could hear as the policeman got out of his car and shouted after us. Without even a seconds thought, we hastily shut the door on him and locked it back up again. After a quick look at each other, we both knew what to do:

"NICK!"

"JAKE!"

We looked into a couple rooms for them, but there was simply no response. We didn't have time to keep looking. "There's cops outside!" I warned them, hoping they could somehow hear through the huge school.

Running all the way down to the main entrance, we sneaked through one of the doors and into the music room. Eric went to exit, but I stopped him. "Wait," I said, pressing my ear against the door. Slowly, I creaked it open a smudge and peered outside... Sure enough, there was a police car coming down the road. Keeping my eyes glued to the headlights, I watched it as it got closer and closer and then turned into the main parking lot. "Okay," I told Eric, "there's a police car in the front, and another in the back." Our situation was a shitty one.

"Let's run across the street," Eric proposed, "and into the forest on the other side."

I nodded and then creaked the door wide-open. Sneakily, we ran down the small patch of grass and onto the sidewalk. "Act casual," I advised, but us acting casual would no longer be of any use... A large bang came from the closest door to us—one near the end of the building. *BANG*, came the noise again. A door—boarded up from the outside—was trying to get busted open.

"Oh my God," I said as the banging got louder. *BOOM!*

The door successfully smashed open, sending the boards that held it shut flying through the air. Jacob and Nick appeared from the wreckage, running towards us.

"Come on!" we shouted.

Catching up to Eric and I, the four of us ran across the street and jumped into the thick forest on the other side, hoping to God the police hadn't seen us... Once we were deep enough into the forest, we looked back and saw that no one was following. Jacob and Nick subsequently fell flat to the ground, dead-tired; Eric leaned up against a nearby tree, hiding in the shadows.

Crouching down, I then caught my breath, watching as the cop cars drove in and circled around the school. We were safe.

All of a sudden my phone vibrated. Pulling it out of my pocket, I used a hand to shield the light from giving our position away to the on-going police investigation. It was a text—from Anna. *'Listen to Sparks by Coldplay,'* it read, *'It's everything you are to me.'*

After reading it through once more, I snapped the thing shut and laid down on the ground with Jacob and Nick, panting alongside them. I never knew what to think. What was I doing out here, being chased by the police? How did I get myself into these kinds of things? And now, with the text from Anna—well, that was just the cherry-on-top. What was it about Anna and I that made us act this way? The further we pushed one another away, the closer the other wanted to be.

Truth be told, I did miss talking to her. She was the highlight of my evening. Just reading a couple of texts from her made the night easier to get through. She was my lullaby—and the texts she sent made me feel apart of her life. But how could I ever move on with that dangerous attachment? I hadn't seen her in a year, and yet she was still the most important thing to me.

The thought that plagued me most was that I would never know exactly how important I was to her. In all the time I knew Anna, I always had to convince myself that her unspoken love for me truly *was* there; that it was only hidden below the surface, said in hints and riddles; and that a day would come that she could no longer resist holding in that affection. But what if her affection wasn't as strong as I believed? What if she never cared at all? Girls were like that. Even boys like me were.

Everybody craves attention. Obviously there was something more to Anna—she wasn't *just some girl*—but she couldn't be too far off, could she?

"Let's go," Eric told me, giving my arm a quick tug. I could tell he was scared, but his voice was tough. "If we get to the end of this forest, we'll end up by Railway."

"We can't leave the vehicles," Jacob stage-whispered over to us, knelt beneath a flurry of branches.

"We've got to—"

"Fuck," Nick groaned, keeping his eyes peeled on the police officers strolling around the school-grounds. The revolving flashes—from the sirens across the street—lit his face up all red and blue through the shadows of the trees.

"Let's just stay here," I told them, "and stay quiet. They haven't found us yet and they won't if we keep quiet. Let's just stay here—"

"This was so fucking stupid," Jacob said, lying down on the roots and leaves. "What the fuck were we thinking?"

"It'll be okay," Eric assured him. "Give it ten minutes and they'll drive away."

Luckily, Eric's prediction came true. Eventually the police flicked off their sirens and drove off, letting us finally scuttle out of the thick forest, over to the nearby suburb. Each in our prospective vehicles, we sped our way back towards Highway 16.

My heart never stopped beating until we fell among those passing through our town. Blending in with the rest of the cars and trucks, we dissolved into nothing with the rest of society. We just drove and never stopped—not for a long, long time. It felt good to be safe. Though it may have been nice to feel the adrenaline danger offered, nothing beat the feeling of safety afterward.

Chapter Eight: Ceremony

I'm sitting on main street, it's two o'clock and I've gotta work in the morning... Oh well, I couldn't sleep. I've been looking for a connection this past hour. I eventually found a signal by Subway and so I'm here, sitting on main street, stealing someone's wireless internet connection on my laptop. Just so I can listen to Sparks. Good song. (A little sad, though, maybe..) So I'm not sure when exactly you'll get this. We may have spoken in person by the time you do. So who knows what this might mean by the time you read it. What might we say to each other while this floats around in cyberspace? I don't know how often you check your email these days. Everybody's got Facebook, so I hear.

Thing is, I don't know what I'm doing , sitting on main street, listening to Sparks. I don't know why you do the things you do. But then again, I don't know why I do what I do, either. Why are we so confusing? WHAT ELSE CAN WE BE? You're like my cat. Sometimes you want to be alone and then sometimes you don't. I guess we're all like cats that way, aren't we? We're just a bunch of metaphors.

But I don't want my life to be a poetic device! I want you to be Anna and I want to be Drayvn... in the most uncomplicated way ever. But we can't be together and we clearly can't be friends. We suck. Things could've played out a million different ways...

The signal will probably fade by the time I'm done writing. So this email will probably just stay in the drafts of my hotmail account forever. It will be like nothing ever happened. But that doesn't matter.

Even if you do read this, it won't make a difference. It's crazy how it all ends. You made my life feel like a movie and it ends here, on main street. The camera is drifting away from me. The music gets louder.. the credits roll.
Love always,
    Dray

[SENT: July 20th 2008]

✳✳✳

The day after the night I sent the email, I was as tired as I knew I was going to be. After staying up so late on Friday and Saturday, I knew there was no way I would be able to get to sleep at a decent hour—what better way to spend the night other than wandering around town with my laptop, listening to music and meditating over my current situation? Normally I was used to being stoned while wandering around after dark, and so it was refreshing to finally have a clear mind-space this time around.

"They changed the schedules up a bit this week," said Eric, returning from the bulletin board. We were in the staff room. On our break.

Keeping me up and going, I was drinking a large Rockstar energy drink—even though I'd already drank four cups of coffee.

What's the change?" I asked.

"I don't work tomorrow." He shrugged. "Apparently I work Sundays now."

"Shit, that sucks." I quickly thought it through and told him, "You won't be able to party on Saturday nights anymore."

Considering that, he replied, "I can just come to work tired."

"I guess."

"Like you did today," he added. "How much more caffeine do you plan on drinking?"

I laughed and took a big sip of my Rockstar.

"What were you doing last night?" he pressed on.

"Well, since I don't have internet, I decided to find a signal somewhere up town, and that ended up taking me all night."

"What did you need internet for?"

"Tons of things."

Eric could tell there was something else to the story I wasn't revealing, but he gave up. Reaching over to the middle of the long staff-room table, he grabbed one of the newspapers and probed through it.

A moment later, Carli and Tyler came chasing each other through the door, giggling as they opened their lockers for their lunch. After they finished a flirty argument, Carli asked, "When are we going to The Dark Knight?"

"I dunno," he said. "Is it playing?"

Eric joined their conversation, saying, "Still not here."

Tyler cursed. "It was supposed to come out last week, wasn't it?"

Since we were in such a small town, it sometimes took a couple of weeks after the movie's release date for our theater to actually have it playing. This usually made a lot of people mad, but I never cared; I usually never went to the theater. The only time I did was if there was a big blockbuster that happened to interest me, which wasn't often. Most blockbusters annoyed me. The Dark Knight, however, was a must-see. "I'll bet this Tuesday," I told them. "Tomorrow, or Friday."

"Wanna go opening night?" Tyler asked.

Carli: "Sure. But don't stand me up!"

He laughed. "I'll pick you up at your house—how about that?"

"You got a vehicle?" she cheerfully investigated.

"My brother's lending me his jeep next week while he's out at camp."

She bounced up and down in excitement. "I can't wait."

As they turned to sit down at the table, I quickly averted my gaze back down to my lunch. There was something that bothered me deeply when I saw couples together, kissing or flirting. I hated watching romance bloom in real life. Everyone made it seem so simple, so ordinary.

✳✳✳

Eric would usually drop me off at my house when we got off work, but looking around in the direction we were headed, I sensed there was a different plan he had in my mind. Instead of turning off near 7-eleven, he turned onto the street before, onto the opposite side of the highway as my basement suite. "Where are we going?" I asked.

"I'm picking Trent up," he explained. "He's got a day off tomorrow and wants to get drunk." I remained quiet so he spoke again, saying, "I feel bad we forgot to invite him to Cameron's."

"What the hell!"

Eric turned to me, startled, squinting through the sun's glare. "What?"

"I have to work in the morning and you guys are going to party without me?"

"You're welcome to join."

I considered it. "I'm never gonna get a good night's sleep, am I?"

With a laugh, he replied, "Just get a little drunk and go to sleep by twelve or something."

Realizing it, I said, "That could work."

After pulling into the cul-de-sac Trent lived in, Eric parked the car into the empty driveway at the end. We waited a moment to see if Trent was ready and waiting for us, but it never seemed as though he was.

"Knock on the door and get him," Eric told me.

"Well aren't you bossy!"

Pause. "We're gonna be here for awhile if you don't."

Without notice, I lunged over and honked the horn for one long steady tremor.

"Dude!" Eric pulled my hand off the steering wheel but I fought him off and then honked it repetitively, stopping only when I heard—through my honking—a dog barking from the house next door. With a laugh, I laid back into my seat. Up the driveway, Trent stepped outside his front door and gave us a bewildered glare.

"It worked, didn't it?" I expressed to Eric.

Eric shook his head at me, not finding my antics one bit funny.

"Do you *want* my neighbors to hate me?" Trent asked, getting inside the car. Quickly, he buckled himself into the middle of the backseats.

"*Sorry,*" I remarked feasibly.

Leaning forwards between us, he spoke carefully, almost like he'd prepared a speech: "Now I know you guys are against weed—*both* of you, now… But what about cigarettes?"

I looked to Eric, who looked back at me. Judging from each others expressions, we had a brief psychic-like conversation and decided, "Cigarettes—okay."

"Awesome!" Trent shouted, reaching into his jacket pocket. "James got me a pack today." He pulled out a pack of Vanilla Primetime's and showed it to us. "You guys sure it's okay?"

"As long as I get one," I replied, to which Trent told me of course.

✳ ✳ ✳

It was a typical summery day for Smithers. Though quaint and breezy, it was still as warm as it ever got to be around here. Over ten years spent growing up in this town, I knew how seldom it was for it to be warm enough to wear shorts and a t-shirt; I knew to take advantage of the days it was possible. We all did. The three of us soaked up the sun together, playing pass with a soccer-ball on the field diagonally across from my house.

Kicking the ball back and forth, Eric and I told Trent the long and full story of our adventure breaking into Chandler Park, which he found hilarious. He chain-smoked cigarettes and laughed through every detail. It *was* an epic story. We all could have very well been arrested—somehow we'd gotten off lucky.

Once we were sweaty and too tired to continue, Eric kicked the soccer-ball up into his hands and proposed a plan for dinner. After we agreed on pizza, I made a call for delivery as the three of us walked back to the house. Finishing the order, we noticed up ahead as Kara's vehicle came and parked into the driveway.

"Is your room-mate upstairs nineteen?" Trent asked.

"She's in her twenties," I replied.

"Would she boot for us?"

"I don't know."

"Hey there!" Trent called after Kara. "You!"

Kara, who was now in the middle of carrying a large bundle groceries from her car up to the door, stopped in her tracks and waited for Trent to say something else. "Uh-yeah?" she urged.

"Can you boot for us?"

Kara laughed loudly, and without answering, she continued up the pathway to the front door.

"Oh Trent," I whispered to him. "Always a treat having you around."

"I thought she'd boot for us," he whined.

Being the nice day it was—and to score brownie points from Kara since she now probably hated me and my friends—I decided to mow the lawn as Eric and Trent hung out in the shade. They sat together on the picnic table while I worked up a sweat, listening to my tunes up and down the front lawn.

As I rolled the lawnmower through the carport—done with the front—the delivery-man pulled up in the driveway next to Kara's vehicle. Quickly putting aside the lawnmower back inside the shed, I told Eric the pizza had arrived. Because Trent said he'd pay for the alcohol, Eric and I paid for dinner.

After paying my half, I went and sat the large pizza box down on the table. Unwrapping the plastic bag with our receipt, I pulled out the three Coke's we ordered. I handed one to Trent and placed the others down in front of me, one for myself and the other for Eric, who was still at the pizza delivery vehicle, using his debit card to pay for his part.

A brief moment later, he came running through the yard and hopped into his spot of the picnic table, the one designated by the Coke I'd placed down for him. He cracked it open, and after taking a sip, turned to Trent and asked him, "So how are we getting the alcohol?"

Trent shrugged, taking a bite of *Hawaiian*, and then told us, "I think we have only one option..."

✳✳✳

Pizza in our bellies we waited by 7-eleven for James' return. Sitting on the benches of the Greyhound station, Trent handed us each a cigarette and lit them for us. The sun had begun its descent, which meant there were only a few hours left until it hit the peaks of our mountains—then the sky would light on fire for one last magic hour before vanishing to black.

Coming from around the building, a pack of young teenage girls we knew came and sparked a conversation with us. I never felt much like talking so I slinked away, down to the end of the parking lot. Over-looking Highway 16, I took long inhales of my cigarette, listening to the chatter behind me as cars roamed by.

Anna was out there somewhere. After a whole year, she was here. And we weren't even on speaking terms.

So I *thought*...

That very moment I received a text from her: *'When will you be alone?'* she asked. Re-reading it over and over, I took one last drag of my cigarette and stomped it out on the ground.

'How do you know I'm not alone?' I asked, and then closed my phone before walking back up to Eric and Trent. The girls were blatantly flirting with them, looking for a party, borrowing their cigarettes for a quick puff. Eric—not into sharing—just let one of them keep his.

'I drove out of the 7-eleven parking lot,' Anna replied. *'I saw you with your friends. Smoking.'*

"Do you guys, um, know of anything going on tonight?" the girls asked.

"Text us later," Trent told them. "We'll let you know."

"That'd be sweet," one of the girls crooned, pawing at Trent.

Sending an almost-apologetic reply to Anna, I was astonished by my bad stroke of luck. The moment I put a cigarette in my mouth she so happened to be around to see. But why should I care? Things were over between us. At least, that's what I said in the email I wrote her last night. Did she even read it?

Apparently—I discovered—she had. But not even that was the most significant part in the next text she sent me. What stood out the most was, *'...Will you see me at least?'* After reading that I knew I had a big decision to make, one that put the pressure on everything. I'd told Anna in my email that our story ended, that things were over... *She still wanted to see me.* I put a hand through my hair and started thinking gravely to myself. I was caught in a desperate situation, in what Mr. Reed had taught me in high school to be called a dilemma. I'd read about it; I'd seen it in movies; and now I was experiencing it first-hand.

Not knowing what to say, I put my phone back into my pocket. When I looked back up to my friends, I noticed Eric staring intently back at me. "What is it?" he asked, cutting off the girl beside him. She was in mid-sentence about something, but she stopped talking and looked back and forth at me and Eric.

"I have to go," I told him.

"Why?"

"I just have to."

✻✻✻

Anna told me to meet her at a very specific spot, somewhere that had a deep and sentimental significance to us, a spot we'd shared an intimate and perfect moment together. It was in the middle of winter a year and a half ago. (We weren't friends at this point—not the way we are now.) We were basically like strangers. It may sound crazy, but it was on this day that I believed us to be soul mates.

I was in the process of being driven from bible study to the school when I saw her up ahead, walking in the freezing cold. As we drove past, I looked out the back window. Just as I did, she looked up and saw me staring back at her. We locked eyes and she stopped dead in her tracks, not looking away until we'd disappeared between rows of houses.

I later referred that day to her as the day it was so cold I could see her breath, and since then it became the pinnacle of our strange relationship. After that day she was no longer just a girl that's locker so happened to be next to mine. She would forever mean more to me than she would probably ever prefer.

'Meet me where it was so cold you could see my breath.' By the hospital. I was there, standing exactly where her footprints had been

that one unforgettable day. Now I was in her position, waiting for her to come down the road I had.

Towards my old church, I saw a figure appear up at the intersection ahead. Was it her? Through the crystal-clear quietness of a Monday night, the footsteps got louder and louder. It *was* her. I never moved any closer. I stood still, watching her as she drew nearer and nearer, letting the moment last as long as it possibly could.

"You're here," was the first thing she said.

After a brief concise pause, I replied, "Of course I am," and threw my arms around her. Unlike before, she immediately returned the embrace, nuzzling her chin above my neck.

"Two hugs from Dray?" she emitted, once we had let go of each other. "What's the world come to? You never even hugged me *goodbye*."

I shrugged, grinning woodenly.

"When I *moved*," she added.

"I... put an arm around your shoulder?"

"That doesn't count."

I laughed and started walking down the street. Anna caught up to me and asked, "Are we going for a walk?"

"What did you have planned?"

"I thought I'd give you my letter... and then you'd just leave."

I stopped walking.

"I thought you never wanted to talk to me."

"No matter how mad I am at you," I informed her, "I'll never say no to seeing you."

She smiled hopefully, a smile tainted with melancholy.

"Can I see the letter?"

She reached into her pocket and handed me a folded up bundle of paper. I took it and started unraveling the pages.

"Don't open it!" she told me.

"Why not?"

"Not with me *here*," she murmured softly.

"When can I read it?"

"When you go back to your friends."

I sighed. As badly as I wanted to read the letter, I wasn't even close to being ready to leave her yet.

"What are your friends up to tonight?"

"Drinking," I announced, and we began walking again. "Well, they're not drinking yet. They're waiting for me to come back, *then* they'll start drinking."

"Do they know you're with me?"

"I never said I was, but I'm pretty sure Eric figured it out. He always figures things out like that."

"He hates me."

I corrected her: "He hates how much I like you. He thinks I care more about you than him."

Anna paused. I could tell she was considering whether or not to ask if that was true. But she never. She probably thought it would have been conceited if she had. "Where are they drinking?" she asked instead.

"My basement suite."

She chuckled. "I have a confession to make."

"What's that?"

"I know where you live."

"Do you?"

"Yes, I went stalker on you."

"Well, I've gone stalker on you before—so I guess we're even."

"Get this, though," she began, "I even went as far as looking *inside* the apartment."

"Really? And how did you manage that?" I questioned, now a small bit confused. "Do tell..."

"There's a peep hole in one of the blinds."

I laughed. "Oh *that*?"

"That," she confirmed.

"*That* was the work of my cat."

"Tell her thanks for me," she said, giggling. "What did you name her? You never told me."

"Esme."

"Esme?"

"Yeah."

"Like, from Twilight?" she challenged. "You named your cat after a character from Twilight?"

I stared at her disbelievingly. "You love Twilight—don't even lie."

She thought about it and shrugged. "I *do* love it."

"Of course you do, it's awesome. There's just something about vampires... Have you seen Interview With The Vampire?"

"I haven't, no."

"You've really got to."

"Is it better than Twilight?"

"It's much different." I shrugged and then said, "What I think makes it really special is how the vampires look to one another. You see, none of them have a sexual drive. Because they get their satisfaction from blood, they yearn for something so much more."

"Like what?"

"Real love. Something bigger than who they are. They're affection goes beyond gender and age. It's a deeper attraction. They're searching for knowledge and understanding." In my mind I momentarily remembered myself watching it for the first time. Smiling in fond memory, I told her, "I think it's awesome. Interview With The Vampire is based off books by Anne Rice and everything she's written is *so* thought-provoking. Watch the movie, though—see if you like it."

After taking a couple more steps, she said, "I love how weird you are."

I laughed. "Never mind me."

"I could see you as a vampire, though," she asserted. "Staying forever young, watching the world around you get worse and worse through the ages. Watching and learning..."

"I think the world's getting better actually, not worse."

"Better and better?"

"We've come a long way over the past hundred years. Abolishing slavery, giving rights to women. In the grand scope of things, that stuff's really recent."

"You are a vampire, aren't you?"

We both laughed.

"Listen to us," I said. "Philosophizing just like the old days."

"Have you been writing much?" she asked, interested.

"Some."

"So no?"

"Ever since I moved out I've been pretty preoccupied."

"I can imagine," she pondered. "But you should keep writing. You're so good. I loved reading the emails you'd send me."

"What about the one I sent you last night?"

"Very well-written," she announced sadly, "but I didn't like it, personally."

We stayed quiet, keeping up the pace of our walk.

"By the way," Anna said, her voice a quiver, "I wrote my letter *before* I read the email. I was going to leave it on your front door—*my letter*—but after reading your email I decided I better scoop up one last chance to see you."

"*Last chance*," I repeated, not knowing what I meant by repeating her.

"If our movie is over," she said, quoting my email, "this must be the epilogue, huh?"

✳ ✳ ✳

After circling around town, we made our way in the direction of her house. My friends were texting me non-stop—eager to start drinking—so I told Anna we had to cut the night short, which was too bad. We were having such a good time together. It was odd. We were determined that we were saying goodbye, but it wasn't like that at all. We kept talking like we'd talk again. That's how we always acted around each other: dreamy and vague. Our conversations went in and out of reality—into our own private world. She was the only person I'd ever met that spoke to me like she too were a character from a Miranda July movie.

Passing Safeway there was now only two blocks left to go. Her father's house was next door to Cliff's. (In a town as small as Smithers, everything was closely connected.) "Princess Street," I said, noticing the street sign as we crossed Eleventh Avenue. "You must have loved that—growing up on *Princess* Street."

"No," she replied.
"You never felt like a princess?"
"I guess not."

Something was wrong. Her face was sad. Up ahead she watched as her house grew ever closer. Once she'd slowed her walk down to a halt, she turned to me and said, "I have to sneak in through the back, through my window."

"You snuck out?"
"I *had* to give you my letter."
"Can't I read it here?"

She shook her head.

"Why don't *you* read it to me?"
"I can't."
"Why not?"

She ignored me and blurted out, "Is this goodbye!?"
"I don't know, is it?"

She exhaled sharply and wrapped her arms around me, burrowing her face on both of my shoulders, back and forth. I could feel her lips braze gently over my neck.

It was unlike anything I'd ever felt before. It was beyond words. It was...

"Should I kiss you?" I asked.
"Want to?"

My answer was a silent one. I put my lips over hers—then and there, on the sidewalk beside her house in front of Cliff's.

Another landmark between us emerged. This spot would forever be known as the location of my first kiss. My first kiss with the girl I'd always wanted to kiss the most: the girl with the locker next to mine; the girl I wrote emails to when she moved away; the girl I could never forget about...

The one that got away.

She was now in my arms, kissing me.

As the sheer velocity dawned on me, I checked to see if it was really happening. I opened my eyes mid-kiss and looked down on her. The expression on her face was solemn, deep into our embrace, which was a surprise for me. I half-expected her to seem disinterested. But here she was, more into me than I ever imagined her to be.

When our lips parted, I closed my eyes and then waited a second before opening them back up again—with Anna as hers fluttered open in tune with mine. She grabbed my hand and put it over her chest. "Feel my heart," she said, and I did—I felt it pulse beneath her pale olive skin, below the structure of her chest. Tugging my hand up to her mouth, she gave my knuckles a long and tender kiss. Her lips were warm and comforting, a small bit damp.

Anna waited a brief moment for me to say something back to her, but I never knew what to say. I never knew what she wanted to hear from me. It was too much to process. This was so unexpected, so bizarre—

"I have to go," she said, letting go of my hand.

She was trying to smile but she couldn't; she was unable the way I was unable to speak. I *wanted* to say don't go I love you, but my mouth couldn't keep up with my thoughts—and so I remained hypnotized by her as she stepped away and then when she did I had another impulse, one to stop her and grab her and tell her to stay... But for some reason I couldn't. Every day of my life led to this moment and yet I was completely unprepared.

Drayvn,
When I moved away you said you'd never give up on me. But I'm going to forgive you, just like I hope you'll forgive me for writing this letter instead of declaring it in person. I wouldn't be able to do it. Whenever I speak to you I become detached from myself. It's as if I'm watching myself in third person. Maybe that's why you are what you are to me... A light, perhaps.

I found a poem I wrote as an english assignment before we met. A line that was repeated several times was: I am a darkened soul who brings light. I think that's why I denied you for all the time I knew and lived here with you. You contradicted that verse. You brought your own light, and I thought I'd lose myself if that soul brightened. But this year, I did lose myself. Many times. So much that I almost lost my best friend. "You don't believe yourself anymore" was the last thing she said before I hung up on her. But she called back like I knew she would. I took most things for granted... like your respect. When we started talking over the phone a few months ago, I stopped... I stopped taking it for granted.

Believe everything in this letter.

I let you be my light. You carried me through some of the hardest times of my life. Without even knowing it. Little by little. "Everything in moderation." My mum made me read an article about a man celebrating his 100th anniversary-- I mean, birthday. That is how he claimed to stay healthy.

I'd cry whenever you hung up, and stare at my call log until I fell asleep. Did I really destruct everything we had for each other? I don't think I did, but I'm willing to take the blame, all the blame. If it helps you sleep faster at night, alone in your home. I find it easier to take the responsibility instead of blaming someone else, because I keep holding on to the hope that tomorrow will be better, that I could be rewarded. Like yesterday when we went to Seymour Lake and my flip-flops were stolen. I said, "That sucks. Oh well. Karma, man." And I was admired for that. It feels so great for consideration and optimism to be appreciated.

I wouldn't change anything about my life. Everything that's happened has made me who I am. Maybe you don't like it, but Dray, you have no idea. You have no faith in me. What kind of relationship is that? "While you debate half empty or half full, it slowly rises, your love is gonna drown."

You've witnessed how flawed I am. Even this letter is flawed. I told you long ago I wasn't perfect. But I'm leaving my heart in your hands. I won't leave you alone until you tell me to one more time. You don't know how incredible it was to read the email you sent in April. I was never going to forget you. But I'm young. I need to grow and learn more before I'll ever know what love is. You were worth the journey. I think we met each other too early, but that's just opinions. Everything happens for a reason.

It's up to you. I won't run forever,
    Anna

Chapter Nine: Standard Liner

I was definitely not in the mood for going to work on Tuesday. Even when I worked at 7-eleven I'd never been as unmotivated as today. It would be my first day at the Wholesale without Eric, who was lucky enough to be able to sleep in after his night of partying. But my lack of energy wasn't because I was tired like Eric probably was. Last night I never ended up getting drunk with the guys like we'd planned. They ended up going on a trip to Houston with Jacob and Nick.

Last night when I got back to the basement suite they'd already left, leaving me all by myself to read through Anna's letter over and over again until I fell asleep. I still never knew what to make of what it said—*or the kiss we shared*—which may very well have had some part in my passive state of mind. My thoughts were not concerned over bags of freezable vegetables or frozen pizzas.

Having to work in the freezers was getting brutal. The switch from summer weather and into sub-zero was more off-putting than anybody at work realized, and today must have been the peak of our summer's warmth. The last thing I wanted to do was go and work in the cold.

But oh well, maybe a day's work was all I needed to clear my head. Lifting all those heavy boxes was beginning to be therapeutic for me—it made me feel stronger and much more healthy. After quitting weed, I started realizing how important my health was to me again. All it took was a week and a half and already I couldn't even imagine myself taking one more inhale of that soul-sucking plant.

Once I'd made the trek to work, I was greeted by Chelsea in the staff room, a warm welcome before having to get into the flow of the day's work. "Where's Eric?" she asked, leaning up against the lockers as I sifted through mine.

"His day off."

"It's Carli's day off, too."

"Really?"

"Yeah." Chelsea nodded her head, frowning. "I think they're trying to split all us up from our friends so we'll work harder."

"Woah," I exclaimed, "I never even thought of that."

"You never?"

"*Those bastards*," I joked. "They expect us to actually work around here?"

Chelsea chuckled as I threw my toque over my head and raised my eyebrows at her, being friendly. She opened her mouth—to kid around with me or something—but there was an interruption: our supervisor came strolling into the staff-room with a cross expression.

"I better get going," she decided, awkwardly making her way around to the door.

"See you," I tried calling back to her.

As she walked off into the store I reached back into my locker and pulled out my work-gloves.

"You're ten minutes late," my boss told me.

"I was here on time," I replied, attempting to be cheerful with him. "I'm just getting ready."

"When the clock hits nine you should be inside those freezers."

In response, I stared at him like the asshole he was.

"What are you waiting for?" he pressed on, pacing backwards out of the room. "I've got a lot of stuff I want you to do today."

"Alright, alright," I muttered, slamming my locker shut. "Tell me what to do."

Turns out he really did have a lot in store for me. The major task I'd been assigned was re-organizing the meat shelves. Eric and I had apparently, 'made a mess of them.' *Prick*. It wasn't like anyone had properly explained what we were actually supposed to be doing.

After only a couple of hours I'd actually begun to sweat in exhaustion. Even in the terrible cold I was heating up like crazy. I'd take off my jacket, get too cold—put back on the jacket, and then get too hot. It was awful.

✳✳✳

During a late lunch in the empty staff-room, I got a text as I was quickly scarfing down some food before having to hop back up to work. Now that I expected to hear from Anna, I thought it was ironic that Rose was finally the one texting me again. It was like the two of them were taking turns in reversing roles.

As funny as I thought that was, reading the text made me realize the situation wasn't funny at all. '*What the fuck, Drayvn?*' it read, one of the most unusual things I'd ever read in my life. '*Seriously. What the fuck.*'

After that it was safe to say that I'd lost my appetite. There was no way I could have another bite to eat after hearing Rose say that to me. Who told her? Someone had clearly told her about what happened last night. I never mentioned a thing to anyone, so it must have been Anna. She'd probably told the whole town by now!

Put it up on Facebook or something...

And poor Rose—she'd watched me throughout all of Grade 11, staring puppy-eyed at Anna every time she walked by in the halls. Rose gave herself to me and I betrayed her last night with the girl she'd always been envious of. '*I'm so sorry*,' I tried explaining, '*I don't know how it happened, but it did. I'll make it up to you...*'

'*What are you talking about?*' was her response. '*I was just joking around. I meant like, what the fuck why haven't you texted me lately... That's all.*'

My heart sunk. Typical. Of course I had to make assumptions and blow things way out of proportion. Setting my phone down on the table, I tried eating another spoonful of mashed potatoes, but they were cold and I didn't care enough to warm them back up again. I tossed them into the nearby garbage. With a sigh, I dropped my head onto the table with a bang. Suddenly my phone vibrated loudly next to my ear. Sitting up straight, I grabbed it and read, '*What happened? Tell me.*'

What could I say? I couldn't think of an explanation and I never wanted to lie, so I put my phone in my locker and went back to work, trying my best to forget the whole thing.

On my way across the store, a customer stopped me and asked for help. "What can I do for you?" I asked, trying not to sound irritated. I was in a bad mood but I never wanted to take it out on a stranger.

"I'm looking for two boxes of ribs," he said. "They were ordered for the Aspen. Are you the guy I should be talking to?"

"*Frozen* ribs?"

"That's right, yeah."

"Yep. I'm your guy," I told him, pointing to the freezers. "I'll go find them."

I quickly pulled open the freezer doors and searched through the cold foggy storage rooms for restaurant orders. After a brief search, I found the two boxes and carried them out. "Thanks," he said, crossing them off his grocery list as I set them down in his almost-full cart.

"No problem," I said, turning back to the freezers.

"Wait, is your last name Emerald?"

I stopped walking and looked back at him. "Yes it is."

"I know you're dad," he explained cheerfully. "I've worked with him before. He's a great man."

"Well"—a pause—"tell him hi for me."

He gave me a puzzled look, waiting for an explanation—probably hoping that I was joking—but all I did was give him a wave and walk off. It gave me an odd satisfaction, seeing his face double-take like it had. Everybody always made assumptions. But who could really blame them? Who would have thought a kid as young as me wasn't on speaking terms with his own parents?

***

After work I plopped down on the couch, flipped on the TV, and tried to engage myself in the cool and hip California world of The OC—but like never before, it failed to interest me. It wasn't a bad episode or anything like that. I hadn't even reached the mediocre second season yet. Something seemed off. There was something stirring through my mind that couldn't be put to rest.

I thought about Anna, I thought about Rose.

I thought about the past two years of my life—the mistakes I made, all the pain and confusion, the love I felt—and things slowly titled into perspective. I had to sort things out, once and for all.

'*For starters,*' I began a text for Anna, '*your letter means more to me than anything else I own. Know that, but know how much it hurts me to hear you say these things now. I don't get it. Do you want to be with me or don't you?*'

I hit send and got up off the couch. The TV blared on as I walked around the apartment, tidying up a few things to keep busy. Much sooner than I anticipated, my phone vibrated with a response. '*I'm sorry it hurts,*' she told me, '*but you know I can't promise myself to you... We live apart from each other.*'

'*That doesn't change how I feel,*' I told her.

'*And what about how I feel?*'

I stopped my pacing and sat down on the old and ratty chair next to my bedroom door. '*I can't make you love me, can I?*' I blatantly asked, and in soft disappointment I realized how true that was. I couldn't do that and I couldn't keep lying to myself, either. I wanted to throw my phone on the ground in frustration. I easily would have, but I wanted to hear what she'd say next.

Her response took too long, so I sent her another one: '*I never had a choice in this, you know. You made me fall in love with you because you needed that from me.*'

'*What are you saying?*'

'*I don't know... Maybe it's that old quote, All who love are blind.*'

'*Where'd you hear that?*'

'*I guess you'll never know. Goodbye, Anna. Enjoy the rest of your stay in Smithers.*' After turning my phone off, I threw it down on the floor, exasperated by the situation, not even knowing what I meant in my texts.

I accidentally frightened Esme, who was lazing around on the carpet in front of the TV. She shot off into the kitchen and never came back. With nothing better to do, I hit play on the remote and went through an entire disc of The OC, which I watched—without really watching—by myself in my ragged chair.

Chapter Ten: Oh Merry Life

I don't know how it happened. The Wholesale went from being the perfect job to the most miserable experience of our lives. Today Eric was waiting for me at the front doors, holding two cups of 7-eleven coffee, looking off into the distance with a fazed and disinterested expression. With the bright morning sun streaming down on us, his eyes held a bit of a squint to them. Giving me one quick scarce look as I stepped up to him, he handed me one of the cups of coffee. Together, we then drank in a brief moment of silence.

"Time's it?" he asked.

"We got five minutes—"

He cursed; I agreed, sighing. It was Thursday—so close to the weekend, yet so far. "Do you know what we're doing today?"

"Hopefully nothing. Let's hide out in the staff room."

"I don't know if we can get away with that anymore," I told him. "They're keeping a good watch on us lately."

"If only we had Brandon and Tyler's job," he wished—and so did I. We both knew Wholesale probably would have continued being a great job if we hadn't been stuck inside the freezers for as long as they were making us.

Today our job was unloading hundreds of pails of ice-cream. Not the small containers that are sold at most grocery stores, but the big fifty pound pails they use at ice-cream parlors. We'd be body builders by the end of summer if they kept up giving us work-loads as big as this.

"I talked to Rose last night," Eric told me, stacking the items up against the back wall as I handed them over to him. "On MSN," he added, which stabbed me with a familiar sting of jealousy. But I ignored myself, turning from him to grab another tub of ice-cream.

"About what?" I simply asked, lifting the pail up to him.

"She wants to see The Dark Knight with you."

"Does she?" I asked, huffing in the cold. "Why didn't she tell *me* that?"

"You don't have internet, maybe?"

"I have a phone, dude."

Eric switched his attention from the shelves and down to me. "Well... I don't know, man... Maybe you should text her more?"

I thought about it and realized he was right. "Is it playing?"

"Is what playing?"

"The Dark Knight."

"I don't know," he said, focusing back on keeping the shelves evenly stacked, "but when it does, make sure you immediately ask her to see it with you."

"At lunch do you wanna drive by the theater and see if it's showing?"

"Promise me you'll text Rose and ask her if it is?"

Cold breath streamed out of my mouth as I laughed, amused by his perseverance. "Whatever you say, Eric."

✳✳✳

With our morning task complete, it was time for lunch. After pulling my white toque off and throwing it in the locker, I went and sat down across from Eric at the staff-room table. He was reading a text message that seemed to be peaking his interest to an alarmingly high level. "What is it?" I asked.

"My sister's moving to Prince George today."

"Just like that?"

"She's lived there before," he explained. "She wants me to drive down with her so I can take some of her stuff in my vehicle."

"There's not enough room in hers?"

"Guess not."

"Well when is she going?"

"In a couple of hours."

I shrugged. "Too bad."

"What do you mean?"

"What do *you* mean?" I inquired.

"Fuck this, I'm going to Prince George."

"What about your job?"

"My sister needs my help." He leaned back in his chair, pondering something. "You know," he began, "why don't I just move there today? Find a place, get a job. I've a bit of money saved—"

"You're being a little brash about this, don't you think?"

"No," he said matter-of-factually, throwing his gloves off. "I hate it here. I've *always* hated living here."

This was true. Ever since I knew Eric he'd always told me his dreams of moving to the city. My response to him was that moving wasn't going to make life any better, but he was always persistent in telling me that it would.

"Move with me."

"I'm not moving to Prince George," I replied. "Not *today!*"

"Why not?"

"For starters," I told him, "I've finally just got settled into my new basement suite."

"Then let's move at the end of summer."

I stared at him with a bewildered and close-to-condescending expression. He rolled his eyes and put his phone in his pocket. Tugging off one of the store's winter jackets, he threw it down on the table and said, "Well let's drive by the theater, then."

✷✷✷

The Dark Knight – 7:30, 9:45

"What are you waiting for?" Eric asked, playfully punching my shoulder in a rapid spurt with both fists. "Text her!"

I fought him off and waved my phone in the air for his eyes to see.

"Alright, alright..."

We were parked in the lot across the street from our local movie theater—right beside Main Street—looking up at the show times together. Usually there were two movies playing, but apparently The Dark Knight was a big enough hit for it to fill up both showings. *'Guess what movie's playing tonight?'* I coolly asked Rose, beginning to get really excited about seeing it with her. The Dark Knight would be a movie to remember, and seeing it with someone who could possibly be the new love of my life could make it even more memorable.

"What are you hungry for?" asked Eric.

"How about Subway?" I suggested. "We could leave the car here and walk over."

"You're not afraid of going in there anymore?"

"Guess not."

We both got out of the car, locked it, and took the stroll down Main Street, representing Wholesale in our shiny-blue uniforms. I honestly was a bit scared of bumping into the lady that hired me at Subway, but luckily there was no signs of her when we got inside. Besides, we were only in there for a quick minute, taking our subs to go. On our way back to the parking lot, I noticed up ahead that an old friend of ours from high school was walking towards us. Her name was Amelia Wallace, a friendly girl who was in the same grade as Anna. I wasn't sure if she would still remember us as being close friends, though—high-school was a long time ago.

"Dray?" She called after us. "Eric?"

Apparently she *hadn't* forgotten about us.

She came running over and gave us each a big hug. "How are you, Amelia?" I asked, smiling brightly at her. What a surprise: Eric and I still did have some friends left over from the golden ages.

"I thought you two, like, *moved* or something," she said.

"We're still working on that," remarked Eric, giving me a sideways look.

"I see, I see," she replied. "What have you been doing in the meanwhile?"

"I got my own place here in town," I told her.

"No way!"

"It's pretty awesome. Right in the middle of town. Perfect for parties."

Her eyes widened in shock. "You two have parties?"

We laughed.

"You two drink now?"

"Some things change," I said.

"And some things stay the same," added Eric.

"Oh my God," Amelia exclaimed. "I've missed you guys so much. Invite me out sometime, alright?" Giving us each another hug, she explained what a rush she was in. "Seriously, though," she made clear, "you two better text me. If you don't *I* will!"

"I still have your number," Eric confirmed.

She gave him her classic, winning smile, gloating in the sun. "Then I expect to hear from you!"

As she walked away, I momentarily remembered how things were in Grade 11. Every guy our age was obsessed with how attractive Amelia was, but she never gave them any attention. She liked being friends with two nice guys like us. I thought after a year she may have changed, but it didn't seem that way at all. She was the same fun-loving girl she'd always been.

✳✳✳

Finishing our lunch, we threw the wrappers away and went outside into the back yard. I brought Esme along with us, just to let her explore a little before we headed back to work. I was usually afraid that she'd run away and get lost, but since I was with her I thought might as well give her the quick chance to see the outside world. As she slowly stepped through the grass I noticed how quickly it had grown tall again. "I'm gonna have to mow already." I chuckled. "How crazy is—"

"Are you coming to P.G. or aren't you?" Eric interrupted.

I sighed. "You're really set on going."

"Well I'm moving there *one day*... This is my chance to scope out which apartment I want to get. My sister told me about this complex that she lived in while she went to college there. She's moving there again. It could be perfect for me, but I want to see it first."

I looked at him quietly, not knowing what to say.

"Please come with me."

"We'll get fired if we ditch work," I warned him.

"They won't even notice we're gone!"

"I don't know about that..."

"Please," he repeated.

Esme, while hunched in the grass, noticed as a bird flew over and above her. Out of fright, she cowered even lower to the ground. Poor thing was scared out of her wits. Quickly, I went and got her, lifting her shaking body up into my arms. Back down with Eric at the picnic table, she snuggled up onto my stomach, hiding her face in my shirt. "There, there," I petted her, and she slowly began to relax.

When I looked up, I saw something I never would have expected... Eric was crying softly, looking down on his hands with a stern expression. He was *that* upset; I never even realized. Then it dawned on me: this past year must have been really hard on him, as well. It wasn't all about me. Somehow I always seemed to forget that I wasn't the main character in everything.

"It was nice seeing Amelia," he said.

"Not everything in Smithers is all that bad," I said.

He sniffed. "We should have stayed in high-school together. We'd be going to college right now."

"We never had plans for college."

"I don't want to be trapped here forever."

"You won't!" I told him. "You think I want to stay here forever? No fucking way. I wanna move to the city too, you know. But right now I can't. I've used up all my money on this place." I pointed to the suite.

He wiped away a couple tears. "Can't we just go to P.G. tonight, though? Just to see it?"

"It's a four hour drive there, and a four hour drive back."

"So? I'm driving; I'll pay for gas."

"What about The Dark Knight?" I asked.

He considered it. "How about this? If Rose can see it with you tonight, we won't go."

"But if she can't?"

"Trip to P.G.."

I agreed with him in spite of myself. I knew what a terrible idea it was (not going back for the second half of our shift) but Eric mattered more than a job. And how could I return to work knowing I could be out on the road instead? There was a small chance that our supervisor wouldn't notice our absence. There were too many employees for him to keep an eye on all of us. We could get away with it and have a great story to tell.

Zzz. Zzz.

"Is that her?" Eric asked, motioning towards the vibrating phone next to us on the picnic table.

I picked it up, saw it was her, and said, "Moment of truth..."

'It's playing!? I really wish I could go with you tonight, but tonight I'm at my father's. How about the weekend?'

After reading Rose's text, I snapped it shut and popped my head up at Eric. He waited eagerly for me to say something, but I decided that I would play with him a little before revealing the news. "I'm sorry, Eric," I began.

"Did she—"

"*I'm sorry* because you're not gonna see your mother again for a long time... We're going to America!" Carefully I threw my phone on the picnic table and shouted, "Full house, boys!"

The sadness left Eric's face all at once, and he laughed in relief, knowing exactly which movie I was quoting.

***

We loaded up Eric's car with the remainder of his sister's things and hit the road, following close behind his sister as we headed down Highway 16. We passed Safeway and the Wholesale and eventually the house Rose was staying in that night. It was five o' clock by the time we left, which meant we had a long night in store. "You know we'll probably be back as late as two in the morning," I told Eric on our way out of Telkwa, the nearby settlement Rose's father lived in.

"Not *that* late."

"Depends how fast we drive," I supposed.

"On the way back I'll drive faster," he replied. "I'll get us back by midnight."

"We *do* have to go to work in the morning."

"That's right," he realized.

"If they don't fire us—"

"They're not gonna fire us." Eric scrunched his face up in disbelief. "They *need* us."

"Right, because we're such good employees," I joked.

He shook his head at me dismissively and reached for his iPod, quickly putting on some upbeat techno-ish music. "Have you heard this?" he asked.

"This is Metro Station, right?" It was. "I've only heard their big hit."

"The album is surprisingly really good. Very PlayRadioPlay-ish, just more poppy."

He turned the volume up to full-blast, and for the next forty minutes we relaxed and enjoyed the drive, watching as forests and mountains slowly whipped by us. The next town we passed through was Houston, which reminded me of the trip Eric took here with Trent on the night of mine and Anna's kiss. "Hey, what happened on Monday night?" I asked, and Eric turned the music down. "You never told me about your trip here."

"Such a stupid night," he remarked, slowing the car down to the town's speed limit. "The whole time Trent was trying to get into Alice's pants." He groaned and continued, "I never cared, but he refused to come back to Smithers with me. I had to wait until Alice went home before Trent would even consider letting me drive us home."

"Alice?"

"Remember the girl you met—friends with Jacob and Nick..."

"Her," I replied, remembering the morning they brought her over.

"Trent's convinced himself that he's in love with her."

I laughed. "Poor Trent."

"You haven't heard the worst of it yet."

"No?"

"Nick's in love with her, too. He drives here to see her basically twice a week."

"Brutal," I said, looking around the town. Houston was almost exactly the same as Smithers: same size, same look, same kind of people.

"You still haven't heard the worst of it," Eric kept on. "Jacob told me yesterday that Alice isn't in love with either of them." Through laughter he explained, "Apparently she's in love with me."

"Jesus!" I shouted, slapping my knee in shock. "This is an episode of The OC. Why the hell is she in love with you?"

"I've no clue. She doesn't even know me."

"I guess she likes the silent brooding type."

"Don't all girls?" he joked.

"You wish," I retorted.

He laughed, cranking the volume back up.

✳✳✳

The apartment complex that Eric's sister was moving into was everything Eric had counted on it being. It was very old—which meant cheap—but in a really nice neighborhood, close to downtown where the action was. Inside, the room was clean and surprisingly well-kept; and the windows had a great view of the city below. "This is it," he said to me, looking through the empty rooms. "One day I'll live here…"

It never took that long to carry in everything—possibly only a half an hour. Eric and I were able to carry the heavy things as she brought in the boxes. We had planned on going to the mall afterward, but by the time she was settled in and we'd said goodbye, the mall was closed. We went for a drive instead, which was quite the adventure coming from our small town. The heavy traffic and large intersections were intimidating. Eric eventually had to pull over and catch his breath, and so we went for a brief walk in preparation for the long drive back. We grabbed some food and a couple of energy drinks to keep us up and going.

"Imagine how different our lives would have been if we grew up here," Eric pondered, unlocking the car.

"Would we have turned out any differently?" I responded, throwing our supplies in the back. "*That's* the real question."

He sat down in the driver's seat and went quiet, looking off into the distance, absorbing it all in as much as possible. The sun had set and the city lights had flicked on, illuminating the vast enormity of Prince George. We'd seen the place many times, but right now for Eric it was a sight unlike anything else. The city was a symbol of hope for him.

Coming here had meant a lot.

Leaving it behind, we realized how awful the drive was going to be. It was midnight, when we usually went to sleep, and it had taken us four hours to get to Prince George in the first place.

Eric hit the gas hard. "We're getting there by three o' clock, at least," he said, taking the car back down the dark highway. "If we're any later we'll die of tiredness tomorrow."

"We'll get a ticket," I said, feeling the rise of speed pull me back against my seat.

"That's a risk I'm willing to take."

And twenty minutes... sure enough, we were pulled over by the police.

"Typical," said Eric, putting the car into park as the police cruiser trailed behind us on the side of the road. "Shit, shit, shit, shit..."

The sirens went off, but the blue and red lights continued revolving, flashing on and off us. "God dammit," Eric said, quivering a little in his seat. Neither of us had ever had the experience of being pulled over before.

"This is your first offense," I said in an effort to comfort him. "They'll just give you a warning." He checked his rear-view mirror as I turned around and looked through the back windows, seeing as the policeman got from his car and lurched towards us. Unnerved, we both went quiet. All we could hear was the footsteps as he slowly stepped up to Eric's door.

With a strong knuckle he tapped on the window. Eric quickly clued in to roll it down for him.

"License and registration," he demanded.

"Of course, of course," Eric replied. He leaned over me and dug through the glove department, pulling out the right legal document. "There you go." He handed it up to him.

There was an awkward pause.

"And license."

"Shit," Eric said, reaching into his back pocket for his wallet. Realizing that he'd sworn in front of a cop, he added, "Sorry."

The policeman coughed and lifted his hand up, awaiting the license from Eric, who was having a terrible time in trying to comply. His fresh new wallet had a crispy leather finish, and it never helped that his hands were shaking uncontrollably, as well. "It's stuck," he attempted to explain.

Suppressing a laugh, I grabbed the wallet out of his hands and tugged the piece of ID out and then quickly handed it to the policeman. "I'll be back in a moment," he said gruffly, taking it from me. He then walked back to the cruiser.

"Well that wasn't awkward," I said, once he'd left.

Eric let his head fall down on the steering wheel. "Fuck my life."

"I thought you may have gotten a warning," I told him, amused, "but now I'm positive you're getting a ticket."

He lifted his head off the steering wheel and glared at me, defeated.

"I'll be surprised if he doesn't ask you to take a breathalyzer!"

Sitting up straight, he ignored me and muttered another swear word. "Now we're gonna have to drive the limit..."

"That's alright," I told him, turning around in my seat. I pulled my phone out and took a quick picture of the police cruiser behind us—the vehicle and the beautiful blue and red lights which continually revolved through the darkness.

***

"Dray, wake up."

Startled, I opened my eyes and found the the car-door ajar and Eric towering over me. Bright beams of white-light jolted me awake, along with the familiar buzz of a gas station. With a quick look at the surroundings, I realized we still had a long ways to go until we reached Smithers. After apologizing, I asked how long I'd been asleep.

"An hour," he told me. "We have a problem."

"What?" I asked, rubbing the sleep from my eyes.

"I can't drive any longer—I'm gonna pass out with you."

"And you're driving," I realized. "That *is* a problem."

"Stop making a joke of things," he scolded me. "I think I need to get a hotel room."

I unbuckled my seat-belt. "No, no," I told him, getting out of the car.

"No?" he questioned, stepping back to give me space.

"All we need are more supplies—that'll keep us going." I pulled out my wallet and made my way around the car towards the store. "We'll talk and talk and forget all about our sleepiness."

Eric looked back at me disbelievingly, but I smiled like it was no big deal, pretending I never had the same doubts as him. But as he filled up the car while I went inside to grab us more snacks, I realized how fucked we truly were. This was a road trip from hell... Eric got a ticket for a hundred and fifty bucks and now we were on the verge of passing out. To top it off, we worked in the morning. Coming to Prince George may very well have been our dumbest idea yet.

Inside the convenient store, I bought the most healthy things they had to offer: a couple yogurts, a few apples, and two bananas. When I returned to Eric, he was surprised. "No energy drinks?" he asked, setting the fuel dispenser back inside the pump.

"I heard a rumor that fruit gives you more of a boost than any form of caffeine."

"Who told you that—Mr. Hennig?"

I thought about it, trying to remember... "I think it actually was," I said, getting inside the vehicle with him.

We got our seat-belts on and Eric started the car back up again. The fuel meter bounced up to full. "You sure we shouldn't try and get a hotel?"

"Yes, yes," I assured him. "In fact, I've got some news I've been meaning to tell you. Some news you might find interesting enough to keep you awake."

"Alright, what is it?"

"Once we hit the road I'll tell you."

Eric smirked and the put the car into drive. "We have two hours left probably."

"Why don't we just speed again?" I asked, chuckling at my own joke.

Eric stopped the car at the end of the parking lot and gave me a quick glance. "Great idea—let's speed!" He drove out onto the highway and then asked, "You want to pay for my next ticket?"

I pretended to think about it. "Deal!"

He laughed, keeping the car at a safe and steady pace.

"But seriously," I told him, "I'll pay for half of that ticket you *already* got. A hundred and fifty bucks is shitty."

"It's my fault," he uttered. "I'll pay for it. Besides, I dragged you on this trip anyway."

"That's very true. You practically kidnapped me."

"Shut up—"

"But I'm glad I came," I told him, being sincere.

He paused, keeping his eyes on the road. "What's this news you were gonna tell me?"

"Brace yourself," I warned. "This is big—"

"Just tell me."

After unnecessarily clearing my throat, I broke it to him: "I had my first kiss this week."

He furrowed his brow, stunned. "With who?"

"Anna."

"Why?" he asked, carefully keeping his composure.

"I don't know," I told him, which was true. "It just... happened."

"You *were* with her that night," he realized. "On Monday!"

"Yep."

"I knew it." He shook his head at himself, wishing he'd pieced it together sooner. "And you kissed her?"

"She kissed me."

"Same thing," he declared. "But how did it happen?"

I then quickly filled him in on everything: the emails, the letters, the texts; how one thing led to another. At first he was mad at me—since I was supposed to be trying to date Rose at the current moment—but as he listened through the whole ordeal he realized what a surprise everything had been.

"The only reason she kissed you was so you wouldn't stop loving her," he said, coming to the same conclusion I had.

"I know," I replied sadly.

"Have you spoken to her since?"

"I sent her a text yesterday, but she never responded."

"Probably for the best."

I agreed with him halfheartedly, grabbing an apple out of the bag of things I'd bought at the station.

"I can't believe her!" Eric blurted out.

"What do you mean?" I asked, peeling the sticker off and taking a bite.

"She's so selfish."

"Everybody wants to be loved," I said through a full mouth.

"Anna *was* loved—by you. And she never loved you back."

"She moved away, though," I told him, painfully swallowing down a piece of unchewed apple.

"But here she is, complicating your life all over again."

"Well, I mean—"

"That stupid bitch!"

"Dude, don't say that..."

"Somebody just needs to slap her across the face!" he shouted, sounding bizarrely unlike himself. My mouth dropped in astonishment. I'd never heard Eric say anything as rude as that.

"Don't say that," I tried telling him, but he took it even further—

"Somebody just needs to slap the living shit out of her. You know? Just to wake her up from her stupid deluded existence!"

By then I couldn't help but laugh. What made it so funny was the fact I found it humorous in the first place. I never thought I'd laugh over anything as awful as that—*let alone about Anna!*—but right now laughing helped. The whole Anna situation had been hard on me this week, and Eric knew that. Besides, we were tired and done with being serious.

"Well I've lost my appetite," I said, rolling the window down and throwing the apple onto the road.

"*I'm Anna,*" he imitated, once I'd closed the window. "*I'm so perfect and everybody loves me! I write hand-written letters because I'm sooo special!*"

"Come on, man," I urged him, even though I was laughing along with him. "Stop!"

"Alright, I'm sorry," he said.

"Thank-you..."

But after an extremely brief moment of silence, Eric felt the need to add, "But she's evil!"

"*Eric!*"

"Alright, I'm done," he said. "I'm done." He relaxed his face into a serious expression, but then dropped it and laughed at himself.

"You've lost your mind," I told him. "We need to get home."

"I'm taking you up on your offer to pay if I got another ticket," he told me, speeding the car up.

"I was joking about that!"

"Too late now," he said, and we ripped our way back to Smithers. Luckily, we never got a second speeding ticket and we never fell asleep, either. In our dazed states of mind, we ended up getting extremely wired in conversation, cracking even more stupid jokes. Now that it was as late as it was, there seemed to be no police cars on the roads—not a single one passed by us. In fact, there wasn't any traffic. It was just us: alone on the highway, talking and laughing, forgetting our troubles.

***

The expected thing happened in the morning. At least *I* expected it. I never even bothered showing up to work. Eric, on the other hand, brought himself there on time and naively began his shift until the supervisor found him in the freezers and told him to go home.

"Are you still in bed?" he asked after breaking the news to me. He was sitting in his car in the Wholesale parking lot, deciding what the next plan of action was.

"Obviously," I disclosed, laying in my nice and comfy bed with Esme next to me. When I got home last night she was ecstatic to see me, running circles around my legs until I turned the lights off and got into the bed.

"I thought you'd at least be on your way here," Eric told me.

"Um, yeah right—"

"Well I'm coming to pick you up, then."

"No," I hushed exasperatedly. "I'm going back to bed."

"I was the one that man'd up and went in this morning—you owe it to me to get up and help me find a new job."

"You don't need a job that fast, do you?"

"I need to save money if I'm moving to Prince George."

"Right," I muttered. "Dammit Eric, why didn't you just sleep in like me?"

"I was responsible."

"Responsible because we were irresponsible?" I rhetorically asked, too tired to even understand what I'd said. After stretching out in my bed, I told him to bring me some coffee.

"Okay, see you in a—"

I hung up and threw my phone on the ground.

***

Being that it was Friday, a usual turn of events began to form. Trent texted me, Cliff texted me, even Rose and Cassidy texted me. Everybody was looking for a party. Both Eric and I were extremely tired from our long travels, but we never wanted to stay home and do nothing. We got a hold of Jacob and Nick to see if there was a party happening at Cameron's again, but no such luck; they then joined everyone else in trying to sway me into hosting that night's party at my house. The consensus between Eric and I was to have a fire in the backyard. We'd keep the party outside, not wanting things to get out of hand.

Trent was the first one to arrive. He was early enough to join us for a home-cooked dinner of pork, rice, and vegetables, a brief moment of relaxation before the rest of the night unfolded. Next came Cliff, right as we were finishing up. The four of us thought the night through and decided what our plan for alcohol was. We still had left-overs in my fridge from Monday night, but we knew we'd need more. Trent got a hold of James and made an order. "You sure you want to drink?" I asked Cliff as Trent went into my bedroom to talk with our boot.

Cliff raised his eyebrows at me and asked, "Why the fuck wouldn't I?!"

"Because," I laughed, "I was wondering if you weren't still hungover from *last* weekend."

"Hangover's last a day, dumb-ass."

"Yeah, but last weekend you were incredibly wasted."

"That's right," Eric said, remembering. "At one point I thought you may have had alcohol poisoning."

He shrugged. "I don't remember."

"No kidding," I answered, winking at him.

"Don't worry, guys," he said. "One of these days you'll end up getting even more wasted than however wasted I was that one night—I can assure you."

"Doubtful."

"Everybody gets fucked up at least once in their life."

"Guys," Trent said, surfacing from my bedroom, "James is on his way—give me the cash."

After we each pulled our wallets out and handed him the money, he went outside to wait and get picked up. Everything was on schedule. It was eight o' clock and about time to get the fire started. We grabbed the newspaper we'd bought to look for jobs, a pack of matches, and headed out to the backyard. In the carport, we found Kara smoking a cigarette on the bench she'd brought to the house upon moving in.

"What are you three up to?" she asked.

"Oh, nothing really," I said, awkwardly making my way up to her as Cliff and Eric scuttled off into the shed for the firewood. "Well I'm having a fire here tonight," I told her. "Some friends are coming over."

"Are you having a party?" she asked, stomping her cigarette out.

"Maybe a small one," I murmured.

She laughed. "It's alright if you are. Just no later than two in the morning, alright?"

"Oh I really doubt I'll be up *that* late," I explained. "Stayed up late yesterday."

"Once you get a couple drinks in you, you forget all about how tired you are."

I laughed. "That's true, isn't it," I realized, pleased to discover that Kara was actually pretty easy to talk to.

"Have fun," she said, getting up off the bench.

"Dray!" Cliff called after me. "We need the matches!"

"See you," I said to Kara as she walked off towards the upstairs of the house. I went up to the fence, opened the latch, and raced up to Cliff and Eric, who had made a nice teepee of kindling over scrunched up newspaper in the middle of the fire pit. I lit up a match and carefully dropped it in.

Moments later, we had a nice warm fire, and moments after that, James arrived with our drinks, along with his duo of friends, Ryan and Sam, who'd come to get drunk with us, as well.

By nine-thirty I felt the first wave of drunkenness hit me. I was sitting in one of the lawn chairs, fixated on the fire, hypnotized by the crackle of the coals and the party chatter around me. Suddenly, someone behind me put their hands over my eyes—a girl, who said, "Guess who."

I was quiet a second, feeling her smooth hands over my face. "Rose?"

She took her hands off me and dropped her head down on my shoulder. "Don't *you* wish!" It was Cassidy.

I got up, stumbling.

"You're drunk already," she noted.

"I know!"

After briefly looking around to make sure no one was listening, she told me, "Rose is coming in just a bit in case you're wondering. Promise me you'll kiss her tonight?"

"I'm drunk, though!"

"She'll be drunk, too."

"Who's going to be drunk?" asked James, walking up and putting an arm around me.

Cassidy held her tongue, not sure if I'd want him to know. I was a private person, but I never really cared now that I was drunk. And besides, James was a friend. "Rose," I told him.

"Rose Miller?" he exclaimed, patting me on the back. "She's gorgeous, man. Are you dating her?"

"Maybe," Cassidy answered for me. "If he decides to *do* anything about it!" My stomach turned in awkwardness. There was too much pressure. All I wanted was to have a good night. Couldn't things be more simple?

Looking up at the slowly growing party, I noticed another batch of people arrive through the large fence-door. Jacob, Nick, and Cameron and Roger poured in, all of them holding large bags of what would obviously carry alcohol inside.

"One sec," I told Cassidy and James.

"How late's the party going?" James asked as I paced my way across the yard.

"Just two!" I called back to him.

Through the crowd of my friends, I reached the new arrivals and greeted them.

"Hey, I hope it's cool we're here," Cameron said, motioning to himself and Roger.

"Of course!" I shouted. "Join the party! There's plenty of booze, but it looks like you guys are covered in that department."

"Oh yeah," Roger said, lifting up one of his bags in the air in which I could see the faint outlines of bottles through.

Cameron and Roger went and sat down at the picnic table and Jacob gave me a hug. Throughout all of high school, he always did that. It was a theater-kid thing to do. "I can't believe you and Eric got fired today," Jacob said.

I shrugged. "It was kind of expected."

"Still," Nick said, "it was cool having you two around."

Sighing, I told them, "I've got to go there tomorrow and get my toque and a couple other things I left behind."

"Hopefully neither of our bosses see you," Nick said, laughing.

I agreed disdainfully. "I'm so glad Eric dealt with it all this morning."

"You're welcome," came Eric. He finished one of his drinks and tossed the bottle at the end of the yard.

"I've got to clean that up, you know," I said, half-annoyed, half-amused. But then I looked around and noticed there was at least twenty more bottles scattered everywhere all the same. "This place is a mess," I realized.

"Relax," said Jacob. "Get wasted and deal with it in the morning."

I did as he said, spending the rest of the night getting as wasted as possible. I forgot about the mess. I forgot about not having a job. I forgot about Anna and I forgot about the pressures there were between Rose and I. She'd showed up like Cassidy said, but we never stayed stuck to each other anything. We briefly said hello, and then let each other enjoy the party separately. I was able to finally catch up with Cliff and Trent and see how things were with them. Cliff was great as always, but I was happy to hear that Trent was pot-free. He'd come to the same conclusion as me after taking a break from it. Getting drunk and rowdy with friends was much funner.

By two o' clock I had to shut the party down. Everyone was disappointed, but I told them I had no choice, that it was out of respect for the other people living in my house. Slowly, everybody gathered up their things and left. After saying goodbye to a few people in the driveway, Rose came up and hugged me. "Walk me home?" she whispered in my ear. Responding, I took her hand and we made our way down the street to where she lived.

The empty streets had never seemed as relaxing as they did that night. I was so tired I was practically falling over. "I'm so glad you had a party," Rose said, holding me up as we strolled down the sidewalk. "I've missed you."

"We only hang out when we're drunk," I noted. "This whole year we've either been stoned or drunk."

"Really?"

"In Grade 11 we used to just hang out—like every day... We'd find things to do."

"I remember."

"I miss high-school."

"I don't," she replied. "I've still got another year to go through."

"Enjoy it while it lasts," I slurred.

We crossed the street into the alleyway behind her house, which made me realize how close our houses were from each other. I was about to mention it, but Rose spoke before I had the chance. "I saw Anna today," she said.

My thoughts paused and my throat swelled, but I played it cool. A *facade* of cool. "Anna? Hmm. Anna... doesn't ring a bell."

Rose fake-laughed. "Whatever happened between you two?"

"Doesn't matter," I told her. "I don't trust her."

"Why not?"

I tried to explain it in a way that made sense, but my words never came out the way they should have. I was normally good with my words—if only I wasn't drunk. "Maybe, because... Maybe she hurt me too many times," I said simply.

Rose let go of me abruptly, letting me trip over my feet. "I don't want to hurt you," she said as I regained my balance.

"You won't. You're not like that. Right?"

"I don't want to hurt you," she repeated, halting her walk down to a stop. We were at her house now—in the darkness of the unlit alleyway. She pulled me close to her, and even through the dark I could see her face staring deeply into mine. It was that moment, I knew. I was supposed to kiss her. But I was drunk, and talking about Anna had put me into a weird mood. The pressure hit me like a punch to the face. Rose always had to be drunk around me! She never looked into my eyes like this when we were sober. No girl ever did. None except Anna.

Rose kissed me—a long and tender kiss meant for my lips, but I hadn't given her that, and so she placed it on my neck. When she pulled away, the wind rolled down my throat, hitting the very spot she kissed me, a freezing mark so cold it gave me shivers. "Goodnight, Dray," she said, grimacing slightly. "Thanks again for the party."

I immediately knew things were over between us.

She turned away from me and without looking back entered through the back door of her house. Looking down at my feet, I took myself back down the alleyway, trying hard to think it all through. The alcohol refrained me in doing so. Nothing made sense. I started walking faster, hoping that might clear my head somewhat but it never did anything. I never cared; I started jogging, going faster and faster until I was sprinting my way home. By the time I got to the house, I was panting, which made me feel substantially more healthy—considering all the booze that was in my system.

In the backyard I was psyched to find that my three best friends had stuck around, lazily hanging out by the fire. After my strange conversation with Rose, the last thing I wanted was to go to sleep. Even though I was dead-tired exhausted, nothing was better than ending the night with final words from the people that mattered most. "You guys are still here," I asserted, grabbing one of the lawn chairs and pulling it up to the dying fire.

"How did it go?" Eric asked.

"How did what go?" I looked back and forth at them, softly panting from the quick run here.

"You were with Rose," Cliff answered. "We saw you walking with her! You were holding her hand, man."

"Did you kiss her?" asked Trent eagerly.

After pausing, I told them, quietly, "No."

The three of them groaned and sighed, and I realized exactly what was going on. The reason they must have stuck around was because they wanted to congratulate me when I got back, thinking that tonight was the night Rose and I would finally start dating.

"James told us you were going to kiss her," Trent said disappointingly.

"I was going to—"

"Why didn't you?" asked Eric, who was rubbing his eyes in aid of staying awake.

"Things never go the way the should," I murmured, standing up and walking over to the picnic table. Through all of the empties and garbage, I found an untouched beer and snapped it open. Slurping the foam off the top, I sat back down and said, "Whatever, guys, I'm glad you're all here—"

"You like beer now?" Cliff asked, amazed.

"I like coolers," I told him, "but right now I don't care."

"Cheers to that," Trent bellowed, reaching over to tap beers with me.

***

I had a hard time sleeping that night. I was too drunk. Not so drunk that I'd pass out, but the level before that—I was just drunk enough to have a hard time sleeping. My thoughts were unclear, bouncing all over the place. And it never helped—in those early morning hours—that the birds had begun chirping. So after a few hours of in-and-out sleep, I crawled out of bed and got into the shower, passing by Trent, who was in my living room, still passed out on the sofa. Last night, after putting the fire out and taking a walk around town, we split ways off in different directions. Trent had come with me and Eric went with Cliff to spend the night at his place. There was no way we were going to let him drive home. The four of us had each drank a more-than-suitable amount.

Showered up and in clean clothes, I walked to 7-eleven and grabbed a coffee, which I slowly sipped on as I picked the hundred-or-so bottles up off the back lawn. Finishing my clean-up, I carried the bags of empties into the carport next to Kara's recycling and went back inside. Trent was starting to wake up—grumbling as he rolled around restlessly—so I threw a few eggs on the burner and prepared us some bacon.

"Fuck!" I heard him say.

I poked my head around the corner of the kitchen, finding him crouched over his phone on the carpet. "What is it?"

"I'm supposed to be at work right now!" He jumped up off the ground and ran past me toward the entrance.

"I made us breakfast," I told him.

He apologized, putting his shoes on. "No time."

"That's alright," I said, "don't get fired like me and Eric."

He smirked, looking like shit with his hair untidy and clothes wrinkled, all hung-over and greasy. "Good night, last night," he declared, his last words before slipping out the door.

✳✳✳

After finishing my breakfast, I started to get a stinging headache. I was finally coming down from the buzz of a great night. But I didn't want to sleep; I hated napping. I thought I might as well go for a walk, get some fresh air, stop by Cliff's or something. Anything. But when I locked up the door of the suite, I remembered that my white toque was still at the Wholesale.

That's what I'd do.

I'd go on an espionage adventure: a mission of sneaking undetected through my old workplace to grab the toque and get out of there as fast as possible. What better things did I have to do? Besides, I loved that toque.

The espionage adventured proved successful, which was kind of a disappointment for me. I was hoping to have had to hide behind shelves or run through the aisles in order to dodge an awful encounter with the store's supervisor, but all I had to do was walk in and walk out.

Such a disappointment—to never be chased.

I put on the toque—my prize—even though it was a warm and sunny day. Taking the walk back to town, I texted Eric and told him I was up and walking around. *'Come on by,'* he said, *'we're just getting up now.'*

The toque was starting to get really hot, but I never cared. Cliff's was nearby the Wholesale and I never felt like carrying it. I left it on, my hands in my pockets, kicking tiny rocks up the street as I made my way up the hill towards Cliff's. Looking up as I sailed a rock as far as the next block, I saw a couple of girl's in the distance walking towards me—a tall one and a girl closer to my age. They were both smiling and talking, wearing sundresses and sunglasses, enjoying the nice morning sun. They slowly came closer and closer into my vision until I eventually realized who the girl my age was.

An appearance from Anna is always imminent...

Always when it's least expected.

The taller girl—who I realized was a sister—never noticed me, and never noticed Anna notice me, either. She was in the middle of telling her a story. Anna took her sunglasses off and smiled weakly at me as they walked by on the sidewalk.

I was on the road, hungover with a stupid toque planted over my head, looking like an idiot in such nice weather. But unashamed I never looked away; I kept my eyes targeted on her for as long as she was in front of me, until she passed me by.

Chapter Eleven: The Green Green Grass

I nodded down towards the pack of cigarettes in my hand. "Mind?"
"Go for it," she replied.
I took one out and lit up.
Sitting together on the trunk of Eric's car in front of 7-eleven, it was me and Alice, waiting for everyone to re-group after scattering across Houston. We'd been at some party, but when the cops came and shut it down we lost track of everyone. Fazed, I stood relaxed in the driveway of the house-party, trying to make out the faces of people running down the street, trying to spot either Eric or Trent.
Alice snapped me out of it. Tugging my arm, she told me to follow her. After taking the beer out of my hand and setting it on the ground—"I was still drinking that," I drunkenly told her—she quickly steered me through the backyard and onto a hidden sidewalk between a few blocks of houses. Eventually the passageway led towards Eric and Nick's vehicles, which had been safely parked in the back lot of the town's 7-eleven. I sent a text to Eric and another to Trent, telling them to meet us there.
"This totally sucks," Alice said.
"What?"

"It's not often Kathy has parties," she replied. "It would have been such a great night."

I shrugged in agreement, politely blowing smoke in the opposite direction as her. Jacob, Nick and Eric and Trent and I had been aimlessly walking around all night, and right as Alice and her friends finally found us all a place to drink, it was shut down before any of us really got the chance to explore. It had been a somewhat pointless night, and the party was my one glimmer of hope that our trip here had been worth it.

"I can't believe I missed *your* party," she sniveled.

"Last weekend, you mean?"

"Jacob and Nick said it was pretty great."

I was a small bit flattered. The few parties I'd hosted really had been good turn outs. "It seems like I have to throw parties," I explained, "or nothing happens."

"Like tonight?"

I snickered. "Maybe."

"I'm hoping to spend my birthday in Smithers," she told me, "so if you happen to have a party that weekend, let me know."

"When's your birthday?" I asked, whisking smoke coolly out of the corner of my mouth.

"The fifteenth," she said.

"I could do that."

Alice smiled, hiding her confusion. "Do what?"

"I'll throw you a birthday party."

"You don't have to make it about *me!*"

"It won't *all* be about you," I said, flicking my cigarette off into a puddle, "but that's in like two weeks—I can prepare."

"Well don't feel pressure or anything," she added kindly.

Coming from 7-eleven, we looked up and saw our troupe of friends emerge from around the building. Alice hopped off the trunk and called out to them: "What happened to you guys?!" In response, Jacob and Trent started drunkenly telling her everything that went down, talking over each other in sloppy explanation. Eric and Nick, the sober ones, slinked over to me and their vehicles.

"How about we get out of this town?" I asked them. In response, they both precociously took out their keys.

***

For the drive back, Trent was in a drunk and bitter mood towards me. It was obvious that he was still in love with Alice—as Eric had told me—and the time I spent alone with her tonight must have been on his mind. I didn't even get this attraction that both Nick and Trent supposedly had toward her. To me she was just like any other girl, nothing special. She was nice, sure. Good-looking, maybe. But there wasn't much more to her than that.

"So what's this party that you're having for Alice about?" Trent asked roughly.

"Oh she mentioned it to you?"

"Right before I got in..."

"She wants us to throw a party for her birthday," I explained, turning around in the passenger seat to look back at him. "I was hoping you could help me throw it?"

This seemed to cheer him up a considerable amount. "Her birthday's coming up?" he asked excitedly.

I flipped around in my seat and chuckled to myself semi-silently. Trent was still unaware of Alice's apparent crush on our best friend, Eric.

"Going to buy her something?" Eric inquired, trying not to laugh.

"Maybe," Trent murmured, going quiet, obviously now molding it through his head over what would be the best possible gift to give her. Eric looked over at me and we both smiled guiltily, feeling bad that we'd still left him completely clueless. But it was better for Trent to dream than to confront him with the reality of the situation. It was better this way. After all, there was always a chance things might work out for him.

"I can't believe you're starting back up at 7-eleven," I said to Eric, changing the subject.

"I have to."

"Why?!" I implored.

"One week without a job is hurting my bank account," he grumbled, "especially since we've been going out drinking basically every single night."

"But 7-eleven?"

"It's just temporary," he defended, "until I save up enough to move."

"At the beginning of the summer it's easy to find a job," I concluded, "but by the end, all positions are filled."

"You should ask for your job back there too, you know... *Soon*, or you're not going to have any money for rent next month."

Eric was certainly right about that. All of our funds were running low. Basically all the money in my account had been depleted over the past couple weeks. "I'll give it this weekend," I told him. "If I don't find anything by then..."

"You won't," he said. "Nowhere is hiring."

"Come back to Zellers," said Trent. "I don't even know why you quit there in the first place."

"I don't know either."

If I was a small bit braver—or had a bigger ego—I probably would have followed Trent's suggestion. With all the jobs I had this summer, I couldn't believe I was going to end up back at 7-eleven. I clearly seemed to have run out of options. In any case, I decided to take the weekend off and spend it worry-free. With Eric working both Saturday and Sunday, I'd have a couple of days off to clear my head. Come Monday, I'd figure out what I would do for sure.

In the meanwhile, I made use of the spare time by returning to an old writing project. Throughout the entirety of high-school I'd worked on trying to write a novel based off a dream I had when I was in elementary, but so far all I had was bits and pieces of it done. Nothing was tied together. I never knew where to start. Every time I tried to make sense of the story it seemed to make less and less sense. All I had were the images from my childhood.

But Saturday morning, after our pointless venture to Houston, something clicked together in my brain. I knew where to begin and I knew what mood to follow. Sitting in the ragged but comfy chair next to my bedroom, I sat with my laptop and wrote the first chapter.

It's amazing how one day something can suddenly make sense. One day, one chapter. A good start. *Maybe this summer I might actually be able to accomplish something worthwhile, after all.*

Like a writer—or the idea of a writer I have in my head—I went outside for a cigarette upon completing the chapter. But as I took in my first celebratory drag, Kara came around the front door entrance into the carport, shocked to find me standing there in the darkness with a flaming cigarette hanging out of my mouth. "You smoke?"

I shrugged. "I don't, um, actually smoke."

"Then why are you?"

"It makes me feel intellectual, I guess."

Kara burst out laughing. "You should find another way to feel intellectual."

I lifted my half-empty pack up to her. "Want one?"

"No, no," she replied, pulling out her own. Lighting up a cigarette, she went and sat down on the bench she usually sat on while smoking. "I actually came down here to talk to you."

"You did?"

"I wanted to tell you that me and my sister are going out of town in a couple of weeks." She exhaled, then continued, "We leave on the twelfth and we won't be back for a couple of weeks."

"Really?"

"I know you've been taking care of the lawn, doing the mowing, but I'm also going to need you to water our plants for us. You up for that?"

"Of course," I told her. *Anything!* If she was going to be out of town that meant I could have parties as late as I wanted.

"And I know what you're thinking," she began mind-reading. "You're thinking of all the crazy parties you're going to throw, aren't you?"

I coughed up smoke, laughing.

"Don't let them get too crazy!" she yelled, serious but friendly. "I don't want to come home at the end of August to find the house in ruins and all the windows broken."

"I can't promise that," I played around, "but I can promise you the plants will not die under my watch."

"Well as long as the plants don't die..." She sociably rolled her eyes, but something crossed them. "I got a question," she began.

"Okay."

"Why don't I see any girls coming around here for you?"

I chuckled. "I'm a fag like that."

"No," she dismissed. "Seriously...."

"I have a hard time with girls," I explained, hunching my shoulders together.

"How?"

"I don't know," I told her, "you'll have to ask them."

"Try harder," she told me, putting her cigarette out in the ashtray next to the bench. "Work at that while we're away. Think about it, you can be as loud as you want."

Embarrassed, I laughed and threw my cigarette on the ground.

"If you're gonna be dumb enough to smoke," she said, "at least put the butts in the ashtray."

I apologized, still laughing as I picked it back up off the ground to put it with hers.

***

After all the parties and road trips we endured over the past week, we decided to take it easy on Monday night. We were still going to get drunk all the same, but tonight it would be just the three of us, and in that respect we were taking it easy. Sure it would have been nice to kick back and watch a movie or something, but how exciting would that have been? It was summer, and it was August—we only had one month left before Trent went back to school and the cold temperature of our northern climate returned.

Summer was coming to a close.

Getting alcohol this time around proved harder than most nights, being that James—our regular boot—was busy on a date with some girl. We had to improvise. Our first attempt was a major failure: we spent an hour in the parking lot of the Twin liquor store, asking strangers to go in and buy it for us. That, we discovered, was completely pointless. Even while offering a twenty dollar tip, nobody would put their ass on the line for us. Why would they? We were just a bunch of dumb teenagers.

As a last resort, I went inside the liquor store myself. Cliff had gotten away with it before, hadn't he?

Trying not to look suspicious, I quickly walked through the aisles until I found the coolers we usually drank. After grabbing three packs of four, I went and casually sat them down on the counter of the till. The lady working asked for my ID, and without a beat I pulled it out and handed it to her, hoping that she might not take a proper look and just assume the date of my birth made me out to be nineteen. With one glance, she handed it back to me. I thought I was in the clear, but she then picked up the phone and dialed a number.

"Yes," she said, glaring at me with the phone up to her ear, "I have a boy here who tried illegally purchasing alcohol—did you want to send someone down here?"

At that, I finally realized it was 911 that she had called... I was *not* in the clear.

Flapping my arms to life, I ran out of the store at full-speed. ("He's running away, now," was the last thing I heard her say.)

Eric and Trent, who were waiting outside the doors, caught on to what happened and without a word they followed me running through the parking lot and all the way back to my basement suite.

Up the driveway, we went and sat together on the bench, remaining quiet long enough to regain our strength. "Well that was stupid," I said, spitting up a large loogie.

"Wait," said Trent, "how did you two get alcohol on those nights you were at Cameron's?"

Together, Eric and I responded, *"Roger."*

"Do you have his number?" Trent asked hopefully.

We never, but finding it was easier than any of our other ideas...

Texting Nick we got Cameron's number, and texting Cameron we got Roger's number. Texting Roger, we got the alcohol.

A night such as this was an annoying procedure, but when we finally had a case of alcohol in our grasp it was completely worth it. It was like a scavenger hunt, and the idea of winning a prize is always more enticing than what the reward actually is—kind of like the stupid bouncy balls won at arcades, usually lost or discarded by the end of the day.

"When are you going to call and ask for your job back?" Eric asked me, opening his cooler.

I groaned. "Don't remind me."

"Yeah," Trent agreed, "let's just drink."

"I can't believe we only have four coolers, though," Eric said, "and *this* shit." He reached over my kitchen table and grabbed the two-six of Jack Daniels that Roger had decided to buy us. We tried it, but it was too much... We could hardly drink beer, let alone whiskey.

"We're going to have to drink it," Trent said.

"I've got some Coke," I mentioned. "A few cans only, though. They'll have to be strong mixes."

"Better than nothing," said Eric.

✳✳✳

During all of our past drinking experiences, it always felt to me as though I was taking a sip from my drink every twenty-seconds or so. I realized tonight that that was never the case. Gaps of time pass by unnoticed.

If I truly had been drinking every half-minute, I would have been throwing-up drunk every single time. There's always been distractions, safely preventing the possibility of drinking too much.

If someone was nervous, I'd imagine they might binge drink in order to feel more comfortable, but for all practical purposes it's easy to drink the right amount when you're surrounded by lots of things going on.

How We'd Look on Film

But with only a few guys sitting around a table, the main concentration is put on the drinks, and when drinking is the night's main attraction, you really are taking a sip every twenty-seconds or so.

By night-fall, the three of us were sprawled out in my living room, either on the couch or on the floor, half of the two-six of Jack Daniels inside us.

"My head... is spinning..." I told them. "I think I need a cigarette."

"Oh yeah," Eric said, "that'll help!"

"Why wouldn't it!?"

Trent laughed. "Let's get outta here."

We piled out the door, laughing and stumbling, pushing each other over as we sloppily put our shoes on. Outside, I put a cigarette in my mouth and another into Trent's, and as we staggered down the middle of the street I lit us up.

With a sudden burst of energy, Eric dashed off, calling out to the night. Running through the warm summer air, we chased after him, onto the field and into the parking lot by the local college. "Check it out!" we heard Eric say. He was up ahead, standing in front of the entrance of one of the school buses they sometimes left parked over night in the alleyway of the community hall. "It's open."

"What is?"

Slowly, I made out what was happening: Eric had pried open the door of the school bus.

"All aboard!" he shouted.

Trent and I laughed and stepped up the large stairs. From the driver's seat, Eric pulled the door closed once we were inside. I ran to the end of the bus, looked out the window, and caught a brief glimpse of my house in the distance. When I returned back to the front, Trent lifted something up in the air for me to see.

"Look what I found," he said.

It was a small fire extinguisher, and without even a moments thought over it, he pulled the pin out and aimed behind us, toward the back-end of the bus. "Don't!" Eric yelled, but it was too late: Trent sprayed the extinguisher all over the place. When he realized—in awe—what he was doing, he changed aim and directed it over me and Eric, covering us both in a thick, misty powder.

Eric and I freaked out—even inhaling some of it—and jumped out of the bus. Running out into the parking lot, we turned back as Trent surfaced from the wreck inside, laughing his ass off as the fog of chemicals came pouring out of the bus-door behind him. With a cigarette still in his mouth (mine had fallen out) he lifted the extinguisher and shot the remnants up into the air. A large and beautiful cloud formed over our heads, and as it drifted to the ground, we ran through it, eyes-closed, hands out, feeling the powder dribble down our fingertips.

When I made my way out of the vapory gas—to see it from a further angle—I realized exactly how big it was. Our antics could be seen a mile away.

"We got to get out of here!" I shouted after them. "Leave the fire extinguisher, follow me!"

Emerging from the blurry mist, Eric and Trent came sprinting forwards.

We made our way towards Main Street.

There, things got even worse. The flower gardens around the sidewalks were no match for Eric and Trent, who were much too hyper to calm down now. They started tearing out everything, even breaking the hanging-planters onto the middle of the street. Disinterested, I laughed, knowing how stupid and guilty they'd feel about it in the morning.

I casually strolled into a nearby alleyway, pulling out my phone and dialing Anna's cell phone number. All I got was her answering machine. I pretended not to realize: "Anna! What's up! Hello! You there? Hello—"

CRASH!

I pulled the cell phone away from my ear and flipped it shut.

Walking back onto Main Street, I turned the corner and found Trent standing over a mangled motorcycle. "Dude!" I said. "What did you do?"

"I think I may have broken the—"

"You mother fucker!" a voice said, unmistakeably whoever owned the bike. I looked up as a tall and angry-looking man came storming towards us.

Trent ran for the hills, but I stood planted to the spot.

"Get back here you piece of shit!" he yelled, coming closer from the other side of the street.

But Trent was long gone. Even Eric seemed to have vanished. I was all alone.

"YOU!" the man shrieked. "Get over here," he demanded, pointing onto the cement next to the fallen motorcycle.

Shaking, I made my way over there.

"You're staying with me," he informed. "I'm calling the police."

"Any damages done," I tried telling him, "we'll be happy to pay for them."

"No way! Don't you try and weasel your way out of this—"

"I'm not—"

"Shut up!" he yelled violently. (For a second I actually thought he was going to punch me.) "I'm getting the police. This is going to get DEALT WITH!"

He wasn't joking.

He called the police.

"You're fucked, man," he said. *"Fucked."*

"It wasn't even me," I said, "I was just calling a girl—"

"Save it."

The cop that arrived moments later was in no better a mood than this guy. He didn't want to hear my story, either. "Have you been drinking?" the policeman asked, shining a small flashlight into my eyes.

"I'm not going to lie," I said firmly. "Me and my friends had a couple drinks. We went for a walk to catch some fresh air. I went into the alleyway, over there, to call this girl, and when I came back—"

And then the craziest thing in my entire life happened…

The cop turned me around, pulled my hands behind my back, and cuffed me.

Dragging me up to his cruiser—lit up with the familiar blue and red lights—he opened the back doors and tossed me inside. "I'm innocent!" I told him, but he slammed the door shut on me.

Shaking my head, I tried waking myself up from the nightmare I'd found myself in. Did this really just happen? Did I really get arrested?

Through the bars, I looked down on the road and watched as the cop talked with the guy who owned the motorcycle. They were both writing down information, occasionally pointing dismissively at me. I struggled, trying to take the cuffs off, but that just made them tighter, and they were already *very* tight. I started to cry.

When the policeman got into his driver's seat he told me to be quiet, but he then realized I was crying. The look on his face was a wave of puzzlement. He obviously never had that many kids crying in his cruiser before. "Relax, would you?" he said, turning off the flashing police lights.

I whimpered.

"It's okay. I know you never broke the bike. But you're drunk in public and I have to take you to the tank."

"The what?"

"The drunk tank."

"Whas' that?"

"You have to spend the night with us until you get sober."

"Why!"

"You're not allowed to be drunk in public," he told me. "You're under-aged."

"I'm not even drunk!"

He ignored me, putting the car in drive.

✸✸✸

At the station they took all my things. My pack of smokes and lighter. My iPod and headphones. My cellphone. They took my shoes and took my belt.

It was humiliating.

They made me out to be a criminal, which I supposed I might have been, but the way I was handled seemed so bizarre. They'd interrogated me in a dark room, lit up only by the lamp on the desk—as if I were a traitor of the country about to be tortured. It was eerie.

When they finished questioning me, they came to an agreement that they weren't going to charge a criminal fine, which was very lucky. All I had to do was take care of the damages done to the motorcycle. If my friends helped pay that was alright, too. Either way, it was now my responsibility.

"I'm going to call your parents, okay?" one of the officers had asked, a female.

"I don't have any parents."

"Yes you do," she told me. "I know who your parents are." She looked at the two other policeman around her, including the one that had arrested me, and said, "I know his parents—The Emerald's..."

"They're not my parents anymore."

After giving her co-officers another awkward glance, she explained, "We can only let you out tonight in the care of a parent. If not, you have to sleep in the drunk tank."

"Well I don't have any parents so I don't see how I have a choice in any of this."

She nodded to the policeman I never knew, and he pulled me up out of the chair, guiding me out of the room and down the hall. At the end, he put me inside of a cold and dingy room with a small mattress in the middle. No blanket or pillows. "I have to sleep here?" I asked, turning around.

The officer shrugged and shut the door, and I listened as his footsteps went back down the hall. For the hell of it, I tried opening the door—imagining myself breaking out and having to sneak out of the jail house—but the door was locked shut. *These sons of bitches*, I thought to myself. This would definitely be the last time that I ever try dealing with the cops... I should have ran for it with Eric and Trent. I never expected the bastards to haul me away like this. I thought I'd give the man my number and tell him I'd make sure we paid for the damages—if there even *were* any! I thought it would have been that simple. But no, I'd been arrested.

Using the zipper of shorts, I carved my name in the wooden door. That cheered me up a little. Now if anyone else got hauled in here like me, they'd see my name—sloppily scratched in—and know they weren't alone.

***

Pacing back and forth, I started sobering up a considerable amount. I realized what an idiot the three of us had been. Breaking into school buses? Spraying fire extinguishers? Trampling the flower gardens on Main Street? How did we expect to get away with *any* of it? I took the fall for those guys, that was for sure. They owed me big time.

An hour passed of pacing around, and it dawned on me finally that I would have to sleep eventually—here, in this hideously uncomfortable room. If I was a small bit drunker I may have been able to.

I should have drank more, was my conclusion.

The door suddenly swung open, revealing the female officer. She was holding the box full of all my things, which she began handing to me. "Let's go," she said afterward. "Your mom's here."

I was too scared to move. Didn't I tell them I never had any parents? I wasn't ready to face my mom. "Come on," she said kindly. "Follow me."

Taking a deep breath, I stepped out and let her take me back to the interrogation room. My mom was inside, sitting on the chair I'd been in. Surprisingly, she never looked as pissed off as I thought she would. She *genuinely* looked happy to see me. But why? Maybe she expected to find me a whole lot drunker. It must have been that: the relief that my eyes weren't going cross-eyed and that I wasn't falling all over the place...

She stood up and said, "Let's go home." I nodded, and after my mother turned to the police officer to give her thanks, we left.

***

On the drive, I pleaded her to drop me off at my apartment, but she repeated how important it was that she kept me with her. "Police orders," she told me—since I was, as they said, *intoxicated*. "What were you even drinking?" she asked, sounding disgusted. She hadn't had a sip of alcohol in over twenty years. When she met my father—a kind and handsome Mormon back from a mission to England—she quit, eventually joining the church, just to be with him. "How *much* did you drink?"

"Too much, I guess."

She scoffed. "I was going to leave you in there, you know, when the police called. I told your dad, 'Fine, let him spend the night in there and think it over.'"

This was no surprise to me; hence why I told them not to bother calling them in the first place. "What made you change your mind?" I asked, hiding how truly glad I was that they did.

"The kids are out of town, I realized. They wouldn't have to see you come home like this."

"Spares them the horror... Nice."

"And your dad wanted you home," she added. "That's what he said... *Let's just bring him home.*" The SUV pulled into the suburbs, my old neighborhood, down the streets I used to walk on my way back home from school every day. "Are you glad? Are you glad I came and picked you up?"

"Beats jail."

She never laughed, so I gave her my thanks, sounding as sincere as I could.

Turning into the driveway of my parents' mansion, a feeling of dread flipped over inside my stomach. Seeing my dad was not something I was looking forward to. As we walked from the SUV and up the front entrance stairwell, I wanted to make a run for it, but I knew this was something I had to face—sooner or later. I hadn't seen my dad in two months.

Inside the house, I found him sitting at the black baby-grand piano in the living room, one of his fingers placed down on a silenced key. He stood up, walked up to me, and gave me a solemn and simple hug. "What's this on you?" he asked evenly.

"What?"

He stepped back from me, and lifted his hand up. It was covered in a white substance. "Your back's covered in it."

"That's from a fire extinguisher."

"You were in a fire?" my mom asked, setting her keys down on the red-denim couch.

"Um, no..."

They looked down on me for some sort of answer. All I could think to say was, "It's been a long, stupid night..."

"You can sleep in your old room," my father said, questioning me no further as he gave my shoulder a squeeze. "Henry sleeps there now, but he's out of town."

"But go ahead and take a shower before you hop into bed," my mom told me. "You smell pretty bad."

"And you have white powder all over you," my dad added, smiling sadly down on me.

I laughed, realizing how gross I was in contrast to this nice and clean home. Both of my parents were clean-freaks. They hired a housekeeper to come twice a week, and cleaned the place themselves, as well. The place was always spotless, the sheets were always fresh—and here I was, smelling of cigarettes and whiskey. "Well," I said, "*thanks.*"

About to walk down the stairs to my old bedroom and bathroom, my mom stopped me: "Tell your friends they don't have to worry about paying for the motorcycle. I gave the police our information. We'll pay for any damages."

"You don't have to. Trent can pay—"

"It's already taken care of."

I went to say something else, but stopped myself; instead, I gave them one last nod of thanks before stepping downstairs, into my old lair.

✱✱✱

The next day I caught up with Eric and Trent and we talked the whole thing through, sitting in the carport, wearing our hoodies and jackets due to the windy and cloudy day it was. We all agreed how idiotic the three of us had been, how important it was that we smartened our act up. If Trent had been the one arrested, he for sure would have gotten a criminal fine. That meant standing up in front of a judge, which meant possible juvenile detention. What the hell were we doing? This wasn't *us*. We used to make short films and get interviewed by the town newspaper.

People used to respect us. And now, we were nothing. Time had distorted things so deeply the past seemed unrecognizable.

"Want to do anything tonight?" Trent asked.

"Get drunk," Eric joked, throwing a rock down my driveway.

"How about we go see The Dark Knight?"

"Oh my God," Eric shouted. "I can't believe I forgot it was even playing."

"I haven't seen it," said Trent, and the three of us exchanged looks, silently coming to a decision. We would obviously go tonight.

"But weren't you going to see it with Rose?" Eric asked.

"Oh," I exclaimed, matter-of-factually, "I've given up on girls."

The two of them laughed, sitting up from the cement. "Don't tell us that," said Trent, wiping the dirt off the back of his pants. "When's the movie start?"

"We'll have to drive by and check," I told them. "But uh... I have one thing I want to do before we go."

"Alright, what do you want to do?" Eric asked, prepared to help me with anything, feeling bad I'd been put through the awful experience of being arrested. The two of them, I knew, had the guilty conscience that they'd left me behind.

"I gotta ask for my job back at Sev."

Eric nodded, knowing it was true.

Chapter Twelve: Why Can't Sometimes And Always Be Friends?

Twelve o' clock and I was finally off my shift. As I'd planned and anticipated, I quickly went to my house and picked up my laptop for another night of wandering around and listening to music.

For some reason, the spot by Subway I'd caught a wi-fi signal from before never pulled through, so I had to walk up and down Main Street to look for a connection elsewhere. Hitting refresh over and over, I found a hotspot for people staying in the Fireweed, a motel across from the highway. Sitting on one of their cement barricades, I checked the inbox of my email, which was as empty as I expected.

All I really wanted was to get out and walk around after a treacherously long night of work at 7-eleven.

Returning was a blast from the past. My old co-workers were still there, of course, doing all the same things they used to: complaining usually, making mistakes and blaming them on each other. Like before, I worked extra hard and eased them through all the bumps and glitches.

They were obviously glad to have Eric and I back—two strong and energetic guys capable of dealing with anything. When sketchy or creepy-looking men came in, we were usually asked to take the front till while they hid in the back in case anything bad happened (like a hold-up or something.) But we never minded. It made us feel tough—putting ourselves face-to-face with danger.

The regular customers came in as always, barking orders of cigarettes and numbers for potato wedges and chicken wings. It was like a vortex. There, everyday was the same. It had been my third shift today, and each remained a repetition of the last. But it was work. My other jobs were for fun. I practically had nothing else to do. Right now I really needed the money. I couldn't stand it, though, working at 7-eleven...

Eric was right: we had to move to Prince George. Somehow we had to make it happen.

Looking down Main, I noticed a boy turn onto the street and walk towards me. He was close to my age, maybe a small bit younger. In his hands was what looked like a laptop, and the closer he came the more sure of it I was. Once he caught sight of me—as he stepped up to the parking lot of the Fireweed—he slowed his walk down, hesitant to continue.

"Hey," I called out to him.

"Hey."

"What are you up to," I asked, "this fine evening?"

He chuckled, surprised to find that I was friendly. "Same thing as you." He motioned toward the laptop in his hands.

"You came here to steal internet?"

"This is my spot," he told me, now walking through the nearby rows of cars.

"No way! I just found it tonight. The internet is fast here."

"Don't tell anyone," he advised. "There'd be people here every night." Sitting down on the same cement barricade as me, he flipped his computer open and turned it on. "I'm Josh, by the way."

Something whipped through my mind. "Josh?"

"Yeah."

"We were in drama together," I realized.

He laughed. "You remember? That was in like grade eight or something. Mrs. Lytle's class. I remember *you*, but only because you were the star of every class, basically."

"Well, I used to want to be an actor..."

"You always got in trouble!" he suddenly shouted in remembrance. "For doing the most outrageous things on stage!"

"So you really *do* remember me..."

What a random encounter, I thought to myself as his laptop beeped to life. Turns out I wasn't the only one that walked around town at twilight with the excuse of looking for internet.

For a couple of hours, we commiserated back and forth while each of us did our own things on our laptops. With nothing better to talk about, we told each other our situations, all the reasons we had in being out here in the dead of night. I told him that I lived on my own, in a basement suite, that I was working a job I hated, trying to save up so I could get out of town.

"Did you graduate?" he asked, still having another year to go himself.

"I dropped out."

"I see, I see." He weighed it around in his head. "Let me guess—you started smoking weed and got kicked out?"

His nearly-correct presumption made me burst out laughing. "I might as well have been kicked out," I replied, hushing myself. "But yeah, I think weed had something to do with dropping out."

"It always does," he said, thinking sadly of something. "My older brother," he began, "got kicked out of school for smoking weed."

"Really?" I asked, thinking of my own younger brothers. What would they think of me a couple of years down the road from now? Would they think of me sadly? I never even knew what they thought of me in the current moment... "That's shitty," I told him, shutting my laptop closed.

"I learned from it," he explained confidently. "I'm never touching drugs or alcohol as long as I live. But anyway, it's getting late." He began closing down the windows on his screen.

I agreed with him, getting off the bench-like piece of cement.

"Hey, boys," a woman said, somewhere off in the distance.

"Who's that?" Josh asked, standing up with me and looking around to find the voice, his laptop tucked beneath his arm.

"I dunno," I said.

"Up here," the woman called out to us again.

On the second floor of the motel balcony, a woman was peering over the ledge, having a cigarette. She was waving to us and she seemed somewhat drunk. She also so happened to be wearing nothing but underwear.

"Hey!" I yelled up to her.

"Keep it down," she told me, giggling. "Come on up."

I looked to Josh, who was shaking his head at me. "Let's go," I whispered to him eagerly. "It'll be funny!"

Though he continued nervously shaking his head, he followed me nonetheless—up the spiraling stairs to where the girl's room was. "What are you two doing?" she asked. In clear sight I realized she was no more than five or six years older than us, a kind of hippie girl with a pierced nose and dread-locked hair.

"We're just out enjoying the night," I told her, which would have sounded cool if Josh wasn't covering his eyes. Being in the presence of a half-naked woman was apparently far too much for him to handle. He was shocked. I was too, but it was weird moments like these that I lived for. "What are you here in Smithers for?" I asked, ignoring Josh, who was practically hiding behind me.

Opening her mouth, she was interrupted as the the motel door beside her swung open. A man came stepping out. "What's going on out here?" he asked, drunk as well. He wasn't half-naked, though—no, no... He was *completely* naked. Turning to me and Josh, he asked how we were as he offhandedly stroked himself. In the room we could hear moans and grunting.

Only an idiot wouldn't realize what was happening. There was an orgy going on in there.

A big, good-old-fashioned, hippie-fest orgy.

"You guys want to party?" the man asked.

Josh burst out laughing. "I'm out of here!" he yelled, scuttling off.

I listened as his footsteps reached the bottom of the stairs and to the end of the parking lot, all the way out of ears-reach. But me: I was much too curious to leave now. I wanted a glimpse of the party inside. Stepping closer to the man and woman—and the room beside them—the man said, "Come on in!"

"He's just a child," the half-naked woman said, smacking his chest with the back of her hand. "Go home," she told me, walking off into the room. I caught a quick look below, down at the skimpy thong she wore.

"Sorry, man," the guy in front of me said. "Maybe another time," he mused, returning back to the motel room. Shutting the door, the noise from inside subsided to a small muffled chatter. The town was quiet again.

Just another regular Monday night.

※※※

For my fourth shift I'd been put on kitchen duty, and there I was—prepping chicken kebob's in the cooler, dating them for expiration—when my coworker stepped in, a middle-aged woman. Her name was Carol and she was holding a book in her hands. "Someone dropped this off for you," she said, handing it over to me. Shutting the cooler door, she swiftly ran back out to the cash registers.

We were the only people working, even though it was busy enough to have at least four. But that's how things were at Sev: busy, busy. But it made the time pass, which was a perk of some sort.

Who would have given me a book? I thought, looking over the cover. **The Hottest State by Ethan Hawke.** Who knew I was a fan of Ethan Hawke? Although, to be honest, I never actually knew he was a writer; I was a fan of his acting, most notably his performance in Before Sunrise. Anybody that knew me would know that, but no one really did know me to that extent.

Flipping through it, I found an encryption on one of the blank pages at the beginning. First things first, I glanced to the bottom and read the signature. It had been Amy, a girl I knew from my grad class. We hadn't been too close, but we were both similar in the way we kept to ourselves and sat in the back of class. Due to both of our introverted personalities, we got along really well over time.

Dear Drayvn,
I'm a coward who can only tell you this if I write it down. Here goes: I've loved you for the longest time, all through math and science, all through high school. I always envied you, the way you slacked off through each and every class. All you ever did was read and write. I don't know how you got away with it. But now I'm moving to Edmonton and I wish I had even just this parody of bravery sooner.
I was ridiculously devastated when you left school. One day you were there and the next you weren't. What happened to you? I hope things are well.
A friend mentioned to me you work at seven eleven now (again? apparently) so I thought I'd give you this. I imagined the character as you while reading it.
Love and luck, (if you believe in those things)
Amy

I felt the sharp hint of tears wave over me, but finishing the last of her words I shook it off, preventing them from bubbling to the surface. I had to. If a rush of customers occurred, I'd be called out to help, and I didn't want to run the till in a visibly emotional state. I kept my cool, taking a deep breath in and out.

It had meant a lot, especially now. It felt good knowing that I meant something to someone. Being the outsider I was, I'd hardly connected with anyone in high-school. Amy was one of the few. I lent her Death Cab CD's and she lent me Bright Eyes in return. She actually had opinions on things. She knew art.

During tests I'd lean over and copy her and she'd pretend not to notice, even though I'm sure she was strongly against cheating. I failed every class I was ever in, though, so it must have seemed not to matter to her in any case.

High-school was six months ago—why did it feel as far away as years?

Things could have unraveled so many other ways. Right now I could be going to post-secondary with the rest of my grade, moving to the city, preparing myself for a career. Instead I'd gone depressed and turned to drugs. Now here I was: rotting away in a dead-end job, no plan or nothing.

I had to figure something out. I had to—

The doorknob of the cooler suddenly rattled from the outside, so I quickly set the book down and pretended to be working hard. As the door swung open, it revealed my co-worker once again.

"Busy?" I asked her.

"Nope, someone else is here to see you."

"Aren't I popular?" I joked, giving myself a pat over the chest like I was Tarzan or something. And as I followed her back onto the floor she couldn't help but laugh. I always did that—made jokes. I played the comic-relief character surprisingly quite well, not that I was genuinely funny, but because I was good at pretending to be when people were having a bad day (which was *every* day at 7-eleven.)

Rose was waiting for me at the till. She was with her friends, who were huddled in the back of the store. "Hey Rose."

"Hey," she said, her eyes stoned red.

"What are you up to?"

"Just went to Batman."

"Smoke a few bowls before going?" I asked, looking up at her friends, who were stoned as well. One of them was in the middle of pocketing a chocolate bar, but I decided not to care. *Let the lowlife have it.*

"It was so trippy," Rose told me, flushed. "I can hardly remember what happened in it!" She cackled, being cute, but I never laughed with her. *What a waste of a great movie,* was all I was thinking. "I heard you were having a party this weekend?" she asked.

"Where did you hear that?"

"Everybody's talking about it." Someone stepped up to the till, but Carol grabbed it for me. Rose and I slid down to the other end of the counter. "Is it true?" she pestered on. "Are you having a party this Friday?"

Maybe I shouldn't...

"I'd really like to see you," she said. "It's been two weeks since I've seen you. Why haven't you texted me? I miss you."

Even though it went against my better judgment, I told her it was true, that I really was having a party on Friday. In the back of my mind, I knew I should have called it off right then and there, but I couldn't help it. The last couple of weeks had been lonely. The beginning of summer had so much promise—what the hell happened?

"Oh my God I'm so excited," she said seamlessly, like a robot. "I'll see you later!"

Rose ran back to her friends and I went back into the kitchen to finish work, full-knowing what a terrible mistake it was that I'd made.

But what was I to do? Alice expected to stay at my house for the weekend of her birthday and that was all Trent had to look forward to. He'd gotten her a gift and everything. It was all he ever talked about: *Alice, Alice, Alice...* I knew he never had a chance in hell with her; but still, I had to fall through on my promises.

✳ ✳ ✳

After my day off on Wednesday they switched me to morning shifts for Thursday and Friday, which was brutal because I was used to staying up till 4:00 AM the past week. Somehow I pulled myself out of bed and got through them. Maybe it was the texts that helped keep me going, the constant replies I had to send off. Everyone I knew had heard of the party and was coming. Even our co-workers from the Wholesale had heard about it. They continually texted me, checking in on the status, seeing if it was still going to happen. It was the big one, the party everyone was waiting for.

'What time do you get off work?' Alice asked.

'Four,' I told her, sneakily hiding my phone below my waist, making sure my manager couldn't see.

'Nick's coming to get me when he's done work, so I probably won't see you till around seven.'

It worked out pretty well that I had the next two days off. Alice was staying at my house until Sunday, which was when I would return back to a normal schedule: morning shifts from Monday to Friday. This would have been perfect, but Eric was trapped working the weekends. Our manager refused to put us on the same shift together. Brody, on the other hand, sometimes worked mornings with me. But he was part-time, and only around for a few hours at a time.

"Pack of Canadian Classics," a younger guy demanded, stepping up to the till and tapping his debit card on the counter.

"Can I see your ID?"

He scowled. "Obviously I'm old enough."

Oh no, I realized. He was one of *those* guys, the kind of guy who liked to get worked up over nothing and act like an asshole.

"I'm older than you," he said.

"Well I'm seventeen," I replied, "so even if you were older than me that wouldn't mean much because that wouldn't necessarily mean that you're old enough to buy cigarettes. Right?"

"You trying to be tough with me?"

Anger washed over me and my heart started pounding, but I held it all in.

"I have a question," he began. "Are you gay? You seem the type. You like sex with boys?"

I glared back at him—without looking away, without blinking.

"You *are* a fucking queer..."

He waited for a reaction, but all I did was hold my stare, keeping silent.

"Fuck it, I'll go to Petro," he muttered, turning around and exiting through the doors. I exhaled and looked around. There were people in the store, but none seemed to have noticed the guy who'd been at my till swearing at me. Everybody was caught up in their own world.

Oh well, nothing new.

Ending the uncomfortable moment for me, my phone vibrated. I pulled it out and read the text. It was Alice again, asking, *'Do you know if Eric is going to be there?'* I sighed and told her that he obviously would. Why wouldn't he? Of the fifty people coming, Eric was first in line. I considered telling her straight-up that Eric never liked her, that it was Trent who did, but I never cared enough. She was just some girl. I don't even know why I was throwing her a party in the first place.

✱✱✱

"I can't believe you were arrested," Cliff said, untying his shoes at the entrance while I prepared the grounded beef he'd brought me. We were going to make tacos before the night of drinking began. "I mean, *I* haven't even been arrested. You know how many times I've encountered the police wasted? Not once have they sent me to the drunk tank!"

"Just my luck, right?"

"More like *Trent's fault*," he speculated, unloading one of the bags of groceries he'd brought me.

"What do you mean?"

"Eric told me the full story." He scrunched up the empty Safeway bag and tossed it into my garbage. "I can't believe you're not pissed off at Trent."

"I'm over it."

"Such a good friend, you are," he said, giving my shoulder a rough squeeze. "Where was I when all of this was going down?"

"You wouldn't have wanted to be there," I told him. "It was just the three of us drinking."

"Ahh," he exclaimed, "a sausage-fest."

"I thought you'd say something like that."

Cliff was the biggest drinker, but he only drank if there was an actual party happening—if the night was actually *worth* drinking for. He was practically a professional kick-boxer; he didn't like wrecking his health for nothing. Tonight, he said, was a night worth any amount of alcohol. Along with everyone else, he'd been waiting on this party for the last two weeks, since it was first announced.

✱✱✱

Eating tacos with Cliff was the calm before the storm. By the time we finished, people had already arrived with alcohol, ready to party.

The first wave of people had come with Cameron and Roger, and the next set was James, Ryan and Sam, who'd arrived with Trent. Everybody from the entire summer was showing up. It was a mash-up of every group of friends I knew.

Trent made a point in speaking to me immediately. He pulled me away from the people I was talking to by the fire, over to behind the shed. "Has—" He stuttered, then coughed. "Has Alice gotten here yet?"

"Not yet."

"I want to show you what I got her for her birthday," he told me excitedly, digging through his backpack. "Look," he said, pulling out a small pearl-colored box. Opening it, he revealed a small piece of jewelry.

"Tell me that's not made of diamond."

"It is!"

Trying not to cringe, I told him she'd love it.

At the other end of the yard, Ben came strolling through the tall fence-door with a couple of his friends. "Dray, my man!" he hollered. "Come 'ere I got a few guys I want you to meet." As nice as Ben was, him and his friends were a bunch of lowlifes. Tonight he was here with Lance and Taylor. "This is Lance," he said, "and this is—"

"I know who they are," I interrupted.

"Well alright then," he replied, laughing. "Let's get drunk."

"Dray," said Trent, tugging my arm.

Ben and his friends brushed past me towards the fire as I looked over to Trent, who was pointing through the cracks in the fence to the front lawn. A golden car had just pulled up in front. "She's here," I confirmed, and Trent let go of my arm and picked up his drink off the picnic table. In one go, he drank the rest of it down. "You're going to want to pace yourself," I tried cautioning him.

Already I could foresee how the night would turn out for him. He was obviously going to get extremely loaded once he realized Alice wasn't as excited to see him as he thought she'd be.

Once Trent went through the fence-door after her, James stepped up to me and asked, "Did he show you the ring?"

"Sadly."

"I told him not to get it," James told me, shaking his head. "I was like don't fucking do it Trent, don't fucking blow your money on a chick. There was seriously no stopping him." I remained quiet, watching through the cracks in the fence as my poor friend went up to her and gave her a hug. He was wishing her a Happy Birthday. "Does he have a chance at all?" James asked.

After thinking it through, I decided, "What do I know?"

I was going through a similar situation. Rose and I hadn't spoken since my last party—weeks ago. But she told me on Tuesday that she missed me. Was that simply her way of getting me to throw a party? Most likely, but she had to miss me a small bit. At least I hoped she did...

When the sun began its departure, there were at least twenty people in my yard, probably even more.

By ten o' clock, Rose finally showed up.

As expected, she was with Cassidy. I watched from a distance as the two of them joined the party.

(She never even bothered trying to find me.)

Sitting down by the fire, they passed a two-six back and forth between each other. They'd chug the vodka, and then drink from a 2L of Coca-Cola. It was pretty disgusting in my opinion, but I was starting to see that that was how most people got drunk. A lot of people here tonight were using that method.

"I can't believe you got fired!" someone yelled at me.

Turning my attention to the voice, I found my old-coworkers, Brendan, Carli and Tyler.

"Oh," I exclaimed. "Hey guys."

"You find any work yet?" Brendan asked. "I heard nowhere's hiring..."

Before having time to answer, Carli shrieked, "You're so odd!"

"What do you mean?"

"Why'd you and Eric up and leave that day?" she asked.

Truthfully, I explained, "I've no clue."

Carli giggled. "Chelsea misses you."

"She does?" Though I acted doubtful, I for some reason believed it. Chelsea was... *nice*. "Where is she tonight? Chelsea, I mean."

"She doesn't like parties."

"It's so weird," added Tyler, pulling a beer out of his pocket.

"I know, right?" Carli ensued. "She hardly even drinks."

Tyler cracked open his beer and handed it over to her. "Have a sip," he said, and Carli quickly complied.

"Cool party, man," said Brendan. "Any chance that things will go inside when it gets dark?"

I stuttered, about to tell him that that depended on how the party went, but I became distracted. Something caught my eye from across the yard. I drifted away from the conversation I was in, staring off into the distance, through the crowds of drunk teenagers.

"Dray?" Brendan inquired, but Carli said something in my place.

The three of them walked off, leaving me to watch the heartbreaking scene unfold. Rose was flirting with Taylor—Ben's fucking friend. A lowlife. Rose was sitting next to him and they were flirting with each other.

She was flirting—*blatantly!*—right in front of me...

Taking a page from Trent's book, I started chugging back my drinks as fast as possible.

"Holy shit!" Cliff's voice said to me. "Have you seen Trent? He's already puking his guts out."

My eyes—watery from all the carbonation—turned over to him as I downed the rest of my cooler.

"What are you doing?" he asked, laughing.

I set the empty cooler down and smacked my lips with my palm, wiping them dry. "What?" I said roughly.

Cliff stopped laughing. "What's wrong?"

"Nothing's *wrong*." I quickly poked my head up, over the crowd of drunks, glancing at Rose again. Taylor's arm was now around her.

"Shit," said Cliff in realization, now looking off at Rose alongside me. After thinking to himself, he blurted out, "Fuck it! She's like that. It 'aint for real. She's never dated anyone cause she's afraid of that kinda shit. That's why she gets drunk and flirts it up all the time."

Cliff was always a joker, but when it came down to it I could always count on him. In the end he always said the right thing. He lived a different life than me: had more friends, did more things. But he knew me just as well as Eric.

"It's not just that," I said, looking around at the party raging around me. "A couple of weeks ago"—I nervously shook my head—"Anna kissed me, man."

His face double-taked. "Anna?" he sputtered out, realizing how heavy the situation was. Cliff was one of the very few people who knew how long I'd been infatuated with her.

"But she won't date me," I pressed on. "No girl will. They all just... want something else."

"You'll find your girl," he assured me, shrugging. "But right now that's not what matters. Try and just have some fun. Look at this fucking party you're throwing. Enjoy it. If girls want to be bitches just let them be that way. You know? There's no way you can change a girl. Don't bother."

"Who wants some shots?" came Kate, waltzing over to Cliff and I. She had a two-six—not unlike the one Rose had—propped between both hands.

"Pick me," shouted Cliff.

Kate laughed and handed the Smirnoff bottle over to him. As Cliff chugged some and gave it back to her, I cracked open another beer and tried my best to not look up at Rose.

Taking one quick-and-clean sip, Kate put an arm around Cliff and lazed her head against his shoulder. "We should hang out more," she slurred up to him, beginning to nibble at his neck with small kisses.

Cliff looked offhandedly at me, giving me a friendly and encouraging smile, as if to say, *This is what parties are like, this is who girls are.*

* * *

"Where's Eric?" Alice asked me, entering into my train of thoughts. Cliff had walked off with Kate somewhere—probably to make out—and I was now sitting by myself on the picnic table, observing the havoc surrounding me as I drank all the free beer I found lying around. "Why isn't he here yet?"

"Eric?" I was already pretty drunk.

She giggled. "He's your best friend, isn't he?"

"Holy shit," I said, burping, "I can't even keep track of who's here and who's not. I'll go call him."

I got up from the picnic table and walked into the carport. I thought it best get away from the loud party and make the call where it was quiet.

"Uh, Dray," said Alice, stopping me right as I was about to head down the cement stairwell. "Thanks," she said, stepping under the carport with me. "Thanks for letting me stay here this weekend, I mean."

"Not a problem," I told her.

(In my head all I could think of was Rose flirting with the piece of shit next to her.)

"Means a lot," she added, staring deeply into my eyes.

In return, I drunkenly stared back into hers...

But when I realized how long we—without a word—had been looking at each other, I shook my head and slapped my face. "You got any stuff you need to bring in?" I asked, scratching my head.

"Like what?"

"Blankets? Pillows? Extra clothes?"

"No," she replied. "All I brought is my purse."

Sounded stupid to me, but I ignored it, and said, "I better go call Eric."

With a brief smile, she left and joined the party as I headed down into my nice and clean basement suite, a real contrast from the disaster all over the yard. As the phone rang, I looked up through window and noticed how dark it had gotten all of a sudden. I'd completely lost track of time.

"Hey man," Eric answered grimly.

"What's hap— going on?"

"You're drunk already..."

"I'm not having a good night," I said, as though I were correcting him.

"Really? Everyone's texting me saying that it's the most amazing party they've been to all summer."

"I'm sure they're all having a blast."

"Why aren't you?" he inquired.

"Two reasons," I said. "One, you're not here. Second, Rose is flirting with Taylor and ignoring me."

Using his words carefully, he asked, "Are you sure she's ignoring you? Or are you just drunk?"

"Oh no no no," I told him, stammering away, "you see I was sober up until she started ignoring me. That's when the beer started tasting a whole lot better."

"I thought you said things were over between you and Rose, anyway?"

"I know I said that, I know. But tonight I thought there might have still been a chance for us to work out."

"Yeah."

"Will you just get your ass over here?" I pleaded. "There's like fifty people in my backyard. Alice is sleeping here and she didn't even bring anything. And Trent! That guy is on his way to get alcohol poisoning... I mean—*fuck!*—what did I leave out? Shit's going down."

"Sorry, man."

"Fuck you! Come over. I need you here."

"I was excited to come, I really was. But my family needs me home tonight."

"Come on!"

"I can't."

I grunted. "You know someone called me gay today in 7-eleven... Some fucking asshole, piece of fucking—"

"Dray!" he yelled, shutting me up. "Just relax and enjoy the party. Rose is a bitch! Go protect Trent from his impending doom."

"I don't want to go out there," I told him.

"Dray," he said, repeating my name once again, "I need you to. If you don't take care of Trent, nobody will."

"You're right."

"How's Cliff?"

"He's having fun, probably making out with Kate somewhere. He mentioned something about a party that Jack and William were having tonight, so maybe that's where he went..."

"I wish I was there."

"Me too."

"You can do this," he assured me. "People will try and crash there, by the way. I'm positive of it. Make sure they don't."

"Alright, okay," I concluded, readying myself to delve back into the action.

"And make sure you cut down the drinking," he said. "It sounds like you've had enough."

"I don't think I'll be able to stop at this rate."

"*Try...*"

✳✳✳

Everything twisted and turned until nothing made sense. Trent was puking everywhere, falling all over the place. If it hadn't have been for the help of Cameron and Roger I don't know what I would have done. James and his friends would have helped, I'm sure, but they'd left not much longer after Cliff had. They told me the party was too crazy for them. Too many people, they said.

When we carried Trent's unconscious body inside, the rest of the party followed. Suddenly my basement suite was loaded chock-full of drunk and hyper teenagers. I thought the first party I'd thrown here was a big one, but tonight's put the last to shame. There was so many people and I was so drunk; I had no idea what was going on. All I knew was that Trent and Esme were safe and sound-asleep in my bedroom. The only focus I now had was keeping up with the status of the rest of my apartment. I ran back and forth through the crowds of people, cleaning whatever spill occurred or whatever glass had broken.

I ran around frantically for what seemed like hours. But everyone kept trying to keep me chill. They kept feeding me more alcohol. Everybody wanted to do shots with me and I couldn't find the words to refuse.

How We'd Look on Film

Randoms kept introducing themselves to me as though I'd remember their names, handing me beers or sips of hard liquor. Shot after shot, it eventually caught up to me. I slowly stopped caring: I let the house get dirtier and dirtier; I never bothered picking up garbage; I stopped telling people to take their shoes off at the door.

When someone accidentally bumped a lamp down or something, I never bothered picking it up like I normally would have. I decided to give up and let everything unfold on its own. Eventually, it all began to amuse me.

Everything was so interesting. Sitting down on the couch, I relaxed for a moment and just observed everyone. They kept drinking and drinking...

People then started making out in the corners of rooms, eventually in plain sight. From what I heard of the noisy chatter, people were saying the stupidest things. I just sat there and laughed and laughed and laughed.

I need to drink more, I decided, getting up and entering through kitchen to find something else to sip on.

Stepping up to the fridge, I found an unconscious teenaged boy passed out on the floor—which, oddly enough, seemed completely natural. He was curled up in a ball, his mouth wide-open. Even when someone came and pulled open the fridge-door, accidentally hitting his head, the boy still remained unconscious. Like it was no big deal, the person opening the fridge grabbed the boy's legs and dragged him along the floor so that he was out of the way. This amused me more than anything else. "That kid is fucked!" I shouted, and everyone in the kitchen started laughing as though I'd made a clever joke or something. I honestly could have said anything and they would have found it hilarious.

Crshh... something broke, but I didn't even look to see what it was; instead I started dancing through the kitchen. (Someone had brought speakers and was playing shitty rap music.) I took my phone out and began taking pictures of everything: of all the people laughing and falling around everywhere; of all the couples making out.

Even as drunk as I was, I could tell things were beginning to die down. People were now either passed out, or making out. I took one last picture and put away my phone. Right as I did, someone suddenly grabbed my hand and pulled me into the bathroom.

She closed the door and locked it, then turned to me. Her name: Alice... For a brief moments time, she looked at me and I looked at her. And right as I opened up to speak, she threw her lips over mine and squirmed her tongue inside my mouth. She ran a hand over my chest and bit my lip, trying to act sexy.

I went hard, which hurt, but in a feel-good kind of way.

By then, I couldn't stop myself—I started pulling her pants down, feeling her up everywhere.

I was doing the unimaginably stupid, but it already began and there was nothing I could do about it now. In spite of myself, I continued. Like I was someone else, like I was in a movie, I threw her up against the bathroom door and pulled her underwear off, which slowly fell down her legs as I made my way down her body, kissing her neck and cleavage.

She was moaning, which grossed me out; and when I heard that pleasure out loud, I froze. Confusion settled over me, reality sunk in. The sudden rush I'd gone through completely died off, and there she was, standing bottomless in front of me, still moaning, still wanting more of me. So I continued kissing her, complying with the moans of pleasure by awkwardly touching her some more.

I let things take their course.

I kissed her violently—if you could call it kissing—and gripped her tightly, bruising her body as though I were punishing her for putting me in this situation. But she liked it; it made her moan even louder.

As my mind drifted elsewhere, I wished so badly to myself that in real life there was such thing as a fast-forward button. Or even better: a *rewind* button... But there wasn't. I had nothing other than what was in front of me.

Chapter Thirteen: Some Things Last A Long Time

As expected, I was the first one to get up that morning. I had troubles sleeping even when there was no drinking involved—with two people in my bed and a stinging hangover, sleep was an absolute impossibility. Alice and I had passed out here, on my bed with Trent and Esme after agreeing to never speak of our night to each other ever again. We were too drunk, she told me, so to her that meant nothing even happened. It was flawed logic in my opinion, but I wasn't about to argue with her. Forgetting everything sounded good to me.

Flipping onto my side, I coldly examined her as she slept curled up next to Trent. Before today I never thought of her as ugly, but this morning I did. And when I got up and looked in the mirror I hung next to my closet, I too looked ugly.

The sound of birds outside was irritating, and the light from my window was pale and sickly. My basement suite no longer felt like a home; it was nothing but a few rooms full of furniture.

Walking through the the wreckage, I was pleased to see things weren't as bad as I thought they'd be. Nothing looked stolen and the half-dozen people that crashed here last night all seemed to have left already. Nick was alone in the living room, sleeping on the couch, and the only other person left in the suite was Ben, passed out in one of the chairs of my dining room table. He was sitting there, propped up on the table, one of his hands clutched around a pack of cigarettes. I pried them out of his grasp and took one, leaving the pack next to his hand. As I put the cigarette in my mouth, I noticed a strong smell whiff up at me. With my fingertips up to my nose, I realized what the scent was.

Gagging, I ran for the the bathroom and washed my hands. When I looked up at myself in the mirror, I realized what a shit-show I was. In response, I spat the cigarette into the toilet and flushed it down. *Who had I become?*

"I would have smoked that," a voice said, startling me.

Looking over, I discovered that I hadn't been alone. Taylor was inside the bathroom with me—the loser that Rose flirted with all night. He was resting half-asleep in the shower, even more haggard than me. "You comfortable?" I ironically asked him.

He shrugged, tiredly lifting up a can of beer to his mouth.

"You're drinking?"

"Takes the hangover away," he told me, not proud. "I need to get back to sleep, but my head hurts too much."

"Interesting," I said, looking down on him with a repulsed expression. I also thought it was interesting how he—of all people—had managed to stick around in my basement suite last night. He was the *last* person I wanted to see. "How was your night with Rose?" I asked, not even caring anymore. I couldn't feel any worse—no matter what he told me.

"Shit, I'm so pissed," he said, resting his forehead on the wall of the shower. "All night she flirted with me, saying all this shit to me. Then, next moment I look up, she's gone... She left the party. She didn't even say anything to me. Such a bitch."

"Yeah, man. What a bitch."

"So I ended up just getting way too wasted. Typical."

Taylor chugged the last of his beer and sat it down, then closed his eyes. I almost felt sorry for him, for how pathetic he was. It wasn't even his fault: getting hit on by Rose. She had some major issues, that was for sure.

I turned away from Taylor and left the bathroom. Stepping over some broken glass, I stumbled into the living room and sat down on my favorite chair, the loveseat in front of the TV that matched the couch.

Grabbing my remote off the coffee table, I hit *POWER*, flaring the TV to life. Then came the sound of music and the familiar voice of characters, which relaxed me, finally lulling me to sleep with everyone else.

∗∗∗

As the afternoon went on, I realized there was nothing I could do to get rid of all the people that had stuck around the house. Ben and Taylor wouldn't leave; they were stuck to Alice, who, of course, felt the compulsion to be extra-friendly in return. They made themselves at home—lazing about, napping occasionally—while I cleaned up the apartment and the backyard. I could have easily kicked them all out, but I promised Alice that she could stay another night. With everyone else attached to her, there wasn't much I could do. And I couldn't ask Alice to leave, either. Not after last night. That would be beyond rude. That would make me... *a user.*

Just thinking of that term made me shudder.

I briefly tried swaying Nick in driving her back home to Houston, but he was too tired to give it any care. He never saw it as a big deal the way I did. My house had been invaded, and no one understood I needed the space. The only person I actually wanted to stick around was Trent, but he had better things to do than lounge around and do nothing.

"I'll bet you want them to all leave," Trent said as he put on his shoes. He motioned towards the living room, where the group of them were laughing and talking noisily. "You're pissed, aren't you?"

"I asked for it," I replied. "Are *you* pissed? I know last night never turned out the way you wanted it to."

"I thought Alice liked me," he said, shaking his head at himself. "But look at her..." Once more he motioned towards my living room. "She practically ignored me all day. Good thing I never gave her the ring last night."

With effort, I managed a laugh. "Can you return it?"

"Maybe one day I'll find someone else to give it to." He sighed, zipping his coat up. "Last night sucked."

"Tell me about it. I was being ignored too, you know. By Rose."

"I was too drunk to notice," he realized. "Why do we have such bad luck with girls?"

I hunched my shoulders together in response, silently flashing through the memories of last night. I knew I should have felt guilty about what happened between me and Alice, but I never. It was *her* fault. She was the one that took my hand, who pulled me into the bathroom. *Who kissed me.* Wiping my thoughts away, I told Trent, "Don't worry, man. I doubt we'll see much of Alice after this."

"How about we *not* go to Houston anymore?" he asked, smiling. "And fuck these stupid parties. What a sham."

"We never had Eric here last night," I told him. "The fellowship was broken—look what happened."

"You're right," Trent said, snickering as he opened the door. "We have to stick together."

Someone called my name in the living room so Trent and I said our goodbye's. By the time he'd closed the door, the whole group of them were now calling my name. "What is it?" I called out, making my way through the kitchen. When I turned the corner, I saw the four of them—still sitting around in a circle—all with frightened expressions on their faces. "What?"

"Drayvn," Nick said. "Your cat."

I looked over and saw Esme making her way out of my bedroom. She was using only three of her legs, limping towards me, hissing in pain. One of her paws was mangled and crooked. With a loud curse, I knelt down to her.

"What happened?" someone asked.

I picked her up off the ground as she pleaded for me, cradling her in my arms, but in doing so I accidentally brushed my wrist up against her injured paw, making her screech even louder. "Oh my God," I muttered, my voice crackling. *How could this have happened?*

I went into my bedroom and carefully set her down on my bed. After giving her a moment of comfort, I turned to leave. Esme called me back to her, meowing softly, so I made my point to everyone in the living room as fast as possible. "You all have to leave," I demanded. "I need to be alone with my cat. *Just leave.*"

I slammed the bedroom door shut and returned to my crying kitten. How did I not notice? Clearly this had happened last night. Someone, I guessed, must have stepped on her. Busy inside of my own selfish world, I never even realized it.

It was my job to protect her and I'd let her down, all because of some party I felt so compelled to throw last night. How stupid was that? I didn't even care that the four of them outside of my room had seen me cry, or how long it would take for them to leave.

I knew I would remain with Esme, continuously petting her and making sure she never moved and hurt herself more.

Realizing how serious it was, I knew I would have to do something I'd avoided all summer: I had to call my mom. I needed her help—at least, Esme did. It may only have been a broken leg, but if it wasn't immediately taken care of... Who knew? It could get worse, and I couldn't stand to see her in anymore pain.

On the phone, I was pleased to discover that my mom wasn't about to go through her usual questioning. Without any further ado, she plain and simply told me to get myself ready to take Esme to the vet. And luckily, by the time she arrived, Alice, Nick, Ben, and Taylor had all gone.

✼✼✼

By Monday things were as Alice had said—*as though nothing even happened.* For starters, the house was in proper shape again: clean and tidy the way I liked it; no empty bottles scattered about. The place was spotless, returning back to the relaxing and becoming home I'd always meant for it to be.

Looking through my phone at all the pictures I'd snapped—the mayhem of drunkenness in and throughout my apartment—I was honestly surprised the house hadn't been burned down. The breaks and spills were a calamity, but a small one. Considering the time I'd spent huddled in the bathroom with Alice—leaving my apartment to anyone's disposal—it was a miracle, practically, that nothing was stolen. The people from the party weren't my friends, not anyone to be trusted. If it hadn't have been for Esme's injury, I would have considered myself lucky.

As both my mom and I expected, her paw was broken. A cast was needed. Normally this was a simple procedure for the veterinarians, but because Esme was still in her early few months of birth they needed to keep a closer eye on her. They'd kept her these past few nights, making sure the splint wrapped around her front-right leg remained effective.

Off work, I headed for the Animal Hospital to check in on her. On Saturday they'd mentioned for me to come in on Monday afternoon to see how things were. Unfortunately, it turned out they needed to keep her there for one more night. I was disappointed, but they let me into the back room for a quick visit. Though she was stuck behind a cage—scarcely able to move with her large cast—she was still very excited to see me.

"I'm so sorry you're in here," I whispered, sliding a finger through the tiny bars of her cage. And when she licked my finger and began to purr, it was then I immediately knew how important she was to me. She looked so pitiful, her arm slung in a ridiculously big cast.

It was six hundred dollars setting her up, money I never had. Fortunately I had the kind of mom that was happy to pay for things.

✸✸✸

My parents had always been generous people. Throughout my whole life they'd bought me anything I ever asked for. I never asked for much, though. All I wanted was enough money to rent a movie each night. But there were people that came to them for real help. They'd tell them their problems; I'd listen behind closed doors. They often lent money to friends or neighbors, anybody that came to them. Sometimes they got paid back and sometimes they never, but that didn't matter to them.

They didn't care about possessions; they cared about religion. Being righteous was a higher priority than anything else. They used to tell me that because they never cared about money they were blessed with not having to worry about it.

As much as I tried understanding their points of view, their love for God, the less they made sense to me. Though I admired their virtues, I seemed to be living in a different world as them. I was cynical and negative about the goodness of life; they believed in things.

They were happily married, still madly in love after a whole twenty years of marriage. Over the years I watched and observed them, always surprised by how in tune they were with each other. My dad would come home and often step up behind her as she prepared dinner, making playful grabs at her breasts, making her giggle like they were both young again. Once a week or so he usually brought home flowers.

That was the biggest thing I ever learned from them. I disagreed with them so much, but when it came down to love, I was positive they knew what they were talking about. Their love for each other was pure.

And that was all I ever wanted for myself.

I never believed in God, but I did believe there was someone out there that was I destined to be with. That was what always kept me going, what got me out of bed, what kept me going to church. Love was what made me want to keep my parents happy. But when Anna left, nothing inspired me anymore. Romance movies became nothing but melodramatic lies to me. My head was full of such high expectations and they'd all crashed down on each other. I wanted so badly to go back—all the way to Grade 11. *Back when I knew who I was and how to be happy.*

Instead all I'd gone back to was my old job at 7-eleven, the place in time it all went wrong. But then again, maybe I could use that to my advantage. My return to form could begin here. I couldn't rewind my life, but the future was still up for grabs, wasn't it? I was free to do as I chose.

That's why I left home in the first place.

It was up to me to believe in Anna once again, that much was certain. Even if the memories were all I had left of her, I had to put my trust in them. And so finally, during the lunch break of Tuesday's morning shift back at 7-eleven, I sent a text her way, repeating something I once told her years ago, an inside-thing that only she would respond to. And although she never responded, I never let that bother me. I was the one that sent her away; I was the one who changed. So even if we never spoke again, that no longer mattered. The past was all I had, and it was up to me to learn from it. Memories were meant to inspire, weren't they? I couldn't let them discourage me anymore.

Throughout the week I tried my hardest to start the next chapter in the novel I'd finally begun writing, but it seemed impossible. I couldn't concentrate. My mind wandered to thoughts of Anna. Doing all I could, I sent her a small text each night. She may not have replied, but it was therapeutic for me just seeing if she would.

Chapter Fourteen: Hugs From Boys

"Things are going to be so weird now," Eric said, nervously peeling the label off a cooler with the nail of his thumb.

Trent: "I'm the one going back to school…"

"I know," Eric replied. "That's what I mean. It'll take some time getting used to, not having things going on anymore."

"Everyone's got school: Jacob and Nick, Rose and Cassidy," I added, thinking it over myself. The regular flow of life was about to start back up again. Things would move on—without me, without Eric. It was exactly like before.

The three of us, sitting around my dining room table, sighed.

Trent and I had waited around till 12pm—when Eric got off work—to have a few drinks with him. Normally I wasn't up this late, but tomorrow was a day-off and I knew the three of us were long over-due to hang out. Besides, it wasn't going to be anything big. We weren't going to have anyone else over and we definitely weren't going to run around town and get ourselves arrested. With September around the corner we needed to see each other at least one last time. This would be our way of making up for all the shitty nights we wasted in search of something more epic than each other.

"Can I grab another cooler?" Trent asked, nodding behind him to the fridge.

"You paid for them," I replied with a laugh. "Drink as many as you want."

He shrugged, standing up. "But I'm drinking faster than you two," he explained. "I don't want to drink them all."

"There's plenty," I told him. "Don't worry about it."

Trent grabbed a Mike's Hard and came back to the table. After sitting down, he told us, "I've missed you guys. Going back to school is going to really suck. I doubt I'll hardly see you at all."

"Shouldn't have failed grade seven," I joked. "*Dumb-ass.*"

"*I'm* the dumb-ass?" retorted Trent. "Maybe I should have just dropped out with you guys."

"Now there's an idea," Eric spoke, unraveling a fresh pack of cards.

"Are we playing Waterfall?" Trent asked, noticing the cards Eric brought over. "Just the three of us?"

"Why not," Eric replied, sliding the cards out onto the table and shuffling them. "I'm having a hard time getting these drinks down. It's been too long; I need motivation."

We snickered. "Let's play, then."

In brief compliance I picked up the card on top of the deck Eric set down for me. It was a two. "Two is for you," I said, pointing to Trent.

After drinking the two required sips, he picked up the next card. Setting it down in the discard pile, it was revealed to be a four. *Four, touch the floor.*

Scrambling, Eric and I dived off our chairs to touch the floor first, but looking up, we noticed that Trent hadn't caught on. "What are you guys doing?" he asked.

"Four, touch the floor," explained Eric as we settled back into our chairs.

"No," he complained. "*Four is for whores.*"

Eric laughed. "We've never played that way before."

"And besides," I added, "there's no *whores* here."

"Fine," Trent murmured, lifting his cooler back up. "I'll drink again."

Eric's turn was next. He had a nine. *Nine is to rhyme.* "Jump," Eric began.

"Lump."

"Bump," said Trent happily, surprised by how quickly he'd figured out a rhyme. Usually it took a whole lot longer.

"Dump," continued Eric.

"Hump."

As we'd gone around the table, it was now Trent's turn to rhyme again, but he gave up, ending the round by simply taking a drink. "I don't even know why I bother playing this game," he said. "I fucking suck."

"Doesn't matter."

"You're right," he winked, "just means I get the most drunk."

Eric and I laughed and we continued on.

Trent really was terrible at drinking games. He'd lost too many brain cells from all the pot he'd smoked last year. His mind was still clearing.

Thinking that through now it made me glad to know I never got to that point. I'd gotten close. Extremely close. I was inches away from shutting myself away from everything. Luckily, I had people in my life that reminded me to keep my sights higher, that I was worth much more.

It's taken a long time for me to realize, but I think I've finally come to respect myself. The mind truly is a terrible thing to waste, and I would waste mine no longer. It was true that I may have felt like I never belonged anywhere—not in school, not in church—but that was natural. No one really feels like they belong. That's why they go out in the world: to find the life they want and deserve; to find out where they *do* belong. Things change, and eventually for the better.

A couple of months are nothing in the grand scope of things.

I for some reason had it built inside my head that this summer would last forever, that life was going to be one big party, stretching on for eternity. That Anna was never going to leave again. That I had all the time in the world.

But I never.

I never grasped the moments I had.

✳✳✳

The last week of August went as usual. I worked mornings; Eric worked nights. I'd visit with him and then go home where I would cook dinner and watch a couple movies. As night fell, I usually read The Hottest State—the book Amy had given me—until I passed out, but only after sending Anna another one of my daily texts. (She still hadn't replied.)

Some nights Brody would come over and ask if I wanted to go driving, and to break the habit of routine I'd happily join him. We'd drive out to Telkwa and back and listen to music while he told me all that was going on at church—all the things I was missing out on, *he* thought. One night, be broke the news to me that he was moving. "To Utah," he said, driving us back down Highway 16. "There's nothing for me here."

"Utah?"

"Provo, Utah," he explained. "In a few weeks I'll be gone."

"What are you going to do in *Utah*?" I asked, shuddering at the thought. That was an extremely long way south.

"It's too late for me to apply for BYU, but maybe next semester I'll try and get in. For now"—he turned onto my block—"I just want to try living on my own."

I was speechless. This was huge. We grew up together and now he was moving across the continent.

He pulled his vehicle into my uneven driveway and put it into park. "Yeah," he said, breaking the silence. "But you know, I think you might have been the one to inspire me."

"I inspired you?"

"Well... Yes and no," he contemplated. "You're an idiot for drinking and ditching your family, but you definitely got me thinking."

How We'd Look on Film

I smiled uneasily. "Well make you sure you say goodbye before you leave."

"Don't worry," he said. "I still got a couple of weeks of work at Sev with you. We'll see each other around."

Brody pressed the button next to him and unlocked the doors, but before stepping out I decided it was time to finally apologize: "I'm sorry I drank that night while I was staying at your house," I told him. "That wasn't cool."

"I'm over it," he murmured. "I shouldn't have been such a prick."

After one quick moment of silence, I got out of the vehicle and walked up the driveway, still shocked by the revelation I'd just heard. *Brody was moving. He was actually moving...* Life kept on keeping on; so much could change in an instant.

As he reversed out and drove off, I went into the carport, startled to find Kara smoking in the dark a few steps in front of me. "Jesus!" I shouted in surprise.

"Sorry... I had a feeling I might have scared you."

I regained my composure, chuckling. "It's getting dark so much earlier now."

"Want a cigarette?" she asked.

I shrugged, deciding. "That's okay," I concluded.

"Have you quit?" she asked.

"I guess I have."

She snickered. "I'm happy for you—if you do, indeed, quit." She drew in a large drag and blew the smoke out, which eventually drifted towards me. I smelled it, and craved it, but stood strong with my decision. "You haven't had any parties lately," Kara inquired. "What gives?"

"I'm kind of through with throwing parties."

"After what happened at the last party?"

"What do you mean?" I asked.

"The neighbors told us all about it when we got back. Apparently it was pretty huge."

"It was awful," I told her, remembering that terrible night.

"Oh!" she shrieked, remembering something herself. "We also heard that one of your friends tried stealing firewood sometime ago? There's like five hundred logs in the shed—why would he need to steal any?"

I laughed out loud. "I forgot about that."

"Why did they try and steal some?"

"Just drunk."

Kara stubbed her cigarette out and slowly walked towards the front entrance, stretching. With a yawn, she told me, "Your friends are hilarious."

"They're pretty great," I confirmed, and we said good night.

Inside the house, I made my way hurriedly into the bedroom to check in on Esme. Even weeks after the accident, she still had a cast over her front-right leg, which had been a major inconvenience for the both of us. She couldn't walk around. She needed me to carry her to the litter box and to her food. I knew the chances of her peeing on my bed were high, but I never cared. It was my fault that she was hurt. *The same way it was my fault for hurting Anna.*

Peering through my phone, I sadly took another glance at the empty inbox I had. Eric and I were both very busy with our full-time jobs; so were Cliff and Trent. None of us had really kept in touch. With Anna not texting me either, it had been a lonely couple of weeks. August was ending, the summer was over.

'*Text me back,*' I sent to Anna, one last desperate call for her. I knew it was pointless to try, but I had to. One last—

'*Like this?*' she abruptly replied.

Shocked, I pounced out of my bed and flipped on the lights. I was about ready to go to sleep, and now this... After all this time... I thought she'd never speak to me again. '*You replied,*' was the only thing I could think of to send back to her.

'*Do you want to see me tonight? I'm nearby.*'

Out of nowhere, Anna and I had gone from not talking to about to hang out together. Why did I feel as though her actions were always rooted through the element of surprise? She always kept me guessing. Throughout the past two years of my life—the only years that mattered—she'd kept me on my toes, waiting.

'*Of course I'd like to see you,*' I told her. '*When?*'
'*I'll be at your house in five.*'

Breathless, I took off my glasses and ran into the bathroom to put in my contacts. After briefly looking in the mirror at myself, I went back into my room and undressed out of the clothes I had on. I threw on some jeans and a polo shirt, made my bed, and paced nervously throughout my basement suite. It was perplexing, the drastic change that had occurred in only a matter of minutes. At any second, she was coming over. She was going to be inside the house I lived in.

Cantering in and through my bedroom, I realized Rose's message was still plastered up in plain sight, on the whiteboard I'd put over my bookshelf.

Good morning, beautiful. It's a beautiful day.
Rose <3

Without even thinking about it, I raced over to erase it. Using my forearm, I frantically tried rubbing the words out. But through all my efforts, the green print—fading slightly—remained intact. If I were to make it completely disappear, I would need hot water and a warm cloth. But there was no time—a knock came at the door. Two small timid taps, unmistakeably Anna.

The only option I now had left was to yank the entire whiteboard down. After throwing the wretched thing inside of my closet, I forcefully shut it close and went for the door.

Everything was set.

I swung it open, and there she was: the prettiest girl I'd ever seen in my life, standing in the cement stairwell in front of me.

"Can I come in?" she asked.

I clumsily stepped backwards and let her through. She took off her shoes and followed me into the living room.

"Nice couches," she noted, resting a hand over one of the armrests. Something whipped through her mind—she asked, "Where's Esme?"

"She sleeps on my bed."

Anna looked up at the room in front of her and rightfully assumed it was my bedroom. I followed her in. "Oh my goodness!" she shouted.

"What?" I said, looking into the room with her.

"Esme has a broken paw?" She stared at me, her mouth dropped low, and then skipped over to my bed.

"That happened a while back," I explained as she she hunched over the bed and reached for Esme.

"Poor thing," she whimpered, petting her with long strokes around the neck, exactly how Esme liked it. Nobody knew how to pet her properly—it was almost a miracle that Anna somehow did. "Baby..." she whispered, giving Esme a kiss on her brow.

I folded my arms and admired the two of them from across the room. They were both so beautiful. Anna turned back to me—her fingers getting a bath from Esme—and asked me how I'd been. I paused, looking down on my feet. "Did you even read the texts I've sent you this past while?" I replied, sounding upset, but not upset enough that there was a possibility of wrecking the mood. I couldn't help but remain a small bit frustrated that she'd ignored me for so long. But when I mentioned the texts, the expression on her face changed from concerned to confused.

"You've been texting me?" she asked, after a flutter of shock.

"Every night..."

"Seriously?"

"Yes!"

Anna gave Esme one last kiss and stood up and walked over to me. "I haven't had any minutes on my phone," she explained. "I didn't know you wanted to see me... I thought you were still mad at me. Aren't you?"

"I've done a lot of thinking," I told her. "That's what the texts said."

She leaned up against the wall and asked me, "What happened?"

"This summer," I clarified, "a lot."

As we took the walk across town to her house, I told her everything. I told her all about the road trips I'd went on—about

Houston and Terrace, but mainly the story of Prince George: how Eric and I were fired from the Wholesale because we'd ditched work to go. I explained that's how we both ended up back at 7-eleven, that we were now saving up to move out of town.

She thought we were both very brave, which reminded me of the even wilder stories...

In great detail, I narrated the exciting adventure of when we broke into Chandler Park—how we were chased by the police into the forest across the street. Eventually, I told the story of how I really was arrested.

I told her about Alice, about Rose.

I even told her about the naked guy at the Fireweed Motel, and the orgy going on in his room. Embarrassed by my explicitness, she told me, "I've never seen a naked man before." Chuckling, she said, "I don't even know what a penis really looks like."

"You haven't seen one in a movie?"

She was taken aback. "I don't know what kind of movies *you're* watching, but the kind of movies I watch don't have penises in them."

"I'm not talking about porn!"

"I know," she murmured. "But you watch a lot of weird movies."

"Only to understand why *everyone else* is so weird," I retorted, giving her a wink. She smiled and went quiet, looking down on her feet. I joined in—one small moment of quiet—enjoying the night air with her. At the end of the Safeway parking lot, I realized we were at the spot I sat down and read the letter she wrote me. "*That's*"—I pointed—"where I read your letter."

Taking a few more steps ahead, she pointed to a spot further up and told me, "*That's* where I crashed my tricycle when I was five."

"Did you scrape your knee?" I asked, talking to her as though she were a small child.

Melodramatically, she whined, "It hurt so badly."

We both chuckled and went quiet again. Crossing the street, we silently realized how close we were to her house. This could very well be the last time we spoke for a long, long time. "What were you doing tonight?" I asked, sparking conversation. "Before you came and saw me."

"I was at a dumb party."

"Getting drunk?" I pretended to ask.

"I still haven't had my first sip of alcohol," she reminded me. "And I don't intend to any time soon."

"You're the perfect girl, Anna. *Perfect.*"

"Mm!" she exclaimed.

"What?"

"I had the sudden impulse to kiss you right there."

I smiled brightly. "What stopped you?"

"Erika made me promise not to."

Speechless, I stammered out, "She made you promise not to kiss me?!"

"Pretty much."

"Well," I decided, "one more person to put into my bad books."

"You're joking, right?"

"Of course," I assured.

"I'd like to kiss you," she said, sad and serious. "But I'm leaving in a couple of days. I'm just really glad you kissed me that one night."

"My first kiss..."

"I know."

"The summer never turned out the way it should have."

"I know," she repeated, spinning around to face me. I stayed planted to the ground and watched her step backwards down the street. With one last smile, she turned around again and walked up to her house.

✹✹✹

The lack of sleep I had was completely worth it to see Anna. I was on a very good sleep schedule since I was now working morning shifts, and although I was refraining from going out late, Anna was the ultimate exception. Cameron, Roger, and Jacob and Nick texted me through the past couple weeks, telling me about big parties, but

How We'd Look on Film

I was firm on staying responsible. I wasn't going to let myself get fired from Sev. If that were to happen, I'd be completely screwed. I'd probably have to move back in with my parents or something.

For the entire day of work I did my tasks and responsibilities like I was a robot. While I cleaned the bathrooms, ran the till, wiped down the counters, all I thought of was Anna. I was praying that she'd text me. Tonight was the last night before she went back to Vancouver. Would she spend her last hours in Smithers with me? Only time would tell.

"Excited for your check?" the store manager asked me, walking up to the slurpee machines I was busy dusting the tops of.

"Not really," I told her, hopping off the step-ladder. "It's basically all going to rent for next month."

"Are you really that short on money?" she asked, checking the meters on the back of the machine.

"This summer took a lot out of me."

My boss stood on her tiptoes and surveyed the job I'd done. "I still see some dirt up there," she fussed.

As she walked off, I sighed and prepared the step-ladder once again. Getting the last of the dirt, I got down and walked to the other end of the store. With one last stretch of my shift to get through, I needed an energy drink. Four hours of sleep, I decided, was simply not enough while working at Sev. At Wholesale I could get away with it, but here there was far too much to get done.

When Eric switched off with me at four o' clock, I stuck around an extra half an hour as usual. These days it was the only time we ever got to see each other. In the back storage room I helped him flatten the stacks of empty boxes and prepare bags of ice.

"You hear about the big campout happening tonight" Eric asked.

"Yeah," I muttered. "Kate and Cassidy came in this morning and asked if I was going."

"What did you say?" he asked, breaking up the bunches of ice.

"I told them I'd never gone to those things before so I never saw why I would start now."

Every year, before the start of the school year, all the teenagers camped out at a lake that was far out of town—out of police jurisdiction—to drink and party one last time before school began.

"Can you believe we never went to the campouts?" I mused. "Not once throughout all of high school?"

"We were always such rejects..."

"You used to play hockey," I told him. "You had friends. You weren't *always* a reject."

"Right," he said, "only when I started hanging out with you."

"Dick." I tossed the box in my hands harmlessly up at his face, but he quickly knocked it away to the ground. I groaned. "This trip down memory lane doesn't serve me very well. High school sucked."

Eric laughed. "Prince George, man... We'll get out of this town soon enough."

"We'd better," I said, opening the storage room door.

"See you tomorrow."

After taking my uniform off and grabbing my paycheck, I left Sev and began walking to the bank. Up the street, towards Gone Hollywood, I noticed a familiar car come driving towards me. It was Jacob and Nick. They hit the brakes and Nick unrolled his window. "Hop in!" he yelled.

"I'm going to the bank—"

"We'll drive you."

Before the vehicle behind them had to wait any longer, I dashed up to Nick's golden car and hopped into one of the backseats. Talking noisily amongst themselves, they ripped up the streets until they'd reached RBC on Main Street. "This isn't my bank," I told them.

"Well why didn't you say so!?"

"You never asked?"

"Fine," Jacob said, laughing. "What bank?"

"Credit Union."

"To Credit Union it is," said Jacob, signaling Nick to continue driving. "Why don't you come out partying anymore, Drayvn?"

"Yeah!" added Nick as he turned out of the parking spot.

"We never see you anymore."

"Um, well, I work lots," I explained halfheartedly.

"How about tonight? There's the campout happening. You should come with us."

"Yeah!" cheered Nick once more.

"I don't know about that."

"How about instead you have a couple of drinks with us while we have dinner? *It's a barbeque...*" he said, using the kind of tone used to help sway people in being convinced. But he never needed to say anything further. The amount of money I had in my bank account—even after getting paid today—made a free meal impossible to say no to. Besides, what harm could a couple of drinks do?

✷✷✷

After cooking up some burgers and drinking a few beers at Jacob's, we went to Safeway to wait for Roger to come and meet us. They needed a boot to grab them more alcohol for the campout. "Are you sure you don't want to come?" they continued asking me, but I'd made up my mind. I was already exhausted from staying up late with Anna. The only thing I'd want to do other than sleep tonight was hang out with her once more. But that thought made me sad—she was still yet to text me.

Time was ticking and it was getting late...

"Shit," Nick said, looking down on his phone. We'd been waiting in the parking lot inside of his vehicle for the past twenty minutes.

"What is it?" Jacob asked.

Nick showed him the text on his phone. "My brother can't come, apparently. He says they need him at work for a few more hours."

Jacob cursed. "Ask him if it's possible to get a break maybe."

Looking out the window, I breathed in deeply and sighed. My patience had ended, but right as I was about to ask them to drive me home, I saw something at the other end of the lot that changed everything: Anna was headed up to the Safeway entrance, walking alongside a boy my age, laughing and smiling. Together, the two of them went through the automatic doors and disappeared inside.

If I'd blinked I would have missed it. She was with someone else. There was someone else she preferred to be with for her last night in Smithers. I never expected to be her number one choice after the kind of summer we had, but to physically see her with another guy...

My insides crushed together.

Ignoring the pain, I leaned over between Jacob and Nick and said, "I know how we could get alcohol."

"You've decided to come tonight?"

"You want to get drunk?"

"Very drunk," I made clear. *I now had nothing better to do.* "Let's start by picking Trent up."

As we exited the parking lot, I angrily eyed the entrance I'd seen Anna walk through until it was out of sight. Heating up, I tugged off my hoody and threw it to my side.

"Don't you, like, work in the morning?" Jacob asked.

"Eight to four," I said gruffly, trying to feel tough. "But fuck it. Summer's almost over. One last party, right?"

✱✱✱

With Trent added to our troupe, we waited out in the parking lot of the Twin liquor store while he made the call to James: "Hey... What's up... It's me, Trent... We're at the liquor store... Could you— You're a lifesaver, James... Yep... Yep... Okay, see you soon."

With a loud cheer, Jacob turned around from the passenger seat and gave Trent a high-five. We were now one step closer.

Jacob and Nick were eager to get on the road, and so was I.

"Um, Trent," I quietly drew his attention. "Could you pay for the alcohol again? I'm really strapped right now. Bills and all..."

"For sure," he replied. Then thought it through: "How about we each get our own bottle of Fireball? We can see who drinks the most!"

"Whatever you wanna do," I told him. "I'm down."

I continued acting cheerful, but I was dying on the inside. I wanted to scream. Anna was leaving all over again and we wouldn't even be saying goodbye. She never cared. This whole time, this whole year, she never cared. She'd only pretended to. I thought I could be inspired by the memories of her, but what if the memories of her were false? Had it been my imagination, these last few years, that made her out to be a girl she never was? Was there really a connection between us?

When Trent handed me my own bottle of Fireball, I decided to put these questions aside; and as the car reversed out of the lot and lurched down the highway, I began drinking them away until they no longer came to mind. The moment an image of her surfaced through me, I'd put the bottle to my mouth and cringe the thought of it from existence.

The music in Nick's car was shit, but at the current moment it for some reason sounded good. I supposed it was my sudden rush of drunkenness, the escape I was longing for. The loud indecipherable metal chords and screaming lyrics enthralled me. For the whole drive, Trent and I bobbed our heads up and down together. We had no rhythm or anything; we were just enjoying ourselves.

We clinked our two-sixes together and drank.

Driving past Telkwa, towards the campout, I decided that this is where it was at. This is what being a teenager was all about. Forget love, forget romance. Tonight anything could happen. I could go and hook up with some girl if I wanted, and although I knew I wouldn't actually, I began thinking maybe this was the mindset I needed. From now on, I had to forget about love. Rose wasn't looking for love, was she? She was looking for a good time. Same with Anna. As young as we all were, all anybody wanted was to make memories.

I'd wasted years of my life thinking love was right around the corner.

As much as Trent was drinking with me, he was shocked to discover that my two-six was half gone. He stopped headbanging to the heavy-metal music and said, "Dude, you gotta slow down."

"No way!" I yelled, and then chugged it with full-force.

Trent, speechless, grabbed the two-six out of my mouth, spilling some down my cheek and shirt. "No more!" he then shouted.

Leaning between Jacob and Nick, he turned the music down on Nick's sound-system and showed them how much I'd drank.

"Drayvn!" Jacob turned around and glared awestricken at me. "What the fuck are you doing?" He changed his glance to Trent: "Are you sure he drank that?"

"There's no one else here," he condescendingly retorted.

"We're almost at the party," Nick said. "He's going to have to puke there."

"I never puke," I said. "Can I have my two-six back?"

Trent laughed worriedly. "You're an idiot."

"Only you, Dray," Jacob said. "You went from not wanting to drink at all, to getting completely fucked up. And we haven't even gotten to the party yet!"

"Gotta be... different," I remarked, a sour burp in between my words. *Thank God for Trent*, was all I was thinking. I would have drank that whole thing if he hadn't have stopped me. I was still going to be extremely fucked up, but I knew I'd survive.

But then, suddenly, my ears began ringing painfully from the loud music—I started to feel nauseous. *Hopefully I'd survive*, I re-thought.

At the party, I went running around everywhere, talking to everyone, even people I never knew. I didn't care if I was embarrassing myself or anything. Nothing mattered. I couldn't even make out my surroundings. I didn't know where I was or anything—I just walked group to group, trying to make out the faces of people. My vision was a blur of fires and tents, strangers and old friends. I'd get caught up in a conversation with someone, and then find myself moments later somewhere else, with no recollection of how I got there.

Suddenly I found myself knelt on the ground—away from everyone else, down by the lake—puking up the burgers we ate at Jacob's. Even the time I puked up the Colt 45 at Brody's wasn't even close to comparing to this. This puke was coated with so much hard liquor that my mouth actually stung from the burning whiskey.

I fell down on my ass, and reached for my phone. I had to call Trent and see where he was. I needed help; I could hardly move. But when I flipped open my cell, I found an unread text message.

How We'd Look on Film

It was Anna.

'*I rented Interview With The Vampire. Want to come over and watch it with me? I leave in the morning.*'

I tried responding, but I couldn't. My fingers were unable to process my thoughts and my eyes went in and out of focus. There was nothing I could do. How terribly ironic was that? The reason I was drinking was because of Anna, and now that I was drunk, that kept me from seeing her.

How in the hell did I let this happen?

As I passed out on the gravelly dirt path over-looking the lake, I clung to the only happy thought I could think of—the fact that she'd wanted to see me. Even though there was no way of me seeing her now, at least there was that: the knowledge that she really had cared. It made me feel less alone, just knowing that.

✳✳✳

Everything else happened in a series of disillusionment. One moment I was passed out in the trees, the next I was waking up in Nick's vehicle, being flashed in the eyes with a flashlight. It was the police, I realized, staring down on me through the window. "Your friend's pretty drunk in the back there," I heard the officer say. "You should get him home."

"That's what we're doing," Nick said.

"I'll let you go with a warning, then."

We must have, I realized, *been pulled over for having too many passengers inside the vehicle.*

As the car began to speed up again, I started pleading them to stop and let me get out. I needed to puke more.

"Out the window," Trent told me, leaning over to roll it down.

Jacob and Nick told me not to puke yet. "At least wait until we're out of sight from the police!" But I couldn't wait any longer—I immediately drooped my head out the window and began puking again, all across Nick's car. And as I coughed up bit by bit of the Fireball rolling around my stomach, I thought about Anna. She was somewhere out there, safe inside of her house, watching Interview With The Vampire, wondering what the hell I was doing. She was about to spend her last night in Smithers alone, and there was nothing I could do about it.

I fell back into the vehicle and onto Trent's lap. I was conscious, but I couldn't move or speak.

"Give me your key, Dray..."

"Where's your house key?" I heard them ask.

"We're going to have to carry him inside," another said.

"Look through his pockets."

"Drayvn? Are you there? Talk to us." (The most I could manage was a small grunt.) "We're going to get you home," they assured me. "We're almost there."

I stupidly wanted to tell them to drop me off at Anna's, but the words never came. My mouth was stale and it hurt to use any part of body. Everything was spinning. All I could do was shut my eyes and try pretending that none of it really existed, that it was a dream, nothing but a figment of my imagination... The world slowly evaporated into a wavy smoke, getting thinner and thinner, turning dark. Soon enough, as the car continued tumbling down the highway, I passed out into an oblivion of emptiness. Into a deep, deep sleep.

Chapter Fifteen: The District Sleeps Alone Tonight

My eyes jolted open in realization of what had occurred. Through the darkness I searched out my alarm clock. *Please, let it still be early,* I prayed. *Please let there still be enough time...* But it wasn't early. The red numbers—floating in the darkness—read that it was four o' clock. I'd been out for hours. It was closer to being morning than to the night of.

Getting out of bed, I pieced things together. I flipped on the lights and observed my room, pleased to find that Esme was sleeping soundly at the foot of my bed: a small relief, one less thing to worry about.

On the nightstand I found my phone, tidily placed over top of an unopened box of Pepto Bismol, which was next to a large bottle of Gatorade—a complete set of hangover-aid my friends had clearly and kindly left for me and the situation I was in. At once, I realized what they'd sacrificed on my account. They drove out to the campout, and had to come all the way back—all because of me. We hadn't even stayed there an hour. At least I don't think so.

My mind flickered through what happened...

I grabbed my phone and checked the texts. Had it been real—had Anna texted for me last night while I puked my guts out at Tasmin Lake? Checking my inbox, I realized exactly how real the whole ordeal had been. There was at least a half a dozen texts from her.

'Dray? What are you doing?'
'Answer me, Dray!'
'This is your movie. I want you here for it!'
'Where are you? Are you okay?'

After reading the last of her texts, I shut my phone and jumped up and down, cursing hysterically. I felt so terrible, so stupid. How could I have done this? It was her last night in Smithers. Why didn't I text her before deciding to get ridiculously drunk? Why did I have to be such an idiot about everything?

When was it... that I stopped fighting for her?

Since it was four in the morning, I knew the chances of her being awake were slim, but I took my chances anyway. I dialed her number, put the phone up to my ear, and waited. Four rings later she picked up—a miracle. "Hello?" she weakly and eagerly answered, clearly coming out of the same kind of deep sleep I had.

"It's me."

"Dray..."

"I'm so sorry. I don't even know where to start."

"What happened? Where have you been?"

"It's a long story—"

"You want to come and see me? There's still time..."

"I know it's late."

"I'll sneak out," she said. "Run to me."

When the phone clicked off, I immediately did as she said. Not even bothering to lock my door, I ran out of the carport and down the block to 7-eleven.

I sprinted across the highway and dashed past Main Street as fast as I possibly could, running as if I was running for my life.

Through the parking lot, I found her waiting, sitting in the spot I told her I'd read the letter she wrote me. She lifted her head up the moment she heard my footsteps. Smiling sleepily at me, she got up on her feet.

Her hair was a small bit disheveled, but right now it looked perfectly lovely to me. She seemed so real—standing before me. Hours ago I thought I'd never see her again.

"Hey you," I murmured, a small bit drunk. I wasn't wasted like I was earlier though—just drunk enough for the world to have a dreamy over-cast to it. There was a peace to everything. Who cares if I had to work in the morning? Nothing mattered more than this.

Anna delved into my up-and-rising chest as I panted from all the running. "What happened to you?" she whined affectionately.

Putting an arm around her, I apologized once more. "I was a bit of an idiot tonight."

"Really?" she replied sarcastically, curling up beneath me. "What a *shocker*," she expressed, sounding increasingly more frustrated.

"Well you see what happened," I began to explain, but she hushed me to keep silent.

"Let's not talk," she implored. "Just for a bit."

Closing her eyes with a soft hum, she fell even deeper inside the crook of my arm. I held her tightly, but not too tight—the right amount as we walked through the parking lot.

"I'm so tired," she said sadly.

"I can walk you home," I inferred. "I really just wanted to see you one last time before you left. I had to say goodbye."

She looked up into my eyes, holding my body with both arms, thinking hard about something.

"What is it?" I asked.

"Let's go to your house," she replied. "Can we?"

***

We never bothered turning on the lights when we stepped inside the basement suite. The smudge of sunlight storming over the mountains outside was enough; our eyes were too sleepy for anything brighter. She went and sat down on the ragged chair in front of the TV; I went and grabbed my guitar. Sitting on the carpet in front of her, I played a few riffs and asked if she recognized the tune. She looked down on me in admiration and guessed knowingly that it was a Death Cab song. "And you used it one of your videos," she further guessed, "the last one, I'm pretty sure."

She was right about that, too. "Know the title, though?" I asked, setting the guitar back down next to the TV.

"I'm too tired to remember..."

I chuckled and walked over to the matching couch. "Army Corps of Architects," I told her, sitting down.

"Right. From their first album."

"Actually, it was more of a *compilation* album," I corrected her, being the elitist snob I was.

"What are you doing over there?" she asked.

"What?"

"Come sit with me."

I chuckled again and got up to join her, realizing all the tiredness in me was gone. I felt wide awake and I never even seemed drunk anymore. Maybe that was because I'd been lucky enough to puke all the alcohol out of my system. The majority of the Fireball must have left me, I realized. "Do I smell bad?" I asked her, settling down next to her in the loveseat.

She lifted her body up and sat on my lap. "You don't smell bad," she said. "But I do smell alcohol on you."

"I wouldn't have drank if I knew you wanted to see me."

"Of course I wanted to see you," she immediately replied.

"I didn't think you did, though—because, well..." I considered not bringing it up, but went through with saying it, anyway. "I saw you outside Safeway with some other guy."

"My brother?"

"Your brother?" My jaw dropped. "Outside Safeway?"

Anna groaned. "You got wasted because you saw a guy with me, who was my brother?"

"Apparently."

She giggled. "Oh Dray..."

I smacked myself over the head, bemused by my wild antics. "Have you ever seen Before Sunrise?" I asked, the thought of it suddenly coming to mind. The situation we were in was up to Richard Linklater standard. For some reason tonight I woke up right

How We'd Look on Film

in the nick of time. After nearly missing our last chance together, here we were.

"You've mentioned it before, but no, I haven't had the chance."

"This really reminds me of it," I told her. "It's a simple romance movie, but at the same time it's very existential and philosophical."

"I'm not sure what existential means."

"No one really does," I explained.

She laughed and I continued on. "You see... At the very beginning, Ethan Hawke meets a girl on a train while he's in France. They get along really well, but it turns out they're headed to two different places, and so he tries to convince her to get off the train and spend the night in Vienna with him."

"That's a crazy thing to try and convince someone."

"No kidding," I replied. "Especially someone you've just met. But this is what he says..."

Breaking into an Ethan Hawke impersonation, I began to quote the movie as closely as I could: "Jump ahead in your life twenty years into the future," I said, speaking to Anna as though she was the girl on the train. "Think about your future marriage, only right now your marriage doesn't have that same energy that it used to have. And so you start to blame your husband. You start to think about all those guys you've met in your life and what might have happened if you'd picked up with one of them. Guess what, *I'm* one of those guys."

Anna giggled dreamily.

"That's me," I told her, still using the accent. "So think of this as time travel, from then, to now, to find out what you're missing out on. This could be a gigantic favor to both you and your future husband to find out that you're not missing out on anything..." I paused, not sure how the rest of the monologue went.

"Then what happens?"

Switching back into my own voice, I evenly told her, "She gets off the train with him."

As I concluded the story, something triggered in Anna. The expression on her face changed: she stopped smiling and looked dutifully at me, searching my face for some sign of something.

Sliding her hand over my cheek, she then wrapped it around the back of my neck and pulled me in closer. Without a beat I kissed her tenderly on the lips. And with our heads nice and close, I whispered, "I didn't know we were going to kiss when we got here."

"You never?" she whispered back to me. "Right away I knew we would."

Smiling, I kissed her again.

"You're such an actor," she said, running both her hands through my hair. "How do you learn to recite movies and poems?"

"I've nothing else to do. All I ever did through high-school was stay home."

"If you had a girlfriend that probably would have changed, wouldn't it have?"

"Or if I went out partying every weekend," I added.

She thought it through and said, "Probably did you a lot of good, staying home... Instead of ruining yourself like everyone else."

"Well, looks like I ruined myself in any case—just a little later than most."

"You're not all that corrupted," she assured me, getting more comfortable on my lap by wrapping one of her legs in between mine. "You've made a lot of mistakes, maybe. But you can make up for them."

"I hope so."

We stared into each others eyes some more until I said, "Know what I realized?"

"What's that?"

Sadly, I explained, "I never really asked you how things were for you in Vancouver. You never really told me what was going on. Throughout all of our phone-calls and emails—all we ever did was talk about me or whatever."

"I know," she said. "I liked that."

"But why?"

With another kiss on the lips, she said, "Because talking to you was what *made* me forget about my problems. Everyone always asked questions about everything. But not you. Me and you just talked. We talked about whatever came to mind. You told me funny stories and told me about songs. It was calming—to hear your voice. Everybody always expects me to talk, but really I just like to listen."

A couple tears fell down from her eyes, but I brushed her cheek clean with both of my hands. She smiled brightly, not so tired anymore. "Talking to you," she said, her words quivering, "made me feel close to home again. You never swore, you never made dumb jokes. You never gossiped. You cleaned my head of all the garbage."

"I did that?"

"I told you in my letter that you got me through some of the hardest times in my life, and I meant it. You really did."

I scoffed at myself. "I always thought you were the one that got *me* through everything. I never thought I was making a difference to you."

"But you never really told me what was going on in your life, either, you know..."

"I guess neither of us liked complaining."

"We were each others escape," she mused. "You never told me, but I always wondered what it was that made you drop out of school, or what it was that made you run away from home. You used to be full of so much life, like you never cared what anyone thought. When you spoke to me on the phone I knew you were still that person, but I also knew that other things were going on. I never asked because it was nice that way... When we spoke, we forgot all about our real-life problems."

"That's true," I said, smiling tentatively.

"But what was it?" she asked. "What was it that made you leave school and your home?"

"I was sick of being a disappointment, I guess."

"Why'd you think that?" she asked, almost sounding disgusted by the very thought.

"I dunno," I told her. "Maybe because I always had a lot to live up to."

"Such as?"

"My father, mostly. I always felt like I was letting him down. I guess I knew I could never be the man he was, so it's like I gave up."

Carefully, she asked, "So what kind of man are you?"

"Not a real man."

"Not *yet*, you mean."

I smiled down on her as she beamed back up at me.

And it was then that Anna finally opened up to me, fully and completely. After knowing her for two years, she finally told me the secrets of her life. She told me all the beautiful and painful things that had happened to her, letting me deeper and deeper into her world.

She told me what her life in Vancouver was like: the school she went to, the friends she had, the boys she met. She said no one understood her like I did. "Which is crazy," she reflected, "because even when you hardly knew me you seemed to know exactly what I needed to hear."

"I just wanted to see you smiling every morning," I contended. "I tried to make sure you were always happy."

Eventually we fell onto the floor together, onto the warm, wooly carpet. We merged our bodies together, heating each other up, setting each others skin on fire. She pulled her hoody off and then mine. And when she put her tongue in my mouth it was unexpectedly relaxing, not at all disarming. I slid my tongue over hers, and glided along the smooth lines of her teeth. Her mouth and lips were perfect; her kissing was gracious. She hummed softly and passionately.

When we took a break from kissing to catch our breath, I'd lay over her and count how many kisses we now had together.

I'd stare down on her through the pale morning light and tell her how beautiful she was.

There was a piece of acne on her cheek I grazed my thumb over in fascination. I was amazed by its inherence, because I'd never been close enough to see any blemish of hers before. She'd always appeared perfect—a glowing angel in the school hallways. Now she was real. She was living breathing flesh. A real girl. Not a dream of mine, not a character from a movie; a fourteen year old girl, staring lovingly back into me.

I kissed the crooked blue vein on the top right of her forehead and the blemish on her cheek, down to her neck and chest. And when I burrowed my face into her breasts, she giggled and said my name, surprised by my sudden lascivious movement over her body. I chuckled with her—surprised as well—and went across her stomach. Somewhere during all of our fondling her under-shirt had scuttled up, leaving the flesh of her stomach exposed. Closing my eyes, I listened to the birds that were now chirping as I slowly settled my lips over the skin beneath her naval.

Instantaneously, as I felt my body pulse a wave of eroticism, I pulled up and raced back up to her. She whimpered in excitement, absorbing me as I wildly made out with her, but laughed as my kissing became uncontrollable. I accidentally slobbered over the side of her mouth.

I apologized, using a hand to wipe away the saliva dripping down her cheek, but she smiled and pulled my head back down to her as it was now her turn to wildly make out with me. With both hands she pressed my face hard against hers, squishing our noses together. I broke out laughing and she laughed too; but through our laughter we continued kissing.

We rolled around on the carpet, around my living room, between the ragged chair and the matching couch in front of the TV.

The sun slowly dripped brighter and brighter through the blinds—a colorful tint of blue—and the birds got louder and louder... Life was calling us back; we did our best to make the hours last as long as possible.

Chapter Sixteen: Intuition

When my alarm sounded off in the bedroom, I at once realized I was alone, lying there on the carpet of my living room. I called out her name, though, just to make sure, just to see. As I got up off the floor—pathetically calling her name—I discovered a painful ache in my back.

I limped throughout the apartment, trying to bring clarity to things. I'd clearly fallen asleep and she'd had to leave.

On the dining room table there was a piece of paper with a pen on it, left in plain sight for me to see, which I immediately knew had to have been Anna's doing. I ran over to the table—the sound of the alarm clock ever-beeping—and read what she'd left me.

Drayvn,
I know I should have woken you up to say goodbye, but I knew that would make it even harder for me to leave. Believe me, it was hard enough having to pry my eyes off of you and leave in the first place. I stayed as long as I could but my ride was leaving. My dad called me. He went to wake me up and found my room empty. I'm in trouble. But don't worry, it was worth it... I'll miss you. What more can I say than that? I'll really miss you.

The paper trembled in my hand as I stared over it in astonishment. I read it over and over until I'd memorized the words, but no matter how many times I ran it through in my mind, I couldn't quite put my finger on it. The words seemed strange to me; they seemed *off*. Everything was unclear and fuzzy. My head was throbbing, my back hurt terribly, and I knew there was a hangover on its way of surfacing through me.

Into my bedroom, I placed the the note inside the orange cabinet on top of my bookshelf. The only other thing left inside it was the other letter Anna had given me. I knew I'd keep those two scrolls of paper forever, but what I didn't know was what was now occurring this moment. Had something in the universe altered? What did last night mean to her?

What did it mean? I pondered angrily, wishing I had more answers. Her note hardly said a thing and I was so confused.

She was on her way to Vancouver now. She was gone—I knew that. I wouldn't see her for another year. And even then who knew? There was still a chance of her not returning here for her next summer break. For all I knew I might be in Prince George with Eric by that time anyway.

Did Anna want to be with me? Is that what last night meant? I could move to Vancouver if she wanted me to. I'd move in a millisecond. I'd make it happen—

Beep. Beep. Beep.

The sound of my alarm had finally gotten to me, now adding even more pressure onto my throbbing headache. I flicked the thing off and checked the time in doing so.

I had to be at work in fifteen minutes.

My friends had obviously set the alarm for me, which was kind of them. But fifteen minutes? They were definitely cutting it close. After taking some of the Pepto Bismol they'd left on my nightstand, I headed for work, still wearing the clothes I'd wore last night and slept in.

✷✷✷

As I passed the Greyhound station, I remembered who was working with me this morning: Brody. Would he realize how hungover I was? Apparently, I discovered, it was even more obvious than I realized.

When I stepped inside 7-eleven, he stared me up and down from behind the counter, dumbfounded by my appearance. My eyes were half open and my hair was ruffled and greasy. He motioned me to step closer, and in a hushed whisper, asked, "What the hell happened to you?"

"Um," I began. "It's kind of a long story."

"You look terrible."

My stomach turned. The hangover I felt was getting more and more intense. "I better check in before I'm late," I said.

Brody looked at me worriedly, trying to gauge what was going on. He knew I was hungover, but he also knew something else had clearly happened. "I'll talk to you in a bit then," he said. "There's a customer behind you."

Behind me, I found there was someone trying to pay for a coffee. "Sorry," I told them, walking off to the end of the counter. Through the other side, I went into the staff room where my manager was.

"You'll be working in the kitchen today," she said, not even bothering to look up from her papers. "Brody's working the till, but at twelve you'll switch. Sound good?"

"Sounds good to me," I said simply, putting on my red 7-eleven uniform.

After pinning my name-tag on, I walked out of the office and onto the floor. The white fluorescent lighting burned my eyes; to escape, I eagerly dashed into the kitchen. Remembering silently what I was supposed to be doing in there, I began preparing the boiler.

I tried keeping focus, tried not thinking about last night—

But suddenly my stomach turned into a tight knot. Tightening and expanding.

As the pain grew stronger, I realized I had to go back into the store. Hesitantly, I stepped out of the kitchen, into the bright store and past the counter. Brody noticed me. "What?" he implored, but I continued walking. Without even saying anything back to him I made my way to the other end of the store.

Inside the washroom, I locked the door and opened my mouth, huffing. My eyes were watering and I could hardly breathe. I began coughing. I knelt on my knees, on the dirty, piss-stained floor, and leaned over the toilet. I knew it was coming. My stomach was heaving up and down, my chest swelled in pain.

The puke came, and it wasn't as bad as I expected; maybe because this time I *had* expected it.

After puking I began to feel somewhat better, like the knot inside my stomach had released it's clasp. But soon enough, it raveled tightly back up again. Using all my strength, I got up and looked in the mirror. My eyes were bloodshot from puking and I was still heaving back and forth.

I had eight hours of work to attend to.

How was I gonna do it?

I collapsed on the floor, next to the garbage can, and pulled my knees up to my chest. I held my legs, hugging myself, and thought of Anna once more.

She was gone. She'd gone back to the other side of the province. Out of arms-reach, out of sight. The summer was over, and so was the the excitement of living on my own.

Sitting there in thought, I gradually began to weep. For the first time in a long time, I let myself go completely. I wept like I was a child again—loudly and unashamed. I sobbed away, using all the energy I had left inside me.

I'd destroyed my body and destroyed my heart. My insides were dead. There was nothing left to me anymore.

Chapter Seventeen: Every Song Ever Written By Mark Kozelek

This happened exactly one year ago...

I never eat at McDonald's, so this part of the story confuses me. It feels like something that wouldn't have happened. But it did happen. It's no exaggeration. This was real; I'm not lying.

It all happened.

This goes back all the way to when Anna still lived in Smithers. This was the last time I saw her before she moved away to Vancouver.

✳✳✳

The clothes I wore this day weren't as nice as what I usually wore. This may have been back when I was still obsessed with my appearance—even winning Best Dresser in the yearbook—but today I never cared. I was in a simple t-shirt and plain jeans, not in slacks or in one of my sweater-vests. The reason for this was because I thought Anna had already moved away. Since she was the only person I cared to impress, I had no other reason to dress nice and do my hair. The last thing I expected was to see her inside of McDonald's.

She was standing by one of the tills, talking with a girl who worked there, not noticing me until the line had moved up a few customers.

Remaining quiet, I anticipated her reaction.

When she finally looked back and caught sight of me, her face split from a social smile into a real one. She said my name, using a tenderly-spoken emphasis on it, surprised to see me as well. After staring at each other for one ghostly second, Anna's friend over the counter interrupted. "I can help you," she said, motioning down to the till she was working.

"That's alright," I said, staggering closer. "On second thought I'm not that hungry."

"What are you doing here, then?" Anna giggled. "See me through the window?"

I shook my head and told her, "I thought you moved?"

"Tomorrow," she explained.

"But I haven't seen you in like a month."

"I was in Brazil. On vacation," she murmured. "I'm just here one last day to get my things."

"So it's kind of lucky I've bumped into you?"

Her smile broke out even larger. She put a hand over her face, blushing—*still so young.* "Pretty much," she shyly exclaimed.

"There's someone—" Anna's friend said to me, "—someone behind you."

I moved aside with Anna and let the customer behind me make their order. Anna waved a quick goodbye to her friend and then pulled me through the store. At the exit, she pushed open the doors and dragged me out, happy as ever.

"I can't believe you're here right now!"

"I can't believe *you're* here..."

"I've only two hours, though," she said, "before I have to get back home—"

"Two hours?" I speculated. "That's lots of time."

She gave my arm a tug to follow her, and the both of us took off down the street, towards Main. "My one day in Smithers," she said, "and I see you."

"Kind of eerie," I divulged.

"What do you mean?"

"It's so... *fateful*."

"I guess it was destiny."

Suddenly, I blurted out to her, "Why you can't you just stay here!?"

"...My mom needs me in Vancouver."

"Why can't we be together?"

"Because that would be too simple," she made clear, being strong. "Our story needs a much better ending than that."

"Oh, that's right—because what kind of lame movie would that make?"

"A terrible one," she exclaimed, guiding me past the town's Firehall. She was ahead of me by a few several feet, a soft skip in her steps.

"I need to go off to war, just so I can return to you when everyone thinks I'm dead. Something epic like that, right? "

She looked back at me with admiration, walking backwards. "You're so funny."

"I'm glad *you're* amused," I said, sneering. "But really—do you think we will end up together?"

"Do *you* think we will end up together?

"I hope so."

She thought about it for a moment. "It would be make sense."

"*It'd make sense*," I repeated. "Such an Anna Markus thing to say!"

"Such a *Drayvn* thing to say!" she retorted.

"What is?"

"Just coming out and saying you hope we end up together."

"Sorry, but I do!"

She slowed her walking down to a calmer pace, looking me deep in the eyes. Then, with a slight smile, her voice full of affection, she murmured, "I know..."

"Well of course—you know everything."

"I do," she exclaimed, leaving us to smile for a brief moment of silence as we walked across the highway, onto the central side of

Main Street. "But you always did that... You always said those weird things. Stuff nobody else would."

"Sorry."

"No, I loved that about you," she affirmed. "Anybody else—no. But you're different."

"Why?"

"Because you're totally innocent." She laughed. "You don't know any better!"

"Oh, I don't know about that," I said, molding my face into something cold and stern, an attempt to try and appear dangerous-looking. "I'm not that innocent," I uttered, sounding uniformly like a bad-boy.

"Yes you are and you'll stay that way." She put her hand over my face and rubbed away the serious look I had. "Tell me you'll stay that way."

Smiling as she pulled her hand away, I told her, "I'll stay any way you want me to. If that's innocent, sure. Even if innocent is me not knowing any better—sure. I'll be your fool."

"Not a fool."

"Right, just innocent," I said.

"If you weren't innocent I wouldn't love you."

"Anna!" I shouted, shocked. "You just said *love*."

She looked at me angrily, but in a playful way. "Now don't think I just told you that I'm in love with you... I've never said that to anybody—that I loved them."

"I know," I mumbled. "I get it. I get *you*. I can handle the L word."

"No you can't. Love is everything there is to you."

"So what if I loved you?" I came out and asked.

"You're allowed to love me all you want. That love is yours..."

We stopped at a crosswalk and waited to make sure that an oncoming car would stop and wait for us. After we saw it begin to slow down, we crossed over to the other side, back onto the sidewalk. In sudden realization, I asked Anna whether or not she actually believed in love.

She paused, swaying the idea around inside her head. "I'd believe you if *you* loved me."

"What makes me so special?"

"Everything. Everything makes you special," she said.

"I can't be *that* special," I said, but she repeated that I was. "I look so terrible right now," I remembered. "Do you want to come over to my house? I'd love to have a shower and do my hair before we say goodbye."

"You don't look terrible at all," she muttered, "but I'd like to see your house. One last thing I'll see of Smithers for a whole year... But what time is it?"

I pulled my phone out and checked the display screen. "It's five."

"There's still time, then."

"Why don't you have a cell phone?" I asked.

"My dad said I might as well wait until I got to Vancouver."

"That makes sense. You know, when I was your age nobody had a cellphone in high school. Cellphones didn't even have color, let alone a camera."

"Oh, back in your day?" she mocked me kindheartedly.

"Back in my day," I repeated.

"You're such an old man."

"I'm graduating next year," I said sadly.

"How does that feel?"

I sighed and told her, "It's exciting, but it's also very scary."

"It sucks being a teenager," she grumbled, kicking a rock down the street. "Not being in control of anything."

"I guess we should try and enjoy it. This is the only time we're not gonna have any responsibilities. The rest of our lives are gonna be nothing but work and electric heat bills and all of that."

"Not us." Reminding me what I used to tell her, she confirmed, "We're gonna be rich and famous."

"Oh so you believe me now?" I asked.

"No, but to hear you talk about electric heat bills is depressing... How's working at 7-eleven?"

"The first of many lame jobs I'm sure I'll have," I mused.

"I hate growing up."
"Me too."

✴✴✴

It took us an hour to walk to my house. Normally a walk from Main Street took half an hour but Anna and I took our time. We talked and laughed, reminiscing about the past year and all that had happened—funny things mostly. *There was still so much to laugh about.*

On the way Anna convinced me to share some of my writing with her. I'd written hundreds of poems, but no one had ever seen them. I never thought anyone would. But since Anna was leaving... And was coming to my house... I couldn't refuse. This was my last chance to really impress her. This would be her last memory of me.

The moment she stepped through the door of my bedroom she went completely quiet. To her it was like an intimate experience—she looked in and around all my possessions like I wasn't even there. She touched everything.

Felt the fabric of my bed sheets, placed a hand on all my movie posters, even squeezing the bottom of one of the shirts I had hanging off my closet door. She looked through my drawers and out the window.

"I'm gonna take a shower," I interrupted, and she turned her head back to me from across the room. "My poems are in that drawer right there, below the bookshelf," I pointed. "And um, the ones in the red notebook are my favorite, by the way. The ones in the black one suck."

She looked to the drawer I pointed at and over the whole room again, up to the ceiling. Smiling back at me, she said, "Okay."

I nodded, and left the room, carefully bringing along the t-shirt that was hanging off the closet door. I didn't want to change in front of her—even if that meant I would only be shirtless. I've always been perfectly comfortable with my body, but I didn't want her to feel even remotely awkward.

When I returned, I found Anna sitting on the edge of my bed, still sifting through my notebooks. I broke the silence with a chuckle. "I thought I told you the ones in the black one suck."

She ignored me, smiling to herself, and then asked, "What's the story behind the key card?"

"Hm?" I was wringing my head in a towel one final time before tossing it in the corner of the room. "What key card?"

"You use it as a bookmark."

"Oh... My hotel key." I went and sat next to her as she handed it over to me. Looking down on it, I explained, "It's from a hotel I stayed in when I was in Ontario, a really cool one. It was like an island on water but it looked like a ship, like a cruise ship."

"And...? There's got to be a better story behind this card other than that."

I put the hotel key back into its place and Anna closed the notebook shut.

"You really want to hear it?" I asked.

"Yes," she confirmed.

"Alright. Well there was this girl I met when I was in Grade 8." I stopped and looked at her, then clarified: "When *I* was in Grade 8."

"Keep going," she urged on.

"She was an exchange student from Kingston, Ontario." I paused a moment, lost in thought. "Basically she was the first girl I ever had a romance with."

"Did you kiss her?"

"Only on the cheek," I explained. "I told you: I haven't kissed anyone. Not on the lips. I'm waiting for the best possible moment for when I do kiss someone."

"But do you actually think you'll find that moment?"

"That's what this story is about, actually."

"Okay, sorry. Continue..."

"You remember Hockeyville, right? How Smithers was one of the main contenders to be Hockeyville?"

"It was a huge deal—of course I remember."

"Remember how the town was sending a bus across Canada, full of a bunch of people from our town? But only a select few, though, just the ones that best represented the town?"

"One of my friends' dad was on the bus, actually."

"*I* was on that bus."

"You were?"

"Yep. You see, the Hockeyville ceremony that the bus was headed for was being held in Kingston, Ontario."

Anna connected the dots: "Where that girl lived!"

"That's right. And getting a ticket on that bus was my only chance of ever seeing her again. So I found out about this writing contest. Whoever won it got a seat on the bus, and an extra five hundred dollars to spend on the trip there."

"What did you have to write about?"

"Hockey, of course. I worked hours on it and it ended up being pretty good. I won the contest. But I knew what they wanted to hear. I made it knowledgeable, heart-warming, even personal. I had to lie a little, though, just to make it seem like I *really* liked hockey. But anything to see this girl again! We'd been talking online for the past two years."

"And you saw her?"

"Well"—I shrugged—"no."

"No?"

"I ended up not telling her I was coming."

"Why?"

"I told myself that I wanted to surprise her. But that wasn't it."

"What was?"

"I think it was because I thought if I did see her it wouldn't live up to my expectations. It would probably just end up being awkward. What would we talk about? I might have bored her."

"You went across all of Canada for her, but you didn't even see her," she huffed.

"But I liked it that way. I hoped instead I'd see her randomly walking down the street and I could stop the bus and run after her—"

"Like in Lost in Translation?"

"Pretty much... I tried finding her in the phone book when I finally got there, but I didn't know her parents' names, just her last. I called three numbers, gave up, and hung out in the hot tub for a couple hours. All I've got from that experience is this key. It's like a symbol for what could have been."

"Is it a sad symbol?"

"I guess it could be considered a sad symbol. But to me I think it's more than that... It's more of a reminder for everything the future will hold."

"Are you going to fall madly in love with someone else when I'm gone?"

Her remark was meant to sound like a joke, but I knew she was also being serious. "I think I could learn to love someone if they truly loved me."

"Do you need someone to love you?" she asked.

"With you gone... I think my life is gonna be missing something special. Maybe I will need that someone."

"You'll always have me."

"And you'll always have *me*," I echoed back to her. "But I guess our lives are going in different directions, aren't they?"

"We'll keep in touch," she assured me. "And you still have to make those videos on YouTube!"

"That stuff's over and done with," I said plainly.

"Why!?"

"The school board said we had to stop. And besides, who cares? Everyone hates us! Half the guys in our school want to fight me."

"But your videos will make you famous."

"Right now I just want to get out of high school alive."

"Are you gonna be alright?"

"As long as no one breaks my nose," I joked, making her laugh. "I'll be fine. But what about you? You'll be all the way in Vancouver..."

"Hopefully I make some friends."

"Seriously?" I said, exasperated. "You'll make friends the first day you're there I'll bet you."

"You think?"

"I know."

"I think it works well, me leaving," she said, looking out the window. "It'll give us a chance to go out in the world and live."

"Before we're stuck with each other till death do we part?" I remarked.

She turned back to me and said, "Don't ever stop dreaming, okay?" I then noticed a tear in her eye. "Drayvn?"

"Yeah," I said, but she replied no further. She knew I could already tell what she wanted to say.

So waiting not a moment longer, I did as she wished: I put an arm around her and tucked her inside the crook of my arm.

"I'll miss you," I whispered. "I'll miss you and I won't forget about you."

"Promise?"

"I promise."

And then our time was up—I had to walk her home. She moved to Vancouver the next day, letting the rest of the story unfold.

Part Three: Fall

Chapter One: Gone Hollywood

Autumn normally begins with falling leaves, but my fall came earlier than that. My summer ended the morning Anna left for Vancouver once again. Time suddenly took on a new dimension. Though the days seemed to drag on forever, weeks passed by in an instant without ever really making themselves known to me. Soon enough it really was fall.

Eric and I continued working at 7-eleven all the same. We were stuck at work while the rest of our friends embarked on the next stages of their lives. If they weren't returning back to high-school, they were on their way to college. As much as we also wanted to leave, we had bills to pay and minimum-wage jobs. It was impossible to save up a decent amount of money.

Anna did call me the night after she got home in Vancouver. She told me that she was going to call me all the time—that she was going to sign my number up as one of her 'long-distance-top-five'— but I hadn't heard from her since. Even after sending her an email, I received no reply. She was back for another year of high-school... She never had time for me. I tried not thinking about it; instead, I focused on my tasks at 7-eleven. Like a zombie, I went through each day keeping my mind as blank as possible.

As my mom came to regularly stop by, she finally began to realize how sad I was, which was probably because I had lost all the energy to pretend otherwise. She started bringing me home-cooked dinners, which made my shifts a whole lot easier to get through—having some real food in me.

But the real highlight of my days were the new kids at the high-school. Pleased with the freedom of being outside the confinements of their elementary schools, they made use of being allowed to leave school-grounds at lunchtime. Every day they came into 7-eleven. They bought slurpees or whatever; and they all knew me through the old videos I made.

I was still cool to them.

There was one girl that came in and always talked to me. Her name was Samantha and everyone seemed to like her. She was popular among the new crowds of young teenagers. Every day at twelve I anticipated seeing her. I never dreamed of dating her or even talking to her outside 7-eleven; I just liked it when she came in and talked to me.

Sometimes, before her and her friends left, she would run over and give me a huge hug, then dash off before my manager caught her behind the counter. Her friends would giggle at her bravery and Sam would often blow me a kiss on her way out.

Because I don't see her anymore, I often wonder how she's doing—if she's still as lively as I remember her, if she's still happy. I know I could get a Facebook account and find her online, but I'm still hesitant in joining. Like high-school, it feels like something I don't belong in.

✳✳✳

My life finally changed mid-October with a knock at the door. It was my mom, only this time she wasn't bringing me dinner or coming to help with my laundry; instead, she'd come with a proposition. After letting her in through my basement suite doors, she sauntered in and sat down on the couch. I picked up Esme and let her lay on my lap on the ragged loveseat.

"Her leg's all healed," my mom noted happily.

"Still a bit stiff," I explained, petting her neck, "but she can walk around and jump up on the bed." With adoration I looked down on Esme, smiling softly. She was the most important person in my life other than Eric. I spent more time with her than anyone else. I counted on her each night as she crawled into my bed and slept over top of my chest.

"I have some news," my mom began.

I peaked my head up, worried. "Nothing bad, I hope."

"No," she said, and then hurriedly told me, "Gone Hollywood is for sale. We're thinking of taking it over."

My heart thumped. Gone Hollywood was like a home to me. I'd spent my entire teenage life renting movies there...

Esme was licking my finger, trying to nag me back into petting her, but I was shell-shocked by the revelation my mom had just dropped on me. I needed a real job, something during the day I could actually enjoy. This was more than I could ever ask for.

"I know you and Eric have it all planned to move to Prince George, but I want you two to think about staying and working for us. Me and your father want to buy it—but if we do, we want you and Eric as managers."

After scoffing in splendid disbelief, I told her, "I don't think we need to talk about it. Working at a video store is what we've always wanted."

My mom smiled. "Then you should put your two-weeks notice in at 7-eleven immediately."

✳✳✳

And that's what leads me to where I am now in life.

I work eight hours a day, five days a week, and get paid a decent wage—not that I even care about the money. When I wake up in the morning I actually look forward to coming to work. I even get up extra early just to vacuum and make the place look absolutely perfect.

Before turning on the *OPEN* sign, I usually go up and down the aisles and look over all the movies, tidying whichever are out of place. While doing that I eventually find which movie I want to play in the store. We have two flat-screen TV's at each end of the New Release section and we can play whatever we want on them—as long as it's nothing too offensive.

Gone Hollywood is on the corner of Main Street, only a five minute walk away from my basement suite, but even after my shift ends I never want to leave. I like talking to the customers and checking through all the new inventory, seeing what movies rent and what movies don't. Being the manager I'm still getting used to everything, making changes and reorganizing. Eric and I both make all the decisions. We do up the schedule, we do the ordering. My parents completely handed the business over to us and so we take it all very seriously. We act professional. The only wish my parents had was that my brother, Henry, was to work with us, as well. But he was busy a lot of the time—mostly with the plays he acted in—and so we had to hire someone else.

We interviewed lots of people—every high-schooler dropped a resume off at least once—but we were extremely weary of going through with hiring. It was hard to trust anyone. We weren't the best book-keepers and so we knew how easy it would be for a worker to steal from us. When I finally did hire someone I was very unpractical about it.

One cold November day, as I was filing away some papers, I peered up through the large windows of our movie-poster display and saw an old friend of ours walking down the street. It was Amelia, and right as I was about to go outside and call out to her, I realized I never had to. She'd planned on coming in already.

Immediately, I realized what a great employee she'd be. I had it decided before she even entered through the doors. Pleased to find me behind the counters, her face lit up as the door swung close behind her.

"Drayvn!" she shouted. "I heard you were working here now."

"I'm the manager," I proudly told her. "With Eric."

Her jaw dropped. "No!" she exclaimed, but I assured her it was true. "Good for you guys! I always knew you two would do great things out of high-school."

"Want a job?" I asked, right out of the blue.

She giggled, thinking I was joking, but when she saw the serious look on my face, she then asked, "You really want to hire me?"

"Do you need a job?" I asked.

"I'd love one."

"Then you're hired."

She giggled again. "Do you want to see a resume or anything?"

"Not at all."

Eric was a small bit mad when I later told him I'd hired her on the spot like that—without us talking it through and making a fully thought-out decision—but he knew as well as me what a good employee she'd be. She was friendly and smart and she trusted us the same way we trusted her. We were both extremely happy to have her. Not only was she a good employee, but she brightened our days up as things got gloomier and gloomier around town.

✳✳✳

One day, while I was showing Amelia something on the computer, she caught me as I caught myself looking down her shirt. She never made it awkward, though. She wasn't like that. I went red and so she asked another question, side-stepping the moment completely—not out of any personal embarrassment but out of kindness for me. She knew the kind of person I was, and that the last thing I'd want was to mean her any disrespect.

After being friends with Amelia the last few years, I couldn't see myself having any real romantic feelings for her. It was just strange. The way her body had commuted was overwhelming—especially since I'd known her back in the days she wasn't even a teenager yet.

I wasn't the only one who began noticing her. Many men came into the store, delighted to ask her for help—even if they never actually needed it. A guy in his twenties had apparently gotten himself dangerously infatuated with her. On the nights Amelia worked alone, he started showing up like clockwork, coming in more than twice a night. Somehow he'd weaseled his way into getting her cell phone number and had been texting her.

After a couple of weeks it started to really freak her out, and so she told me about it. When I found out who this person was, I gently told him to leave her alone the first chance I got to speak to him.

His reaction was more than pissed off. He started swearing at me, telling me to mind my own business. But I was cool about it; I explained, "She's just shy. Not used to older guys talking to her. I know she seems old, but she's only fifteen."

"*Fifteen?* Oh shit," he said, calming down. "I thought she was older than *fifteen*..."

I knew he was lying. She didn't look any older than fifteen; she was just extremely attractive for a girl that age. But I let him off easy. I didn't want to be an asshole. All I wanted was Amelia to like working at Gone Hollywood with us.

She was my only real source in having a social life other than talking to customers. Amelia told me about school—her friends and whatnot. She was a real talker, and even though I often dozed off to what she was actually saying, I liked listening to her voice.

I seldom saw Trent. He came by and visited me a couple of times, but we never seemed to have much to talk about. I was quite positive he started smoking weed again now that he was hanging out with his other friends. But I didn't judge him. School can be tough—I could understand that more than most.

When summer ended, Cliff was promoted to Assistant Manager at Safeway, and so he was becoming more and more busy with all his new responsibilities. But as he had always been a regular customer of Gone Hollywood, he still came by and rented large hauls of DVD's each week. Cliff was famous for his late fees, but he no longer had to worry about them now. He was always sincere in trying to pay for them, but Eric and I deleted the over-dues without hesitation. He spent lots of money at our store already, ordering rare movies for his own personal collection. Now that Eric and I were managers, we were able to find all those hard-to-get movies we were interested in.

***

Irritating me more than ever before, my acne was starting to act up worse than usual. When my mom came in one day to check how the store was doing, she also noticed the awful condition my skin was in. Though my face was usually quite clear, it for some reason seemed to be going through a bit of an off-stage.

I asked my mom what I should do and she explained a kind of drug that she thought might be able to help. Acutaine: a four-month-long procedure of taking daily pills. Apparently, after making it through four months of taking the required dosage, the acne will disappear once and for all, never to come back again. But not many people can handle it; that's why it's practically unheard of. The side-effects include terrible headaches and skin so sensitive it hurts just to touch. Yet neither of those things worried myself or my mom—it was another side-effect that we found bothersome.

Depression.

Acutaine was so rough on the body it sometimes caused the user to lose all energy for day-to-day life. Even though that made it dangerous for me, I decided to go through with it anyway. My belief was that if I made it through Acutaine I could make it through anything.

Right now I'm still only in my first month of taking it, but even now I can feel the creeping sensation of depression trying to grab hold. Things in my life are wonderful, but they're tainted by the memories of summer.

I think of that night—of me and Anna on the living room floor, of us on the ragged chair in front of the TV—and my heart stops.

And she still hasn't called me. Three months, and she still hasn't called. But I don't think about it. I try not to, at least... I keep my mind on the movies, and they distract me, two hours at a time.

Chapter Two: Eighteen

Amelia and I spent the eve of my eighteenth birthday together. She wanted to wish me Happy Birthday the moment the clock hit twelve, which sounded good to me. In all the time she worked at Gone Hollywood, the two of us still hadn't done anything together outside of work. It would be perfect this way.

November 29th was a Saturday, and Amelia worked the cross-shifts on weekends, helping Henry with the evening rushes before he closed the shop down. Each weekend so far was getting busier and busier. The uglier it got outside, the better it was for renting movies.

As her shift was ending, I came by to meet up with her.

"Ready to go?" I asked.

"Mm!" She looked down at the remaining returns. "Right after this pile," she told me.

"Let Henry do it," I said, pointing to my brother. He wouldn't care either way, but Amelia insisted on finishing up the last of her duties, being the good employee she was. Grabbing the few piles left, she then darted past the counter. "I'll be real quick," she said, running along the shelves of New Releases. ("Can I help you find anything today?" I heard her ask one of the customers.)

"So what are *you two* going to be up to tonight?" asked Henry, lazily cantering over to me with a stern expression. I knew what he'd implied but I ignored him.

"I'm walking her home," I explained.

"Ah," he breathed out. "You know it's your birthday tomorrow..."

"No!" I gasped. "Really? I forgot—"

"And it's *Sunday*," he said. "Why don't you come to church? Just for your birthday."

"That's the last thing I'd want to do on my birthday... I'm coming over for dinner—isn't that enough?"

He chuckled bitterly. "Did you really leave home just because of church?"

"I don't even remember anymore—why I left..."

"Jane misses you."

"She'll see me tomorrow."

"But she's your sister. Don't you think you owe her more than that? You've only come over like three or four times in the last six months."

"Well, Henry, you see," I began morosely, "I spend five hundred bucks a month so I *don't* have to be at the house."

He paused, then looked around to check our surroundings. My assumption was that he was making sure a customer wouldn't hear whatever he meant to say next. "You're an asshole," he said, making my prediction true.

"Well hey," I expressed, shrugging, "maybe you'll learn from my mistakes..."

Stunned by my vitality—not getting the reaction he'd hoped for—I could tell he started to feel bad. He scratched his head and changed the subject, asking me something irrelevant about closing.

I answered his question, even though I was sure he already knew the answer.

"I'm sorry, Henry," came Amelia's voice. She came around one of the aisles and over to us by the counter, holding one last movie in her hands. "I seriously can't find where to put this one."

"That's alright," he said, taking it from her. "I'll find it. You can get going."

"Thanks," said Amelia, glowing happily as she grabbed her jacket from the cabinet below the counter. "I'll see you next week!"

"See you," he said, giving me one last look before taking off through the store, leaving Amelia and I to exit out into the cold night.

✱✱✱

Though my conversation with Henry put me in a bad mood, Amelia had me cheered up in no time at all. She had that uncanny ability. I'm not even sure if she knew the tensions still lingering between me and my family, but that didn't matter. No matter what, she remained upbeat.

"So where is it exactly that you live?" she asked as we made our way across the parking lot of the Community College and onto its small field.

"Right there," I told her, pointing to the house diagonally across the street. The one with the uneven driveway, with the tall-fence around the backyard... The one with all so many memories.

"A house?" she inquired. "I thought you said you lived in an apartment."

"It's a basement suite," I explained. "Come on!"

I took off running down the path of dead grass and she followed, giggling behind me as we J-walked across the street and up the yard. "Down here," I beckoned, guiding her through the carport and to the cement stairwell.

"You live down here?" she said. "Spooky."

"It's like I don't exist," I mused, creaking the door open.

Inside I showed her my things. My living room and bedroom. My cat. My bookshelf and the movie collection I had beneath the TV. She was deeply impressed. I had everything I needed and I was only seventeen—or, *eighteen,* as I should say now.

"Do you play?" she asked, stepping up to the guitar wedged between the TV and the wall.

"I write my own songs, actually," I told her proudly.

She gasped. "You have to show me one!"

Though I acted reluctant, I truthfully did want to play for her. I'd written a song a few days ago that I was itching to show someone. After handing the guitar over to me, Amelia went and sat on the couch where she leaned forward on her knees and waited for me to begin. Checking to see it was still in the right tuning, I gave the strings a few gentle strokes. It was set to go. Relaxing on the nearby chair, I crouched over the thing and started playing.

After plucking the intro perfectly, I then delved gracefully into the verses.

"You're supposed to be singing here, aren't you?" Amelia asked.

I looked up—continuing the sets of chords—and told her, "I'm not actually going to *sing*..."

But she begged me to and so I did as she asked. How could I say no? I never really did sing the words—my voice doesn't live up to the songs I write—but I whispered the lyrics tunefully enough as the song took its ups and downs.

Sad words of regret, nostalgic images from the summer...

To make the scenario less awkward and less serious, I ended my performance by segueing into some goofy song I knew she'd recognize and then improvised a crazy ridiculous, off-tempo outro.

Amelia laughed as I finished with one final G. "You're so good," she exclaimed. "How long have you been playing?"

"Almost a year."

"How often do you get guitar lessons?"

"Never had a lesson in my life."

"I should have known," she gushed. "Lessons are for people without any talent, right?"

I smiled humbly and shook my head, blushing as I put the guitar back in its place.

"I'm guessing the song is about Anna?"

I scoffed, sitting back down on my ragged chair. "How did you know?"

"I remember how in love you were with her..."

I shrugged.

"So if I heard the lyrics correctly," Amelia asserted, "it's safe to assume that you kissed Anna? Your first kiss..."

"I can check that off my list," I told her, falling deeper into the comfy loveseat.

She smiled. "I'm so happy for you!"

"Don't be too happy," I said, now smugly. "She hasn't spoken to me in months, since the summer."

"Well she's dating someone, isn't she?"

My stomach turned; I tried not to show it.

"You don't know?" Amelia cringed. "Right... You don't have Facebook."

"What's his name?" I asked earnestly.

"Steven."

"I guess it makes sense, then—why she hasn't called..." My heart was breaking, and as hard as I tried not showing it, Amelia knew...

"Come here," she said, pointing to the couch. "Don't get all sad—it's your birthday. In one more hour you'll be eighteen."

"I wish I was *nine*teen," I replied, getting up and awkwardly putting my hands in my pockets. I fell down on the couch, defeated.

"You look tired," she said, and then told me to rest. She pulled my head down and placed it on her lap. "Did you ever get around to reading the new Twilight book?" she asked, running her hands through my hair.

"I still haven't finished reading the third," I whimpered, not bothering to ask what brought Twilight up. If it had anything to do with my situation with Anna... *I didn't want to know.* "I think I liked the movie more than the books," I said somberly, looking around my apartment in the new sideways perspective Amelia placed me in. "I'll just wait for the movies."

She shook my head gently. "No way! The fourth book's the best."

"Tell me about it."

"Is it okay if I spoil what happens?"

I nodded my head against her legs. "It's fine," I told her.

And through the last hour before the clock hit twelve—before she wished me Happy Birthday and I walked her home—she went through the entire plot. Everything there was to it. Every sub-plot and every conclusion to every character. She explained it all to me in complete detail.

I listened to her voice, asking questions here and there while she continued softly massaging me through my clean-cut hair. But all the while, my thoughts centered on Anna—that she was dating someone. Not me. It hurt terribly, but I couldn't imagine a better way to have found out than this. I listened to Amelia's words and blocked out the sadness.

I couldn't allow myself to be sad. Not with the Acutaine running through my system. Anna—and *Steven*—was hardly a shock, really. She hadn't spoken to me in months. I had to move on. But how? How could I move on after everything that happened?

✲✲✲

After my birthday dinner, the usual tradition commenced. They turned off the lights and sung the old familiar tune as my mom brought out the cake, lit up with a circular line of candles. When they were done singing, I breathed in—making my wish—and blew the candles out in front of me. Every last one of them went out, turning the dining room as dark as the night outside. My brothers clapped rowdily and a flash from my father's camera went off. "No girlfriends," I heard him say, referring to the lack of a remaining candle.

"Don't remind me," I muttered loudly, making them all laugh.

As my mom flipped on the lights, I felt a tug on my arm, and after adjusting to the brightness, I focused in on Jane, my eight year old sister. She had long silky hair, dark like our father while the rest of us took after our mom. Cal and Henry and I were sandy blondes. But each and every one of us had blue eyes. That was our family trademark.

Jane had insisted on sitting next to me for dinner, knowing how seldom it was for her to see me. No matter what, she never left my side when I came to visit. "Can I give you your present?" she asked, still holding my arm with both her hands.

"I don't know," I said, looking over to my mom, who was now cutting the cake. "Jane wants to give her present to me?"

My mom licked the icing off one of her fingers and said, "That's fine—you know where it is." She smiled to Jane, who smiled back and let go of my arm to race down the hall to her bedroom.

"Can I give him my gift, too?" Cal asked.

"Go ahead, go ahead," my mom urged, to which he ran off like Jane, but downstairs to where his own room was.

"The store's going good, then?" my father said, making conversation.

"Things are running smoother and smoother," I told him truthfully. "Amelia is helping out a lot."

"What about me?" Henry implored.

I laughed but then sincerely told my parents, "Henry's doing a good job, as well..."

"I take it you don't want any cake, Dray?" my mom asked.

"I'll take a small piece," I said, out of respect, since it was *my* birthday she'd made it for and all.

After my mom had handed the plates of cake around the table, I took a small bite and said, "Mm!" as I rolled it around my mouth. She really was good in the kitchen. Baking things and cooking, cleaning and packing lunches. She did everything.

And then there was my dad, the breadwinner. He wore a suit to work every day and came home to a nice home-cooked dinner.

My family came straight out of the fifties.

Jane and Cal came one after the other, placing their presents in front of me and then sat down to start eating their cake.

"Whose should I open first?" I asked.

"Mine!" they both pleaded.

"I'll open Jane's first," I said, throwing Cal an apologizing sneer. Cal was only eleven, but he was surprisingly quite mature.

Even at first glance, I knew Jane had gotten me a book. She usually did.

"What's this?" I asked her, pretending to not be able to tell.

"Open it!" she urged. "You have to open it to know."

After peeling off the sloppily-done wrappings—wrapping she clearly did herself—I discovered a collection of short stories about paranormal happenings.

"A book!"

"It's scary," she told me, tugging my arm again. "Because you like things that are scary."

I knew exactly what she was referring to. When she was just a toddler I used to let her into my room with me to watch whatever I was watching. If she wanted to be calm and quiet, I didn't mind. I even let her watch The Ring and The Grudge with me. She was scared for both of them—mortified, even, by a few scenes—but she continued watching them the whole way through, cuddling next to me as we leaned our backs against stacks of pillows.

She also watched a full season of Buffy The Vampire Slayer with me, as well—her favorite show now.

"Awesome!" I told her. "I needed a new book to read."

I quickly glanced through the pages and then sat it down. "Thanks Jane." I kissed her brow.

"Before I forget," my mom said, "you have an appointment tomorrow morning. It's early enough. Before you start work."

"What for?"

"They need to check your blood at the hospital to see that your body is reacting to the Acutaine properly."

"Do I need to get a needle—"

"My present," Cal interrupted.

"Sorry," I told him, quickly picking it up off the table and shaking it next to my ear. "A Beyblade?" I guessed, remembering the packaging they used to come in. Me and my two brothers used to play with Beyblades all of the time, battling the spinning tops to see whose spun the longest.

"How did you know? How could you *tell*?" Cal pleaded, but all I could do was smirk and unravel the wrappings to discover what type he'd picked out for me. Like Jane, he'd gotten me something that reminded him of a past memory of us. Something that reconnected the past with the present...

My family really did love me, and for my eighteenth birthday I realized how much I loved them, too. I was older and had to move on, but knowing I had a loving family was a greater comfort than I ever realized before.

After hanging out for another hour with my siblings—playing Beyblades together mostly—I went to leave. It was getting late and I now had an early appointment at the hospital to get up for. I said my goodbyes, but Henry came and followed me out into the garage. "I still have a present to give you," he told me as I grabbed my skater-shoes off the shelf.

"You got me a present?"

"Just don't leave yet," he replied, swiftly returning back inside.

By the time I finished tying my shoes, Henry came back through the garage door, holding a movie. "Here," he said, handing it over to me.

It was Unbreakable, the double-disc edition.

"You need it, right? For your collection?"

"The last one," I confirmed. The director, M. Night Shyamalan, was the man who got Henry and I into movies in the first place, who got the two of us making home videos long before Eric, Cliff and Trent and I started making ours. A couple of weeks ago I told Henry I owned all of Night's films, except that I was still searching for a special edition of Unbreakable.

"The last one," Henry repeated, smiling. "But what about Lady in the Water?"

I shrugged, not a fan the way Henry was. "This is perfect," I told him. "I'll see you later."

"Happy birthday," he said, standing tall on the ledge of the door. With his smile crooked and sad, I noticed for the first time how much older his face was getting. I'd bet anything that beneath his shirt there was hair sprawling its way across his chest. Behind his blue eyes I knew there were stories, secrets of his own.

He was starting to remind me... of myself, actually.

✶✶✶

Shivering from the cold, wearing only a hoody, I realized it was time to start wearing a winter jacket as I stepped inside the hospital the next morning. Rubbing my hands together, I sauntered in through the eerie hallway and up to the receptionist.

Tired and distant, the receptionist sipped away on her morning coffee as she searched my name through the old-school monitor in front of her. "Down the hall to the left," she croaked. "There's a waiting room there."

"Thanks."

After a brief search down the hallway, I was pulled into an office by one of the nurses. As she led me through the room, I began to shake, not from the cold but out of nervousness. I hated getting needles. Sitting me down in the chair, she asked, "Are you alright?"

"I'm fine," I told her. "I'm not very good with needles, but I manage."

She closed the door, then sought out her materials. "How many needles have you gotten before?"

"Oh plenty," I said casually, watching her pace back and forth. She was as young as a nurse could be, probably straight out of med-school. "How many needles have you *given*?" I asked her doubtfully.

"Don't worry!" she exclaimed, smiling at me. "*Enough.*" Fully prepared, she sat down in the chair beside me and grabbed my arm. Pulling the sleeve of my hoody up to the elbow, she whispered, "Just relax... Just try and think of something happy."

"What do you mean?"

"*Think of your happiest memory,*" she said grandiosely.

I paused, then looked away from her to the wall in front of me, feeling her hands stretch along my arm, preparing it in a sling.

"Close your eyes," she said. "It'll be over soon enough."

Quickly, I shut my eyes tight. Through the darkness of my vision, Anna appeared in front of me like an actress stepping on stage. And then, the blackness behind her dissolved into our old school.

I'm following her down a deserted hallway, just me and her. She looks back at me and smiles, looking me deep in the eyes...

I felt the nurse gently slap my arm, trying to spot a vein. My thoughts then changed, cutting away like in a music video:

...It's me and her, kissing on the ragged chair in my living room, the way it was three months ago. She's whispering something in my ear, but it's inaudible. I can't hear it; it's just a hushed whisper.

I tried to picture her face, but I couldn't remember... It's been too long.

She's a blur. All I can see now is someone my age. A male. Tall and lean, his shoulders as broad as Eric's. He's holding a girl around his arm—Anna. He's holding her, and he kisses her. And then I see him reach around her, feeling down her back. They kiss, and I can tell they're very much in love.

I tried rewinding my thoughts, but they kept on. I realized, painfully, that I couldn't think of her happily anymore.

Not able to handle the images inside my head for any longer, I opened my eyes and looked down, and right as I did, I saw the needle enter through the flesh of my arm, into one of the blue veins. I was much too stunned to react. I just watched, feeling the blood rise out of me. Breathing was getting harder and harder...

After pulling the needle out, the nurse looked up at me. She gasped, noticing how dizzy I was. I tried to breathe, but my lungs wouldn't take in any air. The room was getting hazy.

"Lean backwards!" she yelled at me. "Lean backwards!"

She knew it and I knew it: I was fainting. Everything had turned white and my body was completely limp. I tried doing as she said—tried falling backwards—but I was already headed the other direction, towards the floor. I fell out of my seat and smacked down on the ground, unconscious and heartbroken.

Chapter Three: The Last Phone Call

I answered my phone carelessly—without giving it thought—expecting to have been called by accident. No one called me these days. Whoever had dialed my cell phone number had clearly made a mistake. It was a random out-of-town number, so it may have even been a telemarketer. The last thing I expected was for it to be Anna.

I'd stopped hoping, I'd stopped praying.

But I should have known—*an appearance from Anna is always imminent when it's the least expected...* That's just how she worked. It was part of her allure. That mysteriousness was what attracted me to her in the first place.

"What are you—" My confusion was at a breaking point. I could hardly compose a sentence. After carefully catching my breath, I said, plain and simply, "You called..."

"I've been wanting to call you for a long time, actually."

After a deliberate pause, I scoffed in disbelief.

She continued, "I dial your number, but I can never go through with calling you."

"What made today different?"

"I guess I just worked up all my courage."

"You don't need courage to talk to me," I told her, irritated and upset.

"No?" she whimpered. "It feels like I do. You mean so much to me."

I huffed, pacing through my kitchen to set away my empty plate from the dining room table. I'd just finished dinner.

"What are you doing right now?" she asked.

"What's it matter?" I replied, tossing my plate angrily into the kitchen sink.

Sensing my hostility, she decided to give up on trying to have casual conversation. "I'm sorry I never replied to your email," she declared tentatively.

"I only sent it—what, two months ago?"

"There's nothing I can say that can top what you said. I read it countless times, Dray. You're so talented with words."

Ignoring her compliment, I asked, "Are you coming down for Christmas?"

"Turns out I can't."

"Really?" I said, my voice tainted with a note of grief, one she immediately knew and understood. How could she not? Even with thousands of miles between us—even if I hated her!—Anna was still a part of me. She knew that, and she knew how much I missed her.

Even if she *was* dating someone else...

"But I'll be coming down for spring break, though. I really hope so. It'd be great to see you again. We could go for another long walk—if you don't get completely drunk again, that is!"

"Okay," I joked, "I'll try not to get *that* drunk."

After we laughed and went silent, I asked, "Tell me what it's like with, um…" I pretended not to remember his name, not wanting to say it out loud.

"Steven?"

My body went rigid, but I let loose, scowling quietly to myself.

"You'd like him, Dray. He's really nice."

"As nice as me?" I asked, surprisingly cheerful.

"Much nicer!"

We both laughed, realizing that neither of us were capable of actually offending the other. We were so close, yet so distant.

"But is he dark enough? Enough to see all light?" I quoted.

"That's Damien Rice, isn't it?"

"Yep."

"But you know," Anna meekly began, "I'm probably going to break up with him by February."

If Anna broke up with that guy by February that meant she'd be single for spring break—for when she might be in Smithers. Was this what she was calling me about—leaving him for me? My thoughts were bouncing, so I spoke my mind: "You're breaking up with him?"

"Well... No," she said icily. "It's just that every relationship I've ever had... They for some reason always end in in January, right after Christmas. It's like this weird trend for me."

What relationships? The ones you had in elementary school, you stupid bitch!?

I was completely pissed off at her. She'd gotten my hopes sky-high and then smashed them all into oblivion... But I had to be cool about it... "Everything ends in January," I said thoughtfully, hiding my disdain.

"For me," she added.

"Just you?"

"I don't know. I think so."

"Maybe January is that perfect time, you know? It's right after New Years and resolutions."

"That's true"

"Things have to change eventually," I told her.

"That's true, too." There was a pause. "Hey! Um... How's your book?" she asked, trying to side-track me from my own thoughts.

"What?"

"You mentioned in your email that you were on the fourth chapter."

"Oh," I hissed. "I realized it was a bunch of bullshit."

"Drayvn! It's not bullshit. Not if *you* wrote it."

"Well it might turn around," I said, striding into my bedroom. "I think I need to clear my mind a bit, though. I watch too many movies, which is good for ideas and stuff." I looked over my bookshelf, envious of every author that ever existed. "I think I just need to read more."

"I'm reading Little Women again," she said cheerfully.

"For like the hundredth time?"

She laughed weakly. "Yeah."

"I should get the movie for the store."

"Gone Hollywood doesn't have it!?"

"I think something happened to it—got lost or something."

"Well it's not *that* good. I just like it because it means something to me, probably because I read it when I was a little kid."

"And then you watched the movie with your family. Every year, right, for Christmas?"

"It made everything seem so happy."

"That's the power of a good story," I told her.

"Is that why *you* write?"

I thought about it.

"That's why I *try* and write. But yeah, that's why I read and watch movies. Isn't that everybody's reason? Like when they go to the movie theater—isn't it all just to get lost in something better, to fill a void?"

"Dray, how come you've got everything so sorted out?"

I laughed, looking at myself in the mirror, the one still hanging next to my closet. "Anna, I'm a mess," I told her, scampering back out of my bedroom. "I'm a complete wreck! I have *nothing* sorted out."

But she was serious. "You will. A lot of people end up with lives they hate, you know..."

"Do you think that's gonna happen with you or something?"

Still serious, now quiet: "I hope not."

"It won't!" I told her out of love. I couldn't bear to hear her talking in such a sad way. "We're Anna and Drayvn! We used to always dream up these amazing futures that we planned on having. We can't stop dreaming!"

"Thanks, Dray," she said. "I'll try and keep dreaming..."

"*Anna,*" a woman's voice—muffled and older—called after her. "*It's dinner,*" she shouted.

She paused and then muttered to me, "Dinner."

"I heard."

"*Anna, dinner's ready,*" I heard the same voice call after her again, this time more clearly. Her mom, I guessed, was now inside her room.

"I know mum, I heard. Can you just give me one moment?" Anna asked, to which her mom complied. I heard a door swing shut, and Anna cleared her voice. "Well, Dray," she said.

"Well…"

"It's been nice—"

"Yeah," I said, and then urgently asked, "Do you want me to call you back sometime?"

"Um," she murmured. "I'll call you," she decided, and we both said our goodbyes, each void of everything we felt inside.

✻✻✻

Even then, as the lines clicked off, I knew we'd never speak again. She said she'd call, but her words lacked the conviction they usually held. There were new things happening in her life. She didn't have the time for me anymore.

…And there were so many things I wanted to tell her… So many things I wanted to express. She was the summation of my entire teenage life, but she had moved on. She would no longer understand, and so it was clear to me that I had to move on, too—no matter how hard that would be for me. There was nothing I could say that could make a difference. The past was the past and I had look forward.

Part Four: Winter

Chapter One: The Future

"Who called it?" Eric asked rhetorically, smiling haughtily at Cliff and I, who were on the sidewalk of a famous downtown street in Prince George. While the two of us had attempted to get inside one of the cool and trendy night-clubs, Eric waited patiently outside, standing around in the shivering cold with the rest of the drunk guys and girls out on the city tonight, those that were as drunk as us but of the legal age, outside only to smoke their cigarettes.

"We were so close to getting in," Cliff droned. "If Drayvn never had such a baby-face we would have got in no problem."

"I played it cool!"

Cliff punched my shoulder as hard as he could and ran off laughing, over to the other side of the street. All night we'd been as rowdy as this. Since leaving the hotel—after downing the drinks we brought for the trip—we'd been racing around the unfamiliar streets of downtown, being as loud as we pleased, causing a ruckus wherever we went. As there had been a snowfall on our drive to the city, the streets and cars were still covered in a thick coat of fresh snow, which came to great use during all of our mayhem.

With both hands, I quickly and effortlessly molded a handful of snow into yet another round and perfectly-sized snowball. Whipping it across the street—over a couple passing vehicles—it smacked Cliff square in the head on the other side. He fell down into the sidewalk's bank of plowed snow, less from the snowball and more from hysterical laughter. He was amazed I'd actually hit him; my aim was usually terrible.

Eric and I nudged past a parked taxi and over to Cliff, who was still trying to get up from out of the snowbank—too drunk to gain his balance. Over and up to him, I grabbed some more snow and rubbed it in his face.

"Gah!" he grunted, knocking my hands out of the way. "Come on! Help me up," he gushed, and with a quick and strong hand, I lunged him back up onto the sidewalk. Playfully swearing at me, he wiped his face dry with his undershirt and whimpered how cold it was.

After shaking the snow out of the hood of his jacket, he leaned over—hands on his knees—and caught his breath, smiling softly. He was excited as Eric and I were to be here in the city with each other. The three of us were all managers. Our opportunities to get drunk and crazy were slim these days. It took a lot of preparation to organize something together.

Standing tall again, Cliff looked longingly at the bar in front of us, at all the beautiful girls streaming in and out of the club, to and from the taxis out in front.

"One more year," Eric said, noticing Cliff's lingering gaze. "Just one more."

"One year is a long fucking time."

"Not that long," I spoke. "A year can whip by pretty fast."

He sighed and brought his flask from out of his pocket. "You're probably right," he replied, taking a sip.

"And we'll probably even live here by then," Eric added.

"Really?" Putting the flask back into his pocket—after offering it to each of us—he asked, "What about the house you guys are getting?"

"That's just temporary," I told him, motioning us to start walking back down the icy street. "Just while we figure things out."

"We've got decent setups," Cliff murmured, following alongside me.

"We're lucky."

"But we can't let that keep us in Smithers forever," Eric said, poking his head in between the two of us.

"Well, yeah, totally," I muttered in agreement. "We'll give it a year, and then who knows? Maybe we'll move to Vancouver."

"Maybe L.A."

"Or Philadelphia."

"Even New York!"

"It's a big world," Eric concluded, and three of us went silent, lost in our own individual thoughts. We had no idea what our futures would hold.

"When do you guys move into the house?" Cliff asked.

"Start of next month, but—"

"But they're letting us move in as early as we want," I said, eagerly finishing Eric's sentence.

The two of us were extremely excited with our new living arrangements. When we got back from our trip, we would then begin moving our things into the house on Railway we were now renting together. We had the keys and everything, and I'd already started boxing up all of my things. By the end of the month I'd have a new home.

✳✳✳

For the drive back to Smithers in the morning, Cliff was hungover and passed out, lying flat in the backseats of Eric's vehicle, a bucket by his head in case he needed to puke. Eric and I were tired, but we hadn't drank as much. We had our coffees and kept ourselves buzzed off conversation.

"The roads 'aint so bad today," Eric mentioned cheerfully.

"Luckily it was warm this morning," I replied, "or it would all be ice. My parents said it was crazy that we made the drive in the first place, that we should have just waited for all the snow to melt."

"It's spring break! There shouldn't be any damn snow."

I laughed. "After living in Smithers our whole lives you'd imagine we'd be used to the weather by now."

"I think we're just ready for something new."

"Yeah—"

"You see Anna yet?" he asked suddenly, in a tone that told me he'd been meaning to ask about her all morning. "She's in Smithers right now, isn't she? This week—for spring break?"

"I haven't talked to her, no. Hopefully she doesn't come into Gone Hollywood."

"Wait," he crooned, "you're avoiding *her*?"

"This winter gave me some time to think," I told him, trying to smile. "That ship has sailed."

"I doubt it actually sailed," he said, knowing me as well as he did, "but if you're trying to ignore her, after all this time... That's a start."

"I miss her lots, though."

"I know you do," he replied, carefully letting a hand off the wheel to reach for his coffee. Taking a sip, he looked to me and then asked about my Acutaine pills as he sat the Tim Horton's cup back down in the holster.

"All finished," I told him. "It definitely helped—taking them, I mean—but I still get a few zits every once in a while."

"Medicine can only do so much," he said, his words as wise as a grandfather's.

"Remember when we made this drive in the middle of the night?" I asked, the memory of it springing to mind. "In the summer... We had to work in the morning and everything."

He laughed and said, "That was so stupid."

"I can't believe we got ourselves *fired*."

"I don't know what we were thinking." He shook his head regretfully. "Wholesale was a pretty decent job."

"Well," I considered, "things turned out, didn't they?"

Eric laughed again, his eyes on the road. "Things always turn out. Eventually."

"Yep. Eventually," I repeated him. Smirking, I looked out the window at the passing scenery. Snow was dripping off the branches of ever-green trees, melting.

"Hey," Eric called my attention back to him, "you want me to make a stop in Houston? We could go visit Alice."

I groaned. "No."

"You totally did it with her, didn't you?"

Scowling, I clasped a hand over my chest and whipped it in the air, saying, "I didn't have *sex* with her..."

"Whatever—you two hooked up. And Trent liked her so much!" His shoulders bounced up and down in muffled laughter, but it was bemusing for me to even think of it.

"I'm such a terrible friend," I said.

He clicked his tongue against the roof of his mouth. "I'm sure you felt terrible."

"I did."

"Well at least she wasn't your first kiss."

"Now that would have been awful," I agreed. I'd thought of that before—how lucky it was I got the first kiss I always wanted. Things turned out so terrible, but at least there was that: one moment to call perfect.

"You ever see Rose at all?"

"Naw," I replied, uncaring.

"It's funny," Eric began, "how everybody forgot about us when they went back to school. Even Trent."

"Everybody's trapped in their own little worlds," I gathered.

"But you know who's awesome?"

"Who?"

"Amelia."

"I know," I exclaimed dreamily, thinking of how great of a friend she'd been the past few months. "She's *so* awesome."

"You ever think of dating her?" Eric asked, but while I thought of an answer, he continued, "It's too bad she's moving."

"What?" I blurted, gaping at him with furrowed brows.

"You didn't know?" he asked.

"No!"

"Hm," he murmured, "maybe she'll tell you when you go in for your shift today."

* * *

When I stepped inside the store, Amelia was spraying the counters down with a blue bottle of Windex cleaner. Hearing the ding-dong noise of the door opening, she looked up, saw it was me, and smiled. "Hey," she called out, setting the Windex down.

"Hey."

"How was your trip?"

"So great," I proclaimed, staggering over to behind the counter. "We went to the movies, played some laser tag—and then got totally wasted and ran around the city!"

"Did you manage to get inside any of the bars?" she asked, remembering how I told her that I planned on seeing if we could.

"We got kicked out, like, a *second* after stepping inside..."

Amelia laughed, amused the way she always was with my crazy stories. With the rag in her hand, she finished wiping the counters down and then checked the time on the computer. "It's early," she said. "You're here early."

"You always come early. I thought I might as well, too."

"I like it here," she told me, looking down the aisles of movies to the other end of the store. The place was as empty as it usually was in the afternoon; it only ever really got busy during the evenings. Turning her head back to me, she said, "Thanks for giving me the extra shifts this week."

"No problem," I told her. "Because of it we got to go to Prince George."

"Happy to be back?"

"I suppose," I said casually, but I knew what she was getting at.

"Are you worried about seeing Anna?"

From the moment I entered through the Gone Hollywood doors, I expected her to bring it up at some point. "I might be a little worried," I told her, sitting up on the counter—something I normally wouldn't do, but as there weren't any customers in the store I never saw it a problem.

"Well you can stop worrying," Amelia said happily, "because she's not in Smithers."

"What do you mean?"

"She never left Vancouver. Something came up and she couldn't make it."

"Really?"

"I talked to her on Facebook just a couple of days back... It sounded to me like she won't be visiting here for a very long time."

I ran a hand through my hair, dazing through all the leftover thoughts in my head. It was her new home—Vancouver. This place meant less and less to her each passing season.

"By the way," Amelia said, carefully making sure she had my attention. "Thanks a lot for hiring me. It's meant a lot. I've learned so much working here with you guys. You and Eric"—she began tearing up—"are seriously the nicest guys I've ever met."

I hopped down from the counter, trying not smile. She was practically saying goodbye to me and she hadn't even told me she was moving yet!

"Is there something you want to tell me?" I asked, stepping closer to her.

"I'm moving!" she cried, flailing her arms around me.

I held her as tight as she held me, but she withdrew quickly. "I'm *sorry*," she said, wiping her tears away. "I didn't mean to start crying on you."

"Don't be sorry."

She looked down at her feet, and then looked back at me, holding her hands over her stomach. "No," she muttered, "I'm being *silly*. I don't leave for another three months."

"There you go," I said gently, gazing over her in a shower of affection. "So it's not goodbye yet."

"That's right," she told me, a sudden burst of cheerfulness attached to her tone. She was full of so much love and life; I don't know what I would have done without her...

With one more hug, she packed up her things and headed out the door to meet up with her friends. Outside the large windows—with the movie posters on display—I watched her disappear down the road towards Main Street.

Ding-dong...

I turned my head to the door, and to my astonishment found a beautiful woman come strolling inside the store. She had dark and thick hair—thick like the girls they put on shampoo commercials—

and was wearing a long and fine trench-coat, to which she unbuttoned as she entered into the warmth of the store. As I lumbered back over to the counter, she spotted me.

"Hello," she said, her voice as equally attractive as her appearance. "Do you work here? Can you help with me something?"

"Yep. For sure," I quickly replied.

The woman stomped her shoes on the entrance mat, clearing them attentively of snow, and then walked over to me. "I'm looking for a movie—you may have heard of it before. It's about..."

And then I dozed off... I couldn't help it.

Lost in her eyes, her words drifted in and through me. Not once did she look away—she had this cool, self-assured presence to her. And as mature as she was, there was a youthful glow beneath her sharp features.

Shocked by such unfamiliar beauty, I felt a surge of adrenaline run up and down my spine, which was as strong of a sensation I'd had since the summer, maybe even more so. It was strange. I'd never been attracted to someone older, and never in this kind of way. My attraction was almost uncontrollable—like a hunger—tip-toeing on the edge of breaking loose. I wanted to reach forward and grab her for myself—

"You're not even listening to me, are you?" she then said, smiling in flushed containment.

Embarrassed, I came clean. "I'm sorry," I told her, keeping cool. "It's just... I haven't seen you around here before. I'm trying to think who you are."

"I'm Lynn," she said, raising her eyebrows flirtatiously at me. "I'm here visiting."

"That makes sense," I said, nodding briefly. "I'm positive I would have noticed you before if you lived around here."

I could tell she knew I was flirting with her—which was more than obvious—but it didn't put her off. "How *old* are you?" she inquired, tilting her head faintly to the side.

"I'll be turning nineteen," I said, stretching the truth.

"So you're just a couple of years younger than me."

"How long are you visiting for?" I asked, walking around the counter, not letting my eyes stray from hers.

"From now till the end of the summer," she told me, taking her gloves off as I approached closer.

"Just till the end of summer?"

"Then I'm moving to Prince George," she explained.

"What are your plans there?"

"Not sure yet—I'm just taking things one step at a time."

"Me too," I said, and the two of us laughed nervously. "Anyways... I'm sorry. Tell me about the movie you were thinking of. I promise to pay attention this time."

After figuring out which movie it was she had in mind, I grabbed it off the shelf and started up her own renting account on the system. It was great. The whole time I made sure I came off impressive to her. She was older, and the stakes were high. If I was to make her fall for me, I had to play my cards right. Once again, I had a time limit.

This girl, Lynn, would be gone by the end of the upcoming summer.

"Thanks for all the help," she said, waltzing over to the door with the Gone Hollywood DVD case in hand. "You know... You should add me on Facebook."

My heart fluttered, and I smiled in realization that I now knew for sure the attraction had gone both ways.

"I'll add you," I confirmed, neglecting to mention I didn't have a Facebook account.

"You have my name."

She turned around and walked out of the store, not looking back at me through the windows until she'd gotten inside her fancy sports car, which was parked directly out in front. With a smile, she put the car in gear and drove off.

Almost instantly, I ran over to the store's computer and booted up the internet browser. It was time to finally sign up for Facebook.

***

Later that night, when I got back to the basement suite, I continued boxing up the remainder of my things. The moment I got home

I'd tried to fall asleep, but it was pointless. My thoughts were still buzzing about Lynn, so I stayed up through the late hours of the night, processing in my head what came before and what I felt would come next.

As time droned on through the haze of my fatigue, the sudden emptiness of my basement suite finally became apparent to me.

Dozens of boxes were packed up by the door, each full of everything I owned. There was nothing left anywhere else. No pictures on the walls, no lamps on the desks, no dishes inside the kitchen cabinets. The furniture was all that remained—that, and the few changes of clothes I'd put in my backpack.

In my bedroom, Esme was sleeping as soundly as she always did. Soon I'd collapse in bed next to her and dream as happily as ever. But not yet. The reality of leaving this place behind was beginning to fully dawn on me.

To mull over the last of my tired thoughts, I went and sat down in the ragged chair in my living room—which, in its significance, brought a whole package of memories sweeping back to me. As I sat there and looked around the empty apartment, I was struck with a surreal sadness. Swiftly, I shrugged it off with an immediate smile, one as hopeful as Amelia's. Like her, I knew how great the future would be.

Last spring, when I first moved here, I told myself I was ready for the next chapter in my life. This time around I feel like I'm ready for a whole new story. There were new characters, new plots, and new meanings I was yet to experience. They were on their way. Another summer of adventures awaited me. And the love that had come and gone would fuel me forever always.

***

CPSIA information can be obtained at www.ICGtesting.com
Printed in the USA
LVOW070758040512

280259LV00002B/1/P